EVERYTHING TO LOSE

NEWBERRY SPRINGS SERIES
BOOK ONE

HARLOW JAMES

Copyright © 2023 by Harlow James
All rights reserved.

No part of this book may be reproduced in any form or by any electronic or mechanical means, including information storage and retrieval systems, without written permission from the author, except for the use of brief quotations in a book review.

This is a work of fiction. Names, characters, businesses, places, events, locales, and incidents are either the products of the author's imagination or used in a fictitious manner. Any resemblance to actual persons, living or dead, or actual events is purely coincidental.

Paperback ISBN: 9798393914790

Cover Designer: Abigail Davies
Editor: Melissa Frey

This book is for the girls who have always been cautious with their heart.
Don't apologize for being guarded.
But don't be afraid of risking your heart too.
Because without risk, there is no reward.
And you might think you have everything to lose, but you also have everything to gain too.

And for Emily.
This book wouldn't be out in the world without you pushing me to publish it. Thank you for making me see what my heart already knew.

"It seems to me that the best relationships, the ones that last, are frequently the ones that are rooted in friendship. You know, one day you look at the person and you see something more than you did the night before. Like a switch has been flicked somewhere. And the person who was just a friend is suddenly the only person you can ever imagine yourself with."

Gillian Anderson

CONTENTS

Prologue	1
Chapter 1	13
Chapter 2	29
Chapter 3	41
Chapter 4	64
Chapter 5	85
Chapter 6	105
Chapter 7	127
Chapter 8	152
Chapter 9	176
Chapter 10	187
Chapter 11	192
Chapter 12	203
Chapter 13	245
Chapter 14	282
Chapter 15	306
Chapter 16	324
Chapter 17	332
Chapter 18	354
Chapter 19	374
More Books by Harlow James	385
Acknowledgments	387
About the Author	391

PROLOGUE

Kelsea

Ten Years Old

"Get those things away from me!" I pump my legs and arms as fast as I can to escape from Wyatt and his bucket of worms. The last time he caught me, I ended up with a worm in my hair, and Wyatt ended up with a fat lip when I punched him.

"Come on, Kels! They don't bite!" I can hear his laugh behind me through the whoosh of the air whipping past as I speed toward safety.

"I don't care! They're gross and slimy!"

"Don't be such a girl!"

"But I am a girl!" I look back over my shoulder through my

curly blonde hair, checking to make sure I still have distance between us. Then I descend the small hill that leads to the edge of the creek on the Gibson's property, the same creek where Wyatt and I play almost every day until the sun sets.

We know better than to not make it back to the house before the lights on their porch come on. The one night we showed up too late resulted in Wyatt being grounded for a week, and since he's my best friend, that week was the longest and most boring week of my life.

My feet stop abruptly at the edge of the water as I fold forward and rest my hands on my knees, trying to catch my breath. But then I flinch and jump backward as I hear Wyatt skid down the hill and land right beside me, sporting his mischievous grin.

I point a finger in his direction as I clench my teeth together. "Don't you dare throw those worms at me again, Wyatt Allen Gibson, or so help me God, I will tell your momma on you this time!"

A heavy puff of air leaves his lips as he plants his hands on his hips and rolls his eyes. "Relax, Kels. I'm not gonna throw a worm at you, all right? I need them to catch a fish, and your girlish screams are just gonna scare all the fish away if I do that."

Letting out a relieved sigh, I allow myself to relax a bit, even though I still don't trust him one-hundred-percent. I've known Wyatt since we were toddlers, and my earliest memories of us running around in diapers marked the beginning of our friendship.

Our fathers grew up together, so naturally, their kids are growing up together, too. Even though I'm an only child, I was born just a few months before Wyatt and his twin brother, Walker, and despite those two boys having their own close bond, Wyatt and I always ended up doing our own thing.

I watch Wyatt find his fishing pole he keeps tucked up in the branches of the old oak tree next to the creek for safekeeping. He pulls it down and fiddles around with the string before reaching for a worm and pushing a hook through it. My mouth turns down, my lips curling with disgust.

"That's so gross." I shudder and then take a seat near the edge of the water, reaching for a few river rocks and arranging them into patterns like I always do. Sometimes, I make a heart or a star, sometimes a letter or two. But no matter what I make, the process is still the same. Wyatt will fish while I play with the rocks and shield my face from the sun. It's just what we do when we're down here.

"You need to get over it. This is how a man catches a fish—using real worms."

"News flash, you're still a boy."

"But I'll be a man someday, and I want to be able to catch a fish the right way." He looks out over the still water. "So do you think you'll be able to stay for dinner?"

His eyes shift back over the water, studying his line as he anxiously waits for something to bite. The truth is, I've never seen a fish in this stream, but Wyatt is convinced he's going to catch one someday. Boys are so dumb sometimes.

I shrug, picking at a string that is slowly unraveling across the knee of my jeans as I reach for a few more rocks. "I don't know. I guess it just depends on what time my mom gets here." My mom works at an office in town as some man's assistant. I'm not exactly sure what she does, but the man she works for pushes buttons on a calculator all the time, and she constantly talks to my dad about something called "taxes," whatever those are.

"Cool. When does your dad get home?"

"I think on Friday. He's been gone for almost two weeks this time." My dad is a truck driver and spends long stretches on the road, far from Newberry Springs, Texas. While he's gone, the Gibson family watches me while Momma is at work, especially since it's summertime right now. When school is back in session, I'll be there during the day, and then I'll stay at Wyatt's house until my mom is home in the evenings. I swear, sometimes it feels like I live with them more than I do with my own parents.

"I don't understand how your parents are married. They are never together," Wyatt says. A funny feeling erupts in my chest, as if his question makes me uncomfortable because it's true.

"Well, my dad always says that he married his best friend. That's why they love each other."

He flashes me a funny look. "You have to marry your best friend?"

Standing up, I brush the dirt from my pants and pull my ponytail tighter. I look at him as he pulls his pole from the water, the worm still hanging on the hook. "I guess. Maybe that means we're gonna get married one day, Wyatt."

"I'm never getting married."

"My dad says that most boys don't want to get married, but then they meet the right girl, and that all changes."

"Was your mom the right girl, then?"

"She had to be. Why else would they have gotten married?"

He shrugs. "Okay. I guess if that's the rule, I suppose it wouldn't be so bad being married to you. We spend every day together, anyway."

My head bobs up and down. "Exactly." I spin around, and then my eyes land on a flat piece of land right below the old tree. An idea sparks. "Well, if we're gonna get married someday, we should practice." I hold out my hand for him to take, but he stares at me for a moment too long.

"I'm fishin', woman," he declares, and I feel my temper flare with his attitude.

"There are no fish in that darn creek, Wyatt. Now, come here," I say with a stomp of my foot. He drops his pole and walks the few feet over to where I'm standing.

With his hand in mine, I show him where to place his feet in the sand, and then I stand directly across from him so we're facing each other. "Now, every time I've seen people get married, they hold hands like this." I gently place my hands in his as we hold them out in front of us like we're afraid to get too close.

"What do we do now?" My eyes land on the dirt smudged on his forehead and a bead of sweat slipping down his temple. Wyatt is a dirty, smelly boy, but no matter what, I'll just plug my nose or pretend he smells like roses since he's my best friend and all.

"We're supposed to promise to love each other forever. ''Til death do us part,' or something like that."

"'Til we die? That's a long time!"

"Are you saying you don't want to be my best friend forever, Wyatt?"

His shoulders rise with indecision. "I don't know."

"Can you ever imagine your life without me?"

"No."

"Then that means forever—or until one of us dies, Wyatt."

I watch him swallow as another bead of sweat appears. "Okay. ''Til death do us part,' then."

"Okay. Now we have to kiss."

His nose scrunches up, and I feel myself mentally do the same. I've seen people kiss, even my parents and Wyatt's parents, but it looks so gross. I don't understand why people do that.

"We have to?"

"Yeah. That's what you do when you get married."

"Fine," he says with a roll of his eyes, "but make it quick."

"*You* make it quick!"

"Why do you have to argue with me about everything?"

"I do not." I stomp back at him as my hands find my hips.

"Yes, you do."

"Just shut up, and kiss me!"

"Ugh! Fine!" He groans and then reaches for my face. His hands cup my cheeks, and then his lips are on mine, the sensation so foreign that it only lasts a second before the two of us jump apart and wipe our mouths with the back of our hands.

But my heart is fluttering wildly in my chest, and a warmth coats my entire body. And as I study my best friend, I swear I don't see a gross, dirty boy anymore. Wyatt suddenly looks different.

"That was weird," he says as his eyes narrow in on me.

Stumbling over these strange emotions, I clear my throat. "Agreed. But at least we'll know what to do when the time comes."

"Yeah, sure," he says before wiping his mouth one more time, pausing to stare at me some more, and then running back to his pole. Just as he bends down, though, a loud crack of thunder rumbles above us. Our heads flick in each other's direction, knowing we're about to be caught in a torrential downpour if we don't book it back to the Gibson Ranch right now.

"Come on," Wyatt commands as he drops his pole, secures my hand, and then takes off up the small hill, pulling me behind him as the thunder booms again and the clouds roll in darker and thicker than they were just a few moments ago. Texas thunderstorms are unpredictable, so it's common for them to come on with little to no warning.

I let him lead me with his hand in mine, our feet dragging across the dirt and through the tall strands of green grass as if I'd trust him to take me anywhere—and I guess a small part of me does. Wyatt Gibson may be infuriating and a gross boy, but I'd trust him with my life.

By the time we reach the wide wraparound porch of the

Gibson's house, we're both soaking wet. Our shoes are covered in mud and chunks of grass kicked up from our running.

"My goodness! I never should have let you two go down to the creek when they said there'd be a chance of rain," Momma Gibson scolds as she stops us right outside the back screen door, holding two towels. "Here, dry off and start stripping, you two."

"But, Mom," Wyatt whines while I silently laugh at him.

"Don't start with that, Wyatt Allen. You know you're not coming in my house covered in that mess."

He rolls his eyes as his mom turns to me and holds a towel around me to shield my body from Wyatt's eyes as I take off my clothes. We watched a video in school this spring about what happens to girls as they grow up and all the changes their bodies go through, and sure enough, a few weeks later, my boobs popped and a few hairs started to sprout down there. Since then, she's been protective of me and insistent that Wyatt and I give each other privacy, even though it's been years since we've shared a bath or showed each other our privates. That was something we did as four-year-olds. I'd rather die than do that now.

When I'm down to my underwear, she wraps the towel around me and lets me inside. "You go use the guest bathroom, Kelsea."

"Okay. Thanks, Momma G." I scurry down the hall and quickly turn on the shower, grabbing my bag of clothes I always bring over with me before locking myself in the bathroom.

After I'm clean and in dry clothes, I find Momma Gibson in the kitchen cooking dinner, where she always is at this time of day. Randy Gibson, Wyatt's father, should be coming in from the stables any time now, ready to eat. Judging by the smells, I'd say we're having enchiladas.

The evening progresses as it normally does while all three Gibson boys tease each other across the table and their parents threaten them with shoveling horse and cow poop in punishment if they don't knock it off. Forrest, the oldest brother by five years, does nothing but roll his eyes at his younger brothers, his teenage attitude shining through and his annoyance for the three of us earning him his own reprimanding.

As much as I love being in this house with this family, a small part of me remains envious every time I'm here that my own parents can't be bothered to show up for dinner with me every night.

As darkness overtakes the sky and the rain subsides, I glance at the clock. I blink when I realize it's way later than when my mother would usually pick me up.

"Hey, Momma G?" I ease into the kitchen as she hangs up the phone, keeping her back turned to me.

"Yes, honey?"

"Did my mom call? It's pretty late. She should be here by now."

She still fails to turn around as her hands reach back into the sink of soapy water, scrubbing at a pan. "No, I haven't heard from her, Kels. But it's okay. Maybe that just means you get to have a sleepover tonight."

"Sleepover? Yes!" Wyatt comes around the corner, dressed in

his pajamas now, his sandy-blond hair messy and hanging partially in his eyes.

"Why don't you two go pick a movie, and I'll make some popcorn?" she suggests, offering us a soft smile over her shoulder. And when I finally see her eyes, I notice a sadness there I'm not sure I like.

"Don't pick anything girly, though," Walker, Wyatt's twin, says as he walks into the living room while I follow Wyatt to the movie cabinet.

"I don't always pick something girly," I fire back.

"You boys will let Kelsea pick what she wants, and that will be that," Momma Gibson declares as she walks into the room and preps the television.

Once we're all settled in, Wyatt, Walker, and I are sprawled out on the living room floor on top of a blanket, munching on homemade popcorn and brownies, enthralled in *The Sandlot*. Forrest is on the couch with his own bowl of popcorn. Even though we've seen this movie a thousand times, it's one of Wyatt's favorites, so I always know he'll be happy with this choice.

Whispering behind us makes my ears perk up as I hear Mr. and Mrs. Gibson talking quietly in the kitchen. The boys are so enthralled with the movie that they're oblivious to the conversation, but the mention of my name makes me strain my ears to listen.

"She's not coming?"

"No," Momma G says, and I can hear her sniffle. "She left me a message, Randy. Asked us to take care of Kelsea. Apologized for leaving but basically said she's not coming back."

"Christ, Elaine. Does Hank know?"

"I don't know," she whispers, lowering her voice as the movie enters a quieter scene. "Maybe you should call him?"

"And tell him what? 'Your wife up and left town with her boss and basically told us to take care of your kid until you return'?"

What? My mom left? She's not coming back?

"I don't know! I mean, I knew Sarah wasn't happy lately, but I never thought she'd do something like this."

I stare at the movie and then flick my eyes to Wyatt, my best friend who I kissed today because my dad always told me that you should marry your best friend. And up until this moment, I believed him.

Even over the next few days, I wanted to believe that he was still right—that when you marry your best friend, you live happily ever after. I wanted to believe that my mother was coming back, that this was just a work trip and everything would go back to normal when she returned.

But after three days passed and my father finally returned home and sat me down to explain to me that he didn't know if she was ever coming back, I realized that maybe you shouldn't marry your best friend. Because when you do, and things don't work or one of you changes your mind, you lose everything, and your world will never be the same.

My father was never the same after that day, and my family as I knew it had crumbled into nothing but dust at my feet.

Sure, the walls of our house were still standing, and my father still loved me and never failed to show me that. But he was absent more, taking longer and longer trips that required me to stay with the Gibsons for weeks at a time.

Wyatt and his family became the closest thing I had to my own, and the thought of that changing made my heart ache twice as hard. So no matter how much kissing my best friend that day made me envision, over the following years, walking down the aisle in a white dress to him under that big oak tree or notice how his chocolate-brown eyes seemed to sparkle more when we'd laugh in the days and weeks that followed, one fact remained: Giving in to my developing crush on Wyatt Gibson would only result in heartbreak in more than one aspect of my life. And that's the last thing I wanted or needed.

If there's anything the ten-year-old me thought was possible, it was thinking that my decision at that time in my life would be an easy one to uphold. Because as time passed and we both grew up, as the scrawny boy I played in the mud with grew into a man, the more I realized how stupid I was to believe that I could stuff my feelings down.

I thought you were supposed to fall in love with your best friend, and that's exactly what I did. But what if falling meant risking everything worthwhile in your life at the same time?

That question plagued my mind for days, months, and years, until one day, when everything changed, and nothing had been the same since—the day that Walker, Wyatt's twin brother, kissed me.

CHAPTER ONE

Kelsea

Present Day

"Ben, go grab some more trays of glasses from the back," I call over the noise in the brewery as the crowd grows larger by the minute. It's Friday night in Newberry, Texas, and business is booming here at the Gibson Brewery & Restaurant.

"I'm on it!" he yells back, blowing through the double doors that lead to the back of the house where the kitchen is pumping out food. The fermenting and aging tanks are all lined up as well, ready for beer to be served straight from the tap.

Greg, one of our regulars, motions to me across the bar as he holds up his almost empty glass, nearly knocking off his white cowboy hat in the process. "Hey, Kels! Another IPA, please, darlin'?"

"Only 'cause you said please, Greg." I shoot him a wink as I spin a glass up from the tray beneath the bar and turn around to fill the cup to the brim with one of our strongest beers.

One year ago, I wasn't sure if Wyatt's venture would make it, but when he decided to open up his tasting room in Newberry instead of the small farming town of Newberry Springs that we call home, we found his intuition was right on the money. The warehouse located just off the main road in town allows for plenty of people to stop by on their way home from work, grab a bite to eat now that our kitchen is fully up and running, and unwind after a hard day at the office or out in the fields.

"We've got a customer complaining about the cloudiness of the beer again." Britney, one of the other waitresses, comes up to me, holding a glass of our IPA to the light so the haziness can be seen in the liquid.

With a roll of my eyes, I start to respond before a warm hand clasps over my shoulder and stops me from moving forward.

"I'll handle it. Most people don't realize that some cloudiness is normal in certain brews because they're used to drinking beer out of amber bottles and don't see it." Smooth like butter and deep like the hole in my heart where I bury my feelings for this man, Wyatt's voice hits my ears. His touch sends a shiver down my arm, as if my body just naturally reacts to him that way. And she does, that traitorous bitch.

CHAPTER ONE

No matter how hard I try to convince my nervous system that we're not allowed to react to Wyatt Gibson that way, she's stubborn as an ox and fails to listen.

"Thank you. It will probably mean more coming from the owner," Britney replies on a breath of relief.

"Agreed. And since you're new, just make sure you bring this complaint to me every time, okay? Of course, I think we know Kelsea could have put him in his place as well without her beaming smile ever leaving her face." He turns to me now, flashing the spread of his lips that highlights his dimples, and the deep brown of his eyes sucks me in like two pools of melted chocolate just waiting to be devoured. "But I don't think it's fair to subject others to her wrath. She saves that for me."

I stick my tongue out at him as Britney laughs. "Hey, it's called killing people with kindness. It's my secret weapon. You don't know if you should be scared of me or if I'm truly being genuine." I shrug before handing off the IPA to Greg and then fetching a towel from the bucket to wipe up my mess since the cup had tipped a bit and a few drops had fallen out. But I'm really just searching for anything to distract me from the tingling still shooting down my arm from Wyatt's touch.

"That's not the only weapon you possess, Kels." His words rattle my mind as he squeezes my shoulder once more before taking the beer back over to table six in the corner, pulling up a stool to the high-top, and turning on his charm to educate the customer on proper beer brewing technique. He's perfected his speech over the past year to appease the customer and keep them coming back for more, and part of me wonders why I find that so damn sexy.

A wistful sigh leaves my lips, apparently just loud enough for Britney to pick up on it. "You are so far gone for that boy."

Startled that she heard me, I reply in my signature rebuttal, "We're just friends."

"Ha, yeah, maybe to him. But you, my dear, definitely want more."

"You're crazy. That will never happen. We grew up together, and now we work together. Hell, he's technically my boss and more like a brother." Placing my hands on my hips, I ask, "Would you wanna date your brother?"

She scrunches up her nose. "Okay, yuck. Point made."

"Exactly."

I roll my eyes and turn my back to her to hide the blush I can feel creeping up my cheeks. Britney hasn't been working here long, but if she already suspects my feelings for Wyatt, then I need to be more careful of my reactions to him around her.

Of course, she's right, though. Anyone with eyes could probably tell I'm lusting after my best friend—except for Wyatt, that is. It's always been that way, though, ever since we were kids, especially when he kissed me goodbye the night before he left for college. Yeah, that night still lives rent-free in my head.

But I'm probably alone in reminiscing on that night and wondering what could have happened if I had told him how I really felt.

CHAPTER ONE

"Hey, Kelsea." Another familiar voice calls to me, and I find the owner perched on a stool at the bar.

A natural smile pulls across my face. "Walker. What are you doing in here tonight?"

He throws his wallet on the counter and then runs his fingers through his hair, the same sandy-blond tint that his twin brother sports. "It was a long shift at the firehouse last night and today. I need a beer to unwind before I go home and slip into a coma for the next twenty-four hours."

"Completely understandable. Although, aren't you supposed to be at the ranch tomorrow for horseback riding lessons?"

He sighs, accepting the pint of our blonde ale I poured for him. He always drinks the same thing when he comes in here. Walker supports his brother's business, but he doesn't venture out to try new things. He's a creature of habit.

"Yeah. I guess that interrupts my plans for a deep slumber, huh?"

"What will you ever do without all of your beauty rest?" I tease.

"Continue being the ugly twin," Wyatt says behind my back as the hairs on my neck stand up. I hate when he does that—comes up behind me unannounced so my body can't prepare for his presence.

"Why do you talk about yourself in front of other people, Wyatt? That's self-deprecation at its finest," Walker fires back.

"Don't start, you two," I interrupt while mentally tallying how many useless arguments I've broken up between the two of them over the years. If I had a dollar for every one, I wouldn't need to work for the next twenty years, I'd guess.

Wyatt slides into the spot next to me along the counter as we both focus in on Walker. "How was work?"

"Long. There weren't any fires, but several calls required us to call in an ambulance. We lost an older woman to a heart attack. It was . . ." He trails off, obviously trying to hide the emotion in his eyes. But I can sense it. Walker hates when he can't save someone, but not everyone can be saved. Unfortunately, he struggles understanding that sometimes, and I watch it wear on him when it's fresh in his mind.

I reach for his hand, placing my own on top of his, forcing him to look up and meet my eyes. But when he does, his eyes shift slightly to my right, narrowing in on his brother before he focuses back on me so I can tell him what he needs to hear. "Walker, you're an incredible person, and I'm sure that you did what you could under the circumstances. Sometimes fate comes in and makes things happen the way they're supposed to. There's no fighting that."

His brow unfurls as he locks eyes with me. "Thanks, Kelsea. You always know how to make me feel better."

"I don't know how you do it, Walker. I couldn't handle that kind of pressure, that's for sure."

His thumb strokes the top of mine as his eyes flick back and forth between me and Wyatt, and then he leans forward, moving his face close to mine. "It sucks sometimes, but it's part of the job," he continues with a shrug of his shoulders.

A throat clearing beside us slices through our moment, and I turn to glare in Wyatt's direction. "We need to get back to work," he commands, throwing a towel down on the counter before traipsing off.

I frown at his reaction. "What the hell is his problem?" My hands find my hips as I watch him walk away.

Walker chuckles and then moves to stand, gulping down his entire beer in a matter of seconds. "One day, you two will figure out your shit." He wipes his mouth with the back of his hand and then slaps a twenty on the counter. It's far more cash than necessary to pay for one beer, but he never falters in his payment each time he comes in. "Keep the change, Kels."

"Thanks, Walker."

"See you Sunday at the ranch?"

I nod. "Yup. Momma G and I have lots of jars to fill."

Every Sunday morning, the brothers and I gather at the Gibson Ranch to help their parents with whatever they need. I usually end up in the kitchen bottling jams and sauces and bagging spice blends that Wyatt and I take to the farmers market each Thursday to sell. The boys help their dad maintain the property they grew up on, now a booming bed and breakfast and entertainment venue specializing in weddings and business gatherings.

Shortly after my mom left, Wyatt's parents decided to pursue their dream of converting their home into a multi-faceted business.

Elaine, better known as Momma G, always dreamed of owning a bed and breakfast. Randy loves his wife something fierce, so he agreed to slowly start opening his home up to more people and more business opportunities.

Now, almost fifteen years later, the Gibson Ranch has become a well-known and sought-after venue for weddings, company parties, relaxing getaways for couples, field trips for elementary classes, and a place for high school students to gain internship experience in ranching and farm-life skills. It's amazing what they've been able to create, but it's been a family effort—and since I'm technically a part of that family, my time and energy has been devoted there as well.

I turn back around and survey the crowd once more. Britney flies past me holding a tray full of food resting on her shoulder, and Ben clears dirty tables, wiping down the surfaces as more people get ushered back from the hostess stand in the front. A smile pulls at my lips while I admire what we've built here. Yes, I said *we*, because no matter what Wyatt says, I know he couldn't do this without me. Hell, maybe he'd even admit that out loud, but sometimes his pride gets too big to manage.

"Kelsea!"

My eyes seek out the voice and land on a brunette I've come to think of as a friend since she first came in here a year ago.

"Sydney!" As quickly as I can manage, I dodge a few people and weave in and out of tables to greet her with a hug. "How are you?"

Her face turns to the man beside her, one I instantly recognize as well. They share a smile reserved for two people madly in love before she twists back to face me. "I've never been happier. Look." She beams as she offers me her left hand. A beautiful diamond flashes in the light.

"Oh my God! Congratulations, you guys!"

Javi and Sydney knew each other in high school but reconnected about a year ago. Their relationship started out a little unorthodoxly, but they ultimately realized they belonged together. It was certainly entertaining to watch, and over the past year, I've enjoyed watching them fall deeper in love with one another.

Javi places a kiss at her temple and pulls her in closer. "Thanks, Kelsea. Can we get our usual, please? We're just gonna have one drink and then head home." The heat behind his gaze leaves no doubt as to how they'll be celebrating. A tinge of disappointment registers in my mind. I can't remember the last time I had sex—not that any of those times were stellar, anyway.

"Of course." I move back behind the bar and fill their glasses, depositing them on the table when I return. "So when did you get engaged?"

"Last weekend," Sydney replies, a mile-wide smile still plastered on her lips.

"Aw. I'm so happy for you."

"Thank you," Javi answers. "And hey, congrats on the one-year anniversary. Sorry we missed the celebration, but it's great to see this place packed." His eyes scan the room before landing back on mine.

"Yeah. Opening up the restaurant and expanding into the next portion of the warehouse definitely made a difference."

"I bet Wyatt's thrilled."

"That I am." Wyatt appears, inserting himself into the conversation.

Javi and Wyatt make small talk as I get whisked away by one of the bartenders when a keg goes empty and needs to be replaced. But as soon as I enter the back of the house, a puddle of brown fluid catches my attention, and I look down to survey the mess on the floor.

"Shit."

"What the . . ." Wyatt says as he comes up behind me, almost crashing into my body, causing yet another flash of heat to course through my veins. "What the hell happened?"

"I don't know, boss. I came back to grab some clean dishes and saw this puddle. It looks like one of the tanks is leaking," John, one of the employees, says as he breezes past us.

"Dammit! Kels, call—"

"—Stuart. I know. I'm on it." I turn on my heel, taking my cell phone out of my pocket at the same time. I locate Stuart's contact information and dial him as quickly as I can.

The rest of the night goes by in a blur as our technician comes in and fixes the hose that had a leak in it. The kitchen pumps out food, and the front of the house keeps our customers happy while Wyatt and I deal with the crisis in the back. By closing time, Ben and Wyatt lower the giant metal doors of the warehouse, sealing us inside as we finish cleaning

CHAPTER ONE

procedures. Wyatt locks himself in the office to finalize some paperwork.

In a matter of an hour, the only two people left in the building are Wyatt and me, like nearly every Friday and Saturday night. Rarely will either of us take a day off—him, the control freak afraid to leave his business to run without him for one night, and me, the faithful employee and best friend who doesn't have anything else to do but torture herself by being in close quarters with her best friend whom she's secretly in love with.

Out of habit, I saunter over to the jukebox in the corner. My eyes move across the song choices until my heart agrees, and I push the button to end the silence around me. The last task of the evening is to lift the stools on top of the tables and the counter to clear the floors for the cleaning crew in the morning. A little background music makes the job go faster.

The melody of George Strait's "I Just Wanna Dance With You" comes over the speakers, and I start to move my body to the slightly upbeat melody. I shimmy my hips and two-step across the floor, only pausing to lift a stool and put it upside down on a table and then move on to the next.

I continue belting out the words before I turn around and catch Wyatt watching me, leaning against the doorway with one leg crossed over the other and his arms folded in a similar position. His biceps strain against the sleeves of his black polo shirt, the one that all of the employees wear. His sandy-blond hair is cut short but tousled from the stress of the evening, and his jaw is covered in a dusting of light-brown whiskers that tend to get darker as the day goes on. His brown eyes lock on me, following my every move. I swear I can feel them drawing a map all over my skin.

But then again, that might just be my wishful thinking.

"You picked George tonight?" he asks, flicking his head toward the jukebox in the corner.

"Yeah. George never disappoints, and after tonight, I needed something I could count on to help the stress of the night roll off."

He sighs and runs a hand through his hair. "It was a crazy night, wasn't it?"

"Yup."

"If business continues like this, I'm going to have to hire more people."

"I think that's smart."

"Would you help me put the word out? And then sit with me—"

"—in the interviews? Of course," I reply, finishing his thought like we always do. We've known and worked with each other for so long, it seems a habit between us, like everything else. Even him being gone for six years didn't prevent us from slipping right back into our roles as best friends.

He pushes off the wall and crosses the room until he stands right in front of me, pulling me into his chest as he wraps his arms around me. "I don't know what I'd do without you, Kels."

"Your life would fall apart, and you'd have a psychotic break to the point where your family would have to commit you." I breathe in his scent while I instinctually nuzzle closer to him, the vibrations from his laugh rumbling through his chest. His woodsy cologne mixed with a hint of sweat sends my pulse skyrocketing.

"I'm serious, Kels."

"I know. But it's a good thing you'll never have to find out, huh?"

I hear the deep inhale of his breath as his chin rests on my head, the grasp we have on each other holding tight until I feel him start to release first.

I can never get enough of these moments—the moments when I fantasize about our hug meaning more than just a sign of affection in our friendship. When his deep breath is actually him taking in my scent the way I crave taking in his and the look in his eyes is not one of appreciation but longing, the way I long for things to be different.

With a kiss to the top of my head that slices another crack through my heart, he steps back from me and reaches up to tuck an unruly curl of my blonde hair behind my ear. "Go ahead and get out of here."

"You sure?" I search his eyes, silently hoping he'll ask me to stay. Visions of us getting too close and an accidental brush of skin leading to a hot and heavy make out session enter my mind before I can push them out.

Sadly, he nods. "Yeah. You work too hard. One of these days, you're going to realize that I overwork you, and you're going to leave me," he teases as a wave of disappointment slides through me.

"Nah. I'll just demand a raise."

"I couldn't afford to pay you what you're worth to me, Kels."

Something about the way he says that has me questioning his tone. "And what is that?"

He pauses, swallowing hard before starting to back away slowly while the corners of his mouth tip up at the same pace. "Everything."

My heart jumps on the trampoline in my chest as I watch him move further away. I desperately want those words to mean to him what they mean to me, but knowing Wyatt, I have to remind myself that our affection is genuine because of how long we've known each other, not because of unrequited feelings.

"Grab your purse, and I'll walk you to your car."

I lift the last stool beside me and then untie my apron as I slide past him. I hurry to the break room in the back of the building where I leave my purse in a locker during my shift. With a look out the back door before we exit, Wyatt leads me to my truck, his hand on the small of my back. Last year, our friend, Sydney, was attacked in the parking lot, and ever since, Wyatt has insisted that each female employee be escorted to her car at night.

"I can't believe you still insist on driving this truck around." His hand moves toward the same red pickup I've been driving since high school. He insists on teasing me about my vehicle at least once a week.

"I think there's something to be said for nostalgia."

"This truck is way past nostalgic—it's moving into the relic category."

"Leave Old Betsy alone," I admonish.

"She's not a cow, Kels. Seriously, I worry about you driving this thing." He pats his hand against the fender, sending the sounds of the vibrating metal into the air.

"That's why I have Triple A and you on speed dial."

"You know you should call me no matter what," he declares like he always does as he opens my door and waits for me to situate myself inside.

"Yes, I know. Goodnight, Wyatt. See ya in the morning."

He nods. "Yup. Rose's at nine o'clock. Unless you want to sleep in for once. I wouldn't be opposed to—"

"Nine o'clock, and don't be late." I point my finger in his direction as I reach down to roll the window up. Yes, this thing still has handles to control the windows.

"Drive safe." He shoves his hands in his pockets as I fire up the engine, waving before I drive out of the parking lot.

My eyes check my rearview mirror, sneaking one last glance of the man I want so desperately but can never have. I convince myself to take the long way home tonight to help clear my head. The dark Texas sky hangs above me, white twinkling lights painting the black canvas, and I roll down the window to soak in the cool air of a summer night.

Later that night, as I lie in bed, I replay that kiss on my head, the lingering touch in his hug, and the smell of him next to me, feeding the ache in my chest. No matter how much I love my best friend, I can never have him.

And as much as I think a daily reminder of that fact will help me believe it, the next morning, when we meet for our usual

Saturday morning breakfast, just the sight of him kickstarts the cycle once more. Especially when I see him waiting in our booth at Rose's Diner with the grin that makes my heart trip each and every time I see it.

Yup. I'm definitely a lost cause.

CHAPTER TWO

Wyatt

I tap my fingers on the table in front of me before taking another sip of my coffee, relishing the taste of the diner coffee that always seems to taste better than when I make it at home. Rose's Diner is knee-deep in the Saturday morning breakfast rush. The smell of bacon and greasy food is infiltrating my nostrils and making my stomach grumble louder than before as I sit in the booth in the back corner that always seems to be available when I stumble through the door.

Ever since high school, Kelsea and I make a point to have breakfast at Rose's at least once a week. Since I opened the brewery, that day typically lands on Saturday. Beth, the head waitress, is as dedicated to our weekly meal as Kelsea and I are, and her hospitality ensures we're seated fast and in our usual booth.

Sometimes our entire group of friends will gather on a Saturday morning for brunch, but truth be told, I prefer the meals between just the two of us.

My eyes scour the menu, debating what I'm going to get. Everything is starting to sound good, but Beth, Kelsea, and I all know I'll end up just getting the same thing I always do each time.

Everything is as it should be, the usual Saturday morning routine, except for one thing—it's five minutes past nine, and Kelsea is late, which rarely happens.

I've known the woman since I was in diapers, and punctuality is her vice. She thrives on it—she's the type of person who is fifteen minutes early to every place she goes. The only time she's ever late is when she's so immersed in a project that she forgets where she is. Then you get a panicked Kelsea, who can be as scary as one who's trying to kill you with kindness.

As if my mind conjured her presence, the bell above the door rings, and she barrels through the opening. Her head twists in search of me, even though she knows damn well where I'll be, and the evidence of her distraction hangs around her neck like a flashing red light.

I should have known. She was out taking pictures.

With an exaggerated sigh, she hustles to me at our booth and then plops herself down on the other side. She blows her unruly curls from her face before reaching for the strap of her camera and removing it from around her neck. The smooth, silky skin there catches my eye, but I use the same willpower I exhibit around her every day to shift my eyes to anywhere but a part of her I daydream of pressing my lips to.

Yeah, you heard that right. The woman sitting across from me may be my best friend, but she's also gorgeous, and I am a man, after all. I'd be lying if I said I'd never fantasized about crossing the line I know would be a mistake to cross. Doesn't mean I can't look discretely when she's not paying attention.

"You're late," I tease, fighting my grin as I take a sip of my coffee and wait for her to finish righting herself. Her hands are flying everywhere to correct her naturally wild hair, she's trying to situate her camera and purse in the particular way she likes them, and before she flashes me her boob, she finally adjusts the neckline on her plain white shirt. *Thank God.*

"I know, I know. I'm sorry. I lost track of time." A harsh breath of desperation leaves her lips as she finally settles back into the booth and stares at me with wide eyes. Her hand moves over her heart, probably attempting to slow down the rhythm.

Yeah, my heart beats wildly like that around you every day, too, Kels.

"I figured you were taking pictures if you hadn't beaten me here. It's the only thing that ever makes you late."

She purses her lips in a tempting way just as Beth comes by and fills an empty cup of coffee for Kelsea. "You act like you know me well or something."

I chuckle lightly. "Or something."

"Hi, Kelsea. Nice of you to show up this morning," Beth teases.

"Hey. Normally, it's me waiting on him," she declares, pointing a finger across the table at me.

Beth and I laugh simultaneously as she rests the coffee pot on the table and then takes her pen and pad out of her apron. "You're right. So what'll it be for you two today? The usual?"

Kelsea and I share a look across the table.

"I don't know why you even bother writing down our order anymore, Beth."

"Sometimes I switch it up," Kelsea argues.

"Rarely," I say, rolling my eyes. "French toast for me, Beth, please. And you know how I like my eggs." I wink up at her while she grins. The woman is the same age as my mom, but I know she doesn't mind the harmless flirting.

"And for you, Miss Kelsea?"

My best friend hums as her eyes scour the menu unnecessarily. "Short stack today, Beth. Eggs over medium and bacon please."

"No strawberries and whipped cream?"

"Not in the mood for the sugar." Kelsea smiles up at her as she takes our menus and promises to return.

"Not feeling adventurous today?"

She shrugs. "I had my adventure early this morning."

"Where'd you take pictures?" I ask, taking another sip of my coffee while trying not to act too intrigued. Kelsea developed her hobby of photography when we were younger, but she very rarely shares what she shoots with me. Crazy since I'm supposedly her best friend, huh?

The only reason I've ever seen her pictures is because one time, when we were teens, I stole her camera and flipped through the images after she kept denying me access. Her shots were amazing, highlighting so much detail in the world around her, so I can only imagine how she's improved since then. Still, I wish she'd show me what keeps her busy when we're not working together, the one thing that makes her forget her responsibilities.

"I was down at the river park." Her eyes move away from mine as she seeks out the creamer and starts making her coffee.

A small river runs through town, sidewalks lining both sides before connecting at a bridge. It's a popular place for people to run, walk their dogs, ride their bikes, or just enjoy the scenery. During the spring and fall months, the trees and flowers along the path are vibrant, creating beautiful backdrops I'm sure Kelsea can highlight with a simple picture.

"Get any good shots?"

She nods subtly, still avoiding my eyes. "Yup."

"Care to show them to me?"

"Nope," she replies, emphasizing the p before drawing her lips into a thin line.

"Okay, then." My tone is harsher than I intended, but the fact that my best friend won't share her hobby with me sometimes grates on my nerves. I know neither of us wants to push the subject, however, so I leave it alone.

"So when are you going to finally cave and try the pancakes?"

I appreciate her attempt to lighten the mood by changing the subject, so I oblige.

"When you cave and finally try the French toast."

With a playful smile on her lips, she glares at me above the rim of her coffee cup before taking a drink. I pretend not to notice how her perfect pink lips curl around the mug because that would mean my thoughts are veering into dangerous territory, a place I try like hell to avoid.

And believe me, it's not easy to fight slipping into that quicksand and letting those thoughts pull me under. Hell, just last night, I was barely keeping my head above water at the brewery as I caught myself stalking Kelsea with my eyes as she effortlessly commanded my business exactly like I knew she wanted to when I approached her about the idea.

Her ass in her jeans is one of my favorite sights to get lost in, but before I could pull myself out of my own head, my twin brother came in and absorbed Kelsea's consoling just a little too eagerly after his long shift.

Fucking Walker. If he weren't my brother, I would have considered chopping off his hands right then and there just for touching Kelsea.

But Kelsea isn't mine to stake a claim over like that. And I sure as hell wouldn't act on those instincts in front of Walker. He'd never let me live it down if I did.

"You're missing out . . ." she says, pulling me back to our debate over the reigning breakfast carb.

"That's what you think. Let's just agree that the only breakfast denominator we share is syrup, Kelsea."

"And each other," she corrects me. "Our breakfast dates are something I look forward to every week, Wyatt. It was weird coming here without you before you moved back home."

The emotion in her voice makes my chest tight, just like it does every time she mentions our time apart. That distance was strange but needed at the same time. Now, though, I couldn't picture ever being apart again. "I can imagine. But you're like the syrup to my breakfast, Kels. It never felt the same without you, either."

Her eyes slide up as she fights a smile. "That was so cheesy."

I shrug and then reach for my silverware to unwrap the napkin in preparation for our food to arrive. "Yeah, it was. But it's true."

The first time we came to Rose's Diner back in high school, I ordered the French toast and she ordered pancakes. We debated over who had made the better choice, but once I tried the French toast, there was no way I was going to taint my taste buds with anything else. And even when I left for college and came back for holiday visits and then finally moved back home, I still never swayed in my decision. And neither has Kelsea, I guess.

Have you ever gone to a restaurant and tried one dish and loved it so much that you continued to order the same thing each time for fear of ordering something else and not liking it? Well, that's what happened to me. I mean, I don't know how a diner could mess up pancakes, but the French toast is out of this world.

Before she can come back with a rebuttal, Beth returns and drops off our food. "Anything else, you two?"

Our eyes scour the table, and Kelsea reaches for the bottle of syrup before I can. "Nope, I think we're good, Beth. Thank you."

We each situate our plates to our liking and then dive in.

"So I think I'm going to advertise for help on Monday," I say after a small bout of silence around a mouthful of food.

"Okay."

"We can hold interviews next Wednesday before we open."

She nods, focusing on her food. "I'll be there."

"I appreciate it."

Her eyes finally flick up to meet mine. "I know." Her smile is sweet in that comforting way she's always had about her, the same comfort that makes me appreciate how she takes ownership of the business as well. "But my interest is more for the sake of knowing I'll have to manage whoever you hire, though. You know that, right?"

I laugh at her candidness. "I figured. And if you have to deal with someone who's incompetent, I know you'll let me know. But we need people, Kelsea. These past few weeks have been insane."

"Britney was a needle in a haystack, and Ben has secured his reliability. But we've had a few knuckleheads work for you in the past year who have made me question my faith in the intelligence of humanity."

I take my baseball cap off, tossing it on the booth beside me, and run my hand through my hair before taking another sip of coffee. "Don't remind me. I knew owning a business wouldn't be

CHAPTER TWO

easy. I made sure I knew the logistical side of things before we opened, you know? That's what the college degree was for. But dealing with employees is another thing entirely."

"Good thing you have the employee of the year sitting across from you then, huh?" she teases before shoveling another bite of pancake into her mouth, leaving a trail of syrup sticking to her lips. With a swipe of her tongue, she clears the mess, but the imprint of the move has lodged itself into the back of my mind where I keep the images of Kelsea that stir up those unrequited feelings and longing I refuse to acknowledge. They've always been there, but I've been far too stubborn to listen. It's just better that way.

"More like employee of a lifetime," I volley back, pointing my fork across the table at her.

Honestly, I know I could never manage my business without her. It's part of the reason I never acted on my true feelings for her when I returned to Newberry Springs after college. We'd discussed my ideas here and there over the phone while I was gone, but seeing her excitement about the venture in person made me realize something: This woman, *my best friend*, was just as invested in the brewery as I was. She was so excited and overflowing with ideas that our friendship took precedence over my desires.

The vision of Kelsea standing beside me through it all, through building my business and chasing my dreams, was always there in my mind, and the last thing I wanted was to run the risk of any awkwardness between us when we finally got each other back in our lives full-time.

What if I told her how I felt and she didn't feel the same way? What if she was seeing someone and my confession just made things awkward to the point that our relationship changed entirely? Would we still be able to work with each other, or would a lifelong friendship deteriorate from one confession?

So instead of speaking up, telling her the truth about how I felt, I gave her what she wanted: a stake in my brewery. And that became easier to focus on than all of the what-ifs.

She points her fork across the table at me this time. "I like that. We should get it printed on a sash, and I can wear it around the brewery so everyone knows not to mess with me."

"Well, naturally, you'll need a crown to go with it."

"I'll be the beauty queen my mother always wished I'd be." The moment the words leave her mouth, I see the slight twinge of pain there. She doesn't bring up her mom very often, but when she does, resentment laces through every word.

Fighting the rage that builds in my chest every time I think about what her mother did, I say, "You're one in a fucking million, Kels. And it's your mother's fault for missing out on your life, not yours."

She shrugs but avoids my eyes. If I have to remind her of how perfect she is for the rest of my life, I will. As long as she knows that her mother's decision to leave does not reflect on her at all.

She clears her throat, wipes her mouth with her napkin, and then takes another sip of her coffee. "Okay, so interviews next

Wednesday. I'll put it on my calendar." She removes her phone from her purse and taps away on the screen, finally smiling once she finishes pressing buttons—probably satisfied with programming yet another block of time in her life with something to keep her busy—and then gets back to eating.

"Great. And don't forget that the football league is starting back up in a month, so you'd better start marking your calendar for our games, too."

She shakes her head at me. "I can't believe you boys insist on playing football like you're still in high school."

"Hey, it's only flag football, no tackling. And it's fun. It lets us run out some of our manly aggression." I deepen my voice for exaggerated effect.

"Dear lord." Kelsea rolls her eyes.

"But I need my cheerleader there, Kelsea. I can't win without you screaming my name on the sidelines." *And what I wouldn't give to hear you screaming my name while we were alone.*

"I don't scream."

I shoot her a deadpan glare. "Kelsea, please. You get more into the games than some of the guys do," I tease, loving the way her cheeks blush with my words. And then the thought of how else I could make her blush filters right in and out of my mind.

"Well, football is the great American pastime."

"That's baseball, Kels," I correct her.

She waves me off. "Whatever. They're both great in my book, but you know I'll be there, Wyatt."

"You'd better be."

After throwing a twenty on the table, she moves to stand, grabbing her purse. "All right, I'm a busy lady and have things to take care of. I'll see you tonight at the brewery."

Looking up at her, I flash her the smile I reserve just for her. "Yup, see you there."

"Bye, Wyatt."

"Bye, Kels."

My eyes trail her as she walks away from me, honing in on her ass for a brief moment because again, Kelsea's ass is one of my favorite sights. And then my mind starts counting the minutes until we're back together, performing the same dance we always do. Life just always feels easier to get through with Kelsea by my side, and that's a feeling I refuse to fuck with.

CHAPTER THREE

Wyatt

After showering and changing into work jeans and a navy-blue shirt early Sunday morning, I grab my hat and then jump into my truck, heading for my parents' house in Newberry Springs.

When I decided to open the brewery in Newberry, the main hub of our town about thirty minutes away from my childhood home, I found a small place halfway between the two locations to make the drive from either place convenient. A small community of townhouses was constructed between the two parts of town while I was away at college, making the transition home much easier since I didn't have to live with my parents again for long.

Don't get me wrong; I love my parents. But once you're on

your own, it's hard to come back to being under someone else's roof and rules. I'm a grown man, and I needed my space and privacy, which I wholeheartedly appreciate even more now.

I spent six years working on my MBA. Upon my return, I worked for my brother, Forrest, for a year at his construction company until everything was in line for me to open the brewery. And now, a little over a year later, all of the hard work and patience I put into it have paid off.

As the sun takes residence over the horizon, I flip the visor down in my truck to block out the blinding light. Open fields of farmland stretch on for miles on either side of the road, highlighting the occasional house in the middle of the properties where families like my own reside and fight to make a living each and every year.

Growing up, I remember how scary things got from time to time, but then my mother begged my dad to make her dream come true. Momma's vision of a farmhouse that was more of an experience than a farm came to fruition through years of hard work. I love my family and believe in what we've established here at the Gibson Ranch, and I told my dad I wanted to be a part of it and help expand our brand. After taking such a risk to build upon Momma's dream, he insisted I get a degree so I had knowledge to run a successful business.

Even though my father never formally educated himself on the matter, he helped run his own family's farm back in the day, so he had some firsthand familiarity with the responsibility of running a business. But he'd wanted me to have more than what

CHAPTER THREE

he'd had—and something to fall back on in case I changed my mind.

While I was away working on my education, I also developed an affection for craft beers. While most college boys were happy filling solo cups from a keg with Coors Light, my buddies and I would hunt down local craft breweries and sample original beer we couldn't get at a frat party. Through that experience, I decided just exactly how I wanted to help expand the Gibson Ranch: by opening up my own brewery and restaurant.

Since our ranch is too far from ample civilization needed to make an establishment like that succeed, I ventured into town to set up shop, and the payoff was worth it. We still offer my beer to people staying at the B & B and as an option for the bar at weddings and events, but the main contribution of my idea has been established off the property. Success hasn't come without a learning curve, but I'd like to think I've made my father proud. Plus, it gives us a connection to town that helps filter business out to the ranch.

As I turn down the dirt road that leads to my parents' house—far larger now than it was when I was growing up—I glance back in the rearview mirror to watch the dust filter from beneath the tires of my truck before turning back to the sight in front of me. The sky is much brighter than it was a few minutes ago, providing a crystal clear backdrop to the pristine white farmhouse. It looks more like a plantation home since my parents expanded to incorporate the extra bedrooms and a wraparound porch needed to open the bed and breakfast portion of the ranch.

Patches of grass circle the house, enhanced with various flowers and large trees that have been on the property for as long as I can remember. The parking lot to the left still has a few open spaces, so I pull in one of those before exiting the truck and making my way toward the house. A flick of my eyes over my shoulder grants me the sight of Kelsea's truck, so I know to anticipate her when I arrive—and something about knowing she's already here makes it feel a little more like home. She's practically another sibling in the family, which makes the inappropriate feelings I harbor for her all the more damning.

"Momma!" I call out as soon as I open the screen, and the smell of breakfast hits my nose.

"In the kitchen!"

As I turn the corner, I see her and Kelsea standing side by side at the stove, stirring something in giant metal pots in tandem. The slight sway of Kelsea's hips mesmerizes me for a moment, but I pull myself out of my perusal before I get caught.

Momma turns around, wipes her hands on the towel hanging on the oven door handle, and then walks over to me, pulling me in for a hug. "How is my favorite son?" She beams adoringly up at me.

"You say that to all of us."

"Well, you're all my favorite on different days for different reasons," she tosses back.

I plant a kiss on her cheek and then find the basket of biscuits on the counter, reaching in for a fresh one. If my momma is

CHAPTER THREE

famous for one thing, it's her biscuits. The reviews online for the Gibson Ranch are almost guaranteed to mention the delectable balls of dough, and she takes tremendous pride in that—as well as keeping her secret recipe tucked away in her brain until she can pass it along to her future daughters-in-law. It's a generational tradition that started with her grandmother, and she takes it very seriously.

I bite into the biscuit, groaning as soon as the buttery goodness hits my tongue, and finish chewing before I answer her. "I'm good. A little tired."

"Kelsea said you guys were extremely busy last night," she sympathizes before turning back to the stove to stir the pot. If my intuition is correct, there are two giant batches of jam in the making on that stove.

"Yup, which is good, but I'm gonna have to hire more people. These long shifts and nights are taking it out of me."

"Welcome to getting older, son." Her smile finds me over her shoulder, one of pride, adoration, and teasing. Momma has always had a soft spot for me in a different way than my brothers. I feel this inherent need to never let her down, and I hope to God I never do. "Hey, you'd better not eat all of those. We still have some guests who haven't come down yet for breakfast."

"Don't worry, I'll only eat my usual five."

Momma shakes her head at me, smiling the entire time.

"Watch out, Momma G," Kelsea says behind her, grabbing the handles of her pot and bringing it over to the counter where several mason jars rest, waiting to be filled. She deposits the pot on a crocheted pot holder and then reaches up to brush her curly hair away from her face with her forearm.

"Seems you beat me here today."

She eyes me beneath hooded eyelids. "Well, I couldn't be late two days in a row. You know that."

Momma chuckles. "You were late yesterday?"

"To breakfast, not to work."

"I was gonna say, that's not like you." Momma starts sliding jars to Kelsea as she ladles the cooled jam into them, working like the well-oiled machine that they are. Kelsea has been helping my mom with this task since she came up with the idea to sell products from the farm at the farmers market every Thursday. She and I are usually the ones to work our booth, but Walker will step in from time to time if we need him to. Now Forrest, on the other hand, will not. He's too busy running his construction company to help out around the ranch very much, and most of the time, we understand. Plus, he's always so grumpy, the less time we spend around him, the better.

"Well, I was on time today, so let me be." Kelsea shoots me a glare as I grin back at her.

"Dad and Walker out back?"

Momma nods. "Should be in the stables. The vet is here today checking on the horses."

I readjust my hat on my head and then finish off my biscuit. "All right. I'll see you ladies later."

"I'll bring out breakfast in a bit," Momma says just as I open

CHAPTER THREE

the door and venture outside, where the rest of my day will be filled with manual labor.

Walking across this land always brings a sense of pride in seeing how far my parents' dream has come. To the right of the house are the stables where we keep the horses. Walker plays a large part in making sure the horses have everything they need, and he even works on his weekends off giving horseback-riding lessons to kids.

Just beyond the stables is the pasture where the cows, pigs, and chickens reside in their individual areas. To the left, a barn made from a combination of steel and wood, a design that Forrest and his company completed, is where we hold special events, such as weddings. As my eyes flick in that direction, I see a crew taking down tables and chairs from inside, so something must have been happening here last night. I used to keep up with the schedule more, but now that I have my own place to run, anything that isn't absolutely necessary for me to know or have a part in gets blocked out.

As my feet carry me to the stables, I spot Walker talking to the vet. Clarence has lived in Newberry Springs his entire life and services almost every ranch out here with their animals.

"Hey, Clarence." I reach my hand out to shake his as I close the distance between us.

"Wyatt. Good to see you. How's the brewery going?"

"Brewery and restaurant," I reply proudly, "and it's going well. Busy."

"That's good to hear. Some of the guys down at the feed store say they stop in at least once a week."

"Yup, they do, and that's the biggest compliment we can receive: returning customers."

"Absolutely."

"Hey, little brother," Walker teases as he slaps me on the back.

"By two minutes," I reply out of habit, shoving him off me.

"Still, it counts," he says with a pleased grin when he takes in the roll of my eyes.

"What's left to do?" Wanting to get our work done as quickly as possible so I might have a chance to go home and relax for a bit, I wait for his reply. I take Sunday nights off at the brewery, so the quicker I finish up here, the sooner I can go home and rest.

"Dad wanted me to tell you to drive out and check the fence line."

"What? Where's Forrest?" Forrest usually checks the fence line since he deems himself too important to lift a finger and get dirty. Our older brother is not as invested in the ranch as Walker and I are, but I think part of that has to do with our age difference. Forrest was a junior in high school when the ranch started taking shape. He was on a one-way mission to play college football, so he never really relished the idea of staying in Newberry Springs and working on his family's farm.

But after an injury during his sophomore year in college, he dropped out and moved back home. He started working at a construction company and worked his way up from a grunt into management. Then, seven years ago, he used his knowledge to open his own company. His business is his pride and joy, which is something I can relate to, but it also means that he doesn't put in as much time around here as Walker and I do.

"Hey, I'm just delivering the message," Walker says, holding his hands up.

"Well, I guess there are worse things." I toss my thumb over my shoulder. "Is that crew almost done taking down the wedding from last night?"

"Yeah. And George said they're almost out of beer, so you'll need to bring in some kegs this week for the company picnic next weekend."

"All right. Well, let me go make the drive and then . . ."

". . . meet Dad and me back with the cows."

"Sounds good. Nice to see you, Clarence," I say, tipping my hat down.

"You, too, Wyatt. I'll be sure to stop by the brewery soon. I do love that coffee stout you have on tap."

"You're welcome any time. I'll make sure I have a nice pour waiting for you." I turn around and head back to my truck, catching a glimpse of Momma and Kelsea through the kitchen window. The two of them are smiling and laughing in each other's company. A warmth comes over me knowing that even though Kelsea's mom decided to miss out on her life, at least she has my mom to help fill that void.

And though the sight brings me joy, it's a clear reminder of why I've never acted on my feelings for her.

As I cruise along the fence line, the tires on my truck rolling over the bumpy dirt road, the sun moves higher in the sky. Birds chase each other through the air, and beams of light strike through the windshield, flaring the summer heat to life in the cab.

My eyes scour the land in front of me, flat except for the occasional bush or tree, until the reflection of sunlight on water catches my eye. The creek that runs adjacent to our property before cutting through it glistens in the daylight, steadily flowing as I drive along the edge on the other side of the fence. A few hundred feet later, I turn to avoid driving my truck right through the water.

As if appearing from nowhere, a giant tree that serves as the backdrop to so many memories comes into my line of sight while snapshots of my childhood flash through my brain, images my mind can't ever forget. Almost all of those memories involve Kelsea, when we were screaming little kids chasing after each other until we couldn't breathe or when we sat under the tree talking about anything and nothing at all while I pretended to fish and Kelsea played with rocks.

But the one that pops in my head at this moment startles me, probably because I don't ever let myself dig it up. Perhaps being out here for the first time in months is bringing it all back.

∽

"I can't believe you're leaving tomorrow." Kelsea slides up next to me on the ground beneath the tree, right at the water's edge. Our

CHAPTER THREE

toes are bare and dipped in the water lapping at the edge with each pass of breeze that surrounds us.

"I know. It seemed so far off at the beginning of the summer, and now it's here."

"I'm going to miss you, Wyatt." She leans her head on my shoulder and then wraps her arm through mine. And although her touch is something I've longed for more than I care to admit, it serves as a reminder of why it's good that I'm leaving. Because somehow, over the years, Kelsea shifted from being my best friend to a girl on the cusp of womanhood. She makes me want to abandon the gentlemanly ways I've been raised with and touch her everywhere, claiming her as mine.

"I know. But I'll be back at Thanksgiving. And Christmas."

"It's just going to be so weird. I swear, I've seen you almost every day since we were born." She chuckles slightly, but I can sense the emotion behind it. She's been strong so far, not letting me see her cry, but I'm afraid she'll let her tears flow freely tonight. It's going to kill me.

But this is how it has to be. Not only do I need my degree so my father will take me seriously, and I'm desperate for some freedom from them as well, but I think we need this time apart. Even though I know staying here is the safe thing, my feelings have me constantly on the brink of crossing that line—the line my father advised me not to step over months ago.

"I see the way you look at her, Wyatt," he told me one night, back around Christmas. "I know that Kelsea means more to you than just the friendship you two have built since you were kids."

"You . . . you can tell?"

He laughs. "I wasn't born yesterday, son, and I remember what it was like to be seventeen."

"So what are you saying, Dad?"

He clasps his hand on my shoulder. "I'm saying that you're too young to explore those feelings. You're only going to hurt her."

"But . . ." I plead. I feel like, for just one second, the thing I've fantasized about for years was finally within reach, but then it was snatched away from me just as quickly. All the plans I've developed in my head over the past few months instantly go up in flames.

"You both have your entire lives ahead of you. You need space, time apart to create your own lives and hopes and dreams without the other person within reach. You need to fail and not have her to fall back on the second things get hard. And she needs to figure out her future as well—what she wants, who she is. You two can't do that together, especially when you're leaving in a matter of months." He sighs. "I'm not saying that you can't ever go there with her, son. But you also need to remember that our family—you, your brothers, me, and your mom—we're all Kelsea has besides her dad. If you start dating and things go south, she won't only lose you, but she could feel like she's lost us all."

I slump down in my chair, letting his words sink in as I realize he's right. I can't do that to Kelsea, because even though I want to believe that I could offer her the world, that's my seventeen-year-old brain talking right now. That's the naïve boy who's yet to experience the real world and the harsh reality that comes with it.

"I understand, Dad," I say, even though I feel like someone just popped my prized balloon from the fair right in my face.

"Wyatt?" Kelsea's voice pulls me back to the present as her blue eyes peer up at me from my shoulder, her chin resting there comfortably.

"Sorry. Got distracted." I sigh and then focus back on her. "It will be okay, Kels. Yeah, it'll be weird, but I'm always just a phone call away."

She nods and then looks out toward the water, the moonlight reflecting in her eyes where moisture is building.

"Oh, Kels. Please, don't cry." I wrap my arm around her and pull her into my side as her hand finds my shirt and grips at the fabric. The shudders rolling through her body cause her to bump up against me as my body reacts. She's upset, and all I can think about is how good she feels up next to me, how I imagined this situation unfolding so many times. But now I can't act on my feelings, not after listening to what my dad said and taking his point to heart.

But what if for tonight, I give myself something to hold on to, a glimpse of what the future could be? I know my plan is to come back, but what if I don't? What if something happens while I'm away and I regret never feeling her lips on mine? Could I live with never knowing what it would have been like to touch her the way I've wanted to forever?

"Kels," I say quietly, rubbing her back until her head pops up.

I can see the redness on her face even in the dark. Her eyes are glossed over and her lips are turned down, but she still looks so freaking beautiful.

"Sorry."

I reach out to cup her face with my other hand, turning slightly to get more comfortable, and then focus on her lips. "You have nothing to be sorry for. This sucks, it does. It is a lot of change, and you've always been there my entire life. But we will always remain friends. And my family will always be there for you. You know that, right?"

Her chin bobs up and down, and her eyes drop to the ground between us. But then I direct her line of sight back to me with a finger under her chin.

"Kelsea . . ." *I choke out, clearing my throat as I watch her swallow and her eyes zero in on my lips.*

"Yeah?"

"Can I kiss you goodbye?" *The second the words leave my lips, my heart lodges itself in my throat. But I can't take them back now, and for all she knows, this is just me saying goodbye to her as a friend, nothing more. Kelsea has never known about my feelings for her because I've obviously never said anything to her —or anyone, for that matter. My father is apparently a goddamn mind reader, though.*

"Are you sure?"

"Yes. I don't know why," *I lie,* "but I feel like I need to kiss you right now."

"Um, okay," she whispers and then sits up tall, waiting for me to make my move.

I stroke my thumb across her cheek, savoring the feeling of her skin beneath my hands, skin that I've been dying to touch reverently for years. I lean in, anticipating the press of her lips on mine, wondering if it will live up to the fantasy. A small gasp leaves her lips just as we make contact.

It's soft, sweet, and so much better than I ever fucking imagined. The gentle moan that leaves her throat is like music to my ears as I fight the urge to pull her into my chest and do a hell of a lot more than kiss her goodbye.

But I can't. I can't take that from her, knowing it would be months before we see each other again, knowing that I have no future to offer her right now.

Kelsea pushes forward, applying more pressure behind the kiss, so I sweep my tongue out to see if she'll open for me. I've only kissed two other girls from school, but one was during a game of spin the bottle. Samantha wanted me to do more with her in the closet afterward, but I politely told her no. My other kiss and first time having sex was with my ex-girlfriend, Janise. We dated for about five months during our senior year, and she was pressuring me to go all the way. Naturally, my dick thought it was a good idea, so I went along with it.

But nothing I did with either of those girls even compares to this kiss with Kelsea.

Until a few months ago, when my father told me not to go there, I always thought Kelsea and I would lose our virginities to each other. Hell, I don't even know if she's still a virgin, but I can't imagine when she would have found the time to cross that rite of passage since we're pretty much together all the time. Besides, Kelsea likes to keep herself as busy as she can with the five clubs she's a member of at school. I don't even think she's admitted to liking a boy at all.

When her tongue touches mine, a bolt of arousal zings down my spine, and I fight the urge to push for more. But Kelsea lets me take control, and so I do my best to give her a kiss that we'll both always remember, always cherish, no matter what happens from here.

I hold her head to mine, threading my fingers through her thick, blonde curls, her wild hair that reminds me how carefree she can be when she lets herself be. Right now, she's letting me fulfill my desires, though she'll never know that.

As I slow the kiss, I force myself back to the present and reluctantly pull away from her. When I open my eyes, Kelsea's are still closed, her mouth is slightly parted, and I can hear her breathing as I wait for her to come back to the present.

When her eyes pop open, I register shock in her bright blue orbs, and silence falls between us. "Wyatt . . ." she starts but then swallows hard again before she finishes. "What was that?"

And so I tell her what I need her to know. "That was the perfect way to say goodbye."

∼

CHAPTER THREE

"Are you staying for dinner?" my father asks as I stand beside him and my brothers, the four of us resting our forearms on the fence enclosing the cows.

"Might as well at this point." The sun is moving down fast in the sky, bringing a cooler breeze with it, thank God. This heat has been monstrous, and it will be months before it lets up.

"I might have to take mine to go," Walker chimes in. "I have to be at the station in a few hours."

"You'd better let your momma know, then." My father narrows his eyes and then turns to take in the three of us.

"Things look good, Dad," Forrest says, a man of few words as always. He may keep his emotions close to the vest, but deep down, I know he cares about the ranch as much as Walker and I do. He just doesn't have the time to dedicate to it.

"There are days when I wonder what the hell we were thinking, that I couldn't believe I let your mother talk me into this." His chuckle is low, but I catch it. "And then there are days where I couldn't be more proud of what we have here, what we can leave to you three and your children one day."

"Whoa. No children for me yet, Dad." Walker widens his eyes at my father, who just rolls his back at him.

"Yeah, don't you have to meet a woman for that to happen? I'm pretty sure Walker still doesn't know he has a dick." Forrest laughs beside me as I see the irritation flicker in Walker's eyes, but I can't help but laugh as well. Walker likes to pretend he has his shit together, but when it comes to women, the word "serious" isn't in his vocabulary.

Although, I guess I can't really talk shit. I can't remember the last time I had sex or a girlfriend. Pretty sure my business has become my significant other for the past year. And the one woman I want I can't have, which doesn't make me the most pleasant man to be around some days.

"Hey, my dick gets plenty of action, all right?" he fires back. "I bet I have kids before the two of you." Everything has always been a competition with my twin. For some reason, he feels like he has something to prove. Not sure why.

"Will you stop talking about your dicks, for crying out loud?!" Dad turns to us with his spine straight and a command in his voice. "I raised you better than that."

"Sorry," we all mutter as my dad visibly tries to cool down. But when he turns away from us, we cast side-eye glances at one another, smirking discretely.

"Look, I know you're grown men, and I know you're not innocent. But maybe it's time you all start looking for someone to share your lives with."

I'm pretty sure all three of our heads spin toward him at the same time.

"Uh, what are you saying, Dad?" I ask, unsure of how we got on this topic this afternoon and where he plans to go with it. But my guard is up, and I'm not sure I want to hear what he has to say next.

"I'm saying that you're all doing well for yourselves—owning your own businesses, working at the fire station," he says while pointing at Walker. "But life is lonely without someone to share it with. I just think it's time you all start thinking about your futures and who you want in them."

"Are we seriously getting pressure from our dad to settle down right now? I'm only twenty-six," I mumble out of the corner of my mouth.

"Yeah, isn't this the type of conversation that should be coming from Mom's mouth?" Forrest adds.

"Dad, are you okay? You're not dying, are you? I mean, that would explain why you're telling us to find a woman to marry . . ." Walker starts, but my dad just shakes his head and looks back out at the pasture. However, my intuition says something else is going on.

"You three think this is some big joke, don't you?" We remain silent as we wait for the moment of clarity. He turns to face us again, and I can tell this isn't a laughing matter at all. "You know why we have all this, right?" His hand sweeps out across the land stretching for miles all around us. "Because of your mother."

"Okay . . ." I venture.

"I never knew what was possible until I met her. I never knew what I was missing. I thought I was content living my life as it was—running my family's ranch, working from sun up 'til sun down, seeking company of the female variety when the mood struck," he says, giving us the side-eye. "But when she came along, I realized everything I was missing—companionship, someone to share the ups and downs of life with, intimacy. She made everything better. I guess I just see a lot of my younger self in you boys, and I don't want you to miss out on what I have with your mother because of your own stubbornness."

"You think we're purposely not settling down?" Forrest questions.

"Well, I'd imagined by now at least *you'd* be married," he replies, a sure way to cause Forrest's hackles to rise.

"I've been busy," he grates out.

"Exactly. And if you keep this up, you'll be forty and alone and wonder where the hell your life went," my dad fires back.

"Dad, where is this coming from?"

He blows out a breath, lifts his cowboy hat from his head, and runs his fingers through his dark hair sprinkled with grays, the same dark hair that Forrest inherited. It's so unlike mine and Walker's—we got our blond from Mom. "Your mother is worried about you all and wonders if she'll ever have someone to pass her biscuit recipe down to someday." He shakes his head as he chuckles. "She just wanted me to talk to you, and I thought it was a good idea, too, but I guess I'm not doing a very good job of getting my point across."

"No, I think we get it," I answer, not bothering to look back at Walker and Forrest to see if they agree. "But I think I can speak for my brothers when I say love can't be rushed or forced, Dad."

"No, but it can be fostered if you're willing to finally go after it." His eyes are locked on me when he says those words, and I can't help but feel like he's trying to tell me something.

My dad moves toward the house. "Dinner will be ready soon. Don't keep your mother waiting," he calls over his shoulder as my brothers and I just stand there, trying to process what the hell just happened.

"Is anyone else feeling like we just got mind-fucked?" Walker stands next to me with his hands on his hips.

"Uh, to put it bluntly, yes," Forrest interjects.

"Something must be going on." I purse my lips, wondering why he and Mom would be so worried about us while hoping that I'm wrong.

Forrest grunts. "I don't know. Maybe. But I'll be damned if some parental pressure is going to make me settle down any time soon."

"Yes, we know, Grumpy Gibson. You like to be alone and plan to stay that way." Walker mocks him with the nickname we gave him after he came home from college. It was fucked up since we knew part of his surly attitude had to do with his injury and part from a broken heart, but after a few years, he just stayed that way.

"Fuck off." He spins on his heel and then starts heading for the house, too.

"I bet if Shauna was still in the picture, he'd feel differently." Walker leans in and speaks in my ear, referencing Forrest's girlfriend from high school. They both left for college thousands of miles away from each other, so they agreed to part ways, even though we all know that's not what Forrest wanted.

I shrug. "Maybe. Or maybe some people just aren't meant to be together at all."

Walker lifts a brow at me as we start to head back to the house ourselves. "Is that supposed to be as ambiguous as it sounded?"

I stare off to the side, avoiding his eyes, pretending to look out over our parents' property once more. But really, the memory that came to mind earlier of that kiss I shared with Kelsea makes its presence known again, stirring a restlessness within me that's getting harder to ignore. Alongside that conversation with my dad all those years ago, too.

"Nope. Just stating facts." I can feel Walker's bullshit meter reading my body loud and clear, but I do my best to ignore it, just like my feelings for Kelsea that like to pop up at the worst times.

Although, after Dad's comment, I wonder if he was trying to tell me that there's no time like the present to go after what I want, what I've *wanted* from a very young age.

But then I think about where we are now—our friendship that picked back up right where we left off when I returned home, the kiss that neither of us ever spoke of, and the fact that she now works for me and my parents and is an integral part of our lives.

So I've done what any self-respecting, avoidant man would do: I've buried my feelings, pretended like everything could be as it was before, and ignored the instances when I felt like crossing the line.

The notion that we could be together seems laughable at this point because our lives are so intertwined. Furthermore, if we were meant to be together, it would have happened by now, right? I mean, I don't even know if Kelsea feels the same way about me, which is an obstacle in itself. I mean, I swear I catch her staring here or there, and the shot of electricity that zips through my body each time we touch can't possibly be one-sided, can it?

But taking the risk to find out could be catastrophic.

And that realization right there tells me to ignore my father's warning, bury those feelings sparking to life again, and keep doing what I'm doing: focusing on my business and helping my family keep theirs alive.

CHAPTER FOUR

Kelsea

"You'd better relax your face before it gets stuck like that."

My head spins to the side to see Evelyn studying me with laser focus, much like I'm using to line up the jars of jam on the table in front of me. I have to make sure each of the labels is facing the same way and the flavors are organized in rows.

"What are you talking about?"

"You look like you're either constipated or woke up on the wrong side of the bed."

I arrange the last few jars, brush the hair from my face, and then stand tall to face her head on. "I'm fine. Just busy."

CHAPTER FOUR

She shrugs and then moves back into her booth. "Whatever you say."

"I take it you're all ready?" I eye the racks of clothes behind her and admire a few pieces I wouldn't mind adding to my collection, even though I don't have anywhere to wear something that nice.

She rests her hands on her hips. "Always. I have a system down now, girl. You know that."

Evelyn owns her own fashion boutique in town and sets up her booth next to the ranch's booth each week at the farmers market. Her clothes tend to bring in the younger crowd, but she really carries something for women of every age. Fabrics of all colors and textures make up dresses, shirts, and even denim jeans, a staple in any woman's wardrobe. And I love that she's not afraid to carry items that are classic and trendy.

Shortly after Wyatt left for college, she and I met and hit it off. I have never been so grateful for friendship, especially of the female variety, until I met her. She filled a void I didn't know I was missing. Having a boy as your best friend means you miss out on a lot of girl talk, comparing stories and feelings that a man could never understand. And since my mom wasn't around, I missed out on even more in that respect.

"Well, would you mind grabbing the last two boxes from the bed of the truck for me then, please?" I throw my chin in the direction of the truck where the bags of spice blends still sit.

"Sure." Evelyn jumps up in the truck just as Wyatt comes over with two cups of coffee.

"Here you go, Kels." He hands me the sweet nectar of life and I take a sip, moaning out loud at how good it tastes. Roasted, a local coffee shop in town, has a truck that comes out to the farmers market each week. I know it might seem sad, but sipping on a cup of their coffee while I'm out here each Thursday is something I think about all week.

"Thank you. God, I could drink this coffee all day." I close my eyes and take another drink.

Wyatt's face contorts when I open my eyes, his tense jaw ticking while he stares at me.

"What?"

"Nothing." After his short, sweet, and to-the-point non-answer, he turns on his heels, grabbing the boxes Evelyn had pushed to the tailgate from deeper in the bed of the truck.

"Help me down?" Evelyn pulls my attention to her, reaching out for my hand so I can help her return to the concrete.

I stretch out my hand and hoist her down just as she whispers in my ear, "Your boyfriend looks like he has something on his mind."

"He's not my boyfriend," I grate out, glaring her direction before we make our way back to our booth.

"But that's exactly what you wish were true," she sings playfully while stepping around me and skipping back to the booth right next to ours.

Evelyn knows about my crush on my best friend because girls are supposed to tell each other everything, right? Well, sometimes, I wish I'd kept my mouth shut about this morsel of information.

Evelyn has come very close to outing me multiple times in front of Wyatt, which may or may not have ended in a dead leg for her once or twice.

The farmers market is bustling this morning as the temperature in the air rises along with the humidity. Fall is coming, though, which means a little reprieve from the Texas weather that plagues us all summer. At least the nights cool off enough to enjoy some time outside.

"Please, tell me you have the blackberry jam today." The familiar voice that makes my insides twist has me turning to take in the face of Janise Brown, the daughter of the mayor and Wyatt's only full-fledged ex-girlfriend—at least that I know about.

"Good morning to you, too, Janise." I plaster on my best smile as I take in the only woman I can actually say I'm jealous of. She and Wyatt dated for a few months in high school, and I don't know for sure, but I'm pretty sure he lost his virginity to her. Either way, she always likes to throw that they once dated in anyone's—aka my—face, even though that was almost ten years ago.

"Blackberry or no?" she declares, bypassing my attempt at being polite and snarky at the same time.

"Well, hello there, Janise." Wyatt comes up beside me now, his right hand stuffed in his pocket while his left holds a cup of coffee. "I think what you meant to say is, 'I would be so grateful if you still had enough blackberry jam to fulfill my order.'"

"Wyatt!" she exclaims, her tone changing to upbeat and fake in an instant. "How are you? I missed seeing you here last week."

"Walker and I take turns at the market sometimes, you know that." He lifts his coffee to his lips, and Janise's eyes lock on his mouth as quickly as I'd like to lock my fist on her face.

"Oh, yes. That's right. Well, I need three jars of blackberry jam if you have it, please." With a bat of her eyelashes, she leans forward, planting her hand on the table in a blatant attempt at flirting and giving Wyatt a peek down her blouse.

I roll my eyes and turn away, pretending to reach for something on the ground so I can still eavesdrop on the conversation but don't have to stare at her face any longer.

"Coming right up."

A rush of hot air blows past my face as Wyatt leans down to the box just to my right, getting dangerously closer to me than necessary. My body doesn't hate it. "Excuse me, Kels."

"Yeah, no problem." He reaches for the jars in the box my hands are currently in, and I can feel my pulse in my neck as his fingers brush against mine.

Just as quickly as he came, his muscular body retracts. Then the telltale sound of a paper bag opening signals that Wyatt is depositing the glass jars, topped with red-and-white-checkered fabric squares and the Gibson Ranch signature logo on top, into the bag. The sound of them hitting the table mimic the staccato of my heart.

"That will be eighteen dollars, Janise."

She cackles. "What's it going to take to get that girlfriend discount?"

"Ex-girlfriend," he retorts. When I turn around, I have to fight

CHAPTER FOUR

the smirk pulling at my lips from how annoyed he sounds. But Janise catches it anyway, shooting me an icy glare before turning her attention back to Wyatt.

"That can be fixed easily," she says with an arch of her brow.

"Sorry, Janise, I'm just here to sell jam. And you owe me eighteen dollars, please."

She huffs and rolls her eyes while opening up her wallet and grabbing a twenty dollar bill, placing it in front of him on the table. "You know, you've been home for two years, Wyatt. When are you going to call me so we can pick up where we left off?"

Wyatt moves to reply, but Walker comes over at just the right moment. "When pigs fly and you can learn to take a hint, Janise." Smiling proudly, he casts his gaze in her direction where I'm sure there's smoke coming out of her ears.

"No one asked you, Walker. It's impolite to butt in on people's conversations."

"It's also impolite to ask for a discount and then hit on my brother after he's graciously turned you down numerous times."

Wyatt and I watch the dispute in front of us as if all we're missing is popcorn.

"Your brother just doesn't know what he wants. We were good together. He just needs a little reminder." She tosses a wink at Wyatt over her shoulder.

"God, could you *be* any more clueless, woman?" Walker asks in his best Chandler Bing impression. "If a man wants to date you, he'll make it happen." He shoots a definitive stare in my and Wyatt's direction, which has me retracting slightly.

Oh God, is he implying something?

"Well, maybe your brother just doesn't know what he wants yet!" she fires back.

But Walker's eyes find mine, and then the corner of his mouth tips up. "Yeah, I think you're right about that."

"If you don't mind, Janise, we have other customers waiting to make their purchases, so you can just move on along now," I taunt her in my best honey-coated southern drawl. The death stare she gives me back is worth every ounce of sweetness I coated my words in.

"Wyatt. Call me." She holds a finger phone up to her face and blows him a kiss, scowling at Walker and me. Then she grabs her bag from the table and saunters off.

"Dear lord," Wyatt mutters. "I really dated her, didn't I?" he asks Walker and me.

We both answer in unison. "Yes, you did." I add, "Unfortunately."

"The girl just doesn't know how to take a hint."

I huff. "Well, some girls can be extremely determined, especially when someone tells them they can't have something." *Just like I'm determined not to ruin our friendship because of the feelings I have for you.*

"Yup. And some men can be blind to what's right in front of them," Walker adds, grinning as his eyes bounce between Wyatt and me.

Wyatt clears his throat and then moves around the table and out from under our pop-up tent. "I don't have the energy for this shit today." He pushes a hand through his hair and then continues, "If you don't mind, Kels, I'm gonna go say hello to a couple of the other vendors. I think we're going to need to increase our produce order from Mr. Wilkens to keep up with the increase in customers."

"Yeah, sure. I'll hold down the fort."

He stares at me long and hard before squeezing my shoulder. "I can always count on you, Kels." With a nod, he tosses his coffee cup in the trash and then walks away, shoving his hands in his pockets, his denim Levi's hugging his ass like they were made to fit his body.

"Would you like me to let you finish, or can I say something?" Walker interrupts my perusal of his twin brother, causing flames to crawl up my neck.

"I was just admiring the flowers at Mrs. Aguilar's stand. She has some beautiful blooms today." Spinning around, I bury my head under my unruly blonde curls, trying to hide the blush on my cheeks.

"No, you weren't. You were checking out my brother's ass."

I spin to face him, my eyes wide, but then I recover. "I have no idea what you're talking about."

Walker rolls his eyes and crosses his arms over his chest. "Kels, anyone with eyes can tell you have a thing for my brother."

"You're crazy," I huff out.

"Well, what I'm about to suggest is a little crazy, but I think it just might be the best way to get him to see what's right in front of him."

My brow furrows as I study him. "What are you talking about, Walker?"

"Yes, Walker. Please, enlighten us with your crazy scheme," Evelyn says as she walks up to us, stepping away from her booth for a minute.

Walker checks our surroundings, making sure we're alone before speaking. "I have an idea."

"Yes, we've established that," Evelyn snipes back.

He flattens his lips. "Listen, I know my brother better than anyone, right?"

"Sure, although I might argue that I know him better than you," I retort.

"Well, then you and I both know that the two of you have feelings for each other but are too chickenshit to talk about it," he declares as my heart slams against my ribcage.

"I don't know what you *think* you know," I say, turning in preparation to walk away and stand firm in my denial, but Evelyn reaches out and grabs my hand before I can take a step.

"Kels . . ."

"Kelsea, I'm not stupid. And neither is anyone with a brain who's been around you two."

With my head hanging down, I side-step his accusation and encourage him to continue. "Just say whatever it is that you need to say."

He clears his throat. "As I was saying, I know you're in love with my brother. And I know he has feelings for you, too. But for some reason, neither one of you will act on it." My eyes pop up to find his, and my pulse thrashes violently in my veins. "And I don't know why."

Sighing but not confirming his suspicions of love, I answer him. "Crossing that line of friendship to something more is risky, Walker. You guys are like my family. If something were to happen and we didn't work out, I don't think I could live without your family in my life."

"See, that's where I think you're wrong. You don't have everything to lose here, Kels. You have everything to gain."

"So what's your plan?" Evelyn asks, moving this conversation along as his words swirl around in my brain.

"Well, I think my brother needs a wake-up call."

"Okay. How?" Evelyn adds.

"We make him afraid."

"Afraid of what?" I ask.

"Afraid of losing you."

I huff out a laugh and then turn around. "You and I both know that I'm not going anywhere, Walker. I've lived in Newberry Springs my entire life and will probably die here." *I'll probably never get to see New York or go to that photography program I applied to in the spring, either.*

He reaches out and clasps his hand around my bicep, forcing me to face him again. "I'm not talking about moving, Kelsea. I'm talking about seeing you with another guy." He pauses, swallowing roughly before finishing. "Me."

"What? Walker, are you crazy? You're like my brother." I retract my arm from his grasp. I mean, the last thing I want is to date Walker, but the idea that it would make Wyatt jealous is . . .

"I'm in total agreement, Kels," he answers. "Dating you would be like dating my sister."

Evelyn leans over and talks out of the side of her mouth. "Oh, I kind of like this idea."

I stare back at her like she's crazy.

"Listen, Kels, I need you to focus. Wyatt will be back soon. Seriously, I think this could work."

"You think that he would be jealous if *you* asked me out?"

He grins like he just won a hundred dollars. "Hell yeah, he would. Look, there's always been an unspoken competition between me and Wyatt since we were born. Twin thing and all that." He waves off his thought. "Anyway, yes, I *know* he would be jealous. If he saw me touch you, hug you in a non-brother-sister way, perhaps even kiss you . . . he would lose his shit. Hell, he growled at me the other night when I put my hand on yours at the brewery."

I could have sworn I heard him growl, but I thought I was just conjuring up random sounds in my mind.

Anyone else do that? No? Just me?

"So . . ."

"So it would cut him in half knowing I would get to touch you the way he wants to."

"Uh . . . do you want to touch me that way, Walker?"

He scrunches up his face. "Ugh, no. Listen, Kels, you're beautiful, but you *are* like my unofficial sister. When I tell you I don't feel anything for you, I mean it—not to hurt your feelings or anything."

"No, I'm good. I just—"

"We make him jealous, make him realize that you won't be single forever. And because I'm the threat? He won't last a week." He nods his head, his smile deceptively convincing.

"I don't want to hurt him. I don't . . ." I reach up to run my fingers through my curls. "Hell, Walker, I don't know if this is such a good idea."

"No, I think he may be on to something," Evelyn interjects, tapping her chin with her finger. "I've seen it, too, Kels. You guys both share these stolen glances, but they're just never at the same time."

"See? It's like some secret lovers type of shit," Walker adds.

"Yes. Only instead of them both knowing that they could get caught, they both think no one else exists and can see them because they're all alone in their blurry bubble."

"Yes! Yes!"

"Jesus, you two!" I shout, shushing them both before turning to Walker. "I honestly don't know what to think about your proposition this morning. With only one cup of coffee in my system, I'm not sure I'm capable of making such a crazy decision. So can I just . . . think about it?"

Walker nods. "Yeah, sure. But I'm telling you, Kels. I know I'm right." With a parting nod this time and a tip of his ball cap, Walker saunters away from us, leaving me reeling.

"I think you should do it, Kels," Evelyn says just as customers come up to both of our booths.

"We can talk about this later, Evelyn," I grit out between the clenched teeth of my smile.

"Oh, we will," she fires back.

But all I do is think about it for the rest of the day and up until I start my shift at the brewery the next night.

※

With our usual Friday night crowd except for a few new faces, I plaster on my southern smile and do my job, convincing myself once again that Walker is crazy. If that arrangement idea of his got out of hand, all hell could break loose. I could lose the two people who always felt like my real parents, brothers who are not related by blood, and my very best friend.

As convinced as he is that seeing us together would rile Wyatt up, I can't take that risk.

But God, do I want to.

"Kels, can you hold down the fort for a minute, please? I need to go make a phone call," Wyatt calls out to me from the other side of the bar.

"You got it." I toss my towel over my shoulder and start making my rounds—checking up on customers, assessing the connections on each of the taps to the kegs, and making sure the kitchen isn't running behind.

When things start to slow down a minute, I fill a glass with

CHAPTER FOUR

water and drain it just as Walker comes in and finds a seat at the bar. "How's it going, Kels?"

"Just trying to take in some water before I die from dehydration. What about you? You want your usual?"

"You know it. Yes, please." He takes off his hat, running his fingers through his hair. It's crazy how he and Wyatt can look so similar but I'm not attracted to him in the least. However, that doesn't stop other women from looking in his direction. The Gibson men are all handsome in their own way, which then reminds me that it's only a matter of time before Wyatt finds someone to date. And I don't know if I'll be able to handle it.

Seeing him with Janise in high school was bad enough, but my feelings weren't at the level that they are now. Back then, it was more annoyance and irritation that we couldn't hang out because he was spending time with her or how seeing them kiss made me want to give her a black eye.

But now? If I saw Wyatt fall in love with another woman in front of me, I don't know how I would live with that ache in my chest. I don't know how I could watch that unfold.

And that thought has me saying something I never thought I'd say.

"So I've been thinking about your proposition," I declare as I set Walker's beer down in front of him.

"Have you?" He smirks at me over the rim of his glass.

"Yes. And I'm . . . interested," I say, trying not to sound too enthusiastic.

But the smile playing on his lips tells me he knows I'm all in.

"Hot damn, Kels. I didn't think you'd cave this quickly. What changed your mind?"

"That's not important. What *is* important is that I don't want this to make either of us look bad, and I don't want to hurt him." I lean over the counter so our faces are inches apart, so close that it probably looks like we're about to kiss even though that couldn't be further from the truth. I just don't want people overhearing our conversation. "You know how people talk, Walker. I don't want it to look like I'm bouncing between two brothers. That's not my style."

He nods in agreement. "Understood. Don't worry, though, I think I have a way to make him jealous without making us look bad."

"What's going on over here?" Wyatt's voice has my spine straightening instantly as I turn to see a scowl on his face, his eyes bouncing back and forth between me and his brother.

"What's up, little brother?" Walker asks, gleefully smiling as he takes in Wyatt's reaction to what he just witnessed. The hammering of my heart has me second-guessing the decision to follow this through, even though I'm pretty sure Wyatt is frozen in shock right now, his hands clenched at his sides.

Is that because he's jealous?

"I was just telling Kelsea how beautiful she looks tonight," Walker adds as I feel my stomach begin to roll.

"Okay . . ."

"And, well, I think I've convinced her to be my date to Schmitty's birthday hoopla next week."

CHAPTER FOUR

Walker's best friend, Schmitty, wanted a big group of us to go to The Jameson in Fort Worth to celebrate his birthday. He's only turning twenty-seven, but the man is always down to have a good time, and his birthday is the perfect excuse. The Jameson is known for being one of the world's largest honky-tonks (leave it to Texans to be proud of that), a hundred-thousand square-foot building that contains bars, dance floors, and a full bull-riding arena.

"Date? Why do you need a date?" Wyatt asks, the tick of his jaw becoming more apparent as he stares at the two of us like Walker had just spoken a foreign language.

"Well, I've kind of been thinking about what Dad said last week," Walker says, which has me intrigued, but I know now is not the time to get clarification on that topic. "And perhaps it's time to start putting myself out there. Plus, the guys at the station all agreed to bring someone."

I swallow hard as I watch Wyatt assess his brother, arching his brow. "Kelsea isn't someone. She's . . ." His brow furrows more. "She's Kelsea," he finishes with a wave of his hand.

And instantly my shoulders drop.

"Exactly. She's beautiful, kind, and looks dynamite in a dress. Say, Kels?" Walker hams it up. "When's the last time you got dressed up and had a night out?"

"Uh . . . I honestly can't remember."

"Exactly. You're always so busy working for this guy." He tosses his thumb in Wyatt's direction. "But since you'll be there that night, I think it would be fun if we go together. Let me show you a *good time*," he says, emphasizing the last two words.

Wait. Do I hear growling again?

Sure enough, my eyes find Wyatt, and if looks could kill, Walker would be a dead man right now.

"Uh, thank you for the offer, Walker. Can I maybe . . . think about it?" I've told him this already, and I know my mind is convinced that maybe this could work, but actually agreeing to this in front of Wyatt is making my skin crawl and my stomach somersault.

"Absolutely." Walker stands and drains the rest of his beer, placing his customary twenty dollar bill on the counter. "You know where to find me, Kels." He comes around the counter, reaching for my hip and pulling me into him so fast that my hands move to his chest on instinct and my heart pumps wildly.

"I do." I fake my most genuine smile, but then Walker does something he's never done before. He presses his lips to mine, a soft and innocent kiss that has me widening my eyes from the shock. The kiss ends as soon as it begins, but the tension radiating around us right now is thick and palpable, and I'm deathly afraid of twisting around to see Wyatt right now.

"Call you later, Kels." Walker winks in my direction and then throws a glance at his brother, a hint of mischief in his eyes. "See ya 'round, bro."

The two of us watch Walker stride away, and then, reluctantly, I focus back on Wyatt.

CHAPTER FOUR

But he doesn't say anything. He just stares at me, the tick in his jaw getting harsher with each passing second.

And just when I think he's finally going to utter a few words, he spins on his heel and marches away, shoving the door to the back of the restaurant open with such force it slams against the wall, startling everyone around us.

Suddenly, reality slams back into me—the brewery is full of people and things that need to be done, and someone could have just witnessed Walker kissing me and Wyatt's reaction to it. Before I start to have a panic attack, I shake off the moment and turn on my ability to function as I plaster a smile back on my face and refill drinks for our customers.

By the time closing hits, my nerves are creeping back up on me. The only people left in the building are me and Wyatt, like normal. But he hasn't said a word to me since the incident earlier, and now I'm not sure if he will address it or just let it slide.

Out of habit, I walk over to the jukebox in the corner and flip through the choices at my disposal, feeling particularly nostalgic. "Strawberry Wine" comes out of the speakers as I move to stack the stools on the tables like I do every night, swaying my hips to the melody and singing along with Deana Carter.

"Hey."

My head spins to locate Wyatt leaning against the doorway to the back of the restaurant, watching me intently, his forehead scrunched up. "Hey."

He pushes off the wall and then walks right over to me as I feel myself begin to choke on my tongue. Luckily, I remain stoic and intact. "Are you really thinking about going to Schmitty's birthday party with my brother?"

I can hear my pulse in my ears, but I fight to remain composed. "Uh, maybe? I mean, I don't see the harm in letting him pay for my drinks all night," I attempt to joke, but Wyatt's face doesn't change.

"What if I told you I needed you to work that night after all?"

I narrow my eyes at him. "Well, then I'd tell you that I already have plans and you need to find someone else to come in. You're going, too, you know, so why would you even say that?"

"Kelsea . . ."

"Wyatt . . ."

He sighs in frustration. "You can't be serious about dating him. You *don't* date. You focus on work and live your life the same way you've always done. I don't understand why all of a sudden you're looking to go out for a night, let alone with someone like my brother."

And just like that, my pulse that was racing from nerves is now roaring with anger. "Excuse me?"

"You don't date, Kels. And neither does my brother. He's—"

"What? Good-looking? Has a noble job? Cares about me and my happiness?" I'm fuming, my hands flying up in the air. "And since when can't I go out and have fun with my friends?"

And then it clicks. Perhaps Walker was on to something here. I've been pining after Wyatt for so long that I've forgotten there are other men out there, and maybe he needs to see that, too. I've forgotten to have fun and take a break from life, letting life essentially pass me by.

Maybe this little experiment will serve as a reminder that if I won't make a decision about my crush on my best friend, I need to move on and start living for me.

"You think my brother is good-looking?"

"Well, I'm practically staring at his doppelgänger right now, but yes. He's handsome."

I swear I see his brown eyes darken. "You're attracted to him?"

No, I want you, dumbass. But right now, you're just pissing me off, making me see how you truly feel about me dating someone else. "Is it so far-fetched that he could want me? Am I not good enough for him?" I'm fueling this fire, but at this point, I'm way beyond irritated. How dare he think that I couldn't find someone to date me if I wanted?

"That's not what I'm saying. I just—"

"—don't understand?" I shake my head. "Yeah, apparently, you don't."

He sighs heavily. "Fuck. Just . . . just forget it. I've got it from here." He pulls the stool I was holding from my grasp and then moves to lift it up and flip it over on top of the table.

"Yeah, I think I'm done for tonight." I untie my apron and traipse off to the employee room to grab my purse, shaking from my fury. And even though I wasn't sure he would, Wyatt still meets me at the back door of the brewery to walk me out to my truck.

"See you tomorrow, Kels."

"Yeah. You, too, Wyatt."

And that's all we say before I drive off, fuming with frustration and hurt, losing hope that Wyatt will ever see me the way I see him.

But then I get a text just after one in the morning, right as I'm about to fall asleep.

Walker: *The plan is working. I just got a text from my brother that makes me think he might murder me in my sleep.*

I fling myself up in bed.

Me: *Really?*

Walker: *Yup. Time to really mess with his head. Find something sexy and alluring to wear to The Jameson, Kelsea. We're going to make my brother admit he wants you if it's the last thing we do. Good night, Sis.*

He closes the text message with a kissy-face emoji, and then I throw myself back on my bed, knowing that perhaps making Wyatt jealous was the key to turning this tide all along. And even though he pissed me off beyond reason earlier, all I could think about was smashing my lips to his and drinking him in, absorbing every molecule of air surrounding us. Because when it's just him and me, it feels like there's no air around me to breathe.

I'm officially crazy. I've agreed to play with fire—and with a firefighter, no less.

I just hope it's worth the risk.

CHAPTER FIVE

Wyatt

"Fuck," I mutter as I watch the taillights on Kelsea's truck disappear down the road, shining bright red before dulling out against the pitch black of the night.

I reach up to tug on my hair, wondering how the hell the events of the evening unfolded like they did and why the uneasiness in my stomach is now at an all-time high.

Tonight was insane. The number of customers coming through our doors had me grateful I decided to hire a few more people. I already have several interviews scheduled for Wednesday.

But no matter how chaotic business becomes, there's always been one thing I can count on: Kelsea. Like a magnet, my eyes found her in the brewery multiple times tonight, smiling at customers at the bar, her blonde curls hanging loosely by her face, her perfect lips highlighting the smile that lights up the entire room.

And then that familiar pang of longing rested in my chest when I realized that this is all we'll ever be: two friends who exist around each other but not together.

I feel like there's a forcefield surrounding her, an invisible barrier that I can't break through no matter what tool is at my disposal. Maybe I've fought the instinct not to touch her the way I want to for so long that now I'm afraid to even try to slay those dragons.

And then there's the other question that plagues me several times a day as well: Would Kelsea even want me to cross over that threshold? Is she willing to cross that line with me? Or does she still just see me as her best friend and that's all I'll ever be?

Seeing Janise at the farmers market yesterday reminded me how long it's been since I've dated anyone, let alone had sex. Don't get me wrong, I wasn't a saint in college, but I wasn't promiscuous, either. However, as soon as I knew I was moving back home, women weren't a center of focus for me anymore. It's as if my heart knew I was headed back to the one it wanted.

And as soon as I saw Kelsea again, no other woman seemed to exist.

But how can I want someone I can't have? How can we transition from friends to more, and how do I even broach that subject with her?

My mind had been spinning this past week after that conversation with my dad, but nothing could have prepared me for the intense rollercoaster I unwittingly jumped on when I saw my twin brother put his lips on Kelsea's earlier tonight. Walker's move was out of left field but also felt calculated, even though it was something he's never done before. He pressed his lips to hers for only a second, but I could tell by Kelsea's face that the move caught her off guard.

But for me? Watching his lips land on hers, even if it was just for a fraction of time, had my stomach dropping to my feet and red clouding my vision as if someone had shown me my worst nightmare. But it's even worse because it was my brother kissing my best friend, the girl that I know in my heart should be mine.

But I couldn't say anything. I was speechless. My heart was in my throat. My knees felt like they were about to buckle. My skin was crawling, and my ears were starting to buzz.

So I did the only thing I knew was best in that moment—I walked away.

I knocked my fist into the swinging door as I made my way back to my office, slamming that door shut as well before hunching over in my seat, calming my body down before a panic attack ensued.

But as I was sitting there in my office, it hit me: Kelsea won't be single forever.

Someday, some guy—*who'd better not end up being my fucking brother*—will want her, see how incredible she is, and make it his mission to be the most important person in her life. And where would that leave me? The best friend who only gets to see her at family functions while pretending that it's not ripping my heart into shreds to see her happy with someone else?

Maybe Walker is right. Maybe it is time to contemplate what Dad was talking about, thinking about *what* and *who* I want in my life.

It's never been clearer to me than it is now what I need to admit: I want Kelsea. A life without her in it is one I can't imagine, but the one we're living currently—where we pretend that there isn't electricity every time we're near each other—is keeping us stagnant. As my father has also said so eloquently numerous times in my life, it's time to "shit or get off the pot."

I spent the rest of the night avoiding her, but then when closing time came, I knew I needed to say something.

Lesson learned: Sometimes it's just better to keep your mouth shut.

That conversation did not go well.

No shit, Wyatt. You basically told her she was undatable, moron.

But despite knowing that Kelsea needed time to cool off, I'd be damned if I let her walk out to her truck by herself. My momma taught me better than that and would castrate me if she ever found out I let her do so.

Like a gust of wind, Kelsea whirled right past me in the hallway, her chin held high, her purse slung on her shoulder, and her keys in her hands. I followed her to the back door of the brewery, looking in both directions in the dark parking lot as she

CHAPTER FIVE

faced straight ahead and walked to her truck. The bright security light on the top of the building surrounded her in a beam of light.

And that all led me to where I am right now.

With renewed anger building as I watch her drive away, I walk back inside and stew in my misery as I finish up the rest of my to-do list. I place the rest of the stools on the tables, balance the cash drawers from the registers, and lock up before getting in my own truck and heading for my place.

Cold beer in hand, I slide onto my couch after a shower, needing to unwind before trying to go to sleep. I can never go to bed right after I get home. My body has become so accustomed to the late hours, and I always need a little bit of time to decompress after work.

Reaching for my phone, I open up my text messaging app, debating whether or not I should text Kelsea and try to apologize. But then I see Walker's name right under hers and bring up our thread instead.

Me: *Hey, fuckface. What the hell was that about earlier?*

It takes him a minute to reply.

Walker: *Whatever are you talking about, little brother?*

Me: *Don't play stupid with me.*

Walker: *Seriously. I think I need you to be more specific.*

Me: *You. Kelsea. Lips touching. WTF?*

Walker: *Oh. That. Well, I guess a man can realize he's been a moron and finally go after what he wants.*

Me: *And you want Kelsea?*

Walker: *Why wouldn't I? She's beautiful, kind, hard-working, and our parents already love her. It's like it was meant to be.*

Pain starts to radiate in my temples from the clench of my jaw.

Me: *She's not just some girl you can fuck around with, Walker. Kelsea is . . .*

Walker: *Please, brother. Tell me what Kelsea is.*

I shake my head, wondering how the hell this has become my life.

Me: *Just . . . don't fucking hurt her, Walker.*

That's not what I should have said, but it's the only thing I could think of that wouldn't give me away.

Walker: *Don't worry, Wyatt. My only plan is to give her exactly what she needs.*

Without thinking, I chuck my phone across the room, watching it slam to the ground when it hits the wall. My chest is rising rapidly with my shallow breaths while visions of my brother and Kelsea together filter through my mind.

"This can't be happening," I mutter out loud, even though I'm the only one in the room.

With anger still raging through me, I head for my bedroom, not even bothering to get ready for bed as I toss myself on my mattress. I stare up at the ceiling, wondering if I'm too late—if I've waited too long to make my move.

And now, I might have to accept that Kelsea could fall in love with my brother, leaving me and my feelings behind.

∾

CHAPTER FIVE

The next morning, I stumble out of bed, feeling anything but well-rested, and opt to go for a run to help relieve some of this tension in my body. Plus, the Newberry Springs football league is starting up again soon, so I need to make sure I stay up on my conditioning. I don't want to be the slow man on the field.

Feeling slightly more relaxed than I was last night after running five miles, I show up at Rose's Diner for our weekly Saturday morning breakfast, wondering if Kelsea is even going to make an appearance. We didn't exactly leave the brewery on the best of terms last night, but we've never missed a breakfast together, other than when I was away at college.

I drink down the rest of my second cup of coffee, knowing I'll probably need two more before I feel fully functional today. I barely slept last night as dreams of Walker and Kelsea getting married plagued my mind, a fear that has me conjuring up thoughts of moving away from the town I call home.

But my business is here. My family is here. So leaving isn't really an option.

The chime of the bell above the door alerts the restaurant to the arrival of another customer, and my eyes drift in that direction on instinct. But my heart does a somersault when I see Kelsea walk through wearing a light-pink sleeveless sundress.

I can probably count on one hand how many times I've seen the girl wear a dress, most of which were when we were much younger. Now, she lives in t-shirts, jeans, and boots.

But the way the soft pink highlights her tanned skin, the way her curls bounce as she walks, giving her a more feminine look, and even the flip flops she has on her feet have my tongue lodging itself in the back of my throat so it doesn't flop out onto the table, creating a puddle of embarrassing drool.

Forget girls who are so into their looks it's obvious they're trying too hard. I'm all about the girl walking toward me, the one who's so damn beautiful in a simple pink dress and her natural appearance that she doesn't even realize she's giving me heart palpitations.

"Miss Kelsea!" Beth says in a shocked, high-pitched voice. "You look so lovely today!"

Kelsea's cheeks pink as she arrives at our booth, removing her purse from her shoulder while sliding into her seat. "Thank you, Beth."

"What's the occasion? Normally, you come in here with jeans and boots on—not that there's anything wrong with that," I say, sounding like an ass instead of a friend. But honestly, I'm wondering if she's meeting up with Walker later. Like for a date.

"No occasion. Just wanted to mix things up." Her eyes lift and catch mine for a moment before reaching for her menu and opening it, raising it to cover her face.

"Change can be good. In this case, I think you look beautiful," Beth continues.

"Thank you, Beth." She's still hiding behind her menu, which only has my nervousness for this meal building as we wait for her to make her decision.

"You know what I'll be having, Beth," I say. "And I'll take some more coffee when you get a chance, please."

CHAPTER FIVE

"You got it, Wyatt. And what about you, Kelsea?"

She plops her menu down on the table, staring directly into my eyes when she says, "I'll have my usual, too, Beth, please. Although this time, let's make them chocolate chip pancakes. I'm in the mood for something a little different but still notably the same." With an arch of her brow, she hands Beth the menu and then shifts her gaze to her coffee, moving to fix it just the way she likes.

Something different but notably the same, huh? Is that her assbackwards way of alluding to the similarities between me and my brother?

Beth nods and then saunters away, leaving us alone for the first time since last night. My throat becomes scratchy as I debate what to say.

"You do look absolutely beautiful, Kelsea." I decide flattery is always a good start to any tough conversation. And she looks better than beautiful, but I'm having a hard time filing through the thesaurus in my brain right now for a better word.

"Thank you." Her eyes are still down and focused on her coffee before she lifts the cup and takes a drink.

"I—I wasn't sure you were going to show up this morning," I continue, hoping that maybe we can fix our miscommunication from yesterday.

"I thought about not coming; I did." Her gaze moves back to me. "But I'm not one to break tradition."

"I'm glad you feel that way. Look, Kelsea—"

She puts her hand up to stop me. "I don't want to talk about it,

Wyatt. It seems you said what you needed to last night. Let's—let's just move past it, please."

But I don't want to move past it. Hell, the idea of her dating my brother is all I can think about right now. And she still seems pissed. I know her well enough to know she's harboring some animosity toward me, but I can also sense that maybe now is not the time to discuss it.

Well, shit. Then what do we talk about?

I feel like our friendship has changed in the last twenty-four hours, and I'm almost nervous being around her. I've never felt that way before, and that's exactly what I was trying to avoid by not acting on my feelings.

But those feelings are present now, beating against the iron door I keep them behind, fighting like hell to be heard and freed.

"Fine. Well, then, uh . . . how's your dad?" I reach for my mug, thankful that Beth came over and filled it while we remained silent.

"Doing well, actually. I spoke with him this morning. He'll be home this week for a few days, so that's always nice."

"Do you want a few days off so you can spend time with him?"

She glances up at me beneath her lashes that look darker than normal, reaching up to tuck a curl behind her ear. *Is she wearing more makeup than usual?* "Um, maybe?"

"Just let me know." I flash her a tight-lipped smile, and then the crickets between us start chirping again. But the silence is

CHAPTER FIVE

killing me, so I keep trying to start small talk. "Did you take any pictures this morning?"

"No."

More crickets.

"What are you doing after this?"

She sighs. "I was thinking of going to see Evelyn at her boutique."

"Shopping for more dresses?" I tease, but the look of defeat that accompanies the drop of her shoulders has me regretting my question.

"Um, maybe. I haven't decided yet. I do need something for The Jameson, though . . ."

Fuck. Did she say yes to my brother? "Kelsea—"

"Here you are, you two!" Beth stalks over to our booth before I can get another word in, setting down hot plates of sizzling food, warm pancakes and French toast. "Anything else I can get you?"

"No, this looks great. Thank you." Kelsea smiles up at Beth, but I know that wasn't one of her genuine smiles.

She starts arranging food on her plate before cutting off a piece of her chocolate chip pancakes, sliding the fork between her glossed lips. She closes her eyes and moans as she extracts the fork from her perfect mouth. "Dear lord, those are good."

Apparently, my dick agrees with her because I'm instantly as hard as a rock.

"Oh. Cool." *Fuck, does my brain know any words this morning?*

"I've been trying to tell you, Wyatt. You're missing out on the pancakes here."

I stab a piece of my French toast, lifting it to my lips. "And you're missing out on the French toast, Kels." I shrug before moaning a little around my bite.

Kelsea straightens in her seat, her eyes locked on mine while we both finish chewing in a silent stand-off. But she doesn't say anything else, and we finish the rest of our meal in uncomfortable silence.

With a toss of her napkin and stack of our plates, Kelsea moves to stand from the booth. When she starts cleaning the table as if she's about to bus it herself like she does at the brewery, I know she's done. "All right, well . . . I guess I'll see you tonight?"

I stand on my own two feet as well, though the ground beneath me definitely feels shaky—and we don't have earthquakes in the great state of Texas. "Yeah, I'll be there. I'm always there."

She smiles, and this time it feels genuine. "Me, too, it seems." She shrugs and then starts to walk away, but I reach for her forearm on instinct, startling her. Her bright blue eyes flick up to mine, wide and rampant with curiosity. "Wyatt?"

"You'll always be the syrup to my breakfast, Kels, all right?"

Her brows pinch together, and then she tilts her head at me before relaxing. "Yeah. Seems that's never gonna change."

I release my grip on her and watch her walk out of the restaurant and out to her truck before hopping inside and taking off down the road. And I'm left standing there, wondering how the hell I'm going to make my move.

Because Kelsea may be my best friend, but she's also the girl who is meant for me. Not my brother.

And I need to make her see that.

∼

"Dad?" I step into the barn just after eleven, eager to speak with him, especially after that intense and awkward breakfast with Kelsea.

"Wyatt? I'm in the back!" His voice echoes against the wooden walls as I take in the scenery around me. Tables and chairs dressed with white linens are stationed around the room in preparation for what looks like another wedding on the ranch. Burgundy and pale pink flowers sit in vases in the center of each table. Flecks of gold accents adorn the china, and silverware frame each place setting. Giant bulb lights hang from the center pole in the barn that will bathe the room in golden light later this evening when the sun goes down and the party truly starts. I can even see the bar is being stocked by a few servers shuffling bottles of beer from my brewery into the refrigerators and placing bottles of champagne on ice.

It's amazing to see the dreams my parents create for others just by reaching for their own.

"What's going on?" I find my father hunched over, adjusting a few plugs in a power strip. Once satisfied with how they fit, he slowly rises with his hands on his knees then turns to face me when he's extended his spine all the way. My father has always stood as tall as all three of us boys, but as I'm staring at him right now, I'm beginning to see the wear and tear years of hard work on this ranch has done to his body. There's a slight hunch in him now, and the wrinkles on his face are getting deeper, but he still boasts that same Gibson smile the three of us all inherited.

"Oh, just another wedding. Sheila should be back in here in a few minutes to make sure everything is just the way the bride wanted it to be." A proud smile lights up his face.

"That woman is a saint to plan as many weddings and parties as she does," I reply, referencing the event coordinator my parents hired about five years ago.

"Yes, she is. Sadly, she's talking about moving. Wanted to let us know just in case we needed to find someone." His smile falls, and then he plants his hands on his hips. "Nothing ever stays the same for too long when you're running an operation like this one."

"I'm beginning to understand that in many ways, Dad."

He turns to take me in, assessing me with a slow dip of his eyes. "What are you doing here on a Saturday, son? I mean, I'm not *unhappy* to see you, but this is definitely a day when I don't typically see that ugly mug of yours." He laughs as I follow the twang of his voice, his long legs carrying him across the room.

"Well, I kind of wanted to talk to you about something," I say as we head for the barn door.

We step out into the sun, and he puts his black cowboy hat back on his head. Then he looks at me over the shoulder of his red t-shirt and under the brim of his hat. "All right. Is this an office

CHAPTER FIVE

type of conversation, or can I fix a hole in some chicken wire while we talk?"

I chuckle. "How about I help you fix it while we talk?"

"Deal."

All of our supplies in hand, I follow my dad out to the chicken coop, and we get to work. "Okay, so what's up, Wyatt?"

Letting out a heavy sigh, I decide to just dive right in. "It's Kelsea."

He arches his brow as a knowing smile graces his lips. "Okay, what about Kelsea?"

"Well, since I moved back home, things have been . . . I feel like I . . ." I slap my palm to my forehead. "Shit, I don't even know what I'm trying to say."

"I'll wait." He nods and continues clipping the section of wire we need to replace. I notice his hand twitch, and then he's blinking his eyes rapidly, pausing in his movements.

"You okay, Dad?"

"Uh. Yeah. Fine." He clears his throat and readjusts his footing. "Here. Can you do this?" He hands me the wire cutters and then stares down at the ground.

"Yeah, sure." I finish what he started, suddenly uneasy about the way he's acting but opting not to press him for information just yet. "As I was saying, I think she might be dating someone," I continue, choosing not to mention my brother because it could make this even more awkward.

"Well, Kelsea is a beautiful woman."

"Yeah, I know. I just feel like . . ."

"You missed your chance?" His eyes find mine again, his smile growing.

"Fuck. Yeah, I do." I blow out a breath. "I just remember you warning me away from her before I left for college, and I thought my feelings would go away with time. But then I came home, and they all came back with a vengeance. And now we work together, so that makes saying anything risky. Plus, I don't know if she feels the same way."

"You know why I warned you away from her, right?"

"Yeah, I mean . . . I think I do." I hand him the wire cutters again. He grabs them from me and then hands me a set of pliers.

He rests his butt on his heels as we continue to crouch down. "Wyatt, you were leaving, and she wasn't. Asking that girl to stay here and wait for you was inconsiderate, even though I'm fairly certain she would have."

"You think?"

He nods and then shakes his head. "You and Kelsea have always been thick as thieves, and your momma and I have always wondered when you'd cross that line. The love you two have for one another is so blatantly obvious. It wasn't time back then. But maybe it is now."

"But I don't want to hurt her. I don't want to lose our friendship if things go wrong."

Dad tilts his head. "Then don't. *Don't* hurt her. *Don't* let things go wrong. You fight like hell for her, for you both. That's what makes a long-lasting relationship, anyway. You think things have always been easy for me and your mom?"

"Well, yeah. I mean, you guys make it look easy," I say with a shrug of my shoulders. My parents have always had a sparkle in their eyes for one another. I know they fight, but for the most part, I can always sense the love between them.

"It only looks easy when you love the right person, but choosing to love someone every day requires work. It requires the desire to do so. And it doesn't magically become easy one day and stay that way forever. Life still throws challenges at us, even now."

I swear he's alluding to something else. "Well, I don't think I can imagine a day in my life without Kelsea in it, Dad."

"I kind of figured you'd come to your senses one of these days," he says smugly.

"Is that why you brought up the fact that we should be thinking about settling down last week before dinner on Sunday?"

He teeters his head. "Not necessarily. Part of it is knowing that I can't do this forever and wanting to have family to pass it down to, for you all to have women and children who can be a part of this. But mostly, you all needed that reminder for various reasons. Walker is still a little too wild for my tastes. He needs a good woman to settle him down and make him feel needed. And I'm afraid your brother is going to end up being a recluse at this rate. That injury in college changed my son, and even though he's done well since then, he's still carrying around a lot of anger."

"Yeah, I can see that."

"But you," he says, laughing. "You have the woman you want

right in front of you and have just been too chickenshit to do anything about it."

"Hey! *You* told me not to go after her!"

"Yeah, because you were eighteen. You needed to live your life, and so did Kelsea. Hell, part of me feels like she still does. That girl has never known this world outside of Newberry Springs. But you're both older now, and I say you stop wasting your time, son. The days are long, but the years are short." He reaches over with his own pliers to tighten the wire together and reconnect the pieces. I help him pinch the metal all the way around the hole, ruminating on what he said just as his hand begins to shake again and the pliers fall from his grasp.

"Dad? Are you all right?"

"Shit," he mutters, closing his eyes before falling back on his butt in the dirt. His head is down, so I can't read his face under the brim of his cowboy hat, but I'm certain he's contemplating his answer to me. With a lift of his head, his eyes meet mine. Fear rushes through me from the conflict I see in his eyes. "Wyatt. I—I need to tell you something, son."

I swallow hard as anxiety builds in my chest. "Okay . . ."

"And I need to know that this stays between us. I haven't really discussed this with your mother yet, but I plan to. However, I know that I can count on you to pick up the slack if I need you. And I'm afraid I will."

"You know I'll be here, but you're kind of freaking me out."

"I'm not trying to, but the truth is, I'm a little scared, too." He takes a deep breath and then dives in. "I've been having issues with my sight for the past few weeks."

"What?"

"My vision will go blurry, and then my hand starts shaking, and I lose my grip on things. Sometimes a headache will accompany the blurriness in my vision, but that's not every time."

"Holy shit, Dad. You need to go to the doctor."

"I know. I have an appointment next week. It's the soonest they could get me in. But you know how hard it is to get away from your business. You feel like everything will fall apart if you're not there."

He's right. It sucks. "I know, but this is your health and eyesight we're talking about here. The ramifications could be life-changing."

"I know. But I'm getting it looked at, okay? Believe me. If I had it my way, I'd ignore it just like I've done with many other health issues I've had over the years."

"But Momma would never let you."

"I know. And this is one issue I can't sweep under the rug. No amount of ibuprofen and Icy Hot is gonna fix this."

I clasp my hand over his knee. "Just let me know what I can do. I won't let you down, okay?"

"I know you won't, Wyatt. You're dependable and loyal, and I know you can keep this to yourself. Please do so until I know more, okay? Don't tell your brothers. And please, don't tell Kelsea."

"Now your little talk and encouragement to go after Kelsea makes a bit more sense," I mutter.

The corner of his mouth lifts. "When you think your life is about to change, it's easy to put all your doubts and fears aside. And I want that for you. I know your mother will be there for me no matter what happens, and not everyone is lucky enough to find their person like that. But I'm fairly certain that Kelsea is yours."

Getting this news from my father today was the last thing I expected when I came here, but the other knowledge he shared with me only solidifies that he's right. Time passes no matter what. Life can change or end in the blink of an eye. Why should I waste any more time being alone and pining after her? I might as well take a risk and go after what I want. And if she doesn't feel the same, then at least I'll know. I'll have the knowledge I need to move on.

And if she decides that Walker is the man for her . . . well, I guess I'll just have to learn to live with that.

Or find a new family.

I'm joking . . . kind of.

CHAPTER SIX

Kelsea

"So you're saying it worked?" Evelyn is unpacking new outfits and sliding hangers through the sleeves of rompers and dresses as I pace her store, which is currently empty except for the two of us.

"Yes! I'm flabbergasted, but you should have seen him, Evelyn. I thought his head was about to explode." I'm currently filling her in on what happened last night since all I sent her was a text this morning telling her that Walker kissed me at the brewery and the plan was on. Even though it has my stomach tied in knots.

Naturally, she had to offer her advice as well, so I followed her suggestion to wear a dress this morning to breakfast, which seemed to also have an effect on Wyatt that I wasn't anticipating.

I'm not a dress-wearing type of girl, but apparently Kelsea

Baker in something other than jeans can turn heads and catch the eye of even my best friend.

"I told you. And Walker was right." She places the last dress on the display and then turns to face me. "So what happens now?"

"I have no idea!" I shout, tossing my hands in the air for emphasis. "This was Walker's plan, so I'm kind of just flying by the seat of my pants right now."

"Well, how was breakfast?"

"It was . . . odd, Evelyn. Like, we didn't know how to be around each other. I'm still pissed about what he said last night, but I can tell that something has definitely shifted. He tried talking about it, but I politely asked him to drop it. I don't want him to end up saying something else that he can't take back, or worse, I'll say something I can't take back. You know I tend to go off at the mouth when I'm feeling feisty."

"What? You?" she mocks with her hand on her chest. "I could never imagine sweet, sweet Kelsea giving someone a good tongue lashing."

I roll my eyes and continue to pace. "See? This is exactly what I was afraid of. What if nothing else happens with Wyatt and me, but that kiss with Walker ruins our friendship? Twenty-six years. Twenty-six years of friendship and a second family could all be thrown away for nothing!"

Evelyn crosses the room, placing her hands on my shoulders and forcing me to stop in my tracks. "Kelsea, just breathe." She inhales deeply, and I mimic her a few times. "I know this is scary, but dammit, girl—you need a little excitement in your life. And because I love you, I can't watch you pine after the man any more. This is your chance; you have to take it. See it through. Trust Walker."

My chest rises and falls with each breath I take in. "I know, but this is terrifying, Evelyn."

"Sometimes the things that scare us the most have the potential to be the most life-changing." She smiles, which instantly helps me relax. "You don't want to live with regrets, do you? Do you want to wonder for the rest of your life what could have been if you'd just put your big girl panties on and told the guy how you feel?"

I shake my head reluctantly, even though I know in my heart that she's right.

"And I know it probably would have been easier for you to have just done that instead of getting his twin brother involved, but hell, you're knee deep in this shitshow now. Might as well see it through." She shrugs and then squeezes my shoulders.

"Okay. You're right." I nod more confidently this time. "It's time for me to go after something I want. And I know that having a man isn't everything, but wanting Wyatt to notice me and be with me is the first thing I can remember *ever* wanting in my life. The next was my mom coming back. And now, that photography program accepting my application would be the icing on the cake."

Evelyn steps back a few paces. "Have you heard back from them yet?"

"No. The deadline for a response isn't for a few more weeks.

But as it gets closer, I get even antsier. I seriously can't handle all of this change and unknowns in my life at the same time, Evelyn. My hair is gonna fall out!"

Evelyn laughs just as a customer walks through the door. She starts making her way back behind the register, and I follow her. "Girl, you have so much hair, I'm sure you'll be fine. And you know what? I'm glad you feel that way. You need it. Your life has been so boring. It's time for some change."

We both say hello to the customer, and then I lower my voice before continuing. "Not boring, just monotonous."

"You are the *definition* of monotonous. Maybe these circumstances are just the push you need to spread your wings and fly a little." She winks in my direction as the girl in the store asks a question, drawing Evelyn across the space to help her.

My friend is right. Perhaps it is time to come out of the shadows, stop hiding, and chase my dreams. I'm beginning to think I'm losing out on life by not taking chances I need to be taking, just like I do when I choose a different setting on my camera for a once-in-a-lifetime shot. It's a risk I'm taking that the moment will be forgotten or missed if I click the wrong button. But there's also a thrill in that, too—that maybe I made the right choice in that instant and the end result could be even more magical.

This plan could either work perfectly or blow up in my face, but again, at least I'll know. And maybe if I get in to that photography program in New York, I'll at least have somewhere to run if things don't work out.

CHAPTER SIX

I go to work Tuesday morning like normal, helping Wyatt process and put away the food order that gets delivered every week. Other than that, I have the rest of the day off, which is perfect since my dad will be arriving this afternoon.

We step around each other like everything is normal, but my insides are clearly still in turmoil. I guess we've gotten pretty good about pretending on the outside, but now my heart and stomach are at war, brewing a hurricane that rivals one preparing to grace the coast of Texas and leave destruction in its path.

I swear, working around him and seeing him pretty much every day is my very own personal form of torture. But a life without Wyatt Gibson in it is one I can't fathom, so I plaster a smile on my face and act as if life is peachy keen. I leave my truly tortuous daydreaming for when I'm alone in my bed at night, harboring daydreams that seem both closer and further from becoming reality since Walker instigated his plan.

And even though things are awkward, Wyatt remembered that my dad would be home today, so he encourages me to leave earlier than I normally would. I leave without a second thought, focusing on the other man I love.

I race home to make sure that I am there when he arrives, and when the sound of that diesel engine comes up the dirt road we live on, I run out the screen door, waiting on bouncing feet for him to park his rig and hop down from his seat.

"Daddy!" Like I'm ten years old again, I sprint down the porch steps and across the gravel to greet him with the tightest hug I can muster.

"There's my girl!" With a hug only a father can give, he squeezes me so tightly, so warmly, that it causes tears to flood my eyes. And I don't even fight letting them fall. They just do. It's been so long since I've seen him, and every time he comes home is still just as exciting as it was when I was a kid.

"Are you crying, pancake?"

I sniffle between sobs. "Yes."

"Aw, did you miss your dad a little bit?" he teases while stroking my back softly.

"Maybe."

His chest bounces with laughter. "I missed you, too, baby." With a kiss to my temple, he slowly releases me. I reach up to swipe away my tears and take him in for the first time in almost a month.

Hank Baker is a truck driver for a company based in Texas, but he frequently travels all over the country delivering goods. I remember him being gone for short stretches of time when I was younger, but after my mom left, his trips got longer and longer. As if being back here was too painful, when he got the chance to, he ran away—a feeling I'm beginning to sympathize with and understand. This small town can suck you in and keep you here if you let it, just like it's done to me for my entire life.

When he comes home, I always make it a point to spend as much time with him as I can, especially considering his aging appearance. His tan cowboy hat rests atop the thick hair he's

CHAPTER SIX

always had, but now it's far more gray than it was when I was younger. He's wearing a navy-blue t-shirt with the logo of his company on it, dark blue jeans, and of course his brown cowboy boots.

But it's the wrinkles around his eyes that scrunch as he smiles down on me that remind me my father is getting older, that every day I have with him is precious, and that I truly missed him more than I thought.

"Are you hungry? I can make us some lunch. I haven't eaten anything yet."

"That sounds perfect, hun. Let me grab my bag from the truck and meet you inside." He kisses my cheek, and then we part ways. I rush up the porch steps of the home I grew up in and head straight for the kitchen to make us a couple of sandwiches.

After grabbing everything I need from the pantry and fridge, I get to work assembling two roast beef sandwiches. I hear the screen door slam shut.

"I need to tighten those hinges while I'm home," he says, setting his duffle bag by the door and then joining me in the kitchen.

Our home isn't huge since just me and my parents made up our family. But it's comfortable and ours, simple and reassuring, especially after memories of my mom were removed by my father.

Pictures of him and me sit atop the mantle to the fireplace and hang symmetrically on the beige walls. The same few potted plants lie in the bay window that overlooks the driveway. The same creaks in the floorboard squeak when we walk on them. And the same dark-brown couch sits in the living room across from the television that still works and my father refuses to upgrade until it finally dies. I've offered to buy a new one, but he insists on me saving my money for something more important. And in all honesty, I don't really watch too much television, and he's rarely home, so I can see his point.

"So where did you drive to this time?" I ask as I spread the mayonnaise and mustard on pieces of bread.

"Let's see." He takes a seat at the dining room table, removing his hat and brushing a hand through his hair. "Louisiana, Mississippi, Alabama, Florida, Georgia, Tennessee, Kentucky, Missouri, Arkansas, Oklahoma, and then back down to Texas."

"Nice. See anything interesting?"

"Actually, I saw the biggest bug I've ever seen before."

I lift my head to make eye contact with him. "That's what you remember?"

He shrugs. "I've driven around this country so much, nothing really surprises me anymore."

A pang of jealousy radiates from my heart. I love my dad, and I'm glad he has a job he seems to enjoy, but I've never left the county, let alone the state. He gets to see so many new places every day, and I feel like he doesn't appreciate it. Although, I honestly don't know if that's true.

"I guess I can see that."

"So how is my girl doing? Anything new going on in your life?" he asks as he takes a drink from the glass of sweet tea I placed on the table for him.

CHAPTER SIX

Anything new going on in my life? Oh, lordy—do I even try to explain the past week to my dad?

"Uh, not really. Just work, helping out at the ranch. Taking pictures . . ." I reply.

"How are Randy and Elaine? I'll need to stop by and say hello before I leave again on Saturday."

"You're leaving again so soon?" I look up from slicing a tomato to see him surveying the house.

"Yeah, but I won't be gone as long this time. Only a few weeks. But maybe I can knock out a thing or two that needs to be done around here before I take off again."

That makes me feel a little bit better. It seems he's always in a hurry to leave once he gets here, and I have a list of things that need fixing during his short stints at home. "Okay. Well, the Gibsons are doing well. Business has never been better."

"Good for them. What about Wyatt and the brewery?"

I clear my throat before answering, hoping I don't accidentally unload everything on my dad. I love him, and we have a good relationship given the circumstances of his job and my childhood, but he's not the one I speak to about my love life—or lack thereof. "Business is booming there, too. In fact, tomorrow I have to help Wyatt interview and hire more people since our staff can't keep up."

He nods appreciatively. "That's good. I'm happy for them all. I'll have to stop in and get some food and beer to support them before I leave."

I grab the two plates with finished sandwiches and potato

chips and walk over to the table, placing the lunch in front of him. "That means a lot, Dad. Thank you."

"Anything for my little pancake and her friends." He winks and then reaches for his sandwich.

"Don't you think I'm a little too old for you to still be calling me pancake?" I ask as I take my seat across from him.

"Nonsense," he mutters around a mouthful of food. "You'll always be my pancake. There was nothing else I could get you to eat for such a long stretch of your childhood, especially after your mom left."

I can feel my face fall, my appetite suddenly dropping with it at the reminder of my mom, but somehow the term of endearment comforts me from the inside out. "Yeah, they just always made me feel better. And now, that's all I order at Rose's, too." I can feel him staring at me, but I keep my eyes on my plate, reaching for a chip and popping it in my mouth.

"Has she added anything new to the menu since I've been gone?" He wipes the corner of his mouth with a napkin before grabbing a few chips and chomping them to pieces.

"Has she added anything new since I've been born?" I reply sarcastically, which makes him chuckle.

"Good point."

"Everything stays the same in this town. You know that, Dad."

"Yes, it's part of its charm, I suppose. My favorite part is knowing that you will be here, though, when I return." He smiles genuinely across the table at me.

"What if I wasn't here?" I pick up a chip from my plate

before lifting my eyes to take in my dad's reaction to my hypothetical question. And as I would have guessed, his brow is furrowed.

"Why wouldn't you be here? Where are you going?"

"Nowhere, right now." I continue to shuffle chips around my plate. "But I applied to that photography program in New York that I told you about months ago . . ."

"Did you get in?"

"I don't know yet. And I mean, the chances that I will are slim. But . . . I don't know, Dad." I sigh, warring internally with this sudden need for change in my life that has assaulted my senses and my mind in the past week. "I just don't want to look back and wish I would have left Newberry Springs at some point, you know?"

"I can understand that. It's how your mother felt often," he admits, which has me trembling through my response.

"Really?"

He stares down at his sandwich, shuffling his own chips around now. "Yeah, although I think falling for her boss had more to do with her leaving than just feeling trapped."

My pulse is pounding. My father never brings her up, so I'm not sure how to act. "How come you never talk about her leaving?"

He's quiet for a moment, lost in thought. But then on a whisper, he says, "Because it makes me feel like a failure, Kelsea."

"What?" I stand from the table and walk around to sit on his lap, hugging him in his chair. "How on earth could you think that, Dad?"

I watch his Adam's apple bob as he swallows. "Because I wasn't enough for her to stay."

"You know, I feel that way, too . . . like I wasn't enough for her to stay, either." My admission rests in the air between us.

But then he smiles up at me, tears clouding his eyes. "Well, it was her loss, huh? Because I happen to think we're two pretty outstanding people."

And now tears are filling my eyes, too. "I agree."

"But listen to me, Kelsea," he starts, reaching for my hand. "I don't ever want you to feel that way. I don't want you to feel like you have to stay here because of me. Hell, this house is practically yours at this point since I'm never here. But if there's something out there that you want to see, that your heart is pulling you toward, go after it. Don't live with regrets. Don't worry about anyone else. Be selfish now, so when you do find the man you're supposed to be with, you don't end up feeling like your mother did. Okay?"

My throat is tight, but I manage to say, "Okay, Dad." However, my heart is being pulled in two directions—toward both the man I love and the city I've been dreaming of at night.

He pulls me in for a tight hug and then releases me before I make my way back over to my seat. "Now, am I going to see you while I'm home, or are you too busy being the hardworking daughter of mine—whom I am so very proud of—to make time for your dad?" he teases.

CHAPTER SIX

"I'll always make time for you, Dad."

"That's my pancake."

∼

"Do you have any serving experience?" Wyatt asks the young woman sitting across from us in the booth. She's young and upbeat, the perfect candidate for a new employee.

"A little. My current employer has me waiting tables two nights a week, but I'm really looking for more hours."

"That is something we need, too, someone to work multiple nights a week, someone reliable."

"I've never missed a shift except when I was extremely sick," she replies proudly, her back straightening in her seat.

Wyatt's eyes scan her resume one more time before lifting up again. "Well, thank you, Sally. We have a few more interviews to conduct, but I'm very grateful you put in an application." He reaches across the booth to shake her hand as she stands. "We'll be in touch soon."

"Thank you. The Gibson name is becoming quite popular in the state of Texas. I would love to be a part of that." She waves and then moves to walk away.

"I like her," I say, breaking the silence.

"Me, too. She's definitely at the top of the list." He moves her application to the bottom of the pile after putting a star at the top.

I watch him move the papers around while adjusting myself in my seat next to him in the booth. I still showed up today for the interviews. Because even though the tension and discomfort between us is still there, I am not one to let people down. It's simultaneously one of my faults and one of my attributes I'm most proud of. Funny how those two descriptions can be used at the same time regarding a personality trait.

"So how's your dad?" he asks while checking his watch.

"Good. Great."

"That's great."

More silence.

"I bet it was nice to see him. How long was he gone this time?"

"A month."

"And when does he leave again?"

"Saturday morning."

"That's not very long to be home."

"No."

We both pause, waiting for the other person to speak. "How's my brother?" he finally asks, which causes my heart to trip over itself.

"Uh? I wouldn't know. I haven't talked to him."

"Really?" He turns to face me now, arching his brow.

"No."

"Interesting," he says, shifting his attention back to the stack of resumes in front of him. "I thought you two would be talking more since apparently he wants to date you now."

I ponder my response, but a voice pulls our attention to the door.

CHAPTER SIX

"Hello. I'm here for the interview." A tall and muscular man with tattoos up and down his arms approaches us, his dark hair clean cut and shaven on the sides. The guy is massive, but he carries a calmness in his presence as he walks over to our booth and extends his hand. "I'm Clay."

I forget to speak for a minute as I admire the colossal man standing before me. He's definitely good-looking, but my heart knows what it really wants, and it's not him. "Hi, I'm Kelsea, and this is Wyatt, the owner."

Wyatt stands from his seat, intercepting his handshake, his spine straight and his chin tilted up. If I didn't know any better, I'd say Wyatt is slightly intimidated by Clay's presence. Clay definitely commands the room, but Wyatt has always had a heart under his brash exterior, which I find to be the most attractive part of him.

I fight to hide my smirk as they both take their seats and I start asking questions. "So, Clay, what made you put in an application here?"

He rubs his palm along the back of his neck, his eyes dipping down to where just a hint of cleavage plays against the neckline of the white v-neck t-shirt I'm wearing.

I swear I hear Wyatt growl low under his breath.

"I'm new in town and need a job. I love beer and have bartended in the past, so I figure why not work here? Word around town is this place is the place to be on the weekends."

"That it is," Wyatt replies before reaching his arm over the back of the booth. He's not quite draping it over my shoulder, but

I'm definitely fully aware he moved in that way. Suddenly, I feel like the temperature in here rose ten degrees. "What kind of beer do you like?"

"Big craft beer guy. I love a good stout or IPA. Not big on sours, though." He flicks his eyes back over to me, smirking in a mischievous way. "But I know the ladies tend to like those, so that's always my suggestion." He finishes his statement with a flirtatious wink.

Wyatt's finger grazes my shoulder just then, the touch so out of left field that I catch myself gasping. *Holy hell.* Did he mean to touch me right now? Or is he trying to deter Clay's blatant flirting?

"That they do, Clay. So what brought you to town?" Wyatt asks, but Clay's eyes remain on me.

"Needed a change. Dallas felt too big. I wanted to live in a place where people could get to know me. I love meeting new people." His tongue darts out to lick his lips while he stares at me, but all I can concentrate on is the way Wyatt's fingers are pressing firmly into my shoulder now, dragging along my shirt before hitting my exposed collarbone.

My entire body is on fire, his touch singeing my skin and shooting tingles up and down my spine. I swear my heart is thumping so hard the two of them can hear it.

"Well, Newberry Springs can be a very welcoming place as long as you don't step on anyone's toes," Wyatt replies, squeezing my shoulder now and pulling me closer to him. My eyes widen but then I look away, trying to hide my shock.

CHAPTER SIX

"No, I agree completely. Look, I just need a job. I'm eager to work and will do whatever I need to do to help run your business. I have experience and know my way around a restaurant, among other things." He chuckles and then stares back at Wyatt, who is squeezing my upper arm so tightly now, I think he might leave a bruise.

"Well, I think we've heard enough," he says, releasing me slightly and then pulling his hand away altogether as a rush of air leaves my lungs. "We'll be in touch," he continues before standing along with Clay, shaking his hand and staring him down intensely.

But Clay shifts his gaze back to me one last time. "I look forward to it." He gives me a final wink and then marches right back out the door, both of us watching him until the door slams shut.

"Wyatt?"

He looks down, grabs Clay's resume, and tears it in two. "We will not be hiring him."

"Okay," I state simply.

"Did you see . . . ?" He points in the direction of the door then focuses back on me, his eyes wild and his breathing harsh. This visceral reaction from him is uncharacteristic, but part of me doesn't hate it. He looks like he's about to come unhinged.

But then he reels in his anger and spits out, "You know what? It doesn't matter. He won't be working here." With a toss of the torn papers in a nearby trashcan, he starts to walk off, but then he pauses, turning around to face me again. "Let Sally, Nina, and Geo know they are all hired, and get them in here as soon as possible to fill out paperwork and start training."

"You got it."

"Thank you," he snaps then shoves past the door of the restaurant that leads to the kitchen, leaving me a puddle of goo in the booth and even more confused about what's happening between us.

∼

"Need any more help?"

I turn around in the bed of my truck, peering down to see Walker standing on the ground, looking up at me.

"What are you doing here? Wyatt is supposed to be here with me today."

He winces as I hand him the last box of jam. "Yeah, well, he texted me last night and asked if I could come in his place."

"Shit," I mumble under my breath as Walker extends his hand to me to help me down from the bed of the truck.

"Yeah."

"Jesus, Walker. This isn't good."

He holds up a finger. "Actually, it is. It means this is working."

"But at what cost? You should have seen him yesterday when we were holding interviews for the brewery."

"What happened?"

What happened? Oh, the man basically pissed on me in front of Clay the second he got the feeling he was hitting on me. I mean, it was blatantly obvious that Clay was flirting, but that little maneuver of Wyatt's when he wrapped his arm around my shoulder almost sent me spiraling out of control. "Let's just say he got quite territorial when one of the men we were interviewing kept winking at me."

Walker starts to chuckle as we situate the stacks of jars on our table. It's another beautiful Thursday morning at the farmers market, one which I was supposed to be working with Wyatt. Obviously, he sent Walker in his place, probably based on what happened yesterday. Which doesn't make me feel any better about this idea.

"Oh, shit. If he got that pissed at someone winking, just wait for what I have planned for Saturday night."

I feel my eyes bug out. "Oh God, Walker . . . what do you plan on doing?"

He flashes me a mischievous grin. "Don't worry, Kelsea. Just trust me."

I lower my head into my hands. "How on earth did I get here?"

"Excuse me? Know of any place around here where I can get some mouthwatering strawberry jam?" The voice that interrupts our conversation has my head popping up like a flash of lightning.

"Daddy!" I circle the table and throw my arms around him in a hug. We had dinner together last night, but I told him I would be busy today working the market and then at the brewery later. "What are you doing here?"

"Oh, I just wanted to stop by and visit you. Soak up as many moments as I can while I'm home. Visit my friends from around town since they all seem to be here at this market each week." He smiles down at me while he pulls me in closer. Damn, it sure is good to have him here, being able to hug him whenever I want.

"Hey, Mr. Baker." Walker extends his hand to shake my father's.

"Walker, so good to see you. Where's your brother?"

"Uh, Wyatt couldn't make it today, Dad," I reply sheepishly, which grants me a concerned look from him.

"Huh. You two are always joined at the hip. Seems odd that he's not here."

My eyes scour the ground instead of meeting his.

"Well, I'll never leave Kelsea hanging, sir. She's my friend, too, you know," Walker interjects.

"Mine, too," Evelyn declares as she leaves her booth next to us to come say hello to my dad. "Mr. Baker! So good to see you."

"Same, Evelyn." He pulls her into a hug. "I sure hope you're staying out of trouble."

"Me? Trouble? Nonsense." Her hands cover her heart in mock disgust.

My dad just laughs. "Yeah, well, maybe you should get my Kelsea into a little bit of trouble now and again. She could stand to live a little."

Oh, Dad . . . if you only knew what trouble I'm stirring up right now.

Evelyn smirks as if she's thinking the same thing. "Oh, I think I can manage that. We're actually all going out Saturday night to celebrate Schmitty's birthday, so I'll make sure she has a good time."

"Me, too," Walker adds, both of them smiling from ear to ear.

"Just be safe, pancake," he says, concerned now.

"I know, Dad. You know me, Miss Responsible." I roll my eyes as he pulls me into his arms again and kisses the top of my head.

"I *do* know, but that doesn't mean you shouldn't have fun, too. Remember what we talked about."

I nod, knowing he's referencing our conversation about my mom the other night. And in all honesty, it's been in the back of my mind a lot since then.

"I'll make sure she doesn't have too much fun," Walker says. "Does that help?"

My father looks Walker up and down. "If memory serves me correctly, weren't you the troublemaker of the three Gibson boys?"

Walker's mouth falls open, and Evelyn and I burst into laughter. "How did I get this reputation?"

My dad raises an eyebrow at him. "Do you not remember what good friends your father and I are? I may be on the road more than I'm here, but there is such a thing as a telephone, son."

That has Walker shutting his lips really quick. "Let's just end the conversation right there."

My dad laughs this time and then releases me from his arms. "All right, I'll let you all get back to work. See you at home, pancake."

"You, too, Dad." I wave at him as he crosses the sidewalk and saunters over to Mrs. Aguilar's flower stand.

"I forgot your dad calls you pancake. That is so cute!" Evelyn exclaims.

I point a finger at her as I make my way back to the other side of the table. "Yeah, well, he's the only one who can, so don't get any ideas."

"But he did just give me permission to get you wasted Saturday night, so that I'll definitely keep in mind."

I stare at her. "How did you get that from what he said?"

"Yup. I heard it, too," Walker adds.

I throw my hands up and shake my head. "I give up when it comes to you two."

They share a laugh and a high five, and then we all get back to work because the jam and clothes won't sell themselves.

CHAPTER SEVEN

Kelsea

"Are you sure I look okay? I feel like my lady bits are on display." I twist around in the mirror again, checking to make sure I can't see my vagina underneath the dress that hits at the middle of the back of my thighs.

"You look so smokin' hot, Kelsea! Wyatt is going to lose his ever-loving mind!" She squeals, jumping up and down in the middle of my bedroom. "I swear, I think I'm more excited than you are about tonight."

My stomach is in knots, and my heart is in my throat as I take in the strapless, body-hugging, red cotton dress that my best female friend convinced me to wear tonight. I've never worn so little fabric in my life. I feel borderline naked and afraid, but I'm grateful that at least I'm not trekking somewhere out in the wilderness *actually* butt-ass naked and fearing for my life.

Tonight is the night of Schmitty's birthday celebration, and knowing I'm going on Walker's arm is the closest thing I have to compare that to.

I barely recognize the girl staring back at me—dark makeup around my eyes, a deep natural blush color on my lips, my curls tamed, pulled up on one side of my head and secured with a clip, and cowboy boots on my feet. I don't even think I got this dressed up for prom.

"I feel overdressed. People are going to wonder what the hell I'm wearing."

"No, people are going to wonder why the hell you haven't been wearing this all along. You are gorgeous, Kelsea. You need to own that. Walk into that honky-tonk with your head held high. Believe that you belong there and you look fierce. You are a confident woman, you just need to remember that."

"My entire life has been shaken up in the past few weeks, so forgive me for not joining you on the confidence train," I bite back, adjusting the top of my dress for the hundredth time since I put it on. I don't have the biggest boobs on the planet, so I feel like this sucker is gonna fall down at some point, knowing my luck.

Evelyn steps in front of me, placing her hands on my shoulders. She's wearing her own little blue dress that brings out the hue in her eyes. "Remember why you're doing this, okay? This is so you can get everything you've ever wanted."

I shake my head. "It just feels wrong. Like, why do I have to

CHAPTER SEVEN

go to all of this trouble to get Wyatt's attention—pretending to date his brother, wearing dresses and makeup, wondering if every accidental touch between the two of us is intentional or not?"

Evelyn sighs. "Because men are stupid and sometimes need a little visual stimulation to make them see the light. You and I both know that Wyatt thinks you're gorgeous without all of this fanfare," she says, waving her hand up and down my body. "But Walker was right. He needs to see what he can lose, and the best way to do that is for him to feel threatened by another man. Unfortunately, men aren't all that smart when it comes to listening to their hearts."

She pats her chest. "And we know damn well they can't use their brains half the time," she adds, tapping against her temple this time.

I chuckle. "I know. It just feels . . . weird. Like, for once, I'm acting on emotions I've kept buried for so long, and I don't know how to process it all."

"I can see that. But here's why you need to keep chugging along." She takes a deep breath and looks me square in the eye. "Because this uncomfortable feeling is you going after what you want in life for a change, Kelsea. And yeah, it's terrifying. But it's also exciting, and I will be here no matter what." She squeezes my shoulders.

A heavy sigh escapes my lips. "You're right. Go big or go home as they say, correct?"

"Damn straight, woman. And you are going big tonight!" I

laugh, heading for my door just as she smacks my ass. "Let's go get 'em, tiger!"

"Who are *you* after?"

"Any man with half a brain and a dick double that size."

We giggle down the hallway, and as soon as we arrive in the living room, the doorbell rings.

"Hey, Walker." Evelyn answers the door and lets him inside. He's wearing a black shirt, dark blue jeans, and cowboy boots. His hair is styled neatly and combed to the side, and his bright white teeth sparkle as he smiles.

He looks very handsome. *Too bad he's not the brother I want.*

"Evelyn." He nods at her, glancing up and down her body appreciatively before focusing on me. His eyes light up. "Holy shit, Kelsea. You look phenomenal."

I fight to hide the blush crawling up my cheeks, but it's no use. I'm pretty sure my skin matches my dress right now. "Thank you."

He takes a step forward and then walks in a circle around me while whistling. "Damn. Wyatt is going to lose his shit when he sees you."

"That's what we want," Evelyn chimes in.

"Exactly," Walker replies. "But damn, Evelyn . . . you look smokin' as well." His eyes linger just a few seconds too long to be classified as friendly appreciation.

I glance back at her in time to see her own cheeks blush. "Thanks."

"Seriously though, Kelsea . . . how are you holding up right now?" he asks when he's back in front of me.

"Well, I feel like I'm about to pass out and throw up at the same time." They both laugh. "But based on your reaction, I'd say I'm feeling confident about tonight. I just hope nothing crazy happens."

Walker shakes his head. "My brother isn't stupid enough to throw a punch in a bar, let alone a place like The Jameson. The room will be swarming with security and cops outside. But based on the very passive-aggressive texts I received from him earlier, I'd say he's definitely going to be watching us."

"Which reminds me, no more kissing on the lips." I arch a brow and point a finger at him.

His smirk is instantaneous. "Too irresistible for you?"

I smack his chest playfully. "No. But I don't need anyone talking any more than they already are. And—it was weird, okay?"

Walker throws his head back in laughter. "Okay. You've got it. No more kissing on the lips. But if I see my brother looking at us, I'm definitely going to put my hands on you." He wiggles his fingers. "These babies are ready for some dirty dancing, too."

I feel like my skin is about to break out in hives. "Lord, please forgive me for this," I mutter under my breath, my eyes on the ceiling.

Evelyn and Walker share a laugh. "It's going to be great. If all goes well, this little charade won't last past tonight because Wyatt is going to come to his senses," Walker adds.

"Let's hope you're right and this doesn't blow up in our faces."

He extends his elbow to me as I weave my arm through, taking a deep breath of courage. "Okay, let's go."

After I lock up the house, we step off my porch to an Uber waiting to drive us to The Jameson, about an hour away. We all decided to Uber there so no one has to worry about drinking and driving.

"So what's going on in your life right now besides torturing your brother?" I figure talking on the way there will help settle my nerves. The two of us are in the backseat while Evelyn sits up front, carrying on a conversation with the driver.

Walker grins. "Not much, hence needing a little excitement, too. The station keeps me busy, and you know working at the ranch fills in any extra time I have. But I'm actually looking forward to hanging out with everyone tonight. Especially since Schmitty is my best friend, and I can't remember the last time we all went out."

Walker and Schmitty have been friends since elementary school. While Wyatt and I were attached at the hip, Walker had Schmitty. They now work at the fire station together, but it's been awhile since I've seen him.

"What about you, though?"

"What about me?" He casts me a side-eye glance and then focuses back on the road as the lights of cars and reflections of street signs illuminate his face.

"Is there a woman you have your eye on? I mean, why take me to The Jameson tonight instead of some other girl who you might actually get lucky with, or simply one you actually like as more than a friend?"

Walker flexes his hand in his lap, growing more serious as he does. "You and I both know that living in a small town doesn't provide many options in the dating pool. And besides, I'm not ready to settle down. I didn't meet my soulmate when I was born like you and my brother, so it might take me a little longer to see the light."

"Do you want that someday?"

He nods confidently. "Absolutely. But right now, I'm just living. Working at the fire station, helping my parents, hanging out with my buddies."

"Making your brother lose his mind," I add, which makes him laugh. "I don't get why you care so much about the two of us anyway, you know? I never asked you that when you suggested this little plan."

He clears his throat and adjusts himself in his seat before leaning over and whispering in my ear. "What I'm about to tell you stays in this car, all right?"

I nod, turning slightly to face him, eager for him to divulge his secrets. "Cross my heart," I reply, moving my fingers in an x over my chest.

He takes a deep breath and then exhales heavily, like the weight on his shoulders is alleviated along with it. "I guess I'm just a sucker for love, a romantic at heart. I've always admired my parents, how fiercely my dad loves my mom and vice versa. When one of my buddies at the station finds a girl he's crazy about, I encourage him to go all in. And when I see the way my brother looks at you, I just wish he would do the same." He shrugs. "I know there are reasons you two have held back, but what is life without love? You two are wasting time not giving in to what you both know is right."

"I never realized you were so wise and such a softie, Walker," I tease him.

He grins, his cheeks slightly turning pink even in the darkness of the backseat. "It's true, though. And I know someday I'll find the right woman for me. Until then, I figure I'd better help my brother get his girl."

"You could have just talked to him about it, you know?" I retort. "Instead of going through all of this trouble and taking a big risk."

He tosses his gaze my direction as we continue to coast down the highway. "Oh, I know. But this is *way* more fun. It's our duty as brothers and twins to give each other shit." His eyebrows bounce, and I can't help but laugh.

"I get that. But just so you know, you're gonna make some girl really lucky someday, Walker." I reach over and squeeze his forearm.

He smiles over his shoulder at me. "That's the plan. Who the hell knows when that'll be, though? Life has a funny way of making time pass slowly and quickly all at the same time and then slapping you with a hard dose of reality when you least expect it."

"Isn't that the truth? And I know I haven't said it yet, but thank you."

"For?"

"For doing this, even though I still don't know that it's the best idea. But it feels good to finally feel like he's seeing me as more than his best friend, the girl he used to chase around with worms and shoved so far into the friend zone, I never thought I'd get out."

"You're welcome. But believe me when I say, I'm doing this more to piss my brother off and for my own selfish need to not watch you two tiptoe around each other anymore. You both are giving other people blue balls just by watching you."

Laughter escapes my lips, and we fill the rest of the time listening to the Uber driver's music, reminiscing about growing up together, and talking about all of the events going on at the ranch.

But a little slice of optimism rests in my heart now—and a new helping of endearment for Walker.

I inhale the surrounding air scented with hickory smoke and fried food as I step out of the backseat of the car once we arrive at our destination. Music filters out from the steel warehouse in front of us, and lights shine brightly through the high glass windows around the building. The honky-tonk is in full swing as a line of people wait outside to pay their cover charge and get closer to alcohol and uninhibited choices for their evening.

"I can't remember the last time I've gone somewhere like this," I murmur as Walker comes around the front of the car after settling the bill on his phone. He agreed to pay for the ride here. Evelyn and I are going to split the cost of the ride home.

"It's been awhile for me, too, which is why we need to make the most of it. I'm gonna get you drunk tonight, Kelsea Baker."

I instantly grow more nervous. "I don't want to be drunk, Walker. I'm afraid of what I might say when the alcohol clouds my mind."

"Well, you're at least having a few drinks. It will help loosen you up."

"I second that notion," Evelyn says as we huddle in the parking lot near the entrance, waiting for the rest of our friends to show up. Walker had said it's supposed to be a pretty large group, but I'm not sure how many people that actually means.

Just as those words die on her lips, a few other trucks and cars pull up around us. Schmitty, the birthday boy, steps down from behind the passenger seat in a red lifted Ford, running his fingers through his tousled blond hair and grinning from ear to ear. Two other guys from the station I've seen a few times hop down from the passenger seat and the other side of the truck before they thank their driver and make their way over to Walker and me.

"Schmitty! Happy birthday, man!" Walker pulls him into a manly hug before they step away from each other. Then Schmitty's eyes land on me.

"Thanks, bro." Walker steps around us to greet the other two guys. "Is this Kelsea Baker?" Schmitty, whose real name is John Schmidt, widens his eyes before dropping them down my entire body and back up again. *And yup, there I go feeling naked once more.*

"Yup. It's me."

"Damn, girl. It's been a long time." He leans in and plants a kiss on my cheek. "Thanks for coming out tonight."

CHAPTER SEVEN

"Well, I was kind of coerced, but you're welcome."

Schmitty laughs and then flings his arm around Walker's neck. "Yeah, Walker told me he was bringing someone. I just didn't think it'd be you."

"Me neither," I mumble, staring at the ground as Evelyn fights her way to the center of our circle.

"Well, I think we all need to have a little fun tonight. The more the merrier, right?" She tosses her hair over her shoulder and then sticks her hand out to shake Schmitty's.

"Evelyn, this is John, or Schmitty, as we call him. And that is Gage and Brody," Walker says, introducing his friends.

But I see the twinkle in her eye as she stares up at Schmitty, and I think it's safe to say he's feeling the same thing. "So *you're* the birthday boy?"

He holds up a hand before intercepting hers, smirking down at her. "Guilty."

"Well, thanks for letting me tag along to celebrate you getting another year older."

"Sweetheart, I feel not a day over twenty-one, and I'm even luckier now that you're here to help me not feel so depressed about the creaks in these bones." His lips twist into a pleased grin. "How come I've never seen you around before?"

Evelyn laughs. "I'm around. You're just not there."

"Well, I think we need to change that."

"Oh, dear. Is that how tonight is going to go? Shameless flirting?"

"Depends. Are you going to flirt back?"

Evelyn grins and then sizes him up with her eyes. "You know, I think I just might."

"All right, you two. Now that we all know you'll probably end up fucking each other before the night is over, can we start making our way inside?" Walker interjects.

"But what about . . ." I start just as my skin exposed to the cool night air begins to pebble. But it's not the temperature that's making goosebumps appear on my body. It's Wyatt.

"Hello."

Wyatt's voice pulls my gaze to my left, where I see him wearing an outfit almost identical to his brother's. *But lord have mercy, it looks ten times better on him.*

"Hi." It's the only word I manage to squeak out before I gain my composure. Our eyes lock, and the people around us fail to exist anymore. His piercing brown orbs penetrate me, darkening the longer we stare at each other. He's looking at me the way I always wished he would—like he's about to eat me alive yet will hold me tenderly and never let me go at the same time.

"Well, hello there, little brother." Walker puts his arm around my back, holding me next to him, igniting a fire in Wyatt's eyes that I'm sure everyone can see.

"Sorry I'm a little late. I had a rough time finding a parking spot."

His dark-brown eyes lock on me once more, and I feel my skin flush with awareness again. *My God, my body feels like an inferno.*

CHAPTER SEVEN

"You drove?" I ask, still blocking everyone else around us out as more people start to congregate in our area.

"I don't plan on drinking."

"That's no fun," Walker whines, rubbing his thumb along my hip, which draws Wyatt's eyes to the spot.

"Still, you could have ridden with us," I offer, even though I know that would have made things ten times more awkward.

His eyes land back on mine. "Well, I didn't want to ruin your *date*," he says through gritted teeth, glaring between Walker and me.

"Well, I, for one, thank you for that," Walker adds, which has me looking away and biting my lip. "Doesn't Kelsea look gorgeous tonight?" he asks, smirking over my head at his brother.

But Wyatt just stands there, fuming under the surface. He clears his throat and then looks me dead in the eye. "She looks stunning."

"Thank you." I lick my lips sheepishly, but Wyatt's eyes drop down to catch the movement of my tongue. And suddenly, all I can think about is him kissing me, feeling his tongue tangle with my own.

"Yo! Let's get this party moved inside, shall we?" Schmitty shouts, garnering some hoots and hollers from the group. I recognize a few faces from around town, or even from high school, but most of these people don't seem to be from Newberry Springs. "First round is on me."

"Let's go," Walker agrees, and we all start walking toward the entrance, his arms still around my waist.

"Who are these people?" I whisper in his ear as we walk behind the group.

Walker chuckles. "A lot of the guys are from the station, but the others are from Schmitty's college. He went to the University of Dallas before moving back to Newberry Springs."

"Ah, that's right." I remember Schmitty leaving for college much like Wyatt did. Funny how their small hometown pulled them both back even after they left.

"You're shaking." Walker rubs his hand up and down my arm as we find our place in line. Wyatt is about five people ahead of us, talking to some of the other guys.

"Well, yeah. This isn't easy, Walker." I shake my head as the line starts to move.

Walker squeezes the arm I have looped through his elbow as we inch toward one of the open doors. "Just try to relax. Act like Wyatt doesn't even exist; it will make him even crazier. And don't forget to own the room. You look gorgeous, Kelsea. And it's about time my brother sees what he's missing."

"I'm gonna throw up," I whisper, making Walker laugh.

"Well, this place has plenty of bathrooms, so I think you'll be fine."

∼

"To Schmitty!"

"To Schmitty!" The chorus of everyone mirroring Walker's toast rings out as we all raise our shot glasses and toss them back.

CHAPTER SEVEN

The whiskey burns as it goes down, but I'm hoping some liquid courage will help me start to relax—and that would be a hell of a lot easier if Wyatt would stop staring at me every two-point-five seconds.

"Yes, Kelsea!" Evelyn shouts as she bumps her hips with mine. "This is just the start of the evening!"

"Ugh, don't remind me." I wipe the corner of my mouth with my thumb, eliminating the drop of whiskey that slipped out. "So . . . you like Schmitty?"

Her face lights up. "Dear lord. Where did he come from, and why haven't I seen him around town?" She fans herself dramatically.

"I honestly don't know. But I say go for it."

"Walker won't be mad?"

My brow furrows. "Why would Walker be mad?"

"I don't know. That is his best friend and all."

"Yeah, but he's single and so are you."

"Yes, I am."

Evelyn is the type of girl who sees something and goes after it. Hell, she moved to Newberry at nineteen to open up her own clothing boutique against her parents' wishes. She is constantly working to improve her business, and I know that I can call her about anything and she'll be there for me. She's fiercely loyal, strong, and confident—which is why I'm baffled that she's second-guessing going after a guy she wants.

"I guess I just don't want to cause problems."

I wave her off. "You won't, believe me. Walker isn't like that."

That has her smiling. "Okay. But if he says anything, I'm just going to say that you gave me permission."

"I will gladly admit to that."

She giggles and then walks right over to Schmitty, presumably to continue their flirtatious banter from before.

Walker comes up behind me, placing his hand on my waist again. "Feeling good?"

"Uh . . ."

His lips inch closer to my ear. "My brother is watching us right now, but don't look over there. Just smile and remain calm on the outside."

"Easier said than done." I grab the whiskey and coke the bartender set down in front of me just moments ago and bring it to my lips, drinking more than I probably should this early in the evening.

"Whiskey and coke?" A voice from my right startles me, and I twist to see Wyatt glaring, the tick in his jaw twitching.

"Uh, yeah. Is that a problem?"

"Don't you remember what happened the last time you were drinking whiskey and coke?" he asks, arching his brow.

I move to answer, but Walker beats me to it. "Don't worry, little brother. I'm watching out for her. I won't let her have too much." He plasters a knowing smile on his face as he grips my waist tighter.

The last time I got drunk, which was almost a year ago, I was drinking the same drink. We were at one of the bonfires the Gibsons put on for their employees every three months to thank them for all the hard work they put in to help them run their ranch. Let's just say I spent more time over the toilet that night than having fun with everyone else.

"I know my limits now, Wyatt, but thanks for the concern."

His eyes narrow as he contemplates his next words, but then he takes a step back and shoves his hands in his pockets. "Fine. I hope you two enjoy your evening." I watch his back as he runs away, off to do God knows what.

The rush of air that comes from my lips once he's far enough away is embarrassingly loud. "Walker . . ."

He soothingly strokes his fingers up and down my arm. "Don't stress, Kelsea. It's only a matter of time before he snaps."

"But I don't want him to snap." I turn to face him, my body trembling with fear. "I don't want to make him mad. Can't I just tell him what we're trying to do? That you came up with this stupid idea and I stupidly followed along and how we're both really stupid and I'm sorry?"

He chuckles, which doesn't help calm me. "But that defeats the purpose. Then he's *really* going to be pissed. He needs to snap first. He needs to realize that he doesn't give a fuck about what he thinks is going on between the two of us. He needs to realize that he wants you more than that, enough to fuck me over in the process."

"But you're his brother."

"And you're the girl he's in love with. Sometimes that wins." He shrugs before one of the other firefighters from the station comes up to say hello. Walker's words resonate with me as my eyes land on his brother.

Wyatt looks like he's about to snap, all right—snap Walker's neck and then destroy everything in his path.

"Let's dance." At his voice, I turn to find Walker staring down at me now that his conversation with his friend is over.

"Yeah, okay. That sounds like fun."

With my hand in his, he announces to the group that we're headed for the dance floor. The majority of them decide they want to join in and stand to follow us.

The Jameson reminds me of an open air barn, complete with one of the biggest displays of country culture I've ever seen. We leave the long wooden bar with our drinks as the twenty-something bartenders in cutoff shorts and equally small tops run around filling drink orders left and right for the other patrons. As far as the eye can see, several other bars line the walls, and glossy wooden dance floors are scattered throughout the building. Cowboy boots scuff the ground while couples spin and two-step to the beat of the country music blaring overhead.

Exposed steel beams in the ceiling are lined with HVAC ducts blowing stark cold air to combat the Texas humidity outside, and the walls are covered with shiplap, giving a country feel to the one-hundred-thousand square-foot space. To the left of the entrance is the gate that opens to the bull-riding arena (yes, a bull-riding arena—welcome to Texas), and right behind that is the tunnel that leads to the full restaurant, which serves up authentic Texas barbecue.

CHAPTER SEVEN

The Jameson is the place to have the ultimate good ol' American party experience, and it looks like our crowd is on a mission to make that happen tonight.

"Now, this is just what we needed!" Evelyn squeals as she catches up to us, grabbing my other hand, and we descend the small flight of stairs to reach the largest dance floor in the space. She spins me around when we reach the hardwood, making us both laugh as we dance with each other. But then Schmitty comes over and pulls her away from me, eating her up with his eyes as they begin a dirty dance all their own.

Speaking of grinding, I feel a warm body come up behind me and turn to see Walker smiling at me. "Don't overthink it; just dance. Pretend I'm my brother if you need to," he whispers in my ear.

"That's disturbing."

I can feel his laugh against my skin. "Yeah, maybe a little. But don't worry, soon it will be my brother dancing with you. Not me."

A surge of hope radiates from my chest. *One can only hope.*

"So Evelyn and Schmitty, huh?" he asks, casting his eyes in their direction quickly.

"Yeah. She thinks he's hot. Is that okay?"

All he offers is a simple shrug. "I mean, he's my best friend and one of the most loyal guys you'll ever meet. But . . . I don't know . . . something about the two of them together just doesn't feel right."

"Why?" Our feet keep moving to the beat.

"I honestly don't know."

I ponder Walker's blatant concern as the song changes and more people gather on the dance floor. I try to focus on the music, on moving my hips to the beat of the song, while catching glimpses of Evelyn and Schmitty shamelessly running their hands all over each other's bodies. And then their lips are touching. But all I can feel, all I can sense, is Wyatt staring at me.

Sure enough, I fling my gaze toward the table our group secured just on the other side of the barrier of the dance floor to see Wyatt hunched over the surface, resting his forearms along the wood, sipping his soda and tracking me with his eyes. I'm in a trance as we hold each other's gazes for a moment before I break eye contact and shift my eyes to the floor.

This was a mistake. I shouldn't have agreed to this. I need a second to breathe.

"I'm going to use the bathroom," I tell Walker, spinning around to face him.

"You want someone to go with you?"

I shake my head, my mind feeling fuzzier the longer I stand here. "Nope. I'm good. I might get another drink on the way back, though."

"All right. I'll be right here." He squeezes my hand before I saunter off, feeling shaky in my boots as I walk down a narrow hallway to the left of the dance floor toward the neon restroom signs. And as soon as I reach the door, I breathe a sigh of relief. I've never been more grateful that the bathrooms on this side of The Jameson seem to be single rooms.

CHAPTER SEVEN

I need a moment to recoup, to convince myself for the thousandth time that everything is going to work out the way it's supposed to. That I'm doing the right thing.

Once I'm safely inside, I do my business and then check my appearance in the mirror. Reminding myself that I'm alone, I take my time to gather my wits. My cheeks are flushed, but other than that, I look put together, as if I have no worries at all, as if the very foundation of a lifelong friendship isn't crumbling as I stand here.

I wish Wyatt could be mine. I wish I could give in to these feelings that I thought would go away when he left to accomplish his dreams and I stayed behind in our hometown. I wish I could just say what I want and he would tell me he feels the same way, and that would be it. But now things are so twisted that I'm worried we can never be the same as we were before.

The six years he was gone helped dull the ache in my chest. That ache served as a constant reminder that the boy I grew up loving from the moment I knew what that feeling was could never be mine. It was easier to accept when I didn't have to see him every day, when I had enough space from him to convince myself that my feelings were just a childhood crush and not something more. Yet sadly, when he returned home, so did my attraction to him, and a grown-up and determined version of Wyatt was even more dangerous to my heart and mind.

Now, I'm wondering if Walker really knows his brother as well as he thinks he does. Hell, even I'm questioning how well I know Wyatt right now. Is this little ruse really enough to get him to come to his senses? Or will this plan blow up in both of our faces and cause irreparable damage between the three of us?

God, why can't owning your feelings be easy and not a relentless circle of questions that makes you feel like there's no end in sight?

Mustering up another ounce or two of courage, I fluff my hair and then open the door.

But Wyatt is standing there.

"Oh. Hi."

With intense focus and an unreadable expression, he simply replies, "Hey."

"Um, is everything okay?" I look around him but don't see anything since we're away from the main part of the building. My pulse pounds in my ears when I realize we're alone.

"No." His face is stone cold, his entire upper body is tense, and he keeps rubbing his fingers together at his sides.

"Okay. Is there anything I can help you with—"

"Is anyone else in there?" he asks, cutting me off.

"Uh, no. It's a single," I answer, looking over my shoulder and then back at him.

The next thing I know, I'm being guided back into the bathroom as Wyatt stalks toward me, his eyes concentrated on my face and his body radiating heat. He turns to lock the door from the inside and then spins back around, stepping up to me again as my feet move backward on instinct.

Before I know it, my back is hitting a wall, and Wyatt closes every inch of distance between us, pressing his entire body along mine—a move that he's never done intentionally before unless we were hugging.

I can feel every inch of him—*every freaking inch.*

His hard chest against my breasts. His abs pushed against my soft stomach. His hardening length against my leg.

"Wyatt?" I grate out, eyes wide from our proximity and everything I'm feeling coming off of him, everything I'm seeing in his gaze.

"Kelsea," he rasps, closing his eyes before reaching up and placing his hand on the back of my neck, holding me in place so I can't run. Not that I'd want to or even could at this moment.

His fingers tangle in my hair as he tugs on it slightly, forcing me to look up at him. "Why?" He pauses. "How . . ."

"Why what?" I ask breathlessly, unsure that I want to know what he's thinking but desperate to know, nonetheless.

"Fuck." He sighs before meeting my gaze again and moving his knee between my thighs, parting my legs. My breath catches in my throat as my core throbs and my clit lights on fire from the graze of his pants against my underwear.

I feel like I'm outside of my body right now, looking down at us with a wide open mouth and a bowl of popcorn, shoveling the buttery kernels into my mouth, waiting to see what happens next.

"Why are you here with him?" he finally whispers inches away from my lips. Then he leans into my neck and drags his nose along my skin. "How can you not see that *I* am the one you should be with, Kelsea?"

My entire body melts, my internal temperature rising so high and the throbbing between my legs increasing so steadily that I swear my knees are about to buckle. His words are the confirmation I've been waiting for, and yet, now I don't know what to say.

"Wyatt . . ."

"End it," he growls, picking his head back up and peering down into my eyes, his stare so demanding that I couldn't look away if I tried.

Holy hell. Who knew my best friend had this side to him? And goddamn, is it hot.

"What?" Confusion clouds my mind. I have to make sure I heard him correctly.

He leans back and then crouches down until we're at eye level. "*End it, Kels.*" His eyes dip down to my lips. "End it with him before I make you mine. I won't kiss you knowing you're seeing him, kissing him, touching him." Leaning forward, he runs his nose along the column of my throat again, inhaling deeply and making my breath catch in my lungs.

I'm frozen, barely breathing when I feel his lips press softly against my pulse. "As soon as I know you're done with him, I'll kiss you. Then I'll give us both exactly what we've wanted since we were kids."

"Holy shit . . ." I moan, closing my eyes and gripping his shoulders as I feel his hot breath move over my skin.

But then his presence disappears, and his body moves backward so there's space between us now and his hands are no

CHAPTER SEVEN

longer on me. I open my eyes and take in the sight of him, feet rooted to the ground a few feet away.

"I want you, Kelsea," he admits. "I always have. And I hate that it's taken me this long to admit it. If you want my brother, I think I could learn to accept that. If he is the one who can make you happy, then I guess I'd have no choice but to be okay with it." His eyes never waver from mine when he finally says, "But I don't think that's what *either* of us wants."

And then he turns away, glancing at me one more time over his shoulder before he unlocks the bathroom door and leaves me there, holding my breath. When I finally come back to reality, I release the oxygen I was holding in my lungs and slide down the wall as my knees go weak and my clit throbs with need.

Holy hell. I don't think I was prepared for that.

And more importantly, I'll be damned—Walker's plan worked.

CHAPTER EIGHT

Wyatt

"*F*uck." The Jameson is packed with people from all over, bodies dancing and taking in copious amounts of alcohol, games of pool being played and line dancing orchestrated below a stage to my left. I should be having a good time, I should be joining in on all the fun and letting loose. Hell, that was the point of coming out tonight.

But all I can think about is Kelsea in that fucking red dress and the way she stole the goddamn breath from my lungs the minute I saw her in the parking lot right next to my brother.

And then I saw red.

Not just the dress she was wearing—the one I was envisioning ripping from her body—but the red that clouds your vision as your

CHAPTER EIGHT

blood pumps so furiously you can feel your body shake from the strength of your heart.

I really didn't plan on confronting Kelsea tonight—or my brother, for that matter. My goal was to play it cool and watch the two of them to gauge their connection. But after meeting with my dad today and getting the recap of his doctor's appointment, I've been in a shitty mood ever since.

He has a mass pressing on his optical nerve, which is causing the blurriness in his vision. The doctor says it's operable, but that means downtime and recovery and possibly losing his sight altogether. It's a risky operation, and I know that when he tells my mother tonight, she's going to be a mess.

I didn't want to go out after that conversation, but I made a commitment to come tonight. Regret slammed into me, though, as soon as I saw Kelsea and my brother together, fueling my already sour mood and frame of mind.

But when I saw her go to the restroom, something in me snapped. I couldn't risk her going home with Walker. After ruminating on the circumstances going on in the lives of people close to me, I didn't want to live with any regrets. I had to say something.

It's one thing if they're casually seeing each other right now or even if she would prefer for them to remain friends. But if he touched her intimately—or, heaven forbid, went all the way with her—I'd lose my fucking mind.

So I made a snap decision to put myself out there. I was planning to do it at some point anyway, but it just made sense in the moment. Feeling her pressed up against me like that had me fighting my instinct to act on every desire I possess when it comes to that woman. Visions of me yanking off her underwear and fucking her up against the wall were all I could see once I locked myself inside that bathroom with her. But I'll be damned if the first place I have sex with her is in the bathroom of a bar, not when I've waited years to touch her that way.

It's also why I didn't kiss her, why I didn't give in to the urge to smash my lips to hers and remind my body of the way she tastes —because I never quite forgot. And I wonder if she's as warm and sweet as I remember her being all those years ago.

I'm reeling over what just happened, how I behaved, but I know there's nothing more I can do in this moment. Tonight is about Schmitty, and the last thing I want to do is make a scene. I'm stuck here for at least another hour or two to pay my dues as the guy's friend, but my body is wishing I could smash something like the Hulk to combat the rage running through me. Nothing but unspoken words and thoughts plague my mind.

As I exit the bathroom hallway, I take a deep breath and then remember what I'm doing here: spending time with some friends, trying to remember to act like I'm twenty-six, and trying not to beat the shit out of my brother.

Just as my eyes move around the bar, Gage calls me over to him, standing at the table I'd just left moments ago. "Hey, we're getting a few pool tables. You in?"

"Yeah, I'll play."

Grateful for the distraction—and a break from having to

CHAPTER EIGHT

witness Walker put his hands all over Kelsea on the dance floor—I follow Gage and a few of the other guys to the corner where Brody is already racking the balls for a game. We all chip in forty bucks as a wager and then battle it out in teams of two.

But I can't seem to stop myself from glancing in the direction of the rest of our friends. Kelsea made her way back from the bathroom, looking as poised as always, as if I didn't make her skin flush the same hue of her dress. I felt the heat between her legs. I almost groaned out loud when she dug her nails into my shoulders. I knew she was just as turned on as I was.

I meant what I said, though. I won't touch her if she is with him. But at least she knows where I stand. I just wish I knew where her head is at now.

My eyes trail her the rest of the night, watching her laugh and make small talk with everyone who crosses her path, memorizing the way her hips move as she shimmies to the upbeat songs all the girls are dancing to. I watch other men eye her appreciatively, which only makes me more angry that I can't do anything about it without drawing unnecessary attention to us.

When my phone alarm goes off, signaling that I've put in my time, I say my goodbyes to the crew. I give Schmitty one last "Happy Birthday," shake the hands of all the guys I see on a regular basis with my brother or at the brewery, and lastly, make my way to say goodbye to Kelsea.

I can tell when I walk up next to her that she's reached her whiskey and coke limit.

"I'm leaving," I declare from behind her, forcing her to turn around. Her glazed over expression is followed up by a cheesy smile.

"Party pooper," Evelyn slurs next to her.

Kelsea finally blinks when she looks up at me. "Why are you leaving already?"

"Because it's a long drive back, and I don't want to be doing it at three in the morning."

She retrieves her phone from her pocket and lights it up to see the time. "But it's only twelve thirty."

"I know. Perhaps I *am* just a party pooper." She rolls her eyes at me and almost trips over her own feet. "You should probably stop drinking, you know . . ."

She glares at me. "Why do you care?" And now I'm certain she should stop because Kelsea knows better than to ask me that type of question.

She and I always look out for each other.

"I've got her," Walker says, marching up to us and replacing the whiskey and coke in her hand with a glass of water. She tosses him an evil look as well, which actually makes me feel a little better, and then reluctantly starts to down the water.

I take a moment to study her lips before directing my gaze to my brother. "Make sure she gets home safely."

"I know, Wyatt."

"I mean it." I take a step toward him and then grit my teeth. "If anything happens to her—"

"I've got her, Wyatt. Don't worry."

But that's all I do for the entire drive home. Worry about what

CHAPTER EIGHT

she's thinking, worry that I came on too strong when I cornered her in the bathroom, worry that she's too drunk and she and Walker may do something neither one of them can take back.

When I make it home just before two in the morning, I'm so amped up that I can't sleep. I toss and turn for over an hour, replaying every moment of tonight and earlier today. And then, without thinking, I hop in my truck. The first place I want to go is to her house to finish our conversation and get her reaction, to gauge how she's feeling about what I said. But when I fire up the ignition, my mind doesn't take me to Kelsea's house. It takes me to another place I need to visit, another person who needs to hear the truth from my lips.

"Well, hello, little brother." Walker greets me when he opens the door to his apartment. "You know it's after three in the morning, right?"

"What the fuck are you doing?" I shove him back and slam his door behind me as a shit-eating grin graces his lips.

"I think you need to be more specific. I was about to go to sleep, but now I'm talking to you."

"Cut the shit, Walker. You know what I'm talking about."

He shakes his head slightly. "Nope. I'm a little slow and tired. I think you need to elaborate." I know he's not completely sober, but I also know he's not shitfaced drunk, either, which means he's coherent enough to have this conversation.

"Kelsea, you asshole." I wanna punch the grin off his face. "What the fuck are you doing with Kelsea?"

His smile builds. "What do you mean?"

My hands fist his shirt as I push him back against the wall now, getting dangerously close to his face so I can stare into the eyes that mirror mine. "You can't have her, Walker."

"Why not? She's single. She's beautiful. She's—"

"—*mine*," I finish for him, clenching my teeth through the word. But my heart knows the truth now, and it's time that everyone else, including my brother, does, too. Fuck, there's no going back after this.

"She's mine."

He sighs and then begins to laugh. "It's about damn time you admit it."

I can feel my face fall with his words as I lean back slightly. The rage coursing through my veins begins to dwindle. And then I tilt my head at him, making sure I'm hearing him correctly. "What?"

He shoves me off him, smoothing his shirt down as if he's concerned about his appearance. "I said it's about time you admit it. I know she's yours, Wyatt. She always has been."

Standing there in silence, we stare each other down as I process what he said, blinking slowly. "What the hell is going on here?"

My brother huffs out another laugh and then steps around me, reaching for the glass of water he left on his coffee table and taking a few gulps. When he finishes, he locks eyes with me. "I don't want Kelsea, little brother."

"Then why . . . ?"

"I wanted *you* to finally admit that *you* wanted her."

CHAPTER EIGHT

"That's . . ." *What the actual fuck?*

"The only reason I was giving her attention was so it would grab yours, dumbass. You and Kelsea have been dancing around each other these past two years as if no one else can see how you two truly feel about each other. And after Dad gave us that little talk a few weeks ago, I figured, why not help you out?"

I mentally avoid the comment about Dad for fear of spilling the beans regarding his situation and focus on why I'm here.

"So . . . let me get this straight." I place my hands on my hips while narrowing my eyes at him. "You never wanted Kelsea. You only showed her attention to make me jealous?"

"Yup."

"What the fuck, Walker?" I throw my hands in the air, pissed off yet again for the hundredth time tonight. "Why would you do that?"

His points his index finger at me, raising his voice as well. "Because *you* were too chickenshit to admit what you want. And so was Kelsea, so I convinced her to let me interfere."

"Wait. Kelsea knew about your intentions?"

He grimaces slightly. "Yeah, but don't be mad at her about it. She just . . . she was tired of you just seeing her as your friend, and after we saw how you reacted when I kissed her, she reluctantly agreed to be my date, hoping that I was right."

Holy shit. My mind is spinning right now.

On one hand, the sense of relief washing over me knowing that my brother isn't actually interested in Kelsea is welcoming. But on the other hand, the fact that the two of them felt the need to lie and manipulate the situation isn't sitting well with me.

"Right about what?"

"That seeing her with someone else would make you realize that you could lose her if you didn't admit your feelings sooner rather than later."

I reach up to tug at the strands of my hair. "I can't believe this."

Walker shrugs. "Well, believe it. You know I only did this to help you."

That has my head spinning back to face him. "I was plotting your murder, Walker! I was legitimately thinking to myself how on earth I would be able to sit back and watch you touch her and love her if that's what she wanted!"

"Well, lucky for you, that's not what she wants. She wants *you*."

I grind my teeth together. "Why couldn't she just say something, then?"

"Why couldn't *you* just say something to *her*?" he tosses back at me.

"It's—"

"—complicated, I know," he replies, rolling his eyes. "Except that it's not. You and Kelsea are meant to be together, Wyatt. You always have been, since you were kids."

"Dad warned me away from her before I left for college," I admit, my voice low and my eyes pointed down at the ground, which has his eyebrows lifting. "I wanted her back then, but he advised me not to make a move."

"Well, Dad usually has a reason for saying what he says, and I think that's true when he hinted that it's time to start thinking about our futures." *Yeah, well, his future and all of ours is about to change, too.*

I direct my line of sight to him again, my veins still pumping blood at a furious pace. "So you just took it upon yourself to interfere with mine?"

He laughs. "No, I took it upon myself to get you to finally admit what you want."

"I can't believe she went along with this." Running my hand through my hair again, I keep fixating on that detail, not sure if I'm feeling anger or shock but knowing that the adrenaline running through my body will not allow me to sleep anytime soon.

"Think of it as her being gently coerced." He smiles, clearly pleased with himself. "But I'm telling you, Wyatt, if you don't act on your feelings now, tell her how much you love her and want her, you're going to miss out. Kelsea will *not* wait around for you forever. And other guys aren't going to wait around either to make their move. You say that she's yours, but she's not—not yet, anyway. You might feel that down in your marrow, deep in your soul, but she's not yours until you truly fucking claim her."

Staring at him while still absorbing this turn of events, I finally manage to say, "I need to go." I move for the door, feeling Walker right behind me, but I need space. I need time to process all of this.

"When are you going to talk to Kelsea?" he asks as I freeze in place, my hand on the doorknob.

"I . . . I don't know." My skin feels like it's crawling, my pulse is still thundering, and my stomach is twisted in knots. As grateful as I am that their relationship was a farce, the entire situation still feels wrong.

"Don't overthink this, Wyatt," he says, which has me turning to face him again.

And then I let my thoughts out—the most prevalent ones, anyway. "But she kissed you. She went along with this—"

"No, *I* kissed *her*. *I* convinced *her*. This was *me*." He points to his chest. "Put the blame on *me*."

I shake my head, unsure of what I'm feeling or even thinking right now. But I do know one thing that needs to be said for certain.

Pointing a finger at my brother, I growl out, "Don't ever fucking touch her again, Walker. I swear to God, I won't hold back next time."

He holds his hands up, smirking even though he knows I'm deadly serious. "I don't plan on it. I did what I needed to do. The rest is up to you."

With a curt nod, I open the door, traipse down the stairs of his building, and then hop back in my truck, melting into the seat as I drive home and process all of this information.

Why couldn't we have just talked? Why did Walker have to intervene? Why did Kelsea agree to it?

I mean, I guess I can't be completely angry because Walker's little stunt did grant me the awareness to admit my feelings to myself and Kelsea. But the part that's not sitting well with me is her decision, her agreement to let him, the fact that she felt the need to go through with it to catch my attention.

Well, you sure as hell weren't going to do anything, Wyatt, so isn't that a little hypocritical?

Fuck. My subconscious isn't wrong.

I had every intention of talking with her tomorrow morning at my parents' house when we show up for our usual Sunday duties. But now? Well, this new information is making me question just how we got to this place at all, how a lifelong friendship escalated to her and my brother trying to make me jealous. And part of me knows there are much more glaring issues to discuss now instead of just how we feel.

~

"How's my favorite son?" My mother kisses my cheek as soon as I enter the kitchen around eleven the next morning. I managed to get about five hours of sleep, but I can definitely feel the effects of staying up all night, especially since my sleep wasn't restful.

No, it was filled with visions of Kelsea and I talking about what happened last night—and none of them ended well.

"What did the other two do that makes me your favorite today?"

She grins and then plants her hands on her hips. "Nothing they haven't already done before." Her eyes assess me. "You look tired."

"I'm always tired. And yesterday was . . . a long day," I say, not wanting to get into the details of my love triangle with my mother because the uncertainty I feel today is unwelcome. And even though I wonder how her talk with my dad went, after a closer look, I can tell her eyes are swollen. She's been crying.

"Did you have fun during your night out?" she asks, moving back over to the stove to open the oven door and check on the biscuits. I notice the basket is already filled with some, so I grab one, holding off eating it until after I can answer her. "The company picnic we had here yesterday lasted longer than we anticipated."

"Don't they all?" She nods before spinning to face me again, waiting for an answer from me about Schmitty's birthday. "It was . . . fun." *Tortuous. Intense. A goddamn nightmare.*

"That's good. It's important for you to remember to have fun and act your age every once in a while."

"Yeah, I guess so." I stare off into space before gathering the courage to ask, "How's Dad doing?"

My mother freezes at the stove. "He's . . . okay."

"Just okay?"

She spins around to face me as moisture builds in her eyes. "He told me you knew."

"I did." I stand from my stool and walk over to wrap her in my arms. "I'm sorry, Mom. He made me promise not to tell."

CHAPTER EIGHT

"I know. He told me that, too. I just can't believe this is happening."

"Me, either." I breathe her in, the weight of his health resting between us. "But it's going to be okay. I'm here. Walker and Forrest can step up when they can. We will get through this. That's what family does. We're there for each other when things get tough. And this is the *definition* of tough."

When we part, she reaches up to brush her tears away. "I just can't lose him, Wyatt. He's my everything."

Yeah, I know how that feels. "You won't. We're going to remain positive and make sure we look at all the options before making any decisions, okay?"

Our conversation is cut off by the sight of Kelsea coming around the corner, walking into the kitchen without even granting me a sideways glance.

I saw her truck outside, so I knew she was already here. Just seeing her again after last night has my heart lunging for her, regardless of what I know now. Her jean cut-off shorts highlight her tan legs, her white shirt is neatly tucked in the front but left flowing in the back, and her thick head of blonde curls is pulled up off her neck in a high ponytail. It's a far cry from the fire-engine-red dress and makeup she was wearing last night, but I've always preferred the version of her standing in front of me, anyway.

Mine.

My mother turns away to compose herself as the three of us remain silent for an uncomfortable amount of time. "Why haven't you said good morning to Kelsea yet, Wyatt? I taught you better than that," my mother admonishes, breaking me out of my daydreams and inner turmoil.

"Morning, Kelsea."

"Good morning, Wyatt," she returns with a shy smile over her shoulder before gathering the box of jars from the counter and moving to fill them with jam. I can see the shake of her hands as she transports the glass. She's nervous, as am I.

My mother's eyes bounce back and forth between the two of us. "Everything okay, you two? You're both acting strange."

"Everything's fine, Momma." I stand and kiss her on the cheek before grabbing another biscuit and heading for the door. "I'm going to get to work."

"Don't work too hard. I'll bring lunch out soon." And then she mouths silently, *I love you.*

I love you, too, I mouth back on a nod and then head out the door, stealing one more glance at Kelsea before I leave. I find her looking right back at me, her brow furrowed in thought.

I wonder if she remembers everything I said to her last night.

The sound of my boots slamming against the wooden porch echoes until I hit the soft dirt on the ground. The sun beats down on me as I walk toward the horse stables. Walker is brushing Penny, one of the horses we've had since my parents opened the ranch up to the public.

"Hey," he says, sliding the brush across the horse's shoulders.

"Hey."

"How'd you sleep?"

"Like shit," I mumble.

CHAPTER EIGHT

"You see Kelsea already?"

"Yeah." I take a bite out of one of the biscuits and then rest one of my feet on the bottom rung of the metal fence, draping my hands over the top of it.

"And?"

"And what?"

"Did you talk to her?"

I finish chewing. "No. She's in the kitchen with Mom right now. That's not the ideal situation for us to have the conversation we need to."

"You need to say something soon though, Wyatt. The longer you wait—"

"I said something last night."

His head spins to face me. "After you left my place?"

"No. At The Jameson."

"What the hell? You didn't tell me that!" He tosses his hand in the air.

"Didn't know I had to."

"Back up then." He holds a finger up. "You spoke to her *before* you came to my apartment last night?"

"Yup."

"And what did you say to her?"

"That's none of your business," I fire back.

He drops the brush from the horse and spins to face me head-on. "So what are you waiting for then? Make your move."

"I planned on it until I spoke to you last night."

He sighs heavily. "Fuck, Wyatt. Don't let this little ruse

prevent you from getting everything you've ever wanted, little brother. I'm begging you," he pleads, frustration laced through every syllable.

"It just . . . doesn't feel right," I reply, staring at the horses still secured in their stables. "How the fuck did we get here?"

"It was *my* idea, remember? Not Kelsea's."

"But she agreed to it." I shake my head, which is spinning in circles again with the same argument that's been on my mind since early this morning.

"Well, let me ask you this: If I hadn't asked her to be my date to Schmitty's birthday or showed an ounce of interest in her, would you have made your move?"

"Yeah, I mean . . . maybe. Probably . . . eventually." Even I don't buy the words coming out of my mouth right now, because let's be honest—I probably would have just continued to bury everything I was feeling to prevent anything from changing.

"When's eventually? When you're fifty? When she's about to walk down the aisle and marry someone else?" Walker shakes his head while staring at the ground. "You can be pissed all you want, but you know that my interference made you scared."

I narrow my eyes at him. "I'm not scared."

"The fuck you're not." He tosses the brush in a nearby bucket and then climbs over the steel fence, getting right in my face. "And you should be. Scared to let her slide through your fingers. Scared to live a life without her." He points a finger at my chest, pressing against my sternum. "How was college without her, Wyatt? Has any girl even compared to the one in that house?" He points in the direction of the kitchen window now. "Have you met any other girl who has the heart that Kelsea does?"

No. Not by a long shot.

"It wasn't your place to intervene," I counter. The last thing I want to admit is that I'm scared or that he's right. But the idea of losing her to him, of all people, was something I couldn't fathom any longer.

He shrugs. "Maybe not, but at least I got your blood pumping. At least I got you thinking. But if you're going to *overthink* this now, you're only wasting time, time that you could be spending with the girl you're meant to be with."

"I don't get why the fuck you care. It's not like you have someone you feel the same way about!"

He scoffs. "You're right. I don't. But if I did, I sure as hell wouldn't be wasting time by not telling her how I feel. I'd be giving her all of me. Because that's what a woman deserves, especially a woman like Kelsea." With one more withering glance at me, he turns and jumps back over the fence, retrieving the brush and returning to Penny. "Dad wants you to check the fence line again."

I roll my eyes, toss the last bite of my biscuit in my mouth, and then head for my truck, ruminating on everything my brother so eloquently said to me and hating that I agree with him. But my pride is preventing me from accepting it.

As the sun beats down on me while I drive along the fence line, my entire childhood and friendship with Kelsea revisits me like a highlight reel—chasing each other in these fields, watching movies on our living room floor, having classes together and study sessions in my room, our prom, our high school graduation, and the day I left for college.

The girl is in every flashback, every pivotal moment since we were kids for as long as I can remember, and even the time we were apart never had me second-guessing her presence in my life.

But in the past few weeks, I've never been more confused about what the future looks like. My visions have always included Kelsea, but always as my friend. I never let myself daydream too hard about what it would be like to love her the way I wanted because part of me was learning to accept that I would never get to that point with her.

And now that I have the chance, it's tainted with interference and miscommunication. It wasn't on my terms, it wasn't because we were honest with each other about how we feel—it was because my brother stepped in and played God.

My worst fear is being manifested as I realize that this little stunt may have destroyed a lifelong friendship. What if I can't get past this or the animosity builds to the point that things between us will never be the same?

As soon as the creek that holds so many memories comes into my line of sight, I decide to stop and take some time to think. I park my truck and then climb the small hill that Kelsea and I used to run up and down, racing each other and rolling on our sides through the grass, getting as dizzy as we could because it was fun. The time that we spent together was so effortless and full of joy.

Recollections of our laughter ring out, almost as if they're real.

CHAPTER EIGHT

I take a seat under the tree where we spent many afternoons playing and where we shared our first kisses—the one when we were ten and practiced getting married and the one the night before I left for school.

With my arms draped over my knees, I watch the water trickle past me, the sound of bugs buzzing around me providing background noise to the chaos in my mind.

I told her I wanted her. I told her to end it with my brother. But that was before I knew it was all a lie. I can't take back what I said, though the truth of the matter is I don't think I want to.

But how do we move forward from here? Do I tell her that I know? Will she admit it? Will she tell me she feels the same way I do?

"Wyatt?"

I jump, twisting around to see Kelsea slowly tiptoeing down the slope of the small hill, cautiously approaching me. It feels like the war in my body conjured her into my reality.

"What are you doing out here, Kels?"

"I—I wanted to talk to you." She arrives next to me, peering down with uncertainty in her eyes.

"About?"

"What you said to me last night." Her brow furrows as she studies me. "Why do you look so angry?"

Without any caution whatsoever, I say what's on my mind, what's in my heart, letting all of my anger and frustration out because she's the person who truly needs to hear it all. "Because I am, Kels. I'm really fucking angry right now."

"Okay. What's going on?" I can tell by the look on her face that she wasn't expecting this reaction from me after what happened last night. Hell, this isn't exactly what I envisioned, either, until I talked to Walker. But I can't keep this mounting fury bottled up any longer.

I push myself up off the ground, not bothering to dust the dirt from my pants as I stare down into her crystal-blue eyes. "You were dating my brother."

"Um, yes . . ."

"And I was going insane with the thought of him touching you."

"I know. But . . ."

"But then I find out after I left The Jameson last night that it was all a lie."

Her eyes bug out, and then her mouth drops open slightly. "What?"

"Did you really agree to date my brother to make me jealous?"

Her eyes start to water, and then she's reaching out for me, desperation in her voice. "Wyatt, look, I'm sorry. Please, just let me explain . . ."

Turning away from her so she can't touch me, I reach up to tug on the strands of my hair. "I'm so fucking mad right now, Kelsea. I can't believe you would do this."

"But it was fake, so why does it matter?"

I spin back around. "Why does it matter? Because it was *my brother*. Because you agreed to it. Because instead of talking to me and telling me how you feel, you thought this was a better idea! Instead of me being able to tell you that I was feeling the same way, you guys created a fucking mess!"

She shakes her head, clenching her jaw now. "I didn't think it was a good idea, but Walker convinced me. And you know why I agreed? Because for a second, I wondered what it would be like for you to see me as more than your friend—or even if you could. Nothing was ever going to happen with him, Wyatt."

"But you kissed him."

"*He* kissed *me*." Her icy glare grows stronger. "So does this mean you didn't mean what you said last night? That you don't want me?"

I sigh as my blood pumps furiously through my veins. "I do, but . . . this just changes things."

"How? How does it change things?"

"How can it not?" I shout, glaring at her, confused how I could be so dead set on feeling one way last night and now waver in those same feelings less than a day later.

Kelsea is mine, she will always be mine—that much I know is true with every fiber of my being. But I still need some more time to process this.

She shakes her head at me, her lip trembling as she locks eyes with me. "I'm sorry. I am. But I'm not sorry that my decision made me brave enough, for once in my life, to go after something I want. You of all people should know how much courage it took for me to do something like that," she says, emotion clogging her throat. Seeing her cry right now is making me second-guess going off on her. "I never wanted to hurt you. This was my worst fear in all of this, and now that our feelings are out in the open, we can't go back. And I don't want to." She starts to walk away.

"Kelsea!" I call after her as I watch her march up the small hill.

She stops, looking down at me from over her shoulder. "Don't worry about it, Wyatt. We can pretend like none of this ever happened. I'm sorry we lied, but I'm not sorry for allowing myself to admit that I wanted more with you. I always have." And with those parting words, she disappears over the crest of the hill, leaving me all alone once more.

"Fuck!" I yank on my hair again, pacing in a line, wanting to run after her but holding myself back.

I could see the regret in her eyes, hear the remorse in her voice. And instead of being the bigger person, I allowed my petty competition with my brother to get in the way of letting these circumstances die on the words that we both admitted.

She wants me. I want her. Is it really that easy?

Can we honestly just jump headfirst into a relationship, knowing that the way we got there was laced with deception? Or must we simply accept the consequences of our actions and press forward as if nothing happened?

Once I feel my heart rate return to normal, I get back in my truck, finish scouring the fence line for holes, and then head back to the house.

When I step inside and see Kelsea is gone, my gut drops. Now I feel even shittier for what I said and how I acted.

"Where's Kelsea?" I ask my mother, who's building several

sandwiches on the counter in front of her.

With one flick of her eyes up to mine, she says, "She told me she was going outside for a few minutes but then came back claiming she wasn't feeling well. You don't happen to know why that is, do you?"

I close my eyes, letting out a heavy sigh. "It's . . . complicated, Momma."

"It always is with you, Wyatt Allen Gibson. Why you can't just accept that some things are meant to be easy in life I will never fully understand."

"What do you mean?"

She gazes up at me again. "You know exactly what I mean."

"Momma—"

"Go tell your brothers and father that lunch is ready, please," she commands, ending the conversation that I know could go on longer if needed.

But I think she said everything she's going to allow herself to say, and I said too much when I was talking to Kelsea.

Fuck me.

This is why I kept everything inside. This was the exact fear I had—that everything would blow up, that we would both lose so much in our lives by giving in to what we have been burying inside for years.

But now there's no going back, and I'm afraid that Kelsea is right: Things will never be the same.

I just need to decide exactly what that's going to look like now moving forward.

CHAPTER NINE

Kelsea

"It's going to be okay, Kels." Evelyn rubs my shoulder as I blow my nose once more. I immediately called her after I left the Gibson Ranch, and I'm grateful I even have her to lean on. She was waiting in my driveway when I pulled up to my house, still slightly hungover but ready to be my shoulder to cry on.

"How? How is it going to be okay?" Wiping across my nose, the sting of raw skin alerts me to just how long I've been crying. "This is exactly what I was afraid of!"

"Well, at least it's now out in the open . . . your feelings, I mean."

"Yup. And now nothing will ever be the same." I sigh, shaking

CHAPTER NINE

through the heavy breath. "I knew it. I knew I never should have agreed to this."

"Look, you took a risk. This is what happens when you do."

"Which is why I've always lived my monotonous life, as you pointed out before."

She nods on a tilt of her head. "Yes, but you weren't going after anything by doing that, either. Just give this some time. I'm sure Wyatt is just confused right now."

"No. He's pissed—like, *furious*, Evelyn."

"But didn't he say that he wants you?" I told her all about what happened last night when he confronted me and everything leading up to just a few hours ago.

"Yes, but it seems he's changed his mind." Another round of tears escapes my eyes as I shake my head—I'm disappointed in myself, in Walker, and in Wyatt. "Whatever. I'm just going to go back to living as if none of this happened and accept the fact that Wyatt and I were never meant to be more than friends."

"Can you really do that?" she asks, biting her bottom lip.

"I don't really have a choice, Evelyn. I made my bed, and now I must lie in it." I stand from the couch, attempting to keep my composure as I travel over to the door and kick off my cowboy boots. "I think I'm just gonna hop in the shower."

"Do you want me to stay? I can make us some dinner, or we can order something?"

"I'm not hungry, and I kind of just want to be alone." I turn around to face her. "Is that okay?"

"Of course that's okay, Kelsea. I just want to make sure that *you're* okay."

"I'm not, but I will be. Thank you." I walk up to her and wrap my arms around her shoulders. "Thank you for being here."

"I'll always be here, Kels." She squeezes me back, and we stay like that for a moment before I reluctantly release her, needing to really let my tears flow freely in the shower.

"Call me later, or text if you need anything."

"I will."

I open the door for her and watch her leave before shutting it, locking it up, and then trotting down the hallway to my bathroom. Under the scalding hot water, I let another round of tears flow freely, ugly crying in privacy. There's something about a good cry in the shower that helps relieve the pain.

But when I exit the cloud of steam and see the red-faced woman staring back at me in the mirror, the physical indication of my anguish is clear as day.

I can't sit around and cry anymore, though. I need to feel joy and remind myself that my world isn't ending—the seasons are just changing. So after I get dressed, I throw my wet hair up in a hat and grab my sunglasses. I reach for my camera, climb in my truck, and head to one of the fields I love to visit where I can catch the sunset.

The bumpy road has me jostling in my seat, but I soon find a spot and park. I take in a deep breath of air the second my feet touch the ground.

Peace. Calm. Exactly what I need right now.

And the colors in the sky couldn't be more stunning. Hues of golden yellow, pink, and orange are painted across the sky in front of me, the sun displaying its brilliance in the center. The grass is flowing in the breeze, and crickets are beginning to perform as the day transforms into night.

Without another thought, I check the setting on my camera and then click away, catching nature's beauty in all her glory—the sunsets that prevent me from leaving the great state of Texas because there's no way I can get this view in New York. I've never seen a sunset over the ocean in the Caribbean, though, which is another bucket list place of mine. But the Caribbean isn't home.

Newberry Springs is home.

Wyatt is home.

I mentally slap myself for letting my mind drift there and instead focus on the flock of geese that are flying overhead, the three horses trotting in a pack as a couple and their young child go for an evening ride, and the cloud formations shifting with the breeze up against the watercolor backdrop.

God, I love this land. I love this place.

But is it enough to keep me here?

~

Two days later, I show up for work with a brick in the bottom of my stomach. Except for this morning, I haven't seen or heard from Wyatt since Sunday at his parents' ranch, and tonight we have to work together. It's one of the nights he typically asks me to close for him so he can go home early because he's been here since the food order was delivered this morning. We barely spoke to one another throughout that process, which was agonizing, to say the least. I guess working around him is proving to be worse than I thought.

I fight my instinct to trail him with my eyes, but I fail miserably all evening. The only nice part about being here at the brewery tonight is that there are plenty of things to distract me from the drama of my life right now, including the phone call I made earlier that is certainly going to change things even more.

"How's it going, Kelsea?" Greg, one of our regulars, greets me at the bar.

"Oh, it's going, Greg. IPA for you, sir?"

"You know it, darlin'." The twang in his voice makes me smile as I move to fill up his glass from the tap behind me.

I slide the full glass across the bar to him, wiping my hands clean on a towel when I'm done. "There you go, Greg."

"Thank you. Can I get an order of the buffalo chicken sliders, too, please?"

"Of course. Sweet potato fries or regular?" I ask as I move over to the computer to punch in his order.

"You know what, let's do sweet potato tonight. I'm feeling adventurous."

I chuckle. "You got it." I send the order back to the kitchen and then place a bottle of ketchup on the bar next to him, just in case.

Checking on a few other tables and customers around the

brewery, I almost forget about the fact that my heart is in shambles until Janise waltzes through the bay doors and beelines straight for Wyatt. She's wearing a pink sundress not that different from the one I wore over a week ago and a devious smile on her face. Her goal of catching his attention is blatantly obvious, and all it does is curdle the half of a burger in my stomach that I forced myself to eat earlier.

My stomach drops when she stops in front of Wyatt. He acts surprised to see her but offers her a generous smile when she starts speaking to him. I force myself to look away, concentrating on anything but the interaction going on behind me, and hope I don't break down in front of all these people.

"Kelsea." Walker's voice garners my attention as I lift my head to see him taking a seat at the bar while removing his hat from his head. His eyes are full of concern and regret as he studies me.

I take the few steps closer to him and then lean over the counter to whisper, "Walker, do you honestly think it's a good idea for you to be here right now?"

"I don't give a fuck about my brother and what he thinks. He won't do anything here in his place of business. I just wanted to check up on you."

"Well, since I ignored your texts over the past two days, I'd say you didn't take the hint."

"Don't be mad at me."

I glance over at Wyatt quickly, noticing that his eyes are locked on Walker and me, and then I stare right back at the brother who got us into this mess. "I'm mad at myself for listening to you. Please, Walker, just leave it alone. It is what it is."

I walk away from him as he calls out to me, but I ignore him. I make my way around the restaurant again, cleaning up dirty dishes from tables, refilling drinks, and helping out the food servers, anything to take my mind off of this hell and the way my heart feels like it's trying to escape from my chest right now.

A few hours later, as I'm taking a breather in the employee room, a voice behind me has goosebumps appearing on my skin.

"Kelsea."

Spinning around so quickly that I almost lose my balance, I see Wyatt blocking the doorway, his hands by his side, his eyes still glazed over with anger.

"Yeah?"

"I'm . . ." He clears his throat and then continues. "I'm about to head out. Just wanted to make sure you were still okay with closing up tonight."

"Yup. Fine." I flash him a tight-lipped smile that only lasts a second.

"Okay. Beau will still be here, so he can walk you out when you're through."

"I know the drill, Wyatt. I've done this before."

His brows pinch together, and his curt words sting. "Yeah, I know. I just—"

"You just what?" I ask, even though I'm not sure that I want him to continue. But then I notice pink lipstick on his cheek, the same shade of pink Janise was wearing when she walked in tonight.

Is he going out with her? Do they have a date? Is that why she came in earlier, to see him and flaunt their relationship in front of me before he leaves?

And as my hopes that this mess can be cleaned up deflate once again, Wyatt thinks better of continuing, shaking his head as he eases up his stance. "Sorry. Nothing. Thank you and have a good night."

"You, too."

I watch him leave and then let out the breath I didn't realize I was holding. This is how it's going to be from now on, isn't it? Uncomfortable silence, short sentences, limited communication.

And I have no one to blame but myself.

Once I know he's gone for sure, I walk back out front and help the staff serve the last few customers. Then I go through the customary closing procedures, which includes sitting in Wyatt's office and balancing the drawer.

The leather of his chair sticks to my skin when I sit down and run my hands over his desk. It was handmade for him by Forrest—one of the only true declarations of pride I've seen him exhibit for his brothers. He's a quiet man, at war with his choices and circumstances, but when Wyatt opened this brewery, Forrest was the first to present him with this desk as a gift for all his hard work.

The smell of Wyatt's body wash is still wafting in the air as I take in a lungful of the scent, sighing in agony that the memories this smell will hold may not always be good ones anymore. As I take in the surroundings of his office, remembering the many late conversations and tough decisions that were made in here, I feel my eyes well with moisture again. So I let my tears fall silently as I fill out the spreadsheet Wyatt does each night upon closing and crunch the numbers to make sure they reconcile.

I held it together all night. I deserve to let the dam break open for a few minutes.

Satisfied that everything is complete—and making sure the evidence of my breakdown isn't too apparent—I walk around the corner to find Beau finishing the last load of dishes.

"You ready to leave, Miss Kelsea?" His southern drawl is endearing. He's the sweetest man, an employee I've enjoyed getting to know over the years and will miss terribly when I'm gone.

Because right now, leaving feels like the best option.

"Yes, sir."

He hangs the hose to the giant steel sink back on the wall and then steps out from the humid corner where he washes dishes for us each night. "Me, too. Let's go."

After I lock up, I thread my arm through his, and he escorts me outside to my truck, waiting until I'm situated in my seat before he moves over to his car and waves goodbye. I take off for home, anxious to be alone again with my thoughts and the pain that has been resting in my chest since Sunday. Even though being around Wyatt at work is agonizing as well, there are plenty of distractions to keep me from sinking too low. But when I'm home alone, especially because my dad is still gone, my heart lurches every time I try to pry myself off the couch.

So since I don't want to go home to an empty house just yet, I make a turn down a dirt road that I know will add a few extra minutes to my commute home.

The stars twinkle in the sky as "Friends Don't" by Maddie and Tae plays from the speaker on my phone, and every time I hear this song, I think of Wyatt and me—how every accidental touch from him gives me chills, how my future has always had him in it, how we can have a conversation with just our eyes—how life without him doesn't even seem like a possibility.

But then the song cuts out, which always happens when I lose cell service, and I try not to take that as a sign from the universe that our friendship is about to end as well.

Sighing, I glance at my camera on the passenger seat, knowing that taking a few pictures will help take the edge off this evening. So I find a spot on the side of the road, put the truck in park, and step down into the grass, making sure I change the setting on my camera. I want to capture perfectly the sparkle of the stars against the black sky and the soft glow of the moon that is brightening up the world around me.

More time passes than I realize, which is what always happens when I'm behind the lens of my camera, so once I see that a few hours have passed, I get back in the truck and finish the drive to my house.

As I pull in the driveway, the shadow of someone appears on the porch, warning me away. And then I notice a truck parked in the front yard, obscured in shadow so only its outline is visible. My heart races, my back stiffens, and for just a moment, I say a little prayer that I'm seeing things.

But before I can put my truck in reverse, Wyatt steps out of the darkness, revealing himself, and the look on his face is one I wasn't anticipating at all.

CHAPTER TEN

Wyatt

Guilt slams into me for the thousandth time as I recall the look on Kelsea's face when I left her at the brewery. My heart wanted to say something, *anything* to get her to talk to me after I blew up on her Sunday, but my brain argued that probably wasn't a good idea.

Instead, I went through the motions of the night, pretending like everything was fine, even assuming she'd want to close for me like she normally does on Tuesday nights. But when I arrived home, the last thing I felt was relaxed. Nope. It felt like my heart was being tugged by strings connected to the woman closing up my brewery, and even I don't want to be around myself right now in this surly mood.

Sighing, I fall back onto my couch, gripping my hair and

yanking at the strands as I stare up at the ceiling. I still can't believe how we got here, and I don't see an end to this agony.

I owe Kelsea an apology, but after that, what do I say? Honestly, I'm not sure that I know the answer to that. Every time I think about how this all happened, the memory sullies the visions I've always had of Kelsea and me admitting our feelings to one another.

Believe me, I never thought it would go down like this.

Needing a drink, I head for my kitchen, grabbing a Coke and popping the tab on it as I glance at the clock on my microwave. Kelsea should have left the brewery by now. She's probably home alone, wallowing in this bizarre not-normal we've been in since Sunday.

I could call her. I could go by her house. I could stop all of this nonsense tonight if I really wanted to. The only way to know what's going through her mind is to ask her, which I did *not* do when I went off on her at my parents' house. And the more I sway in this emotional limbo, the more I just want to put an end to it.

But before I can pick up the phone or debate my decision any further, my cell vibrates in my pocket. A local number I don't have programmed in my phone flashes across the screen, and instead of screening like I normally would, something tells me to answer it. So I do.

"Wyatt Gibson."

"Hello, Mr. Gibson. This is Sheriff Vernon with the Newberry Springs Sheriff's Department."

CHAPTER TEN

The hair on the back of my neck stands up, and tense shoulders follow. "How can I help you, Sheriff?"

"Well, I'm out here at your brewery because your alarm system was triggered. It appears there was a break-in." When I glance down at my phone, I realize I never got a notification from the security app. That pisses me off even further, and worry mixes with my fury now.

I don't waste another second, lunging for my keys on the counter and racing out the door. "Was anyone there? Is anyone hurt?"

I swear to God if something happened to Kelsea, I'll never forgive myself. Regret will become my new best friend if I never get the chance to make things right between us, never get the chance to hold her, kiss her, marry her.

Fuck. This can't be happening.

How have I been so stupid? How have I let my own pride stand in the way of making her mine? What if I never get the chance to do that now?

I think living with that regret would be worse than if she were actually in love with Walker.

"No, it appears the place was empty, but we did catch the guy." I exhale, letting my spiraling mind unwind as I process his words. "He's in cuffs, but we need you to come down here and sign some paperwork. And just so you know, you're gonna need to replace a window."

Relief rushes through me as I hop in my truck and speed out of my parking spot, still on the phone. "I'm on my way."

"Excellent. See you in a few."

The call ends, and I toss my phone on the seat next to me before slamming my hands against my steering wheel. "Fuck!" I scream, flooring the gas pedal.

And then, as the brewery comes into view, the single cop car with red-and-blue flashing lights reminding me the aftermath of the break-in is so minor compared to what it could have been—that's when it hits me.

Life is too fucking short to stay mad. Nothing is ever guaranteed, and circumstances can change in an instant. Every pivotal part of our journey is one moment away from changing—one loss, one heartache, one lesson.

And I just learned a big one.

Here's hoping it's not too late to fix the mistakes I've made so far.

Once I clear everything up with the sheriff and assess the damage, I board up the window, knowing there's nothing more I can do until the sun rises. Besides, I have a woman to see and some groveling to do, if nothing else than to just make sure she's still here. I need to know I can still touch her, hear her voice, and see that sparkle in those blue eyes that are more stunning than any crystal clear Texas sky.

When I pull up to Kelsea's house about twenty minutes later, her truck isn't there. I reach for my phone as my heart pounds, but her voicemail picks up as soon as the line connects. I keep trying to call her, over and over, hoping she'll answer eventually even if

I'm being annoying as fuck. But every time, the call just goes straight to voicemail.

Fuck. Why won't she pick up?

Probably because the last time you two spoke, you were an ass, Wyatt.

Still . . . if she's not here and asleep, she'd answer my call. The time of night alone would tell her this is an emergency, although sometimes we'll call each other after work just to vent about a long shift and then end up talking for hours.

But this isn't one of those times, and if she's not currently in bed safe, then the question remains: Where is she?

My heart begins hammering again as I step out of my truck and head for the front porch, peering inside, trying to see through the curtains. But the house is completely dark.

Luckily, only a few seconds later, headlights illuminate the porch behind me as I turn to watch Kelsea pull up to the house.

Feeling like I ran a damn marathon this evening, my heart pounds as I watch her shut off the engine, step down from the cab, and slowly walk toward me. Her hesitance is letting me know that if there's any moment to salvage our friendship and the possibility of our future, it's now.

So I stop thinking.

And for once, I just act.

CHAPTER ELEVEN

Kelsea

"Wyatt?" I step down from the truck, slamming the door behind me as the crunch of gravel sounds beneath each one of my steps. "What are you doing here?" He's still wearing his Gibson Brewery polo, his dark blue jeans, and his brown boots, but the utter distress on his face is what's captivating me.

"Kelsea," he breathes out and then runs down the stairs, across the gravel driveway, and smashes his lips to mine so suddenly that it takes me a moment to register what's happening.

Wyatt is kissing me, and *oh my god* his lips are just as soft—if not softer—than I remember them to be. His hands frame my face as he holds me like a prized possession, like the sun and the moon and the stars, like I'm everything that makes his world exist and keep spinning.

I fist his shirt as he pulls us closer to one another, his lips slanting over my mouth before his tongue darts out and tangles with mine as if we're both searching for answers within the depths of this kiss. We moan, jerking each other closer, fighting for air and control as we immerse ourselves in a moment that has been a lifetime in the making.

Every inch of my body is trembling from his touch. It's a life-changing, galaxy freezing, an I-will-never-be-the-same-after-this kind of kiss. It's the kind that speaks of desperation and unrequited feelings finally being revealed.

It's the one that I've been waiting on forever.

Wyatt moves us back toward my truck, and my spine hits the front bumper, but his grip on me never loosens. And neither does mine on him until I move my arms up around his neck, holding on for dear life just in case I'm dreaming and this isn't really happening.

But it is. And as much as I want to know why, I'll be damned if I'm the one who stops this to find out.

We're both so frantic, so deep in our connection, that the rest of the world ceases to exist—the lies that got us here, the words spoken that we can't take back, the truth that no matter what happened, we still can't fight the way we feel.

Slowly, Wyatt relinquishes his hold on me, morphing from owning and controlling me to savoring and holding me sensually. And then our lips part. Our eyes open.

And I see everything in his that I feel in my heart.

"Wyatt..."

He leans his forehead against mine. "Jesus, Kelsea."

"What's going on?"

"Just give me a minute," he breathes out, leaving us standing there in silence as my pulse thrums, waiting for him to continue. Finally, he says, "I'm so glad you're fucking okay."

"Why—why wouldn't I be okay?"

"Why weren't you answering your phone? I tried calling you a hundred times."

As if on cue, my phone starts to vibrate in my back pocket. I reach back to retrieve it, noticing twenty missed calls from him. "I was in a dead zone and stopped on the way home to take a few pictures, try to clear my mind."

"Fuck. I thought something happened to you, that you—"

"What? Why?"

"There was a break-in," he says, lifting his forehead from mine and staring down into my eyes, those chocolate pools of his penetrating my soul, "at the brewery."

Gasping, I lift my hand to cover my mouth, creating more space between us. "When?"

"It must have been just after you left."

"Oh my God."

"When I got the call, all I could do was think about you being there. That person scaring you, hurting you . . . Fuck." He closes his eyes, taking a moment to gather himself. "They caught him, but I've been going insane, especially when you weren't picking up your phone." He shakes his head, taking a deep breath and then blowing it out slowly, relieving some of the tension in his body.

"So you came here?"

He nods. "I did, hoping I'd find you here, but you weren't. And you wouldn't answer your phone, so my mind was going to the worst place . . ."

"I'm . . . I'm sorry."

"No. *I'm sorry.* I'm sorry for so much, but mostly—" He closes his eyes, squeezing them tightly before popping them back open and gazing intensely into mine. "I'm sorry for pushing you away. For yelling at you. For doubting what I know we feel for each other and have been too fucking stubborn to admit."

His confession has my bottom lip trembling. "I'm so sorry, too, Wyatt. I know it wasn't right, but I can't take it back."

"I know, Kels. And it's stupid that I've been holding it against you."

Pleading, I shake my head. "I never should have agreed. I wish I would have just talked to you."

He grips the back of my neck. "Me, too, Kelsea. But none of that matters anymore. Tonight showed me that clear as day."

"Is the brewery okay?" I ask, knowing that there are more important things for us to discuss, but I want to make sure that he's alright, too.

"I don't give a shit about that right now. All that matters is us." With his hands framing my face again, he plants a soft kiss on my lips, a gentle nip to wake my body up once more to this physical connection we just explored. And it's searing heat through my body, that's for sure. "Let's just agree to move forward from here, okay? If anything, this scare made me realize how obstinate I was being, that something could have happened to you and I never would have been able to kiss the air out of you and hold you like I've wanted to since the moment I came home from college."

I wrap my arms around his neck, resting my forehead on his once again. "You've always owned my heart, Wyatt. You know that, right?"

He takes one of my hands and moves it over the center of his chest. "Do you feel how hard mine is beating right now? That's all for you. You're the syrup to my breakfast, Kelsea. Always have and always will be."

We stand there for a moment, letting our words sink in, feeling them infiltrate the air around us and travel out into the universe, leaving a mark on this moment in time—this moment in our lives that changes everything.

My pulse is so wild, my entire body feels numb, and my mind is reeling over how tumultuous this night has been—hell, how insane this past *week* has been. But at least we're on the same page now. We can figure everything else out later.

"Do you want to go inside?" I ask, hoping that this isn't where the night ends but wondering if his mind is where mine is, too.

He growls, gripping my hip with his hand. "I do, Kelsea. I so fucking do. But not to do anything but hold you."

With his hand tucked in mine, we make our way up the porch steps as I fiddle with my keys, my hands shaking so violently that Wyatt clasps his hands over mine to steady them.

"We're not going to do anything tonight, Kelsea. We've waited too long for that."

"I know. I'm just . . ." I blow out a long breath. "I can't believe this is happening," I admit, chuckling through my nerves.

His smile spreads wide. "I know, Kelsea. Me, too. But no more holding back, okay?" He plants a chaste kiss on my lips and then grabs the keys from me, moving to unlock my door and usher me inside.

Stepping inside my house this time is different with Wyatt beside me, because he's not coming in as just my best friend. He's here as *more*—just how much more, I'm not sure. But for tonight, I'm just going to let that be.

"I'm going to get changed, if you don't mind," I say as I start down the hall.

"Take your time," he calls after me, and I can feel his eyes on me as I walk away.

As soon as I shut my bedroom door, I fight the squeal wanting to escape my lips and the rapid breathing that has me questioning if I'm dreaming again. I rush around to change my clothes, pinching myself every few minutes to make sure this is real. I grab a pair of loose red cotton shorts and a white crop top to change into, opting to wear a sports bra underneath so I'm not completely exposed to him. I know this is everything I wanted, and we agreed not to cross that line yet, but I also don't want to send him the wrong signals.

Once I brush my teeth and pull my hair into a ponytail, I open my door to find Wyatt still in the living room. He's sitting on the couch now, hunched over his knees in thought.

"Wyatt?"

His head pops up and finds mine, and his lips spread appreciatively as he takes me in and stands from the couch. The awe reflected in his eyes has me shaking as I look at him. "Damn." He starts stalking toward me. "Am I allowed to say that now?"

"I guess." I bite my lip, fighting my mile-wide grin.

"I can't help it. I know you're just in pajamas, but you have no idea how many times I've thought about touching you the way I want to right now, Kelsea. And fuck, does it feel good to finally say it."

"I can imagine because I feel the same way."

"I just want to hold you tonight, though, Kelsea. I'm serious about that." He steps through the doorway to my room as I make space for him to slide by.

"I know. I just figured I'd get more comfortable."

"Well, if I get any more comfortable, I'd be in my boxer briefs and shirtless, and I'm not sure that's a good idea."

"I could see if my dad has something you can borrow," I suggest.

"No. It's okay. I am going to take my shirt off, but I can sleep in my jeans. Wouldn't be the first time." He moves to extract his shirt from his body, the black fabric sliding effortlessly over his head as he reveals his chest and abs to me. Wyatt has always had a decent body, but after he came home from college, I could tell he'd put on muscle, and it's only increased in the past two years.

CHAPTER ELEVEN

But this is the first time I'm seeing him without his shirt on since then—and my oh my, what a sight this is.

His broad shoulders are one of my favorite parts of him, but his arms without a shirt on are definitely getting added to that list. His jeans hang off his trim waist, highlighting that sexy v that stretches down below the waistband of his jeans that I've admired a time or two when his shirt would inch up his stomach. And his abs—Wyatt has abs that are made to be licked and scratched, made to flex as he thrusts in and out of me. It's a sight I can't wait to take in for myself.

He has bonafide cowboy written all over him right now, a body sculpted from hard work and manual labor, and my libido is appreciating every contour of his muscles. But then my eyes land on a tattoo on his rib cage, a piece of art I know for a fact he didn't have before he left for college.

"Kelsea. My eyes are up here." He points to his face, and I instantly blush.

"Sorry." Taking a step closer to him, I trace the picture inked on his skin and gasp as my eyes absorb the sight. "Wyatt—"

"I got it in college." He cuts me off. "About two months after I left. I couldn't stop thinking about you, but I knew I couldn't go home. I had to see what I left to accomplish through. So instead, I got this as a reminder of you—a way to keep you with me always."

A beautiful sketch of a camera lies to the left of his pec under his armpit and just above his ribs. It looks just like mine, the one I carry with me whenever I feel the need to capture the world around me, but the strap is a heart made out of stones—just like the ones I used to make as we sat by the creek on his parents' property.

"I—I don't know what to say."

"You don't have to say anything right now, but just know, this isn't a spur of the moment epiphany for me, Kels. You've always been inked on my heart. Now, you're just inked on my skin, too."

We stand there, our eyes trained on one another, mine clouded with tears.

Wyatt pulls me into his chest, staying silent for several minutes. But then I can't hold in my yawn any longer, and it breaks through the moment. My heart is still hammering from his gesture. "We should go to bed," I say.

I feel him nod. "Okay. Do you mind if I use an extra toothbrush?"

"Not at all. There is one under the sink, I believe."

"Thanks."

Wyatt heads for the bathroom as I traipse down the hallway and into the kitchen, reaching for a glass and moving to fill it with water.

He has a tattoo just for me.

As if I couldn't be any more in love with him than I already am.

But then a small detail I was forgetting dawns on me. I slowly turn to locate the piece of paper I've forgotten all about in the last few hours, hoping and praying that Wyatt didn't see it. He mustn't have if he's still here.

CHAPTER ELEVEN

Because if he did, he'd have been long gone.

I stare down at the paper, wondering how the hell I'm going to bring this up to him. How do I tell him I made a decision about my future before he kissed me tonight, back when I thought there was no future for us?

But it can wait. I don't need to tell him just yet. Things may falter again, and then this won't even be an issue.

But in my heart, I know that's not true.

Miss Baker,
We are pleased to inform you that you have been selected to attend our Amateur Photography Program that starts on January 5th. We were impressed with your portfolio and look forward to working on your craft with you. Please respond to our admissions office by phone or email as soon as possible to secure your spot.
Sincerely,
New York Life Photography Institute

I couldn't pick up the phone fast enough. I saw it as a sign. I told them yes the instant I could answer the lady's question of whether or not I would be attending.

But tonight, Wyatt took that break-in as a sign, a sign that life is short and he didn't want to remain just friends with me.

And I want that, too.

I shove the letter into the nearest drawer, vowing to deal with it when the time is right, and instead bask in this moment of sleeping next to my best friend while knowing we aren't just friends anymore.

It was the first thing I'd wanted in my life, even back before I wanted a chance to develop my photography skills. So I'm going to take it—and I'm going to immerse myself in it without remorse, regret, or unrequited longing tainting it this time.

"You thirsty?" I hand the glass of water to Wyatt once I make it back to my room.

"Thanks." He gulps down half of it and then takes a seat on my bed.

I set the glass on my nightstand and then situate myself under the covers with him, my back to his front. His hand rests on my hip as he pulls me into him.

His hard physique presses against my soft curves, and I melt, loving how his touch sends bolts of lightning shooting across my skin. I can feel the heat coming off of him, which isn't helping my body relax, but I won't dare complain. I've waited too long for this.

"You comfortable?" he whispers in my ear, biting softly on the lobe, scattering goosebumps all over my skin.

"Yes. You?"

"I'm exactly where I want to be," he says in return, pressing his hand into my bare stomach where it's exposed between my shirt and shorts and breathing in deeply before releasing his hot breath on my neck. I've never felt more at home than I do in this moment.

"Me, too, Wyatt. Me, too."

CHAPTER TWELVE

Wyatt

I feel bright light seep through my eyelids, pulling me from a deep sleep. And as I blink and lift one eye open, a ball of blonde curls is the first thing I see.

Kelsea.

Realization dawns on me, and I'm instantly smiling, reaching for her hip and pulling her closer to me.

She lets out a moan, and my dick gets painfully harder than he already was this early in the morning. And I know she can feel it, especially as she stirs, slightly brushing her ass against my crotch.

"Good morning," I whisper in her ear before propping myself up and leaning over her shoulder to catch a glimpse of her face. Her entire body twists as she attempts to face me. And when I see those blue eyes staring up at me, my heart thumps hard.

This is how things were always meant to be. And fuck, it feels good to finally listen to our hearts.

"Good morning." Her shy reply escapes just as her cheeks tint with a shade of pink.

I trail a finger over the exposed skin of her hip, warring with the need to push her shorts down and do what we both want. "How did you sleep?"

"Really well."

"Me, too."

"Your body is like a furnace. I forgot about that."

This isn't the first time Kelsea and I have slept next to each other or been close enough to absorb each other's body heat. But it's the first time we've done it intentionally.

"At least you know I'll never let you get cold."

"This is true."

Her eyes bounce back and forth between mine as I do the same, reminding myself this is real. That last night really happened. But instead of speaking, I simply lean down and press my lips to hers for a soft kiss, wanting to taste her again, wanting to make that move so effortlessly without second-guessing myself for the hundredth time. But I don't dart out my tongue to taste hers because, well, you know, morning breath.

"I don't know if I'll ever get used to kissing you," she says when we part, cupping my face in her palm.

"Well, you'd better, because I plan on doing it every chance I get from now on."

CHAPTER TWELVE

She takes a deep breath and then lets it out. "I think we should talk, though."

"I agree, but maybe after we brush our teeth, pee, and get a cup of coffee."

The corner of her mouth tips up. "Sounds good."

We part to do our business, and I even take the opportunity to hop in her shower. I may or may not have sniffed her body wash while in there because that scent has always taunted me when we're around each other, but it brings me immense joy knowing I'll get to drown in it now.

I kissed my best friend last night. I took a leap of faith after realizing that I could have lost her, and the thought of that finally made me override all of the other shit that didn't matter.

My brother took a risk with his plan, and Kelsea did as well by agreeing to it. But if it weren't for their choices, I wouldn't be here with her right now. And that's what I need to focus on.

When I'm done revisiting my epiphany under the water, I throw yesterday's clothes on and then find Kelsea in the kitchen where the scent of coffee, bacon, and eggs hits my nose.

I walk up behind her and wrap my arms around her waist, leaning down to whisper in her ear. "Smells good." I place a kiss on her neck as she tilts her head to give me better access, but then she's twisting around in my arms, biting her lip. "What is it?"

"I guess I'm just . . . confused." She stares up at me. "Last night was—"

"—a wake-up call, Kels," I finish for her.

"Are you sure?" With a flick of the stove knob, she turns off the burner and then focuses back on me. "I mean, I'm happy about it. Very much. So much, it's embarrassing," she says through a chuckle. "But I don't want you to hold the whole thing with Walker over my head and then bring it up later when you're mad about something."

"Do you think I would do that?"

She shrugs. "I don't know. I mean, we've only ever been friends, Wyatt. We've never—"

"—dated," I finish for her again. "Been in a relationship."

"Is that what this is now?"

"Yes," I declare without any hesitation. Bending my knees so our eyes are on the same level, I continue. "I'm tired of fighting this pull we feel. We've danced around each other for two years, and I've wanted you since way before that. No more fucking around, Kels. Let's just be together."

She grins, so I know my declaration made her happy. "Okay, but don't you think it's a little fast? I just feel like we're going from zero to sixty, Wyatt. Which is crazy, because this is all I've ever wanted with you, and now it's taking me by surprise."

I take her hand in mine and lead her over to the couch, where we both take a seat with no space between us. "I know. It *is* fast. But I'm done wasting time—time being mad, time being unsure. I just want *you*. All of you. I want to explore this other side to our friendship. We will always be friends, Kelsea, because that's what you are to me, first and foremost, and I think that's a solid foundation for any relationship. But now I want to kiss you, hold you, date you, and make love to you when we're ready. I want to

CHAPTER TWELVE

talk about our future and stop torturing ourselves by stepping around tough conversations. Look at where that got us."

She smiles while stroking her thumb over the top of my hands. "Okay. I am sorry, though, Wyatt, for everything. I just didn't know if it was all in my head."

"What?"

"The glances, the tingles, the feeling that my heart was going to burst out of my chest every time we were around each other."

I lift her hand and place it right over my own heart. It's thrashing wildly with abandon—but this time in happiness, not longing. "My heart always feels this way around you, Kelsea. That's never going to change." *And later, I'll show you how my dick always feels around you, too.* "Let's do this. Dive in headfirst. Be together and figure out everything else later."

Her smile builds and then she's flinging herself into me, clutching her arms around my neck before planting her lips on mine. I fall back on the couch as she climbs over me, straddling my hips while I grow painfully hard behind my denim. I guess I should just get used to that because the last thing I want to do is pressure Kelsea to cross that line before she's ready.

And honestly, I don't know that I'm one-hundred-percent ready for that, either. I mean, am I ready to feel this woman wrapped around my cock? Fuck, yes. But I also know that sex with Kelsea will be unlike any other experience. It's going to mean so much to both of us. It's a lot of pressure, and I want to make sure that it feels right when it happens, that I make it as perfect as possible for her.

As our tongues meld and our breathing gets heavier, I feel Kelsea start to swivel her hips on top of me. I tighten my grasp on her body and then move my hands down to cup her ass.

"Kelsea," I mumble against her lips. "We need to stop, babe."

"I don't want to," she replies before leaning back slightly, her eyelids heavy with lust.

"I know. But I want to take you on a date before we start this up."

Her eyebrows lift. "A date?"

I push myself up again, holding her to my chest. "Hell, yes. I want everyone to know you are no longer available. I get to show them that I'm the lucky bastard you chose, and I can't fucking wait."

"Take me on a real date then, Wyatt." Her eyes mist over, and part of me knows exactly why she's getting emotional.

This is something we've both wanted for so long, probably since before I kissed her that night on my parents' property. When a yearning you've been living with deep in your chest finally unravels, the euphoria is so intense that you can't trust it won't disappear just as quickly as it arrived.

"This is so fucking real, Kelsea. Trust me on that." I brush my thumb over her bottom lip and then move my hand to the back of her neck, threading my fingers through her hair. "So what about Saturday night? We don't have to be up super early on Sunday since we'll be at the ranch that day, which gives us all night to spend together."

"But we work at the brewery on Saturday."

"Yeah, but I've been thinking about promoting Ben to Manager so that you and I can have more of a life." It's true. It's a thought that's been in the back of my mind before everything that transpired in the past few weeks. "I can work on training him all week, and he should be fine by Saturday night to handle things on his own."

"Are you sure?"

"Yes." I take her hand and press my mouth to her skin, as if her touch keeps me alive. And I'm beginning to think that maybe it does. Or maybe I thought I was living before but really wasn't, and now I know for sure that I actually am.

She nods and then leans in to me so her lips are a centimeter from mine. "Fine, Wyatt. Here's your chance. Show me what you've always imagined our first date would be."

∽

"Wyatt. We need to stop." My lips cut off the rebuttal coming from Kelsea as we hide away in my office at the brewery, desperate to touch each other behind closed doors.

I break our kiss just long enough to say, "Fuck no, woman. Just a few more minutes." And then my lips are back on hers, our pelvises grinding beneath our denim.

This is how we've spent each day since Wednesday morning when we finally agreed on our relationship status.

Kelsea and I ate breakfast and then drove separately to the brewery to check on the break-in damage. She accompanied me as the glass company installed the new window, but I could tell that actually seeing the damage shook her up quite a bit. That was the day I declared that she would never be left here to close by herself again.

Because I wouldn't survive if something happened to her. And after admitting our feelings, I feel a clarity in my heart that has never been there before.

Kelsea is mine to protect now more than ever, and I'll be damned if I fail in that regard.

"Mmm." Her moans spur me on, driving me to press her up against the door to my office and drown in her curves. My hands travel along her hips and reach around to grab a handful of her ass, touching and squeezing every part of her I've been relegated to ignore until now.

I feel like we're making up for lost time, which includes lots of make-out sessions wherever we can. We're sneaking around like teenagers like we never got the chance to do when we were.

"Okay. We do need to stop." I fight to catch my breath when we part and force myself to step away from her. Her lips are swollen, her eyes are heavy with lust, and the rock-hard erection I'm sporting all indicate that we were definitely not just talking in here.

She releases a harsh breath. "Yeah. You're right. Damn you, Wyatt Allen Gibson, and those perfect lips of yours." Her mouth curves up in a smile, and it's all I can do not to rush across the space to her again and shut her up with my own.

"Kelsea Anne Baker, you make me want to do *very* bad things.

CHAPTER TWELVE

The thoughts I've had in my head for so long are itching to become reality." That makes her blush. I walk up to her and pull her into my arms, pressing my lips to her forehead. "But all in due time, babe."

I feel her sigh against me, and then she's retracting from my arms. "Okay. I'll go out first."

"Good idea, since I'm still hard as a rock," I say, pointing down to my jeans where the outline of my dick is clearly visible.

She giggles and then opens the office door. "You'd better take care of that soon."

"I can't wait until you can take care of it for me."

"Me, too." She bites her lip, glances one more time at my dick, and then exits the office, shutting the door behind her.

"Fuck." I run my hands through my hair, fight off my shit-eating grin, and then conjure up every boner-killing image I can think of to make myself flaccid before walking back out to the main floor of the brewery.

It's Friday night, which means we're both working and obviously failing miserably to keep our hands off each other. I spent yesterday with Ben, training him for his new position as Manager, leaving Kelsea to manage the farmers market by herself since Walker had to work. Time is of the essence, because I need to feel confident enough to leave him alone for our date tomorrow.

I called Ben after I left Kelsea's on Wednesday and asked him if he was interested in the promotion, to which he replied with a resounding yes. After I walked him through opening and closing procedures, I had him shadow me during his shift. It was hard to concentrate at times, like when Kelsea would rush past us and her scent would hit my nose. It was even harder acting like nothing was going on, but that's what we agreed to for right now.

That, of course, didn't mean we couldn't sneak away and make out in my office, a fantasy I may have indulged in a time or two and now get to live out for real.

Before I left her house, we discussed not being open about the shift in our relationship, particularly at work—at least, not right away. We know that after Saturday, when we go on our date, people around town will see us and inevitably spread gossip. But until then, it's kind of fun living in our own little bubble with our own little secret.

I was also adamant about us telling the staff together, since we both hold authority here, to assure them that us dating doesn't change any dynamic of the business. I told her, too, that I wanted to clear things up with Walker before we jumped in fully as well. And she agreed.

Lucky for me, my brother happens to find his way inside the brewery on this Friday night like always, although he does look hesitant as he walks up to the bar. Neither of us have spoken to him since Tuesday, so he clearly doesn't know what's happened.

"Hey, Kelsea," he says as I listen from a few feet away, helping another customer. Kelsea leans over the bar, displaying her perfect ass for me as she lifts up on her toes and slides a coaster in front of him.

"Hi, Walker. The usual?" She moves behind her to fill a pint of blonde ale and then places it in front of him.

CHAPTER TWELVE

I can tell by the look on his face that he's surprised by her light and easy-going attitude. "Thanks. Uh, you look happy," he ventures as I watch her fight the curve of her lips into a blinding smile.

Same, babe. I can't stop smiling, either.

"I am. Just having a good day," she replies before casting her gaze over at me and lifting her brow. Walker follows her line of sight and then splits his own lips into a mile-wide grin.

"Aw, fuck." He leans back in his chair and smiles as he takes a sip of his beer.

I take that as my cue to walk over and intercept the conversation. "Hey, Walker. Can you come back to my office with me really quick? I'd like your opinion on something."

Grabbing his beer from the bar and standing from his stool, he takes another sip before saying, "Yeah, I bet you do."

I shake my head and then lead him back to my office, past the kitchen and fermenting tanks and down the hallway that leads to the very back of the building. Once we're safely inside with the door shut, he crosses his arms, still holding his beer, and the knowing grin he gives me only proves he's clearly pleased with himself.

"So . . . anything you want to tell me?"

I roll my eyes and then take a seat in my leather chair, adjusting the hat on my head. "Kelsea and I are together."

His smile grows wider. "Is that so?"

"Yeah." Now, it's my turn to smile like a fool.

"And when did this happen?"

"Tuesday night after the attempted break-in. I rushed over to her house to make sure she was okay since she closed that night."

His faces grows serious instantly. "There was a break-in?"

"Attempted. Just a broken window. No one was hurt, and the person didn't even get inside."

He blows out a heavy breath. "Still, that's fucking scary."

"Tell me about it. Kelsea was here with Beau, and it must have happened right after they left."

"Jesus. So what did you do?"

"I came over here to meet the cops, filed a report, boarded up the window, and then raced to her house to make sure she was okay."

"And . . . ?"

"And I kissed her."

"Fuck, yeah!" He pumps the hand that's holding his beer in the air, spilling the amber liquid all over the floor. "Shit, I'm sorry."

Through my laughter, I reach behind me, pick up a clean dish rag from a stack of towels I've yet to fold, and start sopping up the liquid on the floor. Walker sets his glass on my desk and then cleans off his arm. "I'll let this slide only because I should really be saying thank you."

He stands straight again, grinning down at me. "Oh, yeah? What for?" He's clearly enjoying his role in all of this, and as much as I hate to say it, I'm glad he fucking meddled. But I guess it's easier for me to see now that Kelsea and I are playing tonsil hockey and I get to live out every fantasy I've ever had with that girl in it.

"For being a pain in my ass."

He teeters his head back and forth. "Not exactly the thanks I was anticipating, but I'll take it." Reaching for his beer again, he mutters, "About damn time."

"Tell me about it," I say through a laugh. "I'm taking her out tomorrow."

"Really?"

"Yeah. Ben is now a manager, so he'll be holding down the fort for us."

"Holy shit. Are you nervous?" He rests his ass on a table along the other wall and drains the rest of the beer that didn't end up on my floor.

"A little. But more excited than anything. Fuck, I can't tell you how long I've waited for this."

The corner of his mouth tips up. "I can imagine."

"It's Kelsea. I want to give her a night she'll never forget."

Walker stares up at the ceiling for a moment. "Don't try too hard, though. You know her better than anyone. Make it personal. Make it something the two of you would do, not something fancy because you feel like that's what you *need* to do."

I hate that my brother is right, yet again. But I know his advice is spot on.

"I have a few ideas. I'll figure it out." I mull over a plan for a few moments and then ask him something I wanted to discuss with him. "So Evelyn and Schmitty, huh?"

His entire body tenses for just a moment, but I caught it. "Uh, yeah, I guess."

"You guess?"

"I mean, I know they hooked up the night of his birthday, but I don't know that they're together. He mentioned wanting to take her out but then never said much else."

I narrow my eyes at him. "Why do you seem bothered by that?"

He stands and shifts his eyes to the left. "I'm not. Schmitty is my best friend. Evelyn is a great girl. Why shouldn't they hook up?"

It's my turn to stand now and give him shit. Oh, I'm just tickled pink by how the tables have turned. Perhaps I've found a little sore spot for Walker as well. "Are you jealous?"

His entire forehead scrunches from the rise in his brow. "Of Schmitty and Evelyn? No."

"Yeah, I don't believe you."

He blows out a breath and runs a hand through his hair. "Look, I have no problem with anyone dating who they want, all right?"

"I think you're feeling left out, Walker," I tease, even pouting my lips at him.

And then he's shoving my chest playfully. "Shut the fuck up. I'm fine, okay? I'm happy for my friends. Happy for you and Kelsea."

I grip his shoulder and then reach for the door, ready to get back to work now that I've said what I needed to say. "Don't worry, Walker. You'll find your girl someday soon."

"Yeah, I'm not so sure about that anymore," he mutters as I

follow him back out to the main floor, curious as to why my brother seems so uncertain about the matter.

But then as soon as I walk through the swinging door and see my business full of happy customers, my employees solidifying the Gibson name with genuine southern hospitality and customer service and my girl serving my beer and smiling like she's just won the lottery, I know that everything in *my* life is finally starting to fall into place.

And later that night, after the last customer leaves, I do something else I've always wanted to do.

I was so busy last night training Ben on how to balance the drawers that I missed watching Kelsea choose a song on the jukebox and stack the stools, a habit that used to torture me as much as it brought me joy.

But tonight, I'm going to do what I've envisioned doing each time I watch her.

Ben is in the office, crunching the numbers on his own first before I check them for accuracy, leaving Kelsea and me alone in the main part of the brewery. My feet carry me toward her as she stands in front of the jukebox, debating her song of choice for the night.

"Can I choose this time?"

Her body jumps as I press my chest and hips to her back, helping her relax once she feels me. I can't help but put my hands on her hips and then my lips on her temple as I stand there, holding her in my arms.

With a peek over her shoulder, she smiles up at me, the

fluorescent lights highlighting her beautiful blue eyes. "You want to pick the song?"

"Yeah. I kind of had one in mind. But you can't look." I spin her in my arms so she's facing me now and press two buttons on the screen, waiting for the first few notes to ring out.

"Wow. Really?" She's smiling as I take her hand in mine and pull her to an open spot on the floor, wrapping one arm around her waist and holding the other one up with our hands clasped together. "I Hope You Dance" by Lee Ann Womack plays through the speakers as we gently sway together. "Your mom always played this song when she was cooking for us."

"I know."

"I used to love listening to her sing while she was in the kitchen."

"Me, too."

"So why would you want to dance with me to this song?"

I reach up and tuck one of her curls behind her ear. "Because I remember one night, when we were sixteen, I was watching you in the kitchen with her. You two were singing together, and I recall my heart skipping pretty hard in my chest."

"Really?"

I nod. "Yeah. And then all I could think about was dancing with you like I'd seen my dad do with my mom so many times before."

"Why didn't you?"

Ah, the question I'm sure I'll need to answer fully at some point, but I don't want to waste time on that tonight. "We were

CHAPTER TWELVE

young. I was nervous. I wasn't sure you'd want that. I wasn't sure what it would mean if I did."

She nods. "I get that."

"But the words—they always resonated with me. I kept thinking . . . this song is about taking chances, about getting up and making moves, taking risks in your life so you don't look back with regrets."

I watch her swallow, her eyes alive with a slight twinge of fear.

"And I feel like that's finally what we're doing, Kelsea. We're dancing. We're living. We're . . . doing what we've always wanted to." I rest my forehead on hers, closing my eyes and breathing her in.

"Me, too." I feel her hands squeeze me tighter to her, her head resting on my chest now, and then we finish out the rest of the song, dancing to our own beat, our own story.

"I can't wait for tomorrow," she says when the song ends. She steps back from me slightly, but I don't relinquish my hold on her yet.

"Me, too."

"What should I wear?"

"Something comfortable. Nothing too fancy. And certainly not that red dress you wore to The Jameson."

That comment has her grinning. "And why is that?"

"Because I'll be rocking a hard-on all night if that's the case. And I'd hate for the entire town to know just how big my dick is."

Her head falls back in laughter and then she blushes. "Jesus,

Wyatt. Please don't talk about your dick like that." She turns her head away from me, clearly embarrassed, but I grab her chin and force her to look up at me again. Her eyes widen, her lips part, and I can feel her pulse thrumming in her neck as I keep her gaze locked firmly on mine, holding her reverently but commanding her attention just the same.

"You know that seeing and touching my dick is part of this shift in our relationship, right?"

Her throat bobs as she swallows. "Yes."

"And that includes me seeing your pussy?"

Her cheeks grow pinker. "Uh-huh."

"So don't be afraid of saying the things you're thinking, too, Kelsea, because I want to hear them all. I want to hear how I make you feel, how big my dick feels inside of you, how close you are to coming when we finally cross that line."

"Wyatt . . ." she breathes, closing her eyes and squeezing my forearm.

"I want you so much, Kelsea. And my dick does, too. Get used to it." I place a gentle kiss on her nose, such a contrast to the filthy words I was just uttering. Right now, my body and mind are at war over treating this girl like the precious treasure she is and giving in to every animal instinct I feel when I'm around her. She pulls this different side out of me, the one where I feel like a man staking claim to a woman, where I crave being able to touch her and own her the way I've always wanted to deep down.

And I'm finally letting that part of me free.

"Okay."

CHAPTER TWELVE

Once we finish stacking the stools and I check on Ben, who successfully completed his task, I lock up, and the three of us head out to the parking lot. Ben wastes no time taking off after I give him a set of keys I had made, leaving Kelsea and me alone.

"So no Rose's in the morning?" she asks.

"No. I want all of the anticipation of seeing each other reserved for tomorrow night."

Our lips meet, and it's all I can do not to take things further. But we have time. We got in a pretty heavy groping session earlier, too, and the memory has me growing hard in a matter of seconds.

"I'll pick you up at six," I tell her when we part.

"Can't wait. Goodnight, Wyatt." I open her door, wait for her to start her truck, and then shut it behind her.

"Goodnight, Kelsea." And then she's pulling out of the parking lot, making me wish that tomorrow would come even sooner.

∽

"So we couldn't go to Rose's for breakfast, but you're taking me here for dinner?"

I pull into a parking space and turn to face Kelsea. When Walker said to not overthink our date, I knew that this was the only place I could take Kelsea for a meal. Even though we share breakfast here together once a week, this is the first time we're sharing it as a couple.

It's our place. It's something meaningful to our friendship. And what better way to commemorate our leap of faith than by shifting our habits here, too.

"Yes, ma'am. Breakfast for dinner. But I do have one surprise up my sleeve when we get inside."

Her face lights up as she smiles, captivating me even more, just like she's been doing since the moment she opened the door when I picked her up from her house.

Kelsea is wearing a navy-blue halter top and khaki dress shorts with brown wedges that make her a few inches taller and display her beautifully toned and tan legs. She opted to pull her curls up on top of her head, exposing her slender shoulders and collarbone to me. It's such a fucking tease. Like I'm supposed to be on my best behavior all night. Yeah, that's not going to happen with all of that skin on display.

"Now, don't get out yet. Let me get your door for you." I hop down out of my truck and make my way over to her side, eagerly helping her down once I open her door.

"Such a gentleman."

"You know my momma taught me well."

"Yes, I actually do."

With my hand around her waist, I feel her take a deep breath and then we walk up to the door, walking through this time as a couple, not just friends.

And as if the reality weren't stark enough, the second we walk through, all eyes shift directly to us—or more accurately, to the way I'm holding Kelsea by my side.

CHAPTER TWELVE

"No going back now," I whisper in her ear.

"Nope," she agrees as Beth, our usual waitress, comes up to the door.

"Everything is ready for you, Wyatt." She winks in my direction and then saunters off with her arms full of plates.

"What is she talking about?" Kelsea asks as I guide her back to our booth.

Beth did good. I owe her one hell of a tip.

The otherwise plain particle board table has been covered with a white linen tablecloth. A vase of yellow roses—Kelsea's favorite—is resting in the center. Two place settings rest on top of yellow linen napkins, situated on the same side of the booth because I'll be damned if I'm sitting across from her tonight. I'm going to get as much contact with her as I can.

"Wyatt . . ." She studies the table and then looks up at me, awe in her eyes. "This is adorable."

"Well, that wasn't exactly the word I was looking for, but I'm glad you like it." I hold my hand out, urging her to slide into the booth before I follow her. Once we're comfortable, Beth comes around the corner.

"Hello, you two." She smiles cheekily at us. "I'd like to say that this is a surprise, but I'd be lying if I said I didn't think there was more between the two of you."

I lean over and kiss Kelsea's temple as she rests her head on my shoulder. "Well, we finally admitted it, Beth."

"And I am so glad. So what will we be having tonight?"

"Our usual, please," I reply before turning to Kelsea to confirm. She answers with a nod and then Beth scurries off.

"Be back in a little bit."

"This is really sweet, Wyatt." She lifts the silverware off the napkin and places the cloth across her lap.

"I'm glad you like it." Lifting my fingers, I gently caress the side of her face, allowing myself to truly take her in now that we're settled. "God, Kelsea. You look so fucking gorgeous tonight."

She instantly blushes, and I can't wait to see if her skin turns that same shade of pink when I'm trailing my lips up and down her body. "Thank you. You look very handsome yourself."

I opted for a plain olive-green shirt and jeans with black boots—a little different from my normal attire but still casual.

"So what's going through your mind?"

Beth comes by and sets down two cups of coffee and two glasses of water. No matter what time of day it is, Kelsea and I always have coffee with our breakfast.

She sighs, but it's not heavy—more like she's releasing excitement. "A lot. I guess mostly wondering what you have planned after this."

Oh, this girl doesn't even know how I'm about to turn on the charm. "You'll see, and I'm sure you won't be disappointed."

"In all honesty, I don't think you could do anything tonight that would disappoint me. Just the fact that we're finally on a date together is enough."

I stroke her arm with my palm. "I feel like nothing I do for you will ever be enough, Kelsea. There's no way I could possibly show you all at once what you mean to me, so I'm just going to do what I can every time I get the chance."

She leans over and kisses me softly, letting her lips tell me her response to my words just now. "You know, there's one thing we haven't discussed yet," she says when we part.

"What's that?"

"What we're going to tell your family tomorrow."

Fuck, she's right. I was so busy worrying about the staff at the brewery and talking to Walker that I didn't think about my parents or Forrest or everyone that works at the ranch, too, although my father obviously knows more than anyone.

"Well, since we both have to be there tomorrow, I say we just tell them. My dad already kind of knows I wanted to date you, anyway."

"Really?"

I go to speak, to explain that further, but Beth comes over at that moment with our food. "Here you are, you two." She sets down two plates of eggs and bacon, a stack of pancakes, a plate of French toast, and all of the condiments we'll need. "Is there anything else I can get for you?"

Kelsea's eyes scour the table. "Nope. Looks perfect, Beth. Thank you."

"You're very welcome. Enjoy, you two."

I watch her walk away as Kelsea begins organizing her food and pouring syrup all over her pancakes. "Now, hold on there, Missy."

She freezes. "Excuse me?"

"I told you I had a surprise for you when we got inside."

I see her look over the table once more. "You mean this setup wasn't all of it?"

"Nope. So here's what I was thinking . . ." I take her stack of pancakes and swap them with my French toast. "Since we always disagree about which of these is better, I say we try the other's favorite, since compromise is a key component of any relationship."

Her jaw drops open. "Are you serious?"

"Yup." Narrowing my eyes at her and arching a brow, I ask, "Are you scared?"

She shakes her head at me, but she's smiling. "No way. Bring it on, Wyatt. I'm about to bring you over to the dark side."

"Don't count your chickens before they hatch, Kelsea."

We each cut off a bite of the other's favorite food and hold our forks out, poised in the air.

"You ready?" she asks, smirking at me.

"Yup."

"On the count of three?"

"One."

"Two."

"Three," we say in unison and then deposit our food into our mouths. Our eyes remain locked as we chew, both of us smiling as if we don't want to admit defeat.

And I'll be honest—the pancakes are out of this world. They

may even be better than my momma's, but I won't ever utter those words out loud.

Kelsea finishes chewing at about the same time I do. "So?"

I shrug. "Not bad. What about you?"

"Same. It's good. It's just not—"

"—your favorite," I finish for her.

"Nothing compares to pancakes in my eyes."

"I mean, there's a time and mood for pancakes. I just love the French toast here."

"Can we trade back, please?" she asks, which makes me chuckle.

"Sure." I help her move the plates around, and then we continue to eat before Kelsea breaks the silence.

"Okay, I have a confession to make."

"Oh, yeah? What's that?"

Her eyes shift to the side, and she puts down her fork. "I've had the French toast here before." With a bite of her lip, she flicks her gaze back up to me, but I'm baffled.

"And you never told me?"

She shakes her head, giggling now. "Nope."

Lowering my voice so only she can hear me, I say, "When? I need to know how long you've been keeping this from me so I know just how to punish you."

Goosebumps appear on her skin from my promise. She wipes the corner of her mouth with her napkin and then speaks. "When you were away. I was . . . missing you, so I figured I'd see what the fuss was about." She shrugs, but her eyes are clouded. And suddenly, I'm not irritated anymore. "It was okay. It definitely wasn't the pancakes, but somehow, it made me feel closer to you."

If this girl weren't already buried deep inside my heart, she would be with that little confession.

"Damn, Kelsea." I lean down and press my lips to hers, a soft nip that tastes of cinnamon, syrup, and the woman I've always wanted. My hand travels down her arm, a powerful current running across her skin as I move my mouth over hers. And within a few seconds, whistling and clapping explode in the diner.

I turn from Kelsea to see everyone inside watching us, celebrating the public display of affection we just shared. And when I twist back to look at Kelsea, she's beet red and burying her face in my chest.

And I'm instantly laughing.

"'Bout time, Wyatt!" one man calls out.

"When's the wedding?" another lady shouts.

"Oh, knock it off, everyone!" Beth's voice carries over the noise, effectively bringing it to a slow stop. She pauses at our table with a coffee pot to refill our cups. "The cat's out of the bag, isn't it?" she asks, grinning down at the two of us.

"Yeah." I turn to look at Kelsea again as Beth hurries away. "And I'm so fucking glad."

～

"What are we doing out here? No offense, but the last place I thought you'd take me on a date is your parents' house."

I slam the passenger door on my truck shut and then open the back door to retrieve everything I brought: a stack of blankets and pillows, a bag of her favorite cheddar and caramel popcorn mix, and a few electric tea light candles. The sun has already set, and the last sliver of daylight rests at the bottom of the horizon—the same horizon we've stared at too many times to count throughout our lives.

"Technically, we're not at their house. We're just on their land." Winking in her direction, I walk the length of my truck, reaching with my free hand to lower the tailgate.

"Want some help?" she asks as I hop up inside the bed of the truck and set everything down.

"Nope. You stay right there. This won't take long."

Kelsea hugs herself as she rubs her hands up and down her arms. "It just got kind of chilly."

"Don't worry. I'll keep you warm in a minute." Working as quickly as I can, I spread a blanket on top of the memory foam pad I brought to lay underneath us. The steel bed of the truck is hard, and I didn't want us to be uncomfortable.

Next, I position a few pillows in the corner and then flick on the electric candles, placing them on the edge of the bed, creating a soft glow around us.

"All right. Let me help you up." I reach down for her hand, hoisting her up carefully.

"Oh, Wyatt." Her face lights up as she takes in my work. It's not fancy, but it's us. And there were so many times as a teenager that I envisioned doing this with her, especially given how much time we spent out by this tree. "This is so romantic."

That's right. I took Kelsea to our spot under the tree on my parents' property down by the creek we played in growing up. There are so many memories here, and I figured we could continue to add to them.

My dad knew what I was planning and assured me we'd have privacy—a detail I'm very happy about as I watch Kelsea take a seat and start to unbuckle the straps of her shoes. She places them neatly on the edge of the tailgate and then scoots in further toward the back of the truck, getting comfortable on the stack of pillows. She crosses her long, tanned legs over one another, wiggling her toes that are painted a bright pink.

"Are you gonna take your shoes off, too?"

I look down at my feet. "Probably a good idea." After making quick work of removing them and setting them right next to Kelsea's shoes, I join her in the corner of the bed just as the sky goes completely dark. Wrapping my arm around her, I pull her into my side as she rests her head on my chest, and then I reach for one of the spare blankets and pull it on top of us to keep her warm. It's not really cold, but the first crispness that heralds the season's change is filtering through the air tonight.

"You comfortable?"

She hums. "Extremely. Thank you for this."

"You're welcome. I've always wanted to do this with you."

"Really?" She tilts her head back to look at me.

"Yeah. Ever since my feelings started to change, I kept

thinking about what I would do with you if I ever got the chance to take you on a date."

"When did they change?"

"My feelings?"

She nods. "Yeah. I'm curious about when things started to shift for you."

Speaking of shifting, I twist slightly so I'm laying more on my side, and she mirrors me until we're facing each other. Kelsea moves her hands beneath her head as we stare into each other's eyes.

"I think it was freshman year. I was a horny teenage boy, and you wore a yellow bikini to a pool party we went to at Schmitty's house."

Her body bounces with laughter. "I don't remember that."

"Oh, I do. I remember thinking, 'When the heck did Kelsea get boobs?'"

Now she's full-on laughing, and the sound makes my entire body come alive. "On second thought, I think I know what day you were talking about. I felt so uncomfortable. It was the first time we were all hanging out that summer, and my body definitely changed in the first few weeks of summer vacation."

"Well, believe me, I noticed. But then it wasn't just your body that caught my attention—it was your smile, your laugh, the way your eyes would sparkle when you hung out with my mom in the kitchen." I cup her jaw. "It was the excitement on your face when we went horseback riding on the ranch. You slowly became this girl who wasn't just my friend. You became this girl I wanted to kiss and hold all the fucking time."

She reaches up to stroke the stubble on my jaw. "I wish you would have said something."

"I know that now, but back then, I was scared. I didn't want things to change. I wanted you in my life too much to mess it up. I almost said something during senior year, though."

"Yeah?"

"Yes, but my dad warned me not to."

Her face falls as she pushes her torso up, hovering over me. "What? Why?"

I take a deep breath, preparing to tell her everything. "Well, I had just broken up with Janise for obvious reasons, the biggest being that I realized she wasn't you and no one ever would be."

Her eyes stay wide as she waits for me to continue.

"And then, about a month before the end of the school year, my dad caught me staring at you at our house one day and pulled me aside."

"What did he say?"

"He told me not to act on what I felt because I was leaving in the fall for college, and it wouldn't have been fair to you to ask you to wait for me."

Realization dawns in her eyes. "Wow." She settles back on her side. "I can't believe this. All this time . . ."

"Yeah." I stroke the side of her cheek, dragging my thumb down to play with her bottom lip. "It killed me, but I knew he was right. However, I couldn't leave without tasting these lips."

"So you kissed me goodbye," she finishes for me, and I confirm with a nod.

"I did. I needed to know what it was like to truly kiss you, Kelsea. And I'll never forget that kiss."

The corner of her mouth lifts. "I guess our first kiss wasn't really a kiss, was it?"

"Any kiss between a couple of ten-year-olds can barely be classified as a kiss."

"That day was when my feelings started to shift," she says, surprising me.

"Really? That long ago?"

"I mean, they weren't strong feelings. Those came much later. But I remember when we talked about getting married one day because we're best friends and practicing under this tree. My chest felt funny as soon as our lips touched, but it was such a fleeting moment that I tried to brush it off. But it just kept building over time."

That memory hazily reappears in my mind as she speaks about it. I remember kissing her, but I don't exactly remember how we got to that point.

"So you liked me back before I had muscles and a booming business?"

"Yup. It was the gangly limbs and braces that really did it for me," she teases, bouncing her eyebrows up and down.

"You think that's funny?" My fingers find her ribs, and I begin to tickle her as she squirms beneath me.

"You were such a dirty, smelly boy!" she shouts through her

laughter. "I just couldn't resist!"

After torturing her for a few seconds, I finally clasp her wrists together and pin them above her head, causing her to gasp and stare up at me with wide eyes as I hover over her.

"Well, I sure as hell can't resist *you* now," I grate out, waiting until the last possible second to capture her lips with mine.

Her reply is my undoing. "I don't know how I resisted *you* for so long."

Without another moment of hesitation, I press my lips to hers, devouring her, getting another hint of syrup on her tongue and relishing the feel of her beneath me. I keep her hands above her head with one of my own and then use the other to drive her wild. I trail my fingertip slowly down her face to her neck and then along her collarbone and shoulders as I push the blanket off her to watch her chest rise and fall with each stroke of my finger against her flesh.

"You are so damn beautiful, Kelsea," I murmur between kisses, contemplating where I want to touch her next. I move my finger over the strap of the shirt tied behind her neck to the base of her throat and then down, over the swell of her breasts.

Her throaty moans encourage me to keep going, but I'm dying to take in her entire body. I break the kiss and move my mouth to her throat, licking and nibbling along her tanned skin as I move down to her breasts and gently drag my tongue along each hump that is rising and falling even faster with every move I make.

"I want to touch you, Wyatt."

"Not yet. I'm not done exploring."

CHAPTER TWELVE

She groans, rubbing her thighs together, desperately trying to quell the ache that I'm sure is building between her legs. My own is pulsing through my dick. It's hard as a fucking rock right now, and all I've done is kiss this girl.

I dip my tongue below her shirt, searching for her nipple, pleased to find she's not wearing a bra. My wet tongue finds her tightened bud and swirls around it a few times. And when I lean back slightly, I'm gifted the sight of both her nipples standing hard and at attention.

I move my leg between the two of hers, pushing against the juncture between her thighs, granting her some friction. Lucky for me, she instantly starts grinding on my leg.

"Fuck, Kelsea. I want to touch you. I want to make you come," I whisper in her ear, licking the shell before nibbling on the lobe, "but I'm not having sex with you."

"Why not?"

"Because we're outside. We're not alone and secluded, ensuring I'm the only person who gets to hear you scream my name when you come on my cock."

"Oh my God, Wyatt. Your mouth." She finds it with her lips and kisses me deeply.

"What about my mouth?" I ask, pulling back slightly.

"The words you say to me . . . I never imagined you'd talk to me like this." We part, breathing heavily. "But I love it."

"Don't worry. There are more things I plan on saying to you eventually." My free hand travels under her shirt, stroking against the soft skin of her stomach. Kelsea has curves that are addicting to my eyes and my hands. In my opinion, she's just right, and touching her body is lighting my own skin on fire.

"I'm nervous," she whispers as I move my fingers around her stomach.

"You shouldn't be."

"I just . . ." Her eyes shift to the side. "I don't have a lot of experience with . . ."

The unspoken end of her sentence dawns on me: *sex*.

As much as I hate that someone got to touch her first, I can't be mad because I didn't save myself for her, either. All that matters now is that we get to be each other's last. Because being with Kelsea in any respect is a privilege I'll never take for granted.

"Kelsea, the only thing that matters is what we experience together." I grab her hand and move it down to my cock, letting her feel how hard I am through my jeans. "My body, my heart—it wants you. Everything we do together will be incredible because it's us, and part of the fun of crossing this line together is that we get to figure out what makes us both get off." I lean down and bite her bottom lip. "I want to know every way to make you come, Kelsea. And I won't stop until I do."

On a shaky breath, she says, "Then make me come, Wyatt. Please." The strain of her voice tells me she's teetering on the brink of losing control, that her body is just as wound up as mine.

"How do you want me to make you come, Kelsea? Tell me. Let me hear the words from your lips."

I see her swallow and hesitate for a moment. Then: "With your fingers."

CHAPTER TWELVE

My lips find hers again, and then I slowly pull the tie at the waistband of her shorts loose. The fabric gives way, granting me easy access so I can slip my hand under the fabric and search out that sweet spot between her legs.

Fuck me. I'm about to finger my best friend. I'm about to feel her pussy. I'm about to see what she looks like when she comes apart.

And I can't fucking wait.

My last goal is to torture her, but I'm literally shaking as my fingers descend over the smooth skin of her stomach and find the hem of her underwear. I dip one finger under the band, testing the waters, and I'm granted with a gasp from Kelsea as I watch her eyes flutter shut and her back arch.

"I need to touch you, Wyatt."

Realizing that I still have her hands pinned above her head and that I desperately want to feel her nails claw into my back and shoulders when she explodes, I gently release her wrists, causing her eyes to pop open and find mine. I watch her blue orbs glaze over with lust as my finger dips lower and finds the top of her slit and her freshly shaved pussy. I push down further, groaning when I find out how wet she is as I part her folds and begin to discover what makes her crazy.

"Oh my God," she breathes out heavily, maintaining eye contact with me while gripping my shoulders. My hand gets to work, pushing down as far as the fabric constricting my movements will allow, but I have enough room to move a finger to her entrance and slowly push it deep inside her.

"You're so fucking wet, Kelsea."

She moves against my hand, and I drag my finger in and out of her pussy slowly, trying to keep a steady pace.

"Tell me what you need. What do you want?" My thumb finds her clit once I rearrange my hand, allowing me to touch her where it counts.

"Keep doing that. It's perfect."

I lean down to kiss her again as I work her pussy over with my fingers, adding another finger when I feel her grow wetter and even tighter.

"Fuck." I bury my head in her neck, fighting off every tingle crawling down my spine that makes me think I might shoot my load in my pants right now like a goddamn teenager.

But that's what Kelsea does to me, what I'm allowing my body to feel for her now without self-deprecation and fear. I have had this fantasy since I was a teenager and could barely control my dick. Seems fitting that I'm having trouble controlling it now.

"Wyatt," she warns as I feel the first flutter of her muscles around my fingers, prompting me to continue gently rubbing her clit to coax her orgasm from her. And then she detonates, squeezing her eyes shut as I lift my head to watch her come undone. Her face is strained, her entire body tightened, her chest arched against me as she rocks back and forth against my hand. Her moans are fucking music to my ears. The heat of her heavy breaths hits my face, and I find myself panting along with her.

After what feels like an eternity, she visibly relaxes, melting into the blanket and soft padding below us, squeezing my forearm before popping her eyes open.

"Holy fuck, that was hot."

And then she's giggling, burying her face in my arm in embarrassment. "Oh my God, that just happened."

"Fuck, yeah, it did. And Jesus Christ, I'm surprised I didn't come right alongside you." I slip my hand out from under her shorts and then bring my fingers to my mouth, sucking on the ones covered in her arousal. *Jesus Christ, I'm already addicted to this girl with just one taste.*

"Oh my God . . ." She swats at me playfully and then fights to roll over, but I twist her onto her back again and pin her down with my body.

"Don't be embarrassed, Kelsea. Please." I press a soft kiss to her lips. "I loved every second of that. You just made a thousand dreams of mine come true."

Her face softens, and her lips curve up. "I—I did, too. I loved it. It's just . . . we're crossing so many lines."

"Lines that are no longer there and never should have been. There's nothing wrong with what we just did." My finger trails along her cheekbone. "That's part of being in a relationship, and it's only the beginning for us, Kels."

"Can I touch you now?" she whispers.

I feel myself wince at the thought—not because I don't want her to but because I know if she touches me, I'll blow my load in five seconds. "I would love that, but I'm afraid I might embarrass myself, sweetheart."

Her hand finds the bulge behind my jeans, stroking up and down, making my dick twitch again. "It hardly seems fair that you got to see me come but I don't get to see you."

Fuck. She has a point. "I hate it when you're right."

"Get used to it." She smirks before pushing against my chest, switching our positions so she's now on top of me. Her fingers pop the button on my jeans, and then she slowly drags down the zipper as I fight the instinct to come the second her fingers touch me. Her eyes dip down to my crotch where she opens the top of my pants and dances her finger along the waistband of my briefs.

"Fuck." I shut my eyes and take a deep breath through my nose.

"You okay?"

"Uh-huh." I nod. "Just remember what I said: This might be over quick."

"Why?"

"Because the thought of you touching my dick is making me struggle very hard to control myself." When I open my eyes, Kelsea is staring at me. "What?"

"I can't believe I have this effect on you."

"Well, believe it, sweetheart."

"I always wondered—"

I cut her off. "No more of that. Take what you want now, Kelsea. Don't hesitate anymore. And just remember, when this ends embarrassingly fast, it doesn't mean I can't last longer when it counts."

She grins and then reaches below the waistband of my briefs

with her entire hand this time, curling her fingers around my shaft and shoving the fabric down to expose all of me to her.

"Wyatt . . ." Her hand moves up and down, stroking me slowly.

"Fuck," I grate out between clenched teeth, loving the way her tiny hand looks wrapped around my cock. I watch her, exploring the way I feel, the way it feels for us to touch each other this way.

She leans over, moving her mouth closer to my dick. "You're so thick, Wyatt. I—I wanna taste you."

"If you do, I'm going to be coming down your throat."

"I've—I've never swallowed before," she admits, and the primal part of my brain loves that we found something she can do first with me.

"Do whatever you want, Kelsea. I'm yours." I bury my hand in her hair as she picks up her pace, darting out her tongue to taste the tip of my cock, the one she's rubbing skillfully in her hand.

And fuck me—just her tongue has me worried I might explode all over her face in the next second. I struggle to push my orgasm away. "Fuck . . . fuck . . ."

"Is this okay?" she asks, swirling her tongue around the head, peering up at me as she takes me deeper and deeper, over and over again. And the sight of her lips wrapped around my cock, her blue eyes questioning me in such a vulnerable way, has me about to blow my load in seconds.

"Fuck, yes. Shit, I'm gonna come."

Like a fucking queen, she lowers her mouth over my dick as I shoot my release down her throat, and she sucks me clean until there's nothing left. That image will be imprinted on my mind until the day I die.

When she pops back up, she wipes her mouth with the back of one hand and releases my dick with her other one. "Well, that was—"

"—amazing," I breathe out, feeling utterly spent from just one orgasm. My legs are numb, and I am embarrassed by how quickly that was over, but Kelsea just made me one happy man.

She smiles and then crawls up my lap, straddling me while my dick still hangs out of my pants. "I'm glad you liked it. I hope I made you feel good… "

"I fucking loved it, Kelsea."

She smirks. "Good, because I want to do it again."

"We will. Fuck, there's so much for us to explore, babe." Framing her face in my hands, I pull her down to my lips. "We're going to do whatever you want when you're ready." Taking a deep breath, I continue. "I know I've told you before how much I depend on you, but I want you to know that your happiness means so much to me, too, Kelsea. Please don't feel like we can't still talk to each other about any and everything, okay? Please don't think that just because we're in a relationship now that our friendship isn't there. I will always be your friend, and being with you physically is just a bonus. I fucking mean it, okay?"

I see her pause and then nod slightly, as if the idea still scares her. But I swear, I'm going to do everything in my power to make sure this lasts. Because I know it's right. And I know it's meant to be.

CHAPTER TWELVE

I put myself back together, and then we pull the blanket over us again, snuggling into one another as we count the stars and reminisce about our childhood. The rest of the time goes by in a blur, but that's what's so great about the two of us together—we were best friends before we were more. I can talk to this woman about practically anything, something I wish I would have remembered when I was debating admitting my feelings in the first place.

By the time either one of us thinks to check how late it's gotten, it's after one in the morning.

"I need to get you home."

"Yeah, probably a good idea." Kelsea shoves one more handful of popcorn in her mouth and then helps me clean everything up and put it inside the truck.

By the time we get back to her house, we're both stifling yawns, even though I know it will take awhile for the adrenaline to leave my veins so I can fall asleep.

"Thank you for tonight," she says wistfully as we stand on her porch.

"No, thank you. I hope it was everything you wanted for our first date."

She trails her hands up my chest and then wraps her arms around my neck. "It was more."

Kissing Kelsea is everything I imagined and then some. Holding her out in public was a dream come true. Making her come on my fingers was the icing on the cake. And now leaving her alone to sleep is making my chest ache.

"I'll see you in the morning at the ranch?" I ask her when we part.

"Yup. I'll be there."

"And we can tell everyone together."

"That's if they don't already know." She laughs.

"That's true. Goodnight, Kelsea." I kiss her lips once more and then the tip of her nose.

"Goodnight, Wyatt." She turns to enter her house, maintaining eye contact with me until the door shuts behind her. I wait until I hear the door lock turn before I walk back to my truck and make the drive to my house.

That woman is it for me. She always has been. And now I can't wait to experience everything with her.

CHAPTER THIRTEEN

Kelsea

I don't think I've ever had this much trouble sleeping in my life. And it's not because I'm having nightmares or just can't get comfortable.

No. It's because my body is so alive with excitement and adrenaline that it doesn't want to rest. Internally, all I can think about is the next time I get to see Wyatt, touch Wyatt, kiss Wyatt.

It feels like every day is Christmas Eve right now, and I can't wait to see what's waiting for me under the tree.

It's Sunday morning, the day after our first date, and even though I'm nervous about telling his entire family today, I'm literally counting down the minutes until I can leave and not show up looking unreasonably eager to work today.

But when I glance at my phone to check the time, the screen lights up with Evelyn's name. "What are you doing up this early?"

I can hear the grogginess in her voice. "You know I wouldn't wake up this early if it weren't important."

That makes me chuckle. "Okay . . ."

"Well, I half-expected a phone call or at least a text from you after last night, but sadly my phone remained silent. So I took it upon myself to gather intel about your date."

And there go my cheeks hurting from smiling again. "Oh, well, I got in really late last night, so I didn't think it was a good idea to call."

"And just *why* did you get home late last night, Kelsea? Do I need to go over the safe sex talk with you again?"

Rolling my eyes, I reply, "No, thank you. But we were lying in the back of his truck, looking at the stars and talking for hours, and we lost track of time."

"Were you just looking at the stars?" she asks suggestively.

"There was a lot of looking and . . . touching."

"Yes, girl! Get it!" We both burst into giggles. "Was it amazing?"

"Well, we didn't go all the way, but we did enough to satisfy a lot of my curiosity. And yes, it was amazing." My cheeks burn from my smile, a pain I feel I should just get used to at this point.

"I am so freaking happy for you, Kels."

"Thanks, Evelyn. But today, we both have to go to the ranch, which means telling his family."

"Are you nervous? Because you shouldn't be."

CHAPTER THIRTEEN

"Yes and no. I think it's just a big change that everyone, including us, will have to get used to."

"His family loves you, and I'm sure they'll be relieved that the two of you finally got your heads on straight."

"Yeah, I think you're right. I'm still having a hard time accepting everything, but I'm happy. Really happy." I take a breath. "So how are things with Schmitty?"

I swear I can hear her smile through the phone. "Good. Great. There's been a lot of touching going on over here, too."

"Oh my God, Evelyn."

"He is so hot, Kels. I never realized that firefighters have such amazing bodies."

"That's good, I think. Is it serious?"

"I don't know, and I'm not about to ask. All I know is that it's been awhile since I've gotten laid, and I'm just along for the ride, pun intended."

This girl makes me smile. "Well, I'm happy for you, then."

"And you'll be happy once you and Wyatt start boning, too."

I can feel my cheeks turn red. "I'm nervous for that, though. Last night, I told him that I don't have much experience in that area." Sometimes, I'm so jealous of how candidly Evelyn can talk about sex.

"And how did he respond?"

"Like the man I love. He assured me that it didn't matter and what does is what we experience together. He didn't make me feel like I had to do things, so that just made me want to even more."

"Naturally."

"But I'm still scared. Like . . . what if it's not as good as I've built it up in my mind to be over all these years?"

"Kelsea, it will be, trust me. And do you know why?"

"Why?"

"Because you two love each other. You may not have said the words yet, but you have a connection that is rare. Childhood friends to lovers? How many people can you honestly say have maintained a friendship that long, let alone one with a person of the opposite sex?"

"Well . . ."

"There's bound to be an adjustment period where you learn about what the other person likes. That's normal. Hell, I had to tell Schmitty straight up to spank my ass the other night because I wanted him to and he can't read my freaking mind."

"Oh my God, Evelyn!" I cover my eyes like I can't look at her even though we're on the phone.

"Hey, don't knock it until you've tried it, Kels."

"All right, well, I think that's my cue to get off of here."

"Don't be embarrassed. Sex is a natural thing, and girlfriends should be able to talk to each other about it."

"I'm not embarrassed. I'm not a virgin, you know."

"Yes, I know. But I also know that I held you while you cried after you lost your virginity to that guy because you regretted not waiting for the right person. Little did I know at that time that the person you were talking about was Wyatt."

"I know," I reply, suddenly less excited at her reminder.

"But listen—just because Wyatt wasn't your first doesn't mean it won't be spectacular. It's going to be amazing because it's you two."

I can feel the corner of my mouth rise again. "Thanks, Evelyn."

"Have fun today, and stop by the store sometime this week so we can have lunch and find you a few new outfits to make your man crazy."

"He already said I wasn't allowed to wear that red dress from The Jameson out in public anymore."

Her laughter rings out. "See? I told you that dress would make him go insane!"

"Yup. You were right. Talk to you soon."

"Talk later, Kels."

When I hang up the phone, I notice it's now a reasonable time for me to head to the ranch. So while I'm grateful for her call, Evelyn has also made my nerves hum even more strongly at the prospect of everything that comes next.

One step at a time, Kelsea. Remember, you're getting everything you've ever wanted.

But in the back of my mind, I also know there's another detail of my life that will come into play in a few months, and I don't know how to approach the subject with Wyatt.

Do I bring up the photography program now, when things are new? Or do I wait and risk ruining everything down the road? Do I squash the excitement of experiencing years' worth of daydreams, or do I hope that later Wyatt will understand my desire to do something for myself?

As I drive to the Gibson Ranch, I'm no closer to a decision but one step closer to Wyatt—and that's all I want to focus on right now.

∼

"Are you ready for this?" My heart leaps in my chest as I exit the bathroom at the Gibson ranch and find Wyatt standing there waiting for me, chuckling when he sees my face. "Sorry. Did I scare you?"

"Uh, yeah. A little bit. When did you get here?"

"Just a few minutes ago. I didn't see you, so I went looking for you. I'm sorry that I scared you, Kels."

Taking a deep breath to steady my heart rate, I finally reply, "That's okay, but you might have just taken five years off of my life." He laughs. "And as far as telling everyone, I'm as ready as I'll ever be."

"Come on. It's going to be fine. I bet everyone is probably going to celebrate right along with us. But I'm not gonna lie, the idea of telling them makes me feel like a fucking caveman."

"Really?"

"Fuck yes, Kelsea. You're mine, and I finally get to tell people. It's a rush I can't explain."

A surge of something courses through my veins from his declaration. "I might understand what you're saying more than you think I do."

He grabs my hand, plants a kiss on my forehead, and then

CHAPTER THIRTEEN

leads me into the magnificent farmhouse kitchen that Momma G cooks all of her delicious food in. I swear, someone could film a cooking show in this kitchen and have room for the entire crew and about twenty more people.

Lucky for us, there's a lot less than that many people standing around since we're here a little earlier than usual. A few B & B guests are eating at the farmhouse table in the room to our left, Mr. Gibson is refilling his coffee thermos, Walker is grabbing a blueberry muffin, and even Forrest is standing against the counter with his arms crossed, still-steaming coffee cup in hand.

"Good morning, everyone," Wyatt speaks, gathering everyone's attention.

"Good morning, Wyatt," Momma G replies with her back still turned to us. In fact, no one even directed their attention our way when Wyatt spoke.

"So Kelsea and I sort of have some news."

Oh, that does it. Four sets of eyes all flick our way as Wyatt brings our clasped hands to his mouth and plants a kiss on the back of mine. Momma G's eyes practically fall out of her head, Mr. Gibson smiles proudly, Walker nods his head in confirmation, and Forrest remains stoic to the side, but I catch the lift of his lips.

Momma G lets out a squeal and then rushes over to us, abandoning whatever she was stirring on the stove. "Oh my God! Finally!"

"Right?" Walker echoes.

Momma's arms wrap around us both. "Dear lord, I thought you two would never figure this out."

I laugh as she squeezes us tighter before releasing us. "Well, we did."

Walker clears his throat. "With a little help, of course." He winks across the room at us.

"Yes, Kelsea and I are officially together, and we wanted to let you all know." Wyatt peers down at me, affection and reverence sparkling in his eyes followed by a bolt of lust that I feel down in my core. "And damn, am I happy."

I look right back at him the same way, knowing that my future is with this man. And I will fight like hell to have it—but it might mean sacrificing something else that I want, too.

"So when's the wedding?" Forrest pipes up from his stance in the corner, moving toward us with surprising interest.

"Oh, knock it off, Forrest. Give them some time. But not too much." Momma G smirks at me before returning back to the stove as my heart pounds with excitement and worry.

"Just curious. I figured you two would have been married already, but what the heck do I know?" He reaches for a biscuit from the basket and then moves for the door that leads to the back porch. "Congrats, though. Kelsea, you've always been part of this family. Now, it's just a matter of making it official." With a nod of his head, he leaves, and my body hums with more nerves.

A part of me was anxious about the pressure we were going to feel after announcing our relationship, but I know that ultimately Wyatt and I are in control of that.

"Don't worry about Forrest. You know he can come across as pushy and surly." Mr. Gibson comes up to me, forcing me to break my handhold with Wyatt as he pulls me into his big chest and squeezes me tight. "You are the daughter I never had, and I know you and my son will be happy together."

My entire body melts from his words, bringing on the sting of tears that I refuse to let fall. Because he's right—I've always felt like their daughter. But this is more. This means more. This is building a future as a member of this family, one who is in love with Wyatt.

"Thank you, Hank."

"Always." He kisses my temple and then releases me.

Momma G speaks from her spot at the stove. "You know, I always thought I'd be giving Shauna my biscuit recipe, too, but at least I know that Kelsea will take good care of it."

"Don't give up hope on Shauna and Forrest. If Wyatt and Kelsea can figure their situation out, perhaps they can, too," Mr. Gibson replies.

Momma G shakes her head. "Not easy to do when she's thousands of miles away, Hank. And I don't know. I worry about that boy."

"Me, too, Elaine. But at least we've got one down now. Only two more to go." He kisses her temple, hugging her tightly before releasing her and moving for the door. "See you outside, boys. Don't be too long." And then he's gone.

"Well, you think I should act surprised?" Walker whispers to us so Momma G can't hear, but I can't help but laugh.

"I think maybe it's safe to keep what happened between the three of us," Wyatt suggests, looking between Walker and me.

"Agreed," we say in unison.

"All right, boys. Kelsea and I have a lot of work to do, so I need you to scram." She waves her hands in front of her.

"We're going, Momma," Wyatt says as he turns to me. "Have a good day, babe." He smiles down at me, clearly procrastinating leaving.

"You, too."

"Would you be mad if I kissed you in front of my mom?" he asks.

"I'd be mad if you didn't kiss that girl goodbye," his mom interjects, startling us both. "Just keep it PG in front of your mother, okay?"

Stifling my laughter with my hand, I feel my cheeks turn pink. "I guess we'd better do what your mom says."

"Yeah, but when we're alone, I'm in charge, okay?"

His eyes darken as he utters those words, and my entire body warms up to the idea of letting him boss me around later. "I think I can live with that."

"Have a good day," he says again before pressing his lips to mine, and my skin comes alive from his touch. Every kiss with him gets more intense than the last because each one seems to mean more.

When we part and I'm sure that my eyes are glazed over, he kisses the tip of my nose and then backs away from me. "Have a good day, too."

"All right, lover boy. Let's go." Walker leads Wyatt away by the shoulder, and I watch them shut the door behind them before turning around to find Momma G grinning from ear to ear.

"Come here, Kelsea," she says with her arms open wide. I follow her command and sigh deeply as the woman who was more of a mother to me than my own holds me in her arms. "I couldn't have picked a better woman for my son, I hope you know that."

"That means so much, Momma G."

"Deep down, I always knew you two were meant to be together, too."

"Really?" I ask as we part.

"Oh, yes. I saw it early on. And then Wyatt left, and I thought maybe not. Maybe he'd stay in Dallas or find someone else. But when he came home and I saw the way he still looked at you, I knew it was only a matter of time."

I exhale my relief. "It's scary crossing that line, though."

"Oh, I can imagine. But that doesn't mean it isn't the best thing that could ever happen to either one of you. It's rare to have a relationship based on a solid foundation of friendship. Most of the time, it works the other way around: The relationship based on attraction and lust fades, and then the friendship builds, but only if you foster it. A lot of people will let the excitement and newness fade and then assume that they aren't attracted to the person anymore or there's someone better out there. At the end of the day, this person is not only your companion but also the person you will turn to for everything, if you're doing it right. They *should* be your best friend. You *should* want to spend time with them outside the bedroom. And you and Wyatt already have that."

I feel my cheeks blush again when she mentions the bedroom, but everything else she says is refreshing to hear. "I sure hope so."

"And I'm not stupid and don't want to make you uncomfortable, but please, for the love of God, use protection, okay? I'm not ready to be a grandmother, and you two deserve some time to just be together."

"Momma G!" I cringe at my second sex talk of the day.

She throws her hands up. "I'm just saying, and that's all I'll say on the topic. But believe me," she adds as her face softens, "when you two *do* have a child—and you will because you're meant to be together—I will love that little human with every fiber of my being."

And now I want to cry. "I know you will, Momma G."

I hear her sniffle as she walks away from me. "All right. Let's get to work, young lady. We've got jam jars to fill, spice blends to package, and maybe I'll let you help me with the biscuits this time."

"Are you serious about passing along your biscuit recipe to me?"

She eyes me over her shoulder. "Of course. I always planned on giving it to my daughters-in-law someday—as long as they were women I liked, of course," she jokes.

"Did you really think Shauna and Forrest would have gotten married one day?"

She lets out a long sigh as she moves the pot of jam to the other counter. "I did. But then she broke up with him when they went

CHAPTER THIRTEEN

away to college. I mean, I know long distance relationships are difficult, but I hoped maybe, one day, they'd find their way back to one another. And then Forrest got hurt playing football and came home with this pain and darkness in his eyes. He's never been the same since. I don't know if he's just bitter at the circumstances or if his heart is broken beyond repair. He loved that girl."

"I remember," I say, thinking back to how much time she spent at the ranch. Because Forrest was older than all of us, he and Shauna dated when we were still fairly young. But I remember how his eyes would light up when he saw her, how everything he did revolved around her. And as I got older, I wished Wyatt would have looked at me the way Forrest looked at Shauna. "Well, I don't see her coming back anytime soon."

"Yeah, I suppose you're right." Momma brings the new box of clean jars over to the counter so we can start filling them. "Anyway, I might need your help next month with the bonfire."

"Is it really time for that already?" It doesn't seem possible that summer is coming to a close, but I did just spend the last month or so in emotional limbo, so it makes sense that I wasn't necessarily keeping track of the calendar.

"Yup. Fall will be here soon, and you know we do one at the end of each season."

Every Gibson bonfire is special. Momma cooks one hell of a spread, Mr. Gibson smokes hundreds of pounds of meat, they play music, and Wyatt's beer and whiskey flows freely as everyone spends a night together without work and obligations the next day.

It's always a good time, and this one is even more exciting for me since I get to go on Wyatt's arm. *Finally.*

I used to always wonder what it would be like to sit on his lap around the fire instead of stare at him across it, and I longed to dance with him and feel like he and I were the only people there.

"Of course I can help. Is it the baking?"

She nods. "Yes. We're going to do cupcakes, and frosting them always takes too much time."

"No worries. I will be there. Maybe I'll drag Evelyn here to help as well if she's not busy."

"Oh, how is Evelyn? I haven't seen her in ages! I need to stop in to her boutique and see if she has anything that will fit this well-fed body of mine." Momma G shakes her hips, and her large chest bounces with the movement.

"I'm sure she does. She has something for everybody there. But she's doing well. Her shop is doing great. And she actually is kind of seeing Schmitty."

"You don't say?" She tosses a curious look in my direction.

"I don't think it's anything serious, but they met at his birthday celebration when we all went to The Jameson and kind of hit it off."

"Hmm" is all she says, not giving me any other sort of reaction. "Okay, well, let's get to work, Kelsea. We've got lots to do, and I assume you would rather spend some time today with someone else besides me." She arches a brow, pulling a smile from me.

CHAPTER THIRTEEN

"Time with you is always time well spent, Momma G. But yeah, I kinda wanna see my boyfriend for a bit, too."

"Not like you two don't see each other all the time as it is, though."

"True. But now . . . it's different."

∼

"So we wanted to tell all of you together to avoid rumors and speculation." Wyatt snakes his arm around my waist and pulls me tighter to him. "Kelsea and I are dating."

The employees of the brewery all stare at us with expressionless faces.

"Fucking finally!" Ben shouts, leaning back so his voice really echoes, and then claps loudly while everyone joins in.

"I knew it! I knew you two had feelings for each other!" Sally wiggles in her spot.

Beau then steps up next to us and turns to face the group. "The sad thing is, everyone here lost the bet we had going on how long it would take you two to admit your feelings."

The crowd nods, which only has me shaking my head. "You had a bet?"

"More like a pool going. But we all thought this wouldn't have taken so long." He shrugs. "Oh, well, looks like we all get our money back."

Everyone's heads bob up and down as murmurs start up.

"All right!" Wyatt bellows over the noise, regathering

everyone's attention. "Now that we know you were all rooting for us, too, we just want you all to know that this doesn't change anything with the business, okay? Everyone, including us, will continue to act professional. Our relationship will remain private for the sake of our sanity, but . . ." He turns to face me, peering down into my eyes. "If you see me plant a kiss on this woman's lips, don't be alarmed. I can't help it. I've been waiting to kiss her for a long time."

And then he does as collective hoots and hollers ring out.

I must be the shade of a tomato by the time we part, but as everyone disperses, most come up and congratulate us on our newfound relationship status.

A few hours later, I sneak in the back to prepare to leave and am startled by a voice behind me.

"Are you ready?" Wyatt walks through the door of the employee lounge, and I turn to glance at him.

"Just about." I grab my purse and sling it over my shoulder before throwing my dirty apron in the laundry bin. "It feels wrong leaving this early on a Friday night."

"I agree, but Ben's got this. And remember, the only reason we came in tonight was because of that birthday party." The loft of the brewery is big enough that large groups can rent it out for parties, and it was booked for hours tonight. Wyatt and I came in to help manage the usual business on a Friday night while the normal staff covered the party, but he told me we wouldn't be staying the entire time. And I'm glad, because tonight he's coming over to my house so we can spend more time together.

CHAPTER THIRTEEN

It's been almost a week since our first date, and with each passing day, I feel like I'm living more and more in a dreamlike bliss. I'm also becoming increasingly more aroused each time we're around each other. Wyatt has been riding the line between being the perfect gentleman by not pressuring me to do anything I'm not ready for and fighting his desire to touch me the way he really wants to.

Either way, I'm growing antsy, too, and when I woke up this morning, I just knew I didn't want to wait anymore. We've waited long enough. I want to feel him, all of him, and know that all of this time in limbo hasn't been in vain—that the moment we connect will be as life-changing as I think it will be.

"I know. Still, old habits die hard." I shrug, walking up to him.

He stares down at me with a soft smile on his lips, his brown eyes penetrating me and holding me captive. But it's not like it's a burden to be frozen in place by him. "God, you're beautiful."

A warmth spreads through my chest. "Thank you. You're incredibly handsome yourself," I reply, reaching up to brush a few pieces of his hair from his forehead that have fallen forward before lightly pressing my lips to his.

"Let's go." Commanding me in word and action, he reaches for my hand and pulls me behind him, not bothering to say goodbye to anyone as we sneak out the back of the brewery and out to our trucks. He waits for me to start mine and buckle in before running over to his to follow me to my house. We wanted to spend the night together and opted to stay at my place this time since it's closer to the brewery.

On the drive over, my hands are shaking as I grip the steering wheel. Is this too fast? Am I sure that I want to have sex with Wyatt tonight?

But no matter how much I try to talk my mind out of it, my heart knows what it wants.

It wants him.

When we arrive at my house, Wyatt follows me inside where the cool air from the air conditioning hits our face the second we walk in.

"Feels good in here."

"I know. I like coming home to the house this cold, especially after working." I turn to face him and notice he has a bag on his shoulder. "I definitely need a shower, though. You wanna take one, too? You can use my dad's, or I can use his and you can use mine?"

"Yeah, probably a good idea. I don't want to smell like beer and French fries all night."

"Right? Sometimes the smell is so strong, I swear I sense it even when I'm nowhere near the brewery."

"Part of the job. Meet you back out here in fifteen?"

"Probably closer to twenty."

After I gather my shampoo and soap from my bathroom, I waltz into my father's room—that barely gets used—and head straight for his shower. As I clean and shave every inch of my body, I conjure up hundreds of daydreams of how this will play out.

Do I straddle him and take the reins? Tell him that I want him

CHAPTER THIRTEEN

and let him take me? Or should I wait and see if he's thinking the same thing? Or if he makes an innocent move that could turn into something more?

I shouldn't be this nervous. I mean, it's Wyatt. I've always felt comfortable around him, and hell, he's had his hands between my legs already. But we've both been so busy that we haven't had the chance to fool around much since then—well, except for Sunday, after we worked at his parents' ranch. He took me back out to our spot under the tree, where he gave me another intense orgasm with his fingers in the front seat of his truck during a hot and heavy make-out session.

But tonight is really going to change everything, and I know that no matter how it happens, it's what I want. And it's going to be perfect because it's us.

"All clean?" I walk down the hallway, my hair thrown up in a messy bun, and see him sitting on the couch with wet hair, a plain white t-shirt and black gym shorts on.

"Yes. And hungry." He stands from the couch, and we meet each other in the kitchen. "We should have brought something home from the brewery, but I really just wanted to get out of there."

"I think I have a frozen pizza in the freezer." I walk over to the fridge and pull open the bottom drawer freezer, searching for sustenance as Wyatt walks up behind me.

"You are such a fucking tease, Kelsea," he grates out as his hands find my hips and he presses up against me. I wore the shortest shorts I could find with the intention of teasing him a bit. I slowly stand and wrap my arm around his neck behind me.

"I don't mean to be," I say coyly.

"And that's what makes you even sexier," he growls in my ear, kissing the side of my neck.

"Let me feed you, and then we can revisit this moment."

He playfully smacks my ass and then backs away. "I *am* starving, otherwise I wouldn't give a shit about the pizza."

Smiling, I preheat the oven and then scour the fridge for the fixings of a salad that we can eat with it. It's nothing fancy, but I always feel less guilty about eating all those carbs if I get a healthy bowl of veggies beforehand.

As the pizza cooks, Wyatt and I inhale our salads and go over our day, talking about new menu ideas for the brewery and perhaps hiring a live band to come in and play on Friday or Saturday nights. By the time the pizza is ready, I load up our plates, and we plop down on the couch as Wyatt flips through channels, trying to find something for us to watch.

"Oh, this couldn't be more perfect." He sets down the remote as the opening credits of *The Sandlot* scroll across the screen.

"This is on TV right now?"

"Yup. It was kismet."

"Gosh, it's been so long since we've watched this together."

"I think it was right before I left for college," he says, stuffing a piece of crust in his mouth and immediately digging into his next piece. "But I lost count of how many times we've watched this movie together in our lives, Kels."

CHAPTER THIRTEEN

"I know." I wipe my mouth with my napkin and then set my empty plate to the side once my slice is gone. "I used to pick it for movie night at your house just because I knew it was your favorite."

He looks over at me and grins. "I always wondered."

"Well, that, and I knew if I picked something too girly, Walker would have a fit."

Wyatt laughs. "Sounds about right." His eyes drop down to the space on the couch between us. "Hey, what are you doing way over there? Get your butt over here so I can hold you." He flicks his head back, and I waste no time moving closer to him.

His scent hits my nose instantly, and I breathe him in. I rest my head on his shoulder as he wraps his arm around me, keeping me as close as possible. I don't think I'll ever grow tired of this—his touch—and how it makes me feel protected, cherished . . . at home.

As the movie plays, Wyatt and I adjust ourselves so he's turned, leaning against the corner of the couch, and I'm lying against his chest between his legs. His fingers trail patterns up and down my arms, bringing goosebumps up from under my skin. When he switches to my neck, I let out an embarrassing moan. Then his hand reaches up and pulls my wet hair free from my hair tie, and he runs his fingers through the soft curls next.

"Wyatt . . ."

"Yeah?"

"What are you doing?"

"Touching you."

"Okay." I close my eyes as both of his hands start to massage my scalp and then travel back to my neck, over my shoulders and down my arms, only to repeat the process in reverse on the way back up. The movements are a combination of relaxing and tantalizing because I can feel him grow hard behind me each time he continues the same path, but every second makes me melt more until I'm a puddle in his lap.

His hands move down my chest next, tracing the outside of my breasts before dancing across my bare stomach. I'm wearing another crop top since Wyatt seems to be fond of those, too, which gives him access to even more skin. I groan as his thumb brushes over my nipple, and my back arches, pressing my chest forward as I search for more.

I guess I don't have to worry about making the first move since Wyatt's mind seems to be in the same place as mine.

"You like that?"

"Yes."

Wyatt continues to torture me in the best way, passing over my nipples, drifting back down to my stomach, teasing along the band of my shorts, and then moving up again.

I swear I'm panting, losing control of my breathing and desire to take this slow with each pass of his hands on my body.

And I sure as hell am ready for what comes next.

"Wyatt." I sit up and then turn around, guiding him to shift his back so he's facing the television now, giving me ample room to straddle him. I sink down over his lap, biting my lip, and his eyes meet mine as he awaits my next words. "I want you."

CHAPTER THIRTEEN

"You have me, Kelsea."

"No. I want all of you." I take a deep breath of courage. "I'm done waiting. We've waited long enough, don't you think? And if I don't feel you inside of me tonight, I think I might shatter."

His eyes darken before me, changing in color so quickly I wouldn't have noticed if I'd looked away. The next words out of his mouth send a shiver down my spine. "I'm gonna make sure you feel every inch of me, Kelsea. That's a fucking promise."

"Yes, please," I moan my agreement.

"Fuck, sweetheart. I won't be able to stop once I start." He takes a deep breath before sucking one of my nipples into his mouth through my shirt.

Tilting my head back, I close my eyes and let my body take over, desire running through me at such a lightning-fast speed that my skin feels like it's on fire. "Don't you dare," I sigh, gripping the back of his head to keep him there. But he pushes my shirt over my chest and then latches on to my bare nipple this time, sending a shockwave of intense pleasure right down to my core.

"God, woman. I want to do everything to you." He stares up at me once he removes his mouth from my chest, and we both struggle to breathe. Our bodies are wound tight with pent-up need, and I have a feeling that when we finally release it, we're going to be explosive.

"I want that, too." I cup his face in my hands, moving my lips within an inch of his. "I want you so badly, Wyatt."

We're both trembling and on edge when his lips meet mine, and our hands start wandering all over each other's bodies. Wyatt pushes my pathetic excuse for a shirt up over my head, tossing it to the floor before cupping each of my breasts in his hands as he continues to kiss me. The combination of his tongue moving against mine and the way his thumbs are strumming my nipples has me grinding my pussy shamelessly against his dick.

I make my move this time, lifting up his plain white shirt, parting from him only long enough to extract the fabric from his body before smashing my mouth back to his. We grope and touch, squeeze and pull tighter together, as our mouths move in sync.

"Stand up," he says, helping me off of him while holding my hand. I can see how hard he is through the fabric of his shorts. But then he leans forward and starts kissing my collarbone, licking down the center of my chest. He drops to his knees on the ground, flicking his tongue over both of my nipples and then circling my belly button with the tip. His thumbs dip into the waistband of my shorts, slowly pulling them and my underwear down, leaving me completely naked in front of him for the first time.

And although I'm shaking from nerves and arousal, I know that Wyatt likes what he sees and accepts me. I'm not nervous in a concerning way—I'm nervous with anticipation.

When I finally look down at him, he's still on his knees, gazing up at me appreciatively before his eyes move across my body and to the juncture between my legs.

"God, you are so beautiful, Kelsea." He presses a kiss to my pubic bone, making me quiver. "I can't wait to feel you, all of you. I can't wait to claim you. Part of me wishes I could have done that sooner."

"Me, too. I hate that you weren't my first . . ."

"But I'll be your last, babe. That's a fucking promise, too." His lips find my mound, and then he darts his tongue through my slit, making me gasp and hunch forward at the touch. No other man has ever gone down on me. The only two guys I've slept with did not offer exceptional sexual experiences, and our escapades barely included foreplay. I'm grateful to have this first-time experience to share with Wyatt.

He makes a few more passes of his tongue through me, but then he stands abruptly, pushing his shorts and boxer briefs down in one smooth movement before he stands up again, his cock jutting out proudly toward his belly button.

"You're killin' me, Smalls!"

Our heads whip back to the television. I was completely unaware that the movie was still playing.

"What's the irony that as soon as I take my pants off that line is said?"

Covering my hand with my mouth, I stifle the laughter bubbling out of me. "Pretty ironic."

After composing myself, I sidle up to Wyatt.

"But believe me," I say, reaching for his cock and stroking it slowly, "there is nothing small about you, Wyatt."

"Fuck, babe. Come here."

He kisses me once more, and then we're stumbling down the hallway, a heated mess of limbs and lips as we find my bedroom and tumble onto my bed. His mouth moves back down my body, teasing every spot he can reach with his tongue before he parts my legs again and moves his head between them. With one swipe of his tongue, I moan, closing my eyes to take in every sensation as he licks me from the bottom to the top, flicking his tongue gently over my clit and then moving down to repeat the process.

"Damn. All this time I should have been eating *you* for breakfast, Kelsea."

I can't help but giggle. "Probably wouldn't satisfy *your* appetite."

"This is a different type of appetite we're talking about, sweetheart. The one that will no longer be satisfied even though I'm going to do this to you every chance I get."

"Wyatt." I grip his hair as he pushes his face against me harder, devouring me with every lick and flick of his tongue. I'm soaked, my body is humming with lust, and my legs are shaking as I rest my feet on his shoulders and push my back into the bed. My orgasm is building, my body is preparing for the burst of pleasure to flow through me, and because it's Wyatt bringing me there, I know it's going to be incredible.

"Oh God. Yes, right there." Wyatt slides one finger inside of me, curling it up as he drags it in and out, rubbing against the spot inside that has my orgasm teetering on the edge. I can't think about anything else but how amazing his mouth feels on me. My head is spinning, and my eyes are squeezed shut, preparing for the pleasure to hit me.

With a few more strokes of both his finger and his tongue, I combust, screaming through my climax as I shamelessly ride his

CHAPTER THIRTEEN

face and squirm all over the bed. White-hot ecstasy runs through me from the apex of my thighs down every limb.

It's the most intense orgasm I've ever had. I come for so long that I think I forget to breathe. But then I slowly come back down to earth to find Wyatt hovering over me the moment I open my eyes.

"You okay?" he asks, his eyes full of concern and desire.

I sigh. "Yes and no."

He smiles. "That was so fucking hot, Kelsea. You have no idea what this feels like, seeing you experience pleasure like that."

"That was amazing."

"I almost came just watching and listening to you." His honesty has me blushing. But then he reaches down and drags his cock through my slit. "Do you still want to feel all of me, babe?"

I nod. "Yes."

"Just making sure you're ready, because feeling this pussy wrapped around my cock is all I can fucking think about right now." He presses a kiss to my lips and then launches off the bed, reaching for his overnight bag and taking out a few condoms. He places the extras on my nightstand and then tears one open, covering himself. I lie here watching him, desperately trying to get my breathing under control.

When he crawls back on the bed, his entire face has changed from excitement at the prospect of sex to reverence for the woman lying beneath him. And as he rests between my legs, stroking the side of my face with one hand while the other props him up, I feel my heart lurch in my chest.

"Kelsea," he starts, "you're . . . you're everything to me." He cups my cheek in his palm and then kisses me softly and slowly, matching the emotion flowing through me from his words. "I want you to know that . . ." Staring down into my eyes, a moment of silence stretches between us before he says the words I've felt in my heart since we were ten and he kissed me the first time, feelings that only grew stronger with each passing day. "I love you. So goddamn much."

Surprise and contentment flows through me as I absorb his confession, his declaration that makes this moment come full circle. The space between us is bursting with emotion we've both been fighting for so long. "I—I love you, too," I reply on a trembling breath, letting the fact that I actually got to say those words to this man after all this time resonate in the air around us.

The smile he gives me in return could light up the sky, and then he bites his bottom lip, shaking his head. "I'm not just saying that to you because we're about to have sex," he continues as his fingers move all over my body. "I mean it. You are my best fucking friend, and I've always loved you. But this is different. This is the type of love you hope to be lucky enough to experience at all in life—and I get to experience it with you." On a shaky breath, he reiterates, "I fucking love you, so much."

I reach up to cup the side of his face. "I love you, too, Wyatt. This is all so surreal. You and me. Together."

"We are. We get to experience that love together." He leans forward to kiss me again as I feel him line himself up to my entrance. And as he starts to push forward, the gravity of this moment hits me even harder.

"Relax, Kels. Let me in, sweetheart." He presses forward again, kissing me and encouraging me with his words on each thrust. The first one takes me by surprise. The second one has me moaning in surrender. And the last one has me smiling and sighing out loud when he slides all the way in and drops his head to my chest. "So good . . . God, you feel so fucking good."

"So do you."

"Holy fuck. I'm inside of you right now." He stares down at me as he moves in slow strokes, lighting up nerves in my body that I didn't know existed. I can feel him shaking, so I know he's immersed in the gravity of this moment, too. I always wondered what this would feel like, but the reality is so much more intense than the dream. "You take me so well, Kelsea, like you were meant for me."

"Wyatt . . ." I gasp as I clutch onto his shoulders, our bodies rocking together in a perfect rhythm. "Don't stop."

"I'll never stop." He lowers his mouth to my ear. "I'll never stop wanting you or fucking you, Kelsea." He punctuates his words with his hips. "And I'll never stop loving you. You're fucking mine . . . forever."

I direct his mouth back to mine, claiming him and owning him with my lips, trying to memorize every second of this so that I'll never forget it.

Wyatt moves a hand down to cup my ass, lifting my hips

slightly, changing the angle between us as he slides in and out of me a little faster now.

"Oh..."

"Does that feel good?"

I nod. He pushes in deeper and harder on the next thrust, which has me letting out a long moan.

"Fuck, I can feel your pussy squeezing me." He rubs the base of his cock against my clit, our pelvises slapping together. "How about that?" I feel his tongue trace the column of my neck.

"More."

His hips rear back and push forward again and again with such force that I feel myself grow wetter each time he bottoms out.

Time stands still as I absorb my reality. This man—strong, loyal, resilient, and caring—he's been such a fixture in my life. But now he's taking on a new role: protector, lover, and the person I want to spend my future with. He sees me. Loves me. Wants me. And now we're sharing all of ourselves with each other.

I feel like I'm staring up at the other half of my soul—my forever. The realization has me on the verge of tears. What we have is special. Rare. A life-altering connection with another human being.

And that human being is all mine.

"Fuck, Kelsea. I'm almost there."

"Me, too."

I can feel his hand move down between us, locating my clit and stirring up the peak of my orgasm as he moves over it in small circles. The pressure builds, my body grows tense, and in

CHAPTER THIRTEEN

moments, we're both detonating wildly, fully in sync, clutching on to each other as each wave of our orgasms rushes over us.

Wyatt holds me close to him by our hips, rocking us together while our orgasms subside, and then he stops. I pop my eyes open to find him staring down at me, out of breath.

"Christ, Kelsea."

"Wyatt. That was . . ."

He collapses on top of me, and as I run my fingernails up and down his back, trying to process every molecule of emotion racing through me, he finishes my thought. "Life-changing, Kelsea. That was fucking life-changing."

The warmth of his body radiates off of him, and we don't move for several minutes while I process what just happened.

I had sex with Wyatt. I had sex with my best friend.

It was unbelievable. Phenomenal. World-bending.

And he loves me.

After a few more moments, he rolls off me and props his head up on one arm. "Are you okay?" He kisses the tip of my nose and then pulls me closer to him, burying his face in my hair.

"I'm perfect."

"Yes, you are. And I meant what I said—I love you." He lifts his head again, our eyes locking.

"I love you, too." Staring at him braced above me, I see my entire future, a future that I always envisioned but never knew I would be able to have.

Wyatt plants a chaste kiss on my lips before rising from the bed, heading toward the bathroom to deal with the condom, and the sight of him naked just makes this all so much more real.

But then another vision materializes in the back of my mind—one that is far from Newberry Springs and doesn't have Wyatt in it—an image that is so blatantly clear and bright that the two options stand beside each other like prize doors waiting to be chosen.

Option One: Stay in Newberry Springs. Marry Wyatt. Have lots of babies and be ridiculously happy, but run the risk of living with regrets.

Option Two: Go to New York. Complete the photography program. Be given so many opportunities that may be as far away from Newberry Springs as possible. Also live your life with regrets by potentially giving up the man you love.

"What are you thinking about?" Wyatt asks when he returns, laying down beside me again, pulling me from my internal conflict.

"The future."

"I think about the future a lot, too, Kels."

"Really?"

"Yeah. All kinds of plans. And soon I want to talk to you about them. But right now, the first order of business is having sex with you again because that is something I think we both want." He runs his fingers through my slit. "Burying myself in you is going to be my new favorite pastime, I'm sure of it."

My lips spread into an elated smile, one that my heart controls because Wyatt will always own it. "I like that idea. A lot. But I need something sweet first."

"I already had my dessert." Wyatt arches a brow and then drops his eyes between my legs.

"You have a dirty mouth, Wyatt Allen."

"Yeah, but you love it."

I throw my pillow at him before launching from the bed and locating my clothes in the living room. I move into the kitchen, reaching for a tub of ice cream from the freezer as I feel Wyatt's strong arms grip my hips and spin me around to face him.

"Don't be mad at me. I love the way you taste." He bites my bottom lip. "And I'm gonna devour and worship you every chance I get."

I can feel my cheeks catch on fire. "I'm not mad. Just . . . I'm still getting used to hearing you talk like that."

"Kelsea, this is only the beginning. My only focus in the near future is to figure out every way to make you come apart, to show you how hard you make me, to tell you how badly I want you, and to create the most intense physical pleasure between the two of us." He frames my face in his hands, the deep gravel of his voice resonating between us. "And I'm never going to stop."

I jump up into his arms, and he carries me around the counter, attacking my mouth for a minute before we part, our chests heaving.

"Feed me ice cream, and then take me back to bed, Wyatt," I mumble against his lips.

He lets out a laugh. "Done." He moves back to the freezer, takes out the tub of mint chocolate chip ice cream, pops off the lid, and then hands me a spoon. We both dig in as we stare at each other.

"Why haven't you ever shared your photography with me?"

His question feels like it comes out of left field. "What?"

I watch his eyes shift over to my camera sitting on the counter as his words click into place. "You know, it's one of the only things I don't think you've shared with me in all the years we've known each other."

I fold my lips in, contemplating his question, and then shrug my shoulders. "I don't know. My photography has always been something that is just for me, I guess."

"I get that. But I want to know that part of you, too, Kels. I want to celebrate and encourage you in what makes you happy. You do that for me. So why not let me do that for you?"

My shoulders sag. "It's different. Your business isn't something that people sit back and judge like they do art. It doesn't make you feel as vulnerable as my pictures do to me."

"Why do they make you feel vulnerable?" he asks, taking another bite of ice cream.

"Because I don't think my pictures are any good." *Seems to be a theme in my life.*

"Babe." He sets his spoon on the counter and then grabs my hand, bringing it to his lips. "If I know you like I think I do, I can only imagine the beauty you're able to capture. Because I see the way you view the world every day, and I wish I could see it from your perspective."

CHAPTER THIRTEEN

With a gentle kiss to my lips, his words reassure me that it's okay to let Wyatt into this part of my life—the part that took a chance on applying to that program. A program I may or may not be going through with even though I already committed.

"Please don't doubt yourself, Kelsea. And even if I do hate them, I promise I'll keep it to myself."

I smack his chest as we both laugh. Then he backs away from me. "Fine. I'll show you." I take a deep breath and another bite of ice cream, and then I lead him back to my room where my computer is. The room still smells like sex.

Taking a seat at my laptop, I turn it on and click on one of the folders of edited photos I just took a few weeks ago. There are shots from the river walk, the field I stopped by the night Wyatt kissed me, and a few from the ranch.

"Be gentle," I say as I stand from the chair and motion for him to take my seat. I watch him settle in and then click away, pausing on some photos for longer than others, not uttering a word for several minutes.

The pinch in his brow unnerves me as he continues to click. The silence is virtually eating away at me.

Chewing my thumbnail, I pace the room, trying to distract myself from what his criticism might be. I know my photos were obviously good enough to get into that program in New York, but somehow Wyatt's opinions matter slightly more to me. Okay, a lot more.

Finally, Wyatt spins in the chair and faces me, a slow smile creeping across his lips. "Kels, these are incredible. Magazine worthy. Framed-family-pictures-in-the-hallway worthy, the kind of photos people would be proud to display in their homes or in a gallery." He stands and rushes over to me, cocooning me in his arms, grabbing me by the ass and lifting me to wrap my legs around his waist.

I stare down at him with wide eyes. "You think?"

"I know." His lips find the tip of my nose then my mouth. "I can't believe you've never shared these with anyone. You have talent, Kelsea. Honest to God, real fucking talent. I can almost see your view of the world through your photos. It's fucking incredible."

Lowering my head to his, I sigh while fighting a smile. "Thank you."

"I don't ever want you to doubt yourself with this again, okay?" He tips my chin up, forcing me to look in his eyes. All I can do is nod.

This is where you should tell him about the photography program, Kelsea. Tell him about how badly you want to go.

But like the ends of a magnet, our lips find one another again, and Wyatt's kiss cuts off any words I had been considering.

When we part, he stares at me, my body trembling with adrenaline. This entire night has been a whirlwind. "Please tell me you have pictures from when we were kids, though. You always had that damn camera with you everywhere."

My lips lift into a smirk. "Maybe."

"Now those I have to see. Your pigtails, my braces, all the times we spent at the creek. Those must be some gems."

"They're pretty embarrassing, so just remember that I have some blackmail on you."

"Is that so?" He starts tickling me again as I squirm in his arms, backing up to the bed.

I scream as we both fall into a heap of limbs on the mattress. "Wyatt! Stop!"

His hands keep landing on every ticklish spot on my body, making me laugh so hard I'm fighting to breathe. And just when I think I can't take anymore, he pins my hands above my head and leans down over me so our bodies are lined up perfectly. I wrap my legs around his waist, feeling his erection pressing right against my core.

"I'll never stop, Kelsea," he says, his lips but a few inches from mine. "I'll never stop supporting you, wanting you . . . loving you."

"I love you so much," I whisper back. "I've loved you my whole life, but saying those words now makes everything real."

"This is so real." He thrusts his hips forward, settling his pelvis perfectly between my thighs, making me ache to be filled by him once more. "And I'm about to make sure you realize how real it is all night long."

Our lips meet, Wyatt releases my arms, and I wrap myself around him, getting lost in his body once more—this time more eager, more deliberate, *more everything*. Earth-shattering pleasure consumes us, and as Wyatt makes love to me all night, I latch on to each moment, hoping like hell I won't only have the memories to hold on to.

CHAPTER FOURTEEN

Kelsea

"Yes, right there." I reach behind me, gripping Wyatt's neck as he thrusts deeper and harder into me. We're laying side by side on my bed, his chest to my back, enjoying a round of morning sex before we get ready to go to the farmers market.

"Kelsea." He grips my hip harder and increases his tempo, making the entire bed shake.

Let's just say that in the last two weeks, I've learned that the slow lovemaking between us is just as good as the hard and rough.

His hand tangles in my hair, twisting me to face him so he can capture my lips with his. "I will never grow tired of this. Your body. Your pussy. Your fucking heart."

"Me, neither."

CHAPTER FOURTEEN

"You're the only woman for me, Kelsea. I fucking mean it."

"I know." We kiss and grip as our bodies move together. Then Wyatt stops, slides out of me, and guides me to straddle him. Within seconds, we're reunited, and I lose myself in feeling him inside of me once more.

I've been in a sex-induced haze since Wyatt and I crossed that line. He's all I can think about. He's all I want. Being able to touch him and learn his body now is like discovering my new favorite place to eat. Where there are so many options that I'm afraid I'll miss out on the best-kept hidden secrets.

We've tried so many positions, so many places—hell, we even snuck in a quickie in his office at the brewery last night. I couldn't wait to get him alone, and it seems he felt the same way.

At twenty-six, I can safely say this is the best sex I've ever had, and I didn't even know that sex could be like this. With little to compare it to, I'd thought other people must have been exaggerating about how good it could be.

Well, now I know.

Wyatt smacks my ass, spurring me to move faster.

Oh, and apparently I love being spanked. Who knew that Evelyn was speaking the truth about that?

Wyatt's hand travels down my stomach, landing on my clit. Soon, he's circling the nub in the way he's learned I like, the way I need him to. "I'm gonna fucking come, Kelsea."

"Me, too. Keep doing that."

"Anything to make you soak my cock." He tips his head back, closing his eyes. "Aw, fuck. Fuck!"

The pressure builds, the euphoria climbs, and then we're both reaching our climax at the same time, crying out in pleasure before I collapse onto his chest. I lean over to press my lips to his tattoo, the one he got for me that still makes me teary-eyed every time I see it.

Letting out a contented sigh, I lie there, willing my heart rate to settle down and loving the feeling of just being this close to him.

"Just when I think it can't get any better . . ."

"Right?" I ask through a laugh as I pop my head up to look in his eyes. "I feel like a sex fiend."

He smacks my ass again, making me jump. "But you're *my* little sex fiend." His lips meet mine in a carnal kiss that almost makes me think he could go another round, but sadly, there isn't enough time.

"We've got to get ready."

"Yeah, I know," he whines as I climb off of him. "You know, I could just call Walker and see if he can cover for us so we can stay in bed all day?"

I glare at him over my shoulder. "We cannot do that two weeks in a row, Wyatt."

Yeah, we played hooky last week. I'm not proud of it since I've never missed a day of work unless I was sick. But Wyatt's dick was just too tempting to leave. And the things he did to my body were well worth the guilt.

He rolls his eyes playfully before standing from the bed and locating his underwear, pulling them up. "I know. You're right.

Guess I'll just have to take the time to think about what I'm going to do to you next."

How on earth can my body be ready to go again just from those few promising words?

"Well, perhaps when we get off of work tonight, you can show me."

He walks up to me, still shirtless and his hair a mess from me pulling on it. "Your place or mine?"

"I kind of like staying at your place." I look around his room. "I don't feel like we've spent much time here."

"Deal." With a kiss on my nose, we separate and get ready for another day in our new normal: being boyfriend and girlfriend.

∽

"Oh, I know that look."

"What look?"

"The look of a woman who's been thoroughly sexed up and is in love."

My face turns as red as a tomato, but I can't bite my lip hard enough to hide my smile. "Well, you're not wrong."

Evelyn shrieks and then runs over to me from her position behind the counter in her boutique. Hugging me tightly, she sighs while smiling at me like a fool. "I've missed you, Kels. I feel like I never see you anymore since you have a *boyfriend* now."

"Well, if memory serves me correctly, you have a boy who's

occupying your time now, too." My hands find my hips as I challenge her.

"Yeah, but Schmitty and I aren't as serious as you and Wyatt. I mean, he's a nice guy. Easy on the eyes. Knows how to fuck. But . . ."

"But what?" I follow her back up to the register as a group of three girls walk into her store, setting off the chime above the door.

"I don't know," she continues, lowering her voice so just the two of us can hear. "I do like him. He's fun to flirt with, and the sex is . . ." She rolls her eyes while fanning herself. I giggle and then urge her to continue. "But I don't feel like he takes anything too seriously."

"Well, he's still young. Not all guys are like Wyatt."

"Oh, I know. I can practically see the wedding bells ringing above his head when he stares at you."

Her comment has my chest tightening, reminding me of what I needed to speak to her about today. "Yeah, I guess. We haven't really talked about that."

"Really? I figured you two were halfway down the aisle by now."

"Evelyn," I start but catch my hands shaking as I stare down at the ground. "I—I got into the photography program."

"What?" she shouts, pulling the attention of the browsing girls. "Sorry," she says to them before pulling me to her side. "Kelsea, that's amazing! Why didn't you tell me?"

"I haven't told anyone. Not even Wyatt."

I see the realization hit her as her eyes go wide. "Oh."

"Yeah."

"Well, you're going, right?"

"I called them as soon as I got the letter and confirmed I'd be attending."

"That's my girl."

"But that was before Wyatt confessed his feelings."

"Shit."

"Yeah. I got that letter literally hours before he kissed me that night. I was aching inside at the thought of ruining my chances with him, and I took that program acceptance as a sign that maybe I needed to leave Newberry Springs."

"Well, why can't you still go?"

"The program is four months, Evelyn. But then, after the initial part, there are opportunities to intern with professional photographers, which could mean traveling the world and possibly never returning home, depending on where the job takes me. I could be gone for years. I could get the chance to take photos of some of the most miraculous places on Earth. Could you imagine working for National Geographic or a travel magazine? Having my picture be the reason someone decides to visit a new place on this planet? My heart is pounding at the thought of it."

"I can clearly see your lady boner from here," she teases.

"But what about Wyatt?" My eyes sting at the thought of his reaction.

"What about Wyatt?"

"We just started dating. I finally have the man I've always

wanted. He looks at me the way I always wanted him to. I can see a future with him here in Newberry Springs as well. And he can't leave. It's not like he's going to follow me around the globe when his family and business is here."

"Damn. This is—"

"It's impossible, Evelyn." I finally let one tear escape, rolling down my cheek before I bat it away. "How on earth am I supposed to decide what to do?"

"Uh, hold on, Kelsea." She puts her hand up. "I don't see what the problem is here. You go."

"What?"

She sighs and then pulls me into her, gripping my shoulders and commanding my attention. "You have been talking about this photography program since I've known you. I don't want to see you regret not taking this opportunity you've worked so hard for."

"This isn't just some guy, though, Evelyn. This is the love of my life. What if I lose Wyatt in the process?" I whisper, afraid that if I speak the words loud enough, the universe will hear me.

The bell above the door chimes again, interrupting us. But the person walking through the door just reminds me even more of the obstacles I'll face by leaving.

"Oh. Hi, girls." Janise flips her hair over her shoulder as she walks up to the counter, acting as if she didn't know that this is Evelyn's store.

Evelyn and I don't bother saying anything to her just yet.

With her chin in the air, Janise scours the store, judging every article of clothing with her eyes. "You know, I've never been in here. I've walked past numerous times, but nothing enticed me enough to walk in." She slowly circles one of the tables full of t-shirts, hats, and jewelry. "But I figured I might as well see what all the fuss was about. Guess I'm not missing much." She picks up a t-shirt from the display in front of her, holds it up to read the words printed on the front, and then tosses it back down, far from the way she found it.

"Can I help you?" Evelyn seethes through her teeth, attempting to hold her composure. I'm sure if there weren't other customers in here, she'd let her tongue fly.

"I don't think you have what I'm looking for." She drops her eyes down my body and back up again and then smirks. "At least, not clothing-wise." Her eyes flit around once more before she heads for the door. "Yeah, this store is definitely not worth my time. Say hi to Wyatt for me, though, Kelsea. Remind him that when your little relationship is over, I'll be waiting for him." She winks, pushes her sunglasses onto her face, and then marches right out the door.

"I don't think I've ever wanted to punch another human as much as I want to punch her," Evelyn grates out as the young girls come up to the register to make their purchases. She rings them up one by one and then hands them their bags, waiting until they've left before facing me again. "What is wrong with that girl?"

"She's always been that way—entitled and demeaning to others, narcissistic and conniving. And God, Evelyn. You and I both know that if I were to leave, she'd be figuring out any way to claw her nails into Wyatt."

"She could try, but she wouldn't succeed. The man loves you, Kels."

"I know. And I don't think that he'd cheat on me, but I'd constantly be worried about his feelings. Would he get frustrated with me being gone? Would he get angry if I took an internship of a lifetime instead of returning home? Would he convince himself that life with Janise would be easier and break up with me?"

Evelyn purses her lips. "Kelsea, the only way you're going to be able to answer any of those questions is if you talk to Wyatt about it. See what he thinks. See if this is as much of an obstacle as you think it is. And there is no way in hell that Wyatt would take her back over being with you, so that's not even something you need to worry about."

Inhaling deeply, I close my eyes. "You're right. I just need to talk to him."

"Yes. You do. And if I have to take kickboxing lessons so I can fight off Janise while you're gone, I will. That bitch isn't going to touch my best friend's man if I have anything to say about it." She holds her fists up like she's about to box with me and throws a few air punches.

I break out in a fit of laughter, feeling slightly lighter now that at least Evelyn knows my dilemma. It's only the end of September. The program starts in January, which means New York will be freezing by then, too. I'm not sure this Texas-born-and-raised girl is prepared for a northeastern winter. But then the images of snow-covered trees, bustling sidewalks, skyscrapers, and honking taxis has my heart leaping for the experience.

CHAPTER FOURTEEN

I finally got what I dreamed about, what I never thought I'd get to experience in my life, and now I have to choose. I have to decide between my passion, the other thing I'd love nothing more than to have for myself, and Wyatt. But now I have him. I have everything I've ever wanted lying in bed next to me every night. So why would I leave?

"I still have some time to decide what to do. I'll figure it out."

"Yes, you will. You're a brilliant, talented, beautiful woman who has so much to offer this world. You deserve the chance to prove that."

∼

"Come on, boys! Let's go!" Adrenaline races through me as I clap and cheer for the Newberry Springs Men's Football team as they run out onto the field. Today is Wyatt's first game of the season and the first time I get to cheer him on as his girlfriend.

The teenage girl in me is literally squealing with excitement.

Wyatt and a bunch of the other men from the town created the league last fall after a few of them got drunk and were reminiscing about their days of playing high school and even college football. Seeing as how so many people in this small town have either lived here their entire lives or left and returned like Wyatt, the nostalgia of playing with the pigskin under the Friday night lights again was so appealing, the very determined men heavily influenced by alcohol decided to make it happen. Fridays still hold the spot for the high school games, so Saturday nights became reserved for the older guys.

And here we are for season two.

The Lexington Football team—a town just thirty minutes south of us—are our competitors this evening. Wyatt and the men reached out to neighboring towns to see if anyone would be interested in playing, and I swear, I've never seen men so eager to sign up for something in their lives.

I remember an infinite number of times in high school when I fantasized about holding this role: being Wyatt's girlfriend in the stands, wearing his letterman's jacket and being able to run onto the field after they've won, jumping into his arms and planting my lips on his. Sadly, Janise had the honor of being that person back then. Tonight, I can feel her glare on me as I stand in the bleachers wearing a navy shirt with Wyatt's last name and number on the back. It's not quite cold enough for his letterman's jacket, but I have it on the bench next to me just in case.

Most of the wives and girlfriends wear their man's number on a t-shirt or their jackets, too, something we came together to create while drinking sangria. Even Mrs. Aguilar, the same lady who sells her flowers at the farmers market, made pom-poms for all of the wives and girlfriends with navy-blue, white, and silver streamers—and I am proud to get to shake some this year.

Naturally, our town chose the Dallas Cowboys' colors to represent our team. However, the women quickly agreed we wouldn't dare attempt wearing a cheerleading uniform and go down on the track to cheer the men on, but we have come up with

CHAPTER FOURTEEN

a few cheers we've coordinated together and will shout from the stands.

I don't think the league games are just nostalgic for the men—the women take pride in it, too. Something about partaking in a pastime that can transport you back to another time and remind you of the perks of living in a small town brings a lightheartedness to your chest. It gives you a sense of belonging. It reminds you that your neighbors and the people in your hometown are just as important and vital to the place as the town itself. And celebrating friendship, family, and football is a pretty fantastic reason to come together.

Until someone gets hurt, that is, and then there's plenty of scolding and *I told you you're too old to still be doing this* being tossed around.

Since it's a Saturday night, so much of the town is here. Wyatt is even happier now that Ben is a manager because it freed up more time for him to dedicate to this. Last year, he was exhausted trying to figure out how to coordinate everything and run the brewery. Needless to say, I stepped up for him quite a bit, which meant I didn't make but one game last season.

But now that our relationship is public and we both are here, I don't want to waste another opportunity to make a statement about who Wyatt belongs to, especially after Janise's little stunt in Evelyn's shop a few days ago.

After she left and I went about my day, the challenge in her eyes kept grating on my nerves—as if I have to prove that I'm worthy of the man who chose me long before she was ever in the picture. I'm not only feeling insecure about possibly leaving for a while, but the more I think about her behavior, the angrier I become. Wyatt even asked me if I was okay as I scrubbed the dishes furiously the other night.

My eyes shift to the side, landing on Janise's instantly since she can't seem to stop seething in my direction.

"That's right. Who's got his name on her shirt tonight? Me, that's who. Not you," I grumble to myself. But apparently, I was a little too loud.

"Are you talking to yourself?" Evelyn slides her face in front of mine.

"What?"

"You were mumbling just now."

"Oh. It was nothing." I wave her off, giving Janise one more glare and a smirk, and then focus my eyes back down the field, clutching my camera to my chest. Naturally, I plan on taking pictures tonight. I might have to get closer to the bottom of the stands for some shots, but my lens does a pretty good job at a distance, too. "So why aren't you wearing Schmitty's name on your shirt?"

Evelyn rolls her eyes at me. "I told you. We're not serious. I think it'd probably scare him if I did that."

"Don't take this the wrong way, but I don't know how you do it."

"Do what?"

"Casually sleep with someone."

She shrugs nonchalantly. "We've had this discussion. Not all women can do it, but I'm one of them. I just learned a long time ago not to attach feelings to sex. Hell, I don't typically get attached to most people—except for you, that is," she teases, pinching my arm.

"I know. I remember you telling me why you moved here." I think back to that night, one of the only times I've seen her so vulnerable.

Evelyn puts on a strong mask around other people, oozing with confidence. I used to be so jealous of her. I didn't understand why I couldn't do that, too. But then she told me what happened, why she moved to Newberry Springs, and I realized we all hide scars beneath what we let people see on the outside. And that night, I knew I never wanted to be a person who let her down like her own family did.

"So for now, it's just fun. I'll let you be the doting girlfriend, and I'll just be your sassy sidekick." She wiggles her shoulders.

I wrap my arm around her. "You're the best one a girl could ask for, too."

She hugs me back as we watch the men on the field do the coin toss. Looks like Newberry Springs is choosing to defend the ball first.

"All right, boys," I shout. "Let's go!"

The entire crowd cheers as the men take their positions and Schmitty lines up to punt the ball down field.

"At least the man can kick a football," Evelyn declares as we watch the ball fly through the air and land in the opposing team's end zone.

The men line up, preparing for the first play by the other team, the orange flags on the belts around their waists kicking in the breeze. Naturally, men playing football at this age should not be tackling each other, so they opted for a variation of flag football to keep injuries to a minimum.

Lexington doesn't do much with the ball and has trouble completing a pass, so they punt it down field, giving Newberry a chance to score.

Forrest takes his position as quarterback as the other men line up. It's ironic that even after a career-ending injury, he agreed to play in the league. I remember Wyatt asking me if he thought he should even ask his brother to participate given his history with the game. But surprisingly, it didn't take much convincing on Wyatt's part for Forrest to agree. Given the fact that the game would be contactless for the most part, we knew his knee wouldn't pose a problem and keep him from playing.

"Hike!" His deep voice filters over the bustle of the crowd as the men race off the line. Forrest keeps the ball high, waiting for the perfect opportunity to pass it. He assesses the field, rearing back, and then launches the ball toward the other end where Wyatt is waiting. He leaps up to grab it, and a man on the opposing team snatches his flag when his feet touch the ground.

"Yes!" My voice carries over the cheering, and I blow a kiss to him as he's running down the field. God, he's so sexy. I can't wait to show him just how much later.

The team sets up again, and this time, Forrest hands it off to Walker, who runs through the line and earns another first down.

"Walker can move," Evelyn admits, slowly clapping as the men set up for the next play.

"Yeah. All three of the boys played growing up. Forrest played quarterback, obviously. Wyatt played wide receiver, and Walker was a running back. The three of them would play all the time between chores on the ranch and in high school as well."

"What is it about grown men playing football that makes it hard for a southern girl to breathe?" Evelyn draws out, fanning her face dramatically.

"I don't know, but believe me—I'm a little excited to show Wyatt later just how hot and bothered I am."

"Kelsea Anne Baker! Did you really just say that?"

Laughing, I reach up to cover my cheeks that I know are turning pink. "You're rubbing off on me, Evelyn."

"No, girl. That's just what a really good dick will do to you."

We share a laugh as the men line up just a few yards short of the end zone. Forrest catches the ball after the snap and waits just a few seconds before spiraling it across the short distance, right into Wyatt's waiting arms.

"Touchdown!" The wives and girlfriends all pick up our pom-poms and shake them as the announcer, who just so happens to be Janise's dad, the mayor, shouts the score over the loudspeaker.

"I remember how Wyatt and I would celebrate each of his touchdowns back in high school." Janise suddenly appears next to me, catching me off guard. She's clapping wildly as my cheeriness from before disappears.

"That's nice," Evelyn says, peeking her head around me to glare over at her.

"It was. He was such a good kisser, even when he wasn't kissing my lips, if you know what I mean."

"I swear," Evelyn grates, rearing back her arm like she's about to throw a punch, but I turn to stop her.

"It's okay. I've got this." She arches a brow, and I give her a confident nod in return before spinning around to face Janise. "You know, Janise, I've tried really hard to keep my southern belle composure around you because that's the womanly thing to do," I say, making sure to emphasize my accent even more for added effect. "But I'm done putting up with your crap."

I take two steps toward her, crowding her space, forcing her to look up at me since I have a few inches on her, especially in my boots.

"Wyatt is with *me*. He dated you almost ten years ago and doesn't plan on doing it ever again, so it's time for you to move on, sweetie. He's also told me that dating you was one of the biggest mistakes he's ever made in his life besides not telling me how he truly felt about me. We are in love. And we *will* be getting married one day, so your pathetic attempt at winning him back or lighting up my insecurities is a waste of time." I flash her a smile so fake, I know she can tell. I visibly see her swallow. "Now, do us both a favor, and walk away from me, forget Wyatt ever existed, and find some other unfortunate man to pine after."

Her eyes widen, and then she's stepping back, not even

bothering to refute anything I just said before scurrying away from me.

I blow out the heavy breath I was holding, my hands clammy and shaking at my sides as Evelyn jumps up and down behind me, shaking the entire bleachers. "Oh my God, Kelsea! I am so proud of you. I didn't know you had that in you, sweetheart!"

Blowing out a harsh breath, I say, "That girl has pissed me off one too many times."

"That was like watching you figure out you had a dick and it did more than just dangle between your legs."

"Evelyn!" I twist to face her, hiding my laugh.

"What?" She tosses her hands in the air. "I kind of have a hard-on for you right now."

"You are so ridiculous." My eyes sweep around us as a few people give us puzzled looks. Lowering my voice, I say, "Let's take the penis talk down a notch, shall we?"

"Fine. But damn, you made me proud, kid." She pretends to wipe a tear from her face.

I playfully shove her to the side and then focus back on the game, noticing that Lexington must have scored while I was cutting Janise down a notch or two. "Damn. It's tied."

"Don't worry. Our boys will pull out the win," she says confidently, and then the two of us do what we can from the stands, encouraging the men of Newberry Springs to give it their all while avoiding injury.

∼

"There's my girl!"

I run across the field like we're a couple of teenagers, jumping into Wyatt's arms the way I've always wanted to, smashing my lips to his and fulfilling yet another fantasy I've had about this man.

"You were so sexy," I mutter against his lips. "And now you're all dirty and smelly, so I know you need a shower."

"What are you suggesting, babe?"

"That maybe now I need one, too."

His eyes darken with desire, and then he's tightening his grip on my hips since my legs are still wrapped around his waist. "Fuck, Kelsea. We'd better get home, then."

"Wyatt!" Earl Vance, the hardware store owner in Newberry Springs, comes up to us as Wyatt gently places my feet back on the ground, his hands still claiming me. "Nice game, son."

"Thank you."

"It was just like watching you boys back in high school."

"Well, not as rough as high school, but it got my adrenaline pumping just the same." Wyatt shakes his hand and then pulls me into his side. "You remember Kelsea Baker, right?"

Earl nods. "Of course. How are you, sweetheart?"

I lean my head on Wyatt's shoulder. "Really well, actually."

"I have to say it feels right seeing the two of you together. You always were attached at the hip, so I kinda wondered if there was something more."

"Well, it took us awhile to admit it, but yeah . . . and we're really happy," Wyatt replies, staring down at me with that same look in his eyes, the one that tells me he's holding his entire world in his arms.

"I can tell. Say, how is your dad doing?" Earl continues, and I instantly see Wyatt's face fall and feel his body stiffen.

"Oh. He's doing . . . okay. Business is great. He's working hard."

"Tell him not to work too hard now. Once you get to our age, you realize you can't do things the same way you used to. Body starts giving out on you." He pats his beer belly and smiles.

"Yeah, so I've heard," Wyatt acknowledges, but his body is still stiff. Concern races through me.

"I could never be out on that field and run around like you boys are. But it sure does make for some damn fine entertainment." He clasps Wyatt's shoulder. "Well, tell your dad I said hello, and I'm sure I'll see you around soon. It's been awhile since I've been into the brewery, so I'm due for a visit, anyway."

"Thanks, Earl. See ya around." We watch Earl walk away as people mill around us. But Wyatt's face remains impassive.

"Hey. You okay?"

"What?" He looks down at me. "Oh, yeah. I'm fine."

"You sure?"

"Yeah. Let's say goodbye to the guys and then head home." With his lips close to my ear, he says, "I didn't forget about that shower comment from earlier, and if we're not careful, everyone's gonna get a glimpse of how excited I am about it."

"Then we'd better make our goodbyes quick."

"Bro! Great game!" Walker slaps Wyatt on the shoulder,

drenched in sweat as well. Mud is smeared on his forehead, but he looks happier than a clam. "Those Lexington boys put up a fight, though."

"Yeah, they did."

"No one can compete with the Gibson triple threat," Forrest says as he comes up, wraps his arm around each of his younger brothers' necks, and puts them both in a choke hold. "Huh? I taught you boys well, didn't I?" Walker and Wyatt struggle against him as I laugh at the three of them still acting like the boys I grew up with. Even better is seeing Forrest being playful, being the guy I remember growing up before he left for college and came back a different man.

"Jesus. Big brother is high on football right now, isn't he?" Walker asks as Forrest releases him and Wyatt and then squirts water into his mouth.

"Yeah, I am." He inhales deeply. "Damn, that felt good. I forgot how much I missed that." Forrest brushes his dark, sweat-soaked hair back with his hand, passing his eyes over the field around us.

"Your knee didn't seem to be bothering you too much, either," I chime in as Forrest's eyes land on me.

He looks down at his leg, flexing his thigh, twisting it from side to side. "No. It . . . it felt just fine, actually."

"That's good, Forrest. Just keep it that way, okay? That way we can win the season." Wyatt clasps his hand on his shoulder this time.

"Is there an old man football championship game, too? Like

the Super Bowl, but they hand out tubes of Icy Hot and those lower back patches when you win?" Evelyn says, walking up to us with Schmitty trailing close behind.

I see Walker tense up from the corner of my eye, but then he relaxes again and takes another drink of water before wiping his forehead with the bottom of his shirt, revealing his abs to our little circle. I've seen the man with his shirt off plenty of times, but by the way Evelyn's eyes are bugging out right now, I think it's safe to say she hasn't.

"Hardy har har," Forrest bellows. "I may be thirty-one, but I'll still run circles around these kids."

"Watch it, old man. That kind of trash talk is just asking for karma to come bite you in the ass," Schmitty jokes.

"I'll be fine," Forrest declares, rubbing his hands together and then clapping dirt off. "All right, I need a shower, a cold beer, and my bed. See you guys tomorrow at Mom and Dad's." Before anyone can reply, he walks away.

"Yeah, we're headed out, too, huh, babe?" Schmitty reaches around Evelyn's waist and pulls her close to him.

"Yup. But you need a shower, stat."

"Perhaps we can take one together?" He leans over, speaking in her ear.

"I'm out of here. Catch you guys later," Walker announces, leaving just as quickly as Forrest did, heading for his truck and never looking back.

"Call me later?" I ask Evelyn as her eyes trail Walker before zeroing back on me.

"Oh. Yup. You know it, bestie." She blows me a kiss and then marches off with Schmitty toward his truck since she rode here with me.

"Are you ready to go?" Wyatt reaches up to move my hair out of my face, bringing my focus back to him, the one I want to celebrate with, anyway.

"Yes."

Once we settle into our trucks, I follow him back to his place since it's closer to the high school field than my house is.

"Why do I get the feeling that Walker has a thing for Evelyn?" I ask once we step inside. Wyatt tosses his dirty clothes in his washing machine and then waltzes toward me completely naked.

"You really want to talk about my brother and your friend right now?" He reaches down to stroke his length, making me quickly forget what I think I noticed at the field a few minutes ago.

"Um, nope. Not at all." Slapping my head playfully, I say, "Silly me. What was I thinking?"

I take a moment to dip my eyes down his entire body before settling on the smirk he's giving me.

"I believe I owe you a very dirty shower." I reach up to take off my shirt, tossing it on the floor before unbuttoning my jean shorts and dropping them to the ground as well. As I stand there in my black bra with lace on the cups and a matching thong, his eyes dip down my body, and I see him grow harder in his hand.

"I'm already dirty."

"But I'm not." I reach back and unclasp my bra, holding it out to the side before letting it fall.

CHAPTER FOURTEEN

"I think you like it a little dirtier than you'll ever admit, Kelsea."

"Only with you, Wyatt. I only feel safe and satisfied with you."

"God, that's like music to my ears, babe." He stalks toward me as I lower my thong, leaving me naked as well. And when our lips meet and our arms wrap around each other, I trust him to lead me to the shower and give me the pleasure that I know only he can give me.

CHAPTER FIFTEEN

Wyatt

"You like that?" I gently tug Kelsea's hair, pressing her up against the shower wall and smoothing my hand over her ass as I slide in and out of her. I give her cheek a little smack, knowing she loves when I do, and increase my pressure to smack her again.

"God, Wyatt. Yes . . ."

"Fuck, you're so sexy, Kelsea." I nibble along her neck, listening to her moans. "I love seeing you like this. I love watching you take my cock. And I fucking love watching you come undone."

"Don't stop. Please, don't stop." After the game, I was feeling on top of the world, high on life and the competitive spirit—but nothing compares to being intimate with Kelsea. That will always be the best high of them all.

I keep a steady rhythm. I love how every time we have sex, I feel closer to her, more bold and brave to push our limits, and eager to experience everything with her and see what she'll like. So far, she's been right there with me, vulnerable and ready to experiment, willing to push our boundaries and feel every kind of pleasure there is.

In fact, one of the things we've discovered is that Kelsea likes her ass played with. So I release her hair, sucking my thumb in my mouth for lubrication, and then I push against her puckered entrance and wait for her consent. With a shaky nod from her, I press forward as I continue to slide in and out of her pussy with my cock, my thumb now in her ass.

And fuck, it makes my orgasm build in record time.

"God, you're gonna make me come."

"Fuck, I'm there, too. Drench me, Kels," I growl in her ear, moving my other hand down between her legs, locating her clit as I rub her softly while the water falls down our bodies.

With my name as a cry on her lips, I feel the first flutters of her orgasm spiral around my cock. My lips brush the shell of her ear just as she goes over the edge. "Fuck, I'll never get enough of you." And then the strength of her orgasm has me moving faster, chasing my own.

After we finish cleaning up in the shower and get dressed, we snuggle into my bed. I lean up against the padded headboard with

Kelsea tucked perfectly under my arm, the television playing a rerun of *Friends* in the background.

"Can I confess something?" Kelsea asks, breaking the silence.

"Oh, is it juicy?" I tease her.

She huffs out a laugh. "Not particularly. Just something I was thinking about earlier."

"Do tell."

She looks up at me from my side. "Cheering you on tonight, wearing your name and number, and then running down onto the grass and jumping into your arms . . . it was so many fantasies of mine come true, Wyatt."

"Yeah?" My lips quirk softly as I smile down at her, the blue of her eyes darker, illuminated only by the light of the TV.

"Yes. I can't tell you how much I wanted that back in high school."

My hand lifts to trail a finger down her soft cheek, my heartbeat loud in my ears. "I fucking wanted that, too, Kels."

"God, we wasted so much time." She sighs heavily.

"Hey, no, we didn't." I turn her chin so our eyes connect, making sure she's listening to me. "Things worked out the way they were meant to, okay? We can't look back anymore. Now, we have nothing but the future to think about."

"What kind of future do you see?" she asks, swallowing hard as she waits for my response. And even though I haven't been shy about letting her know that she's the only woman I want until I die, we haven't talked about the steps to get there yet.

Guess there's no time like the present.

I lean down and press my lips to hers, getting lost in the gentle movement of our tongues for a few minutes before we part. "I want an entire life with you."

"What kind of life? Paint me a picture . . ." She trails her fingernails down my abs, avoiding my gaze now.

"I want us to be a team," I start, gently tugging her chin so she's forced to look at me again. "Like my parents. They lean on each other because they know they can. Just like I know I can with you."

"I feel the same."

"I see us getting married—sooner rather than later, if I'm being honest." Her eyebrows lift. "And buying a big house on a piece of land where we can have privacy but still be close enough to the brewery and the ranch."

"Do we have babies?"

"As many as you'll let me give you. I want little girls with your blonde curls and boys who can grow up like me and my brothers did. I want to teach them the value of hard work and how to have manners, how to treat a woman—especially the one they love." I kiss the tip of her nose. "I just want everything life has to offer but with you by my side, Kelsea. I want honest-to-God happiness—not the kind that means everything is perfect, but the kind of life that's perfect because of the person you choose to live it with."

I watch her eyes fall and her brow furrow, which instantly has worry building in my chest. Did I say too much? Did everything I just divulged scare her? I don't see how it could when I thought we were clearly on the same page about our feelings and what us being together meant.

Kelsea is it for me. There will never be another woman who can make me feel the way she does, who knows me for exactly who I am and loves me for all my faults. Every vision of my life has always included her, and that will never change.

"I want that, too, Wyatt," she finally says, staring up at me with tears in her eyes. "I want everything you just said."

My lungs relax as I let out the breath I was holding, grateful that my momentary freak out was just that—momentary. However, the twinge of fear in my chest reminds me of earlier when that same feeling hit me after the game.

When Earl came up to me and asked about my dad, I froze. I knew I couldn't say anything about his health scare right then, but it reminded me of the severity of the situation. I've been so wrapped up in Kelsea that it's been easy to block out the imminent results of his CT scan and ignore how everything will be affected afterward. But now that we're alone and talking about the future, I know I need to confide in her.

I have to share my fears with the one person who deserves to know them and can help me through it all.

"Wyatt . . ." she starts, but I cut her off.

"There's something I need to tell you, Kelsea," I say, her lips freezing as she takes in my tone.

Swallowing roughly, she licks her lips. "Okay . . ."

"But you have to promise not to say anything to anyone. I shouldn't even be telling you because my dad asked me not to, but

CHAPTER FIFTEEN

I can't keep it in anymore." Reaching for her hand, I take a deep breath. "You're my girlfriend, my best friend—I need to tell you because it's going to affect you, too."

She pushes up from the bed, pulling the sheet over her chest. "Wyatt, you're scaring me."

"If I'm being honest, I'm scared, too, Kelsea. Terrified, actually." Swallowing down the emotion I feel bubbling up, I take her hand in mine again and squeeze it for reassurance. "My father has been having trouble seeing lately."

"What?" She sits up taller now, her eyes bouncing back and forth between mine.

Running my free hand through my hair, I nod. "Yeah. He confided in me a few weeks ago and was already in the process of getting an appointment to see his doctor. They think he has a tumor pressing on his optic nerve."

"Oh my God." Her hand covers her mouth.

"My mom knows, obviously, and I do, too. But Walker and Forrest don't yet, and neither do any of the employees at the ranch. My dad said he knew he could count on me to pick up the slack in the event he needs surgery and then recovery time. But . . ." I sigh, squeezing her hand again. "It's a lot of pressure. I don't know if I can handle managing the ranch *and* the brewery. My dad does so much around there, you know that. And I don't want to let anyone down. But fuck. Life is about to get crazier, Kels, and I need to know that you'll be there with me. I can't do this without you."

Just her presence as she listens to me tells me everything I need to know, that I can get through anything with her by my side. Fuck, I should have told her about my dad weeks ago, but we didn't know as much about his condition then as we do now.

"You could never let anyone down, Wyatt," she reassures me, even though there are tears in her eyes. "And you won't be alone. Of course you have me."

I nod and then lean my forehead against hers, feeling like I can breathe for the first time in weeks.

I've been trying not to think about it and worry myself over nothing, but I do know that the anxiety of what could happen has been resting in the bottom of my chest since my dad admitted what was going on. I know we're far from in the clear, but just knowing that Kelsea knows now—that I can lean on her through this and confess my fears—well, it's lifted the brick of anxiety and fear resting on my chest.

"We'll get through it, Wyatt."

"I know, babe. I just hope he's going to be okay. The thought of losing him, what would happen to my mom if we did . . ." Emotion clogs my throat, but I clear it away.

"Hey." She cups the side of my face, zeroing her eyes on me. "Don't think that way, okay? Let's try to remain positive and take this one step at a time."

I nod, taking a few deep breaths. And then I yank her onto my lap, holding her to my chest, letting her warmth and everything about her calm my racing heart. The sheet is tangled between us, but there's no way in hell I'm letting her go just yet.

"Thank you for telling me," she says, kissing my neck and then my temple.

"I had to. Especially when Earl asked about him today. It made it more real, you know?" I feel her nod so I lift my head. "Like other people are going to know eventually, my dad's life is going to change drastically for a while, and my day-to-day life is going to change, too."

"I could sense you stiffening when he was talking, but I thought it was in my head."

Her observation makes the corner of my mouth lift. Fuck, I love her. "See? You know me too well."

The soft curl of her lips has me itching to kiss her, so I do. "Yeah, but it comes in handy sometimes." Her eyes drop as I watch the wheels in her mind turn.

Brushing her curls from her face, I study her, feeling better about my confession but remembering she wanted to speak, too. "You were going to say something before I cut you off, weren't you?"

"Oh." She toys with the sheet between us. "It was nothing. No big deal."

I lift her chin so she's forced to look at me. "Are you sure?"

"Yup. I'm sure."

Not entirely satisfied with her answer but too tired to argue, I stifle a yawn. "Then let's get to bed. I'm beat."

"Same." She kisses my lips reverently, and then we snuggle into our usual sleeping position. "I love you, Wyatt."

"I love you, too, Kelsea. And thank you."

"For what?"

Inhaling her scent, I murmur against her hair. "For always being here when I need you."

She's quiet for a moment, and I think she's fallen asleep already. But then she speaks, her voice barely a whisper. "I'll always be here."

~

"Hey! Pass that moonshine over here!" Tim, one of the ranch hands, calls out over the dance floor set up just outside the barn at the Gibson Ranch.

It's the night of the bonfire my parents throw every season, and the party is in full swing. We played a football game earlier for our league, barely winning by a field goal, and then headed over to the ranch to celebrate and keep tradition alive.

Cheers echo over the music as people rejoice over the moonshine my father has been making since he was younger than Walker and me.

I cast my eyes in my father's direction, taking in his proud smile and position in his chair at the edge of the crowd. My mother is standing behind him, clutching his shoulder.

They got the results of his CT scan and biopsy yesterday, and as far as best-case scenarios go, his is that. The tumor is small, operable, and non-cancerous. The doctor thinks they can get it all with surgery and wants to do it sooner rather than later. Now that

CHAPTER FIFTEEN

we're in the middle of October and the wedding and tourist season is slowing down, the time to schedule it is now.

My mother cried in my arms last night, I suspect both out of relief and fear, when she and my father told me the prognosis. Now, we have to tell my brothers and the ranch employees about the changes that will be occurring over the next few months. But we all agreed to let everyone have one last night of fun before unloading a heavy dose of reality.

"Hey. You okay?" Kelsea sits on my lap, sharing my chair with me, her arm wrapped around my neck and shoulders. I look up to find her blue eyes sparkling in the glow of the strings of lights hung above us. It's a beautiful night with just a slight chill in the air. I should be soaking up every moment with her, but my mind is heavily distracted.

"Oh. Yeah, I'm all right." I try to smile to reassure her, but I can tell it doesn't quite reach my eyes. Any flicker of happiness feels forced right now, drowned by responsibility and unease.

"He's going to be okay, Wyatt. You heard what your mom said. It's the best-case scenario. We'll just remain positive, pray, and do whatever we can to help them, okay?"

Exhaling a deep breath, I rest my head on her chest. "I'm so glad I have you, Kelsea. Fuck. I don't know what I would do if I didn't have you through this."

"I'm not going anywhere." Her hands stroke the back of my head just as I hear a familiar voice above me.

"You two are so boring now."

I lift my head to find my twin brother swaying happily on his feet. "Excuse me?"

"You two act like an old married couple now. You don't join us when we go out anymore, you're constantly attached at the hip . . ."

I arch a brow at him. "Isn't this what you wanted to accomplish with your meddling, Walker?"

A hiccup escapes his lips. "Yes, but that doesn't mean we all can't still have fun." He takes a sip of his beer while rolling his eyes and then reaches for Kelsea's hand, yanking her up from my lap. "Come on, Kels. Let's dance."

Standing, I push him away and wrap my arm around her waist. "Hey. I thought we agreed no more touching."

He holds his hands up, still smiling. "You're right. I'm sorry. I may be slightly intoxicated." He winces and then holds up his thumb and forefinger with barely any space between them.

"Ya think?" Kelsea laughs. "You seem to be having fun, though."

He nods, two-stepping on his feet. "I am fun. And it was a rough week at work. I'm grateful to take the edge off tonight."

"Everything okay?"

"Yeah. It's my own shit. I'll be fine, though." He lifts his glass, scanning the crowd before locking his gaze on something and then freezing in place. I don't get the opportunity to see what's captured his attention before Kelsea pulls me toward the dance floor.

"Spin You Around" by Morgan Wallen begins just as we find

CHAPTER FIFTEEN

our rhythm. "I love this song," she croons as she starts to move. My hands reach out to pull her into my chest.

"And I love you."

Holding her close to me, I savor the moment of dancing with her in my arms. We've done this numerous times since we got together, particularly when we close together at the brewery late at night. But I don't think the feeling of knowing I get to do this with her for the rest of my life will ever get old.

This woman is my peace personified. She's light and heaven, earth's greatest treasure as far as I'm concerned.

And she's mine.

"There she is!" Evelyn slides up next to us with Schmitty trailing closely behind her.

"Here I am," Kelsea replies, taking in Evelyn's inebriated state. "I think we're the only ones who aren't three sheets to the wind, babe," she mumbles out of the corner of her mouth.

Evelyn latches on to Kelsea's shoulders. "I had some of Mr. G's moonshine."

"How much is some?" Kelsea asks, amused by Evelyn's slurring.

Evelyn widens her eyes. "A lot."

"Looks like it." I turn to Schmitty, offering him my hand. "How's it going, John?"

"Oh, you know . . . work, fuck, sleep, repeat. Not necessarily in that order." He smirks and then pulls Evelyn into him. "Have you seen Walker?"

Kelsea and I both spin to look for him. I know he was right

here a second ago, but now he's nowhere in sight. "He was just here. Maybe he went to the bathroom or something."

"Yeah." Schmitty furrows his brow. "He seems like he needs to let loose tonight. He's been in a mood at work all fucking week."

"Really?"

"Yeah. Not the Walker I'm used to, for sure." With a shrug, he leans down into Evelyn's ear. "Ready to get another drink and then find somewhere quiet, babe?"

Evelyn smiles at him over her shoulder. "Yes, sir." Her giggles carry out as Schmitty whispers something in her ear, and then she's staring at Kelsea, her eyes bugging out. "I'll see you later, girl."

"Have fun. Be safe."

"They seem like they're having fun," I say as we resume dancing.

"Yeah, but that's all it is. Just fun, according to her."

"Well, Schmitty isn't the type of guy to settle down, at least not yet. I don't know that he's ever had a serious relationship."

"I don't know that Evelyn wants that, anyway, but she says they get along well, so at least there's that. I'm just worried about her."

"I'm a little worried about my brother, too." I know that Walker can drink and party with the best of them, but lately I feel like he's doing it more to forget or avoid reality.

Music continues to play, drinks continue to flow, and the party carries on for about another hour before my dad finds the microphone and asks everyone for their attention.

"Well, I'd say we all have something to celebrate tonight, right?" Echoes of agreement rise from the crowd gathered around the dance floor, focused on my father on a platform in the corner. "Elaine and I could not be more grateful to this group of people each and every season. Without your help, your hard work and dedication to the ranch, this place wouldn't exist."

He smiles. "It started as my wife's dream," he says, glancing down at my mother, who looks swept away just watching him speak. "But then it quickly turned into mine as well—a place that offered the comfort of home, the atmosphere of adventure, and the overwhelming feeling of love. Together, we've created a masterpiece, a place for others to start their own adventures and an experience for each and every person who steps foot on this land. My wife and I thank you from the very bottom of our hearts, and we hope to see nothing but prosperity and tradition continue here for many years to come." He lifts his glass, and the crowd follows. "To you. To us. To dreams and taking the risk of making them come true." Everyone hollers in agreement and then tosses back their drinks.

My dad grabs my mother's hand and leads her out to the dance floor, twirling her around and then bringing her close to him like I've watched him do so many times before.

Their love is the kind I aspire to have with Kelsea—timeless, unconditional, and everlasting.

Instantly, I want to hold her in my arms, too, but when I turn to take her in, I pause, catching a tear stream down her face.

"You okay?"

"Yeah."

"You don't look like it."

"It's just . . . a lot." She peers up at me, her eyes looking so much darker in the soft light above us, full of sadness. And for a moment, I feel like I'm missing something twirling in her mind. But then she says, "Sometimes I forget how incredible it is to be a part of something like this."

"The ranch?"

"The ranch. Your family. This town." She sighs. "It's one of a kind, Wyatt. It's . . . home."

Spinning her around so she smacks into my chest, I brush her hair from her face and trail my finger down her cheek, absorbing how hard she makes my heart beat. "*You* are one of a kind. *You* are my home. And I love you for loving this life of ours, Kelsea Anne Baker." I dip my head down, searching for her lips. And I'm rewarded with a soft moan the second our tongues connect.

No one else exists around us when we kiss. I feel like nothing can penetrate our bubble when she's in my arms.

And as tomorrow's conversation and reality crash into me once more, so does the decision to make Kelsea mine as soon as my father is well.

I'm gonna marry this girl. I just need to make it through the next few months, and then it will be our turn to make our dreams come true.

CHAPTER FIFTEEN

"You're joking."

"Does this sound like a joking matter, Walker?" I snap, rising from my chair and standing next to my father.

"I just . . . fuck." He drops down on the couch cushion, letting his head fall in his hands. His face is a pale gray, probably from his hangover. But the bomb my parents just dropped isn't helping, either.

"The doctor said the prognosis is good, though?" Forrest interjects, standing against the wall with his arms across his chest. His face is tense and I can see the clench in his jaw, but his usual piss-poor attitude is safely tucked away.

My father clears his throat. "Yes. Best-case scenario. The tumor is small and in the perfect spot for surgical removal. I'll be in the hospital for a week, and then it will take about two months until I feel normal again. I'm gonna be out of it, not able to walk without getting dizzy, blurred vision for a while. But I got damn lucky in the grand scheme of things. This just means that I'm gonna need you boys to help out around here until I'm up and functioning again."

"If I let you," my mother mumbles. "I think we need to discuss hiring more people because I don't see how you can continue going on at this rate, Randy. You're not a young buck anymore."

"I grew a brain tumor. I didn't break my leg, Elaine."

She scowls at him, which has me fighting a grin. "Either way, this is a wake-up call. You need to accept that you can't do it all."

My father sighs. "I know."

Now's the perfect time to chime in and relieve some tension. "We're here, Dad. We will do whatever we can and need to do." I turn to look at my brothers and Kelsea, whose support means everything, now more than ever.

"Of course," Walker says, finally raising his head. "On the stretches when I'm on shift, I won't be much help, but I can pick up the slack where I can."

"I have some employees that I'm sure would be eager for some extra money. Maybe I ask if any of them would be interested in working on the ranch on the weekends when we're the busiest?" Forrest adds. I didn't even think about his construction company and the guys he has on his payroll. He's right. He has an abundance of manpower at his fingertips.

Kelsea smiles enthusiastically, clasping her hands together. "That's a great idea, Forrest. And Evelyn and I can help with cooking and cleaning, Momma G," she says as she turns to my mother. "I can be here early each morning if you need me."

My mom's eyes fill with tears. She's usually so strong, stubborn, and incapable of asking for help. She's always insisted that she can handle anything. And she's always been the true matriarch of our family, the most loyal and loving woman I've ever known. I know this is hard for her, especially coupled with the fear of losing my dad. But I can tell by the expression on her face how grateful she is to have all of us to lean on through these next few months.

"I love you kids."

CHAPTER FIFTEEN

"We know, Mom." Walker steps up to hug her.

"You boys make your mother and I proud each and every day. I hope you know that," my father adds, his own voice full of emotion. "And you, too, Kelsea."

My girl smiles and walks over to my mother for her turn at a hug and then leans down to hug my father as well.

Brushing tears from her cheeks, my mother declares, "I may just have to give you that biscuit recipe sooner rather than later, Kels."

"I promise I'll take good care of it."

"I know you will." She takes a deep breath and then reaches behind her for a dry erase board that is mapped out like a calendar. "Okay. Let's get down to the schedule, y'all, and tackle this challenge like us Gibsons do."

CHAPTER SIXTEEN

Kelsea

"God, how long has it been?" Wyatt thrusts harder, slamming the bed against the wall.

I clutch at his shoulders, moaning with each drive, never wanting this to end because I know that reality is waiting on the other side of this orgasm. But I need this release. Hell, I think we both do more than anything at this point. "I don't even know. Just keep going."

"We're never leaving this bed again, Kelsea. We're just gonna hide in here and sleep and eat and fuck until everything goes back to normal."

I moan as Wyatt hits that spot deep inside of me, stroking it with precision, building my orgasm. "Oh God . . ."

"Fuck."

CHAPTER SIXTEEN

I brace my arms against the headboard, pushing against it, arching my back and pressing my chest to the air. Wyatt leans down and latches his mouth on my nipple as he continues to pound into me, and my eyes close as I soak in every sensation.

It's been a month since Mr. Gibson had his surgery, putting us at the beginning of December now. His surgery was the first week of November and went as perfectly as the doctor envisioned. I remember sitting at the hospital with Momma G and the boys, and I swear they were all about to tear the walls down waiting for the doctor to come out with the results of the operation. And that was the moment I realized that I couldn't leave for my photography program in January even though I accepted months ago and haven't rescinded my acceptance.

My family needs me, and I wouldn't feel right if I left.

I was trying to hold on to the hope that maybe by the time Mr. Gibson was fully recovered, I could leave. But then the vortex of Newberry Springs and my life here with Wyatt kept sucking me in, reminding me of how many people count on me here, how my entire life exists in this town, and I can't just leave without letting people down and slacking on my responsibilities.

Over the past month, Wyatt and I have been running around like chickens with our heads cut off between the ranch and the brewery. I've been working the farmers market by myself, even though I asked Walker to help, but he came up with some excuse about not being able to. However, he's been at the ranch helping out in any way he can when he's available, so I considered that to be sufficient. Forrest found several employees who were eager for extra work on the weekends, so they've been helping clean animal pens, move hay bales, and set up for the last few weddings and events of the season.

Evelyn and I get up early each morning and help Momma G cook and clean for the day so she has less to do as the day goes on. I didn't realize how much baking that woman does before I ever arrive at the house on Sunday mornings, and the laundry after each guest leaves is mountainous as well. But now that I'm there every day, I'm overwhelmed by what she accomplishes on her own—and with a smile on her face, no less.

Mr. Gibson's recovery is going well, but he's getting antsy being stuck in the house, not able to go out and help. Momma G is having a hard time keeping him inside and getting him to rest instead of juggling all of the responsibilities he takes on to operate the ranch, showing me just how stubborn those Gibson boys can be.

Not that I didn't already know that from personal experience.

Surprisingly, things have been running smoothly, but we're all tired. And Wyatt and I have barely had sex since all of this started.

Which is exactly why we're taking advantage of a short break while we're both awake and functioning.

"Fuck, Kelsea. I'm gonna come."

"Yes, I'm there." My orgasm slams into me as we climax together, sparks of pleasure traveling all over our bodies, and then we lie in bed for a moment, savoring the fact that neither of us has to jump up and head out somewhere right away.

My father is coming home today. It's been almost a month

since I've seen him, so Wyatt arranged for us to have the morning free before we arrive at the brewery later tonight. Momma G insisted she could handle the baking this morning, but Evelyn will still be showing up to help her, which made me feel a little less guilty for taking the morning off.

"God, I could fall back asleep right now," I say dreamily, closing my eyes and snuggling deeper into Wyatt's body beside me.

"Same, babe. But I don't want you to miss out on seeing your dad." Just as Wyatt says that, a car door slams outside.

"Oh my God! Is he early?" I jump out of bed, running toward my window, peeking through the blinds to find him hopping down from his truck. "Shit! Get some clothes on!"

Wyatt laughs as he jumps up, deals with the condom, and then finds his sweats and a long-sleeved shirt. "God, I love it when you cuss."

"I'm serious, Wyatt. My dad knows we're together, but I don't want to flaunt that we just had sex in his house to his face."

"I'm sure your father's not stupid, Kelsea. We're twenty-six years old."

"I know. But . . . it's just weird, okay?" I toss my shirt over my head and then pull on some flannel pajama pants as well.

Wyatt walks toward me, kissing my temple. "I get it. Come on, let's spend some time with your dad."

"You two decent?" I hear as we walk down the hall. I find my father peeking his head through the front door.

"Dad!" I run toward him as he steps through the doorway and

intercepts me with his arms while I try to fight the blush of my cheeks.

"Hey, pancake! God, I've missed you." His large stature always makes me feel safe when he hugs me like only a father can. He looks over my shoulder as Wyatt joins us in the room. "Wyatt had better be taking good care of you while I'm gone."

"You know it, sir." Wyatt steps forward to shake my father's hand once we part. "Nice to see you, Mr. Baker."

"Please, son. Call me Hank." His eyes drift between us with a knowing smirk on his lips. "Did you two just wake up?"

"Yup," I answer a little too quickly, and Wyatt grins at me. "We haven't been able to sleep in since Randy had his surgery, so we're enjoying our morning off."

"How's he doing?" My father steps around me, heading toward the kitchen where he could probably smell that a full pot of coffee awaits. I set a timer on it last night so it would be ready for us when we woke up.

Wyatt leads me to a stool at the counter and then follows my father into the kitchen. "Really well. He's going a little crazy not being able to be outside and as active as he was before, but my mother is keeping him in his place."

My dad grabs three coffee cups from the cupboard and then moves to fill them. "Sounds about right. Elaine was the only one who could ever keep Randy in line."

"Well, she's doing a damn good job," Wyatt replies.

"I'll have to go by and see him since the last time I was able to was right before his surgery." He lifts his cup to his mouth, smacking his lips with approval.

"I'm sure he'd love that."

"You two hungry? I can make some breakfast," I offer, hopping off my stool to search the fridge for bacon and eggs.

Wyatt comes up behind me and spins me around to face him. "How about I cook and you go take a nice hot shower or maybe even a bath if you want? We have time."

"Are you sure?"

"Yes, Kels. I can keep your dad company, and by the time you're done, the food will be ready."

I want to fight him. I do. But a bath sounds heavenly. "Okay. If you insist."

Wyatt kisses my lips. "I do. Now go."

"I'll be back, then," I say as I exit the kitchen. "You two behave while I'm gone, all right?"

"Take your time, pancake. We'll be right here." My father lifts his cup in the air assuringly.

I saunter down the hallway and into my bathroom, discarding my clothes as the tub fills up. When I dip my legs into the scalding water, I melt and slowly sink into the tub until the water covers my shoulders, warming my sore muscles and aching joints instantly.

An overwhelming sadness comes over me as I close my eyes and lean my head back, faintly hearing my father and Wyatt talking in the kitchen—the two most important men in my life in the same place.

I should be happier than a pig in mud right now. I should be overrun with an assurance that tells me everything is exactly as it should be in my life at this moment.

But I'm not.

I'd say I'm about eighty percent there, but not completely.

Because that other twenty percent? That other twenty percent keeps dragging up what ifs and what nows.

I feel like I'm trapped, and that panic has been resting in my chest much more over the past week, especially as the photography program looms closer and closer and I haven't outwardly settled on my decision. As far as the program knows, I'll be there in a month. But my mind keeps telling me that I can't go, no matter how badly I want to.

I feel like I'm never leaving Newberry Springs now. I feel like I'm never going to see the world outside of this little town.

Part of me already resigned myself to that fact months ago when Wyatt told me about his dad, but I guess a sliver of me was still holding onto hope that I could attend the program. Back when I showed my photos to Wyatt the first time and he was so supportive of them, I was optimistic that we could find a way for me to leave town but still be together.

How would you be able to do that when you still haven't told him?

I argued back. *It just never seemed like the right time.*

Really? So when you saw him every day, you couldn't find a moment to speak with him about it?

Not when we've been managing everything over the past month, no.

CHAPTER SIXTEEN

I should have told him that night when I showed him my pictures, in that very moment, so he knew how important it was to me.

But now, all I wonder is if that opportunity is completely gone.

Is this all I'll ever have or be?

Will it be enough?

Some days, I feel like it is. Some days, I forget about my other dreams completely and focus on visions of little blonde-haired kids running around and jumping up into Wyatt's arms.

But some days—like today—I mourn, afraid to face the loss of another life, even though I love the one I'm currently living. And all the while wondering if it's really possible to ever have it all.

CHAPTER SEVENTEEN

Wyatt

"So what do you think?" I watch Forrest scour the house, his head tilted back as he studies the ceiling. Naturally, I wanted my construction-company-owning brother to assess the home I'm currently in escrow on just for added comfort.

"Foundation looks solid. There's a crack in the ceiling, but that may just be from the drywall separating. If so, that's an easy fix."

I nod. "I thought so, too."

As his legs carry him around the home and I watch him check doorways, plumbing lines, and electrical, all I can see is Kelsea in the kitchen with a few little kids tucked in around a giant farm table in the dining room. Visions of us watching a movie with our kids on our laps and our brood running around the massive

CHAPTER SEVENTEEN

backyard and the rest of the property have visited me in my dreams, too.

This is it. This is the house that we're going to live the rest of our lives together in.

"Have you turned on the heater yet?" Forrest rubs his arms through his flannel as he makes his way back over to me. It's mid-December, and a stark Texas winter is in full effect.

"Yeah, they did during the inspection. But we'll probably use the wood-burning stove most of the time."

"And Kelsea doesn't know about the house yet?"

I shake my head as my lips tip up in a grin. "Nope. And she doesn't know about this, either," I say, reaching deep into my pocket and extracting the black velvet box I've been carrying around for the past week.

"Aw, shit. You bought a ring, didn't you?" my brother teases, reaching out to grab the box from my hand. When he pops it open, I can see the approval in his eyes along with a little bit of regret.

"I did, and I asked her dad for permission." My thoughts drift back to the conversation I had with him in his kitchen last week while Kelsea was in the bath. It was the perfect opportunity to get his blessing, and now there's nothing else holding me back. "I'm gonna marry her as soon as I can, Forrest. I've waited long enough."

He snaps the lid closed and tosses the box back over to me, running a hand through his hair as he spins away. "I'm happy for you."

Really? Because you don't seem like it. "Thanks. I'm getting everything I've ever wanted."

He huffs out a disheartened laugh. "Yeah, you are."

"It's not too late to go after what you want, too, Forrest." I hate seeing my brother like this, masking pain and regret with a surly attitude and burying himself in work.

He spins his head toward me. "Yeah, it is, Wyatt."

"But . . . ?"

"Just leave it alone, okay?" he asks, holding his palm up to me. "This isn't about me. It's about you and Kelsea. And I'm proud of you. This is a big step, but you seem to be ready."

"I am."

"And is Kelsea?"

His question catches me off guard. "Uh, yeah. Why wouldn't she be?"

"I'm not saying she isn't. I guess I'm just wondering if you two have talked about all of this."

Defensiveness roots itself in my chest. "Of course we have. We're on the same page. This is everything we both want."

He nods slowly, taking one more look around the house I bought for us, the home that will hold all of the memories for the rest of our lives. "Then cherish it. Don't take it for granted for a second."

"I don't plan on it."

"Good. The house is in good shape. It's a solid buy. If you want to renovate anything, let me know, and we can work out a deal. But you made a good choice, Wyatt. With this house and with Kelsea."

"Yeah, I know."

"Hey, babe." I walk up behind her at the brewery, wrapping my arms around her waist as she stiffens and then relaxes once she realizes it's me. She's currently in the stock room, gathering more supplies for the main floor.

"Hey. How was your day?"

"Good. Busy."

"Yeah? Where were you?"

"Just . . . places."

She twists in my arms, eyeing me curiously. A few blonde curls frame her face—the rest of them are pulled back in a ponytail.

Fuck, I can't wait to marry her.

"Places? Well, that's vague."

Fighting my need to strip her bare and claim her in this supply closet, I shrug like what I have to share with her isn't a huge fucking deal. "I have something to talk to you about later, okay? Once we're done with this shift."

Her lips slowly spread into a smile. "Okay . . ."

"Nothing to worry about, Kels. It's all good things. We'll talk later, I promise." I press a kiss to her lips, then her nose, and then slowly back away before I blurt out everything I want to say to her—or maul her, since we're actually alone.

"All right. Things are getting crazy out there. I just came back to grab more napkins for out front, and the paper towels are empty in the restroom."

I grab the paper towels from her hands. "I'll take care of these, then. See you out there."

"I love you, Wyatt," she says, almost like she's convincing herself of that fact. And I hate that her tone has my heart pounding now out of concern rather than excitement.

"I love you, too, Kels." I lean in for one more kiss and then exit the room, shaking off the worry that's creeping up my limbs, and get back out to my business, hoping the time goes by quickly so I can talk with her later tonight about everything I've been up to.

Life is happening at warp speed, but it's playing out just as I imagined. Every day feels like living in a dream, a world I envisioned for so long, but one I was convinced could only exist in my mind. But it's now a reality—and yet, I feel like I'm waiting for it to slip between my fingers, robbing me of the fulfillment the last few months have given me after years of emotional turmoil.

By the time Kelsea and I walk inside her house, it's after eleven. We had a late-night rush on a Thursday for some reason, and we both felt guilty enough to stop us from leaving in the middle of it. I had to go back in the kitchen to help the cooks get the food out in a timely manner, so I'm covered in grease and smell like cheeseburgers and French fries.

CHAPTER SEVENTEEN

"God, I need a shower," I mutter as we stumble through the front door.

"Me, too," she replies as we step into the kitchen and a splash of water ripples out beneath our feet. "What the—?" She flicks on the light, and the shine of water all over the floor instantly assaults our eyes.

"Shit." I toss my keys on the counter and move to the kitchen sink immediately, noticing water running from underneath the cabinets. And sure enough, as I open the cupboards, I see the pipe leaking. "Where does your dad keep his tools?"

"In the garage. Is it bad?"

"Well, any leak isn't good." I rise and head for the garage as quickly as I can, looking for a wrench, hoping the ring connecting the two pipes is just loose. Once I find what I'm looking for, I run back inside, crouching down under the sink to assess the issue. "I don't know the extent of the damage, but I'm going to try this first." Tightening the metal ring around the two pipes has the water stopping at once. "Thank fuck. I think that was it."

"How the heck did that get loose?"

"It happens," I reply as I duck out from underneath the sink and notice the water is all over the counter, too. "Shit, maybe there's a disconnection up here, too." Reaching for the faucet, I notice it's swiveling in place. Water has seeped all over the surface around it and down into the drawers surrounding the sink.

"This is just great." Her defeated tone has me irritated, too, when I think about the plans I had for us this evening—which didn't include cleaning up this mess.

"It's an easy fix." Twisting the faucet back in place, I wait to see if any more water is going to leak out. "But just to be on the safe side, maybe we should buy a new one tomorrow. I can install it first thing in the morning before heading to the ranch and then working at the brewery."

She lets out a heavy, frustrated sigh. "This isn't ever going to end, is it?"

"What?"

"The chaos that is our lives right now."

"Hey." I set the wrench on the counter and then pull her into my arms. "Yes, it will. You'll see. Come the beginning of the year, things will start to go back to normal."

She casts her eyes down at the floor. "I guess. I need a shower. Will it be safe for me to take one?"

I toss a look back at the faucet. "Yeah, you should be good. I'll start cleaning up in here."

"Thank you," she says, still avoiding my gaze before kissing my lips and then moving out of the kitchen and down the hall. But watching her go feels strangely like she's slipping away from me, and not just in respect to the physical distance between us.

As I turn back to the flood in the kitchen, I realize some of the drawers are probably going to need to be emptied from the water spilling off the counter. After I locate towels from the hallway cabinet, my feet carry me back into the room to start soaking up the water from the floor and countertops. I open up drawer after drawer, grateful that not all of them had water, even though some were worse than others. When I get to the junk drawer—because everyone has one of those—I start pulling odds and ends out, including a stack of folded papers in the back, spreading everything out on the dry counters.

But then my eye catches on a letter with Kelsea's name in the address line. And as I pick it up, I can feel the wheels start to spin in my head.

Miss Baker,
We are pleased to inform you that you have been selected to attend our Amateur Photography Program that starts on January 5th. We were impressed with your portfolio and look forward to working on your craft with you. Please respond to our admissions office by phone or email as soon as possible to secure your spot.
Sincerely,
New York Life Photography Institute

"What the heck is this?" I mutter to myself out loud, checking over my shoulder to make sure that Kelsea is still in the shower. As if rereading it will make the anxiety go away, I continue to stare at the words, ruminating over what this means.

And then I check the date. This was sent just before Kelsea and I got together, before I pulled my head out of my ass and realized that I'd lose her to someone or something if I didn't act on the feelings I've always had.

Did she accept? Or did she just shove this letter away and pretend it didn't exist?

More importantly, why didn't she tell me?

A wild stampede of horses gallops through my chest as a million questions run through my mind. But I keep coming back to one in particular: *Why on earth didn't she tell me?*

I feel her presence enter the kitchen. And when I lift my eyes to see her fresh from the shower, her entire countenance is terrified.

"Wyatt?"

I take a moment to think about what I want to know next, cautious not to let my anger fuel my reaction. "So you're leaving in a few weeks?" I ask as I hold up the letter.

She shakes her head, her hands trembling as she brings them to her chest and walks over to me. "No. I was going to go, but not anymore."

"What do you mean you were going to go?" *God, she was planning on leaving. What the hell does this mean for us?*

She bites her bottom lip, contemplating her next words, but all I can think is that this conversation feels a lot like losing her despite her standing right in front of me, telling me otherwise.

"I called originally and accepted, but I changed my mind."

"Do they know that?"

Her eyes fall, and suddenly I realize that she's undecided—about a lot of things, and not just this photography program.

I hold up the paper again, warring with myself. Part of me is so fucking proud of her for taking a risk and putting herself out there, especially with her passion.

But the other part is terrified that the inkling of her slipping

CHAPTER SEVENTEEN

away from me wasn't truly all in my head—because part of her really has been holding back. And this must be why.

Breathing out, I take a minute to choose my words carefully. "Why on earth didn't you share this with me, Kels? I'm so fucking proud of you—for taking this risk, for going after your dreams. But . . ." I shake my head, clenching and unclenching my jaw. "I can't believe that you might be leaving. You kept this from me, and it fucking hurts."

I think of all the talks we've had about the future, about the house I'm currently in the process of buying, about the visions of our life together in Newberry Springs that are growing fuzzier with each passing second.

And then her face shifts, the anger I've seen her mask many times before coming out like a lion out of a cage. "I've kept things from you *many* times, Wyatt. Every time you asked if I had a crush on another boy. Every time you'd accidentally or carelessly touch me and you apologized and I told you it was okay—because I told myself I was crazy for feeling things for you. Every time you asked if we'd be best friends forever—because I never wanted to have to choose between having you and *not* having you in my life. But now I finally have you. And *that* is why I didn't tell you."

She stares at me, tears welling in her eyes.

"How do I choose?" she cries through her words now, words laced with sorrow and fury. "How do I choose between you and something I've been dreaming about for years? Another life that is far away from this one in Newberry Springs?"

Her admission smacks me in the heart, twisting the knife,

making me bleed anguish and regret. She wants to go, but she doesn't know if she should.

And even though my heart knows what to do, my head is fighting for everything I've been planning since I kissed her—marrying her, having a family, buying a big house to build a life together in.

Fear comes alive in her eyes as she takes a step closer to me. "I'm not going, Wyatt. I'm staying here for you, your family, and the brewery. I have responsibilities here, a life. I can't just up and leave, even though I want to."

"Do you hear what you're saying?" I back away from her, suddenly feeling like the walls are closing in. "You have to go, Kelsea. I—I don't want you to resent me if you don't. You—"

"Wyatt, please," she pleads, cutting me off. "Can we just pretend this didn't happen?" I feel her try to reach out to me, but I move out of the way before she can touch me. "I can't lose you."

The sting of her wanting to leave is burning a hole in my chest. Her decision to withhold something so important to her from me is only widening it. And hearing her want to pretend this didn't happen, that I didn't see that letter, that she feels trapped here, is only lengthening the crack in my heart.

This means there's something to lose—and it's *us*, just like we feared.

I grab my keys from the counter and then head for the front door. "I think I need some space to process this."

"Wyatt, no! Please, don't go!" She calls out for me, but I just keep moving down the porch steps to my truck. "Are you breaking up with me?" she yells into the night.

Looking over my shoulder at her, I shout back, "No, Kelsea. I love you. But right now . . . I need a minute. I need to come to grips with the fact that I might lose you all over again. And I don't know if I can handle that."

As I drive back to my place, an unsettledness in my body that I hoped to God I would never feel with Kelsea, one thing still remains clear in my mind.

That woman is my soulmate, the person I'm supposed to be with.

But she wants to leave, and I have no idea how to manage all of my feelings about that right now.

~

"It's really early, Wyatt. What on earth are you doing here?"

Running on fumes because I barely slept at all last night, I arrive at my parents' house far too early for a Friday morning. "Couldn't sleep."

"Why?"

Glancing over at my mother, I know I'm better off being honest with her than trying to pretend that everything is fine. Because it's not. And I have no idea if Kelsea is going to show up at the ranch this morning after last night.

God, I was so fucking hurt by her withholding something so important to her that I *had* to leave before that hurt turned to anger. But the second I got home, I realized I should have stayed and talked to her more.

I just needed some goddamn space at the time.

I'm not the type of man to walk out on my girl, especially when she's obviously conflicted about her decision, which affects both of us. She honestly feels like she can't leave because of me and her job. She'd rather stay here than take an adventure of a lifetime, something that she truly wants. I could feel the internal battle she was fighting, see the hope and fear warring in her eyes.

But now, I'm just sad—devastated at the idea of her leaving, empty at the thought of her being hundreds of miles away from me, and missing her already even though she isn't even gone yet.

But I know she's going—because she deserves this, and I'll be damned if she looks back on our life together with regrets. I just don't know what that means for us, though.

Will she want to do long distance? Would it be better to have a clean break and hope she returns to a life with me? Should I back out of the house and buy an apartment in New York so we can be together while she's there?

Or what if she meets someone while she's there or gets a job opportunity that leads her away from Texas completely?

So many questions are swirling through my mind that I feel like my head is spinning and I can't gain my footing again.

"Kelsea and I got into a fight last night," I admit, waiting for my mother's reaction. "I mean, it wasn't really a fight, per se—a disagreement, I guess."

"Well, that happens in a relationship. Is it something you can

CHAPTER SEVENTEEN

discuss with your momma, or is it unsuitable for my ears?" she teases.

"No, nothing inappropriate." I take a seat on one of the stools at the counter and reach for a biscuit from the basket. "She . . ." I exhale and then blurt it out. "She got into a photography program in New York that starts in January, and she wants to go."

My mother's eyebrows shoot up. "Well, holy hell! That's amazing, Wyatt. So why were you fighting about it?"

"She never told me. I found her acceptance letter last night, and she said she decided not to go even after she accepted."

I watch my mother's brow furrow in thought. "That doesn't seem like something Kelsea would do."

"That's what I thought. Heck, Mom. We tell each other everything. Why would she keep this from me?" That question is playing like a broken fucking record, over and over.

"Well, if she lied to you or kept this from you, there has to be a reason."

"I could see it all over her face, Momma. She wants to go, she just doesn't think she can."

"And why is that?" She places her hands on her hips.

"Because of me," I grumble, distraught that I could be the reason she holds herself back from this. I clench my fists against the urge to punch a hole through a wall because I'll be damned if I'm the one who prevents her from following her dreams.

"Let me ask you something, Wyatt." She picks up her scoop and starts filling muffin tins while she talks. "Do you ever regret leaving Newberry Springs and getting a degree?"

Her question has me stumbling in my thoughts. "What? No."

"You left, did what you needed to do, had an adventure, and then came back, right?"

"Yeah . . ." She lifts a brow at me, not continuing at all. And then it hits me. "Kelsea never did."

"Bingo," she says, pointing her scoop at me. "That girl has been here her entire life. She has loved you for most of it, and yet, she hasn't truly lived."

"Shit." I lower my head in my hands, knowing now more than ever that she needs this. "But what if she never comes back, Momma?"

"That's just a risk you're going to have to take. That girl has been here every day, helping us—you, me, and your father—build our businesses, live out our dreams. And now, it's her turn. If what you two have is true love, you'll work through it. You'll find a way for you to both get what you want."

"I just want *her*."

"I know, hun. But that girl needs to fly a little. Spread her wings, soak up something else besides this town. She'll never truly live and be one-hundred-percent happy if she doesn't."

Fuck, I don't want her to end up resenting me, resenting our home, leaving like her mother did when she realizes she wants more than this small-town life.

It would kill me to constantly wonder if she were happy with everything I have to offer her or if she's silently contemplating her exit, if regret and resentment would become her new best friends instead of me.

CHAPTER SEVENTEEN

"I know, Momma. But . . . well, I didn't exactly react to the news very well."

She flashes me a disappointed look. "I guessed as much since you're here sulking and Kelsea already texted me to say she wouldn't be coming by this morning. The good news is, in a few more weeks, your dad and I won't be needing the two of you much more, anyway. His last checkup with the doctor is next week, and then after Christmas and New Year's is over, I'm allowing him to venture back to work. However, he won't be doing things to the level that he was before, that's for damn sure."

It's hard not to crack a smile at her take-charge attitude. "I think that's a good move, even though I know he won't be too happy about it."

Suddenly, her eyes mist over. "All it takes is coming close to losing someone you love once to realize that life can end so quickly, you'd be a fool not to make each day count. It's natural to want to protect someone you love, hold on to them to keep them safe—but that can become stifling, too. As much as it scares me, I know your father is missing a piece of his heart not being able to work on the ranch. And I don't want to be the one to keep him from that, even though this entire thing made me realize how quickly life can change in an instant."

And just like that, I know what I have to do. I need Kelsea to know how apologetic I am, how much I love her, how I only want to support her in anything she wants because that's what she's always done for me.

That woman has always been my rock and my biggest cheerleader, but now it's my turn to be hers.

Standing from the stool, I grab one more biscuit. "Do you really need me this morning, Momma?"

Her smile has me feeling better instantly. "No, Wyatt. I think we've got it handled around here. Go get your girl. Make this right. Kelsea is worth every fight and miscommunication you two will have. You just have to make sure you work through them, that's all."

"Don't I know it." I kiss my mom on the cheek before running out the door, back into my truck, and racing to her house, hoping and praying she'll talk to me, let me apologize and explain.

As I drive, I reach into the glovebox and take out the ring box, popping it open and debating whether I should ask her the moment I see her—once she knows that I'll be here waiting for her and support her in whatever she decides, that is.

I'm not sold on the idea, but I figure it wouldn't hurt to have the ring in my pocket just in case.

By the time I arrive at her house, my body is bouncing with adrenaline. I can fix this. I know what I need to do. I was wrong to walk away from her, and it's time to be the man I promised her I would be.

I knock on the door, looking behind me to see her truck is still here. But she doesn't answer after a few minutes. Walking around the porch, I try to peek inside, but all of the blinds are shut and the curtains over the windows are closed, so then I check the front door to find that it's locked.

CHAPTER SEVENTEEN

My mind goes to calling her next as I reach into my back pocket, bring up her number, and hit send. But the call goes straight to voicemail.

"Hi! You've reached Kelsea! I can't answer right now. Please leave me a message, and I'll get back to you as soon as I can."

I wait for the beep and then frantically speak. "Hey, babe. It's me. Where are you? I'm at your house, and I just . . . Fuck, Kelsea. I'm so sorry. I want to talk to you, to work this out, but not over the phone. Call me, please, as soon as you get this. I love you."

I hang up and then call back just in case, but the call goes straight to voicemail again.

"Fuck!" My hands reach for my hair, yanking on it in frustration, and I pound a fist on the side of the house. But then I realize I can't just sit around and wait for her. I need to find her now.

I pull up my brother's name on my contact list and wait for him to pick up, each ring dragging on and on until I feel like I'm about to snap.

"Hello?"

"Walker, do you know where Kelsea is?"

"Why would I know where she is? She's *your* girlfriend," he counters, the noise from the firehouse in the background.

"I'm aware, doofus. I can't find her, though."

"What? Why?"

"I don't have time to get into that."

"Sorry, man. I don't know where she is. Have you tried calling Evelyn?"

Shit. Evelyn, her best friend. Of course she needs to be the next person I call.

"No, but I'm calling her after I hang up. Thanks."

"Hope everything's okay, Wyatt."

"It will be." *I hope.*

I end the call and immediately scroll back up to find Evelyn's number, hitting the button as fast as my finger will allow.

I have to wait three rings before she answers. "Hello?"

"Evelyn. Hey. Do you know where Kelsea is?" Her silence has my pulse spiking. "Evelyn? Did you hear me?"

She finally clears her throat and then answers me. "Yeah, I heard you."

"So . . . do you know where she is?"

"God, Wyatt. Why did you have to be so stupid last night?"

The fact that she didn't answer my question isn't lost on me, but I'm too flustered to acknowledge it. "I was stupid, Evelyn. I was blindsided, only thinking about myself, when Kelsea should have been the focus. But I need to talk to her, so if you know where she is, you have to tell me."

With a heavy sigh, she grumbles. "I technically don't have to tell you shit, Wyatt. But I will say this—you won't be able to talk to her for at least three hours."

"Three hours? Why?"

"Because your girlfriend is on a plane to New York right now."

My stomach drops in a free fall. "What the fuck?" Nausea swirls in my gut as I blink rapidly, staring out over the field surrounding Kelsea's house.

I'm too fucking late.

"She left, Wyatt. She's on her way to New York. I just dropped her off at the airport for an early flight."

My shock quickly morphs into anger. "What the fuck, Evelyn? Why would you do that?"

Her fire comes out. "Because she's my best friend, Wyatt, and that girl has decisions to make, decisions that you're not helping her make by not supporting her!"

"But I *do* support her. I want her to go!" I drag my hand through my hair. "Fuck, I drove all the way to her house right now to talk to her about it, to make a plan so she can leave and not feel guilty because that's the last thing she should feel."

"How would she know that, though, based on your reaction last night? You made her feel horrible."

"I know. I fucked up, okay? Shit! She's really gone?" The desire to throw up and scream simultaneously comes on strong.

"Yes, she's gone. But only for two days. I wouldn't let her stay longer than that. I told her that if she's not back in two days, I'd fly up there myself and bring her back home."

"I thought the photography program didn't start until January fifth?"

"It doesn't. But she wanted to clear her head, and I suggested she take a trip to the city to see if it was everything she's been fantasizing about." I hear her blow out a breath. "You have no idea how hard it has been for that girl to decide whether or not to leave you here so she can chase her dreams, Wyatt. You have *no* idea."

As I pinch the bridge of my nose, regret infiltrates my mind. "I think I do now, because the thought of her going is crushing me, but I know that she needs to. She deserves this. It kills me, but I fucking want this for her. She deserves to pursue her fucking dreams, Evelyn."

"Yes, she does. See? I knew you weren't a douchebag!" she shouts.

"Does she hate me?" I ask, terrified of the answer.

Her voice softens. "No. She fucking loves you. But she feels like she has to choose and she's letting everyone down if she goes. I wish she could just see that it's okay to want something for herself, that this town and the people in it won't fall apart if she's not here for a while."

"I want her to see that, too. Fuck, she has to know that, right?"

"I think she does. But in the meantime, just give her some time. Let her get carried away in the excitement, and let her heart lead her to what she knows is the right thing for her to do. And then, when she gets home, fucking grovel, Wyatt. Grovel like you've never groveled before."

I let out a laugh that is part relief and part sorrow. "I will. I promise."

"Good. Now, I have my own business to run, so I must get off of here and focus on driving back to our sweet little town to do so."

"Okay. Thanks for letting me know where she is, Evelyn."

CHAPTER SEVENTEEN

"I'll always look out for her safety, Wyatt. And I know you'd go mad if you didn't know she was safe."

"I appreciate it."

When I hang up with Evelyn, my body sags to the porch steps of her house, defeated in the wake of my idealistic views of how this would go.

She left. She ran to New York, and I can't blame her after I ran out on her last night. And now, all I can do is wait and hope that when she returns, she can find it in her heart to forgive me.

Even though I know she'll be back in two days, when she leaves for real in January, it will be months of us apart. Months of not sleeping next to her, waking up with her, seeing her every day at the brewery or for our weekly breakfasts at Rose's. It will be a completely different world without my beacon of light everywhere I turn.

Because Kelsea brightens up my world in every way imaginable.

I just hope she'll want to continue to do so if and when she comes back.

CHAPTER EIGHTEEN

Kelsea

I don't think I've ever made a rash decision like this in my life, but the second I stepped off the plane, I felt like I could breathe.

When I called Evelyn sobbing after Wyatt left, she convinced me to take this opportunity to do some thinking and nonchalantly suggested that I do it in New York. So with her help and a charge on my credit card, I booked a flight to the city that's been calling to me in my dreams.

Snowflakes flutter down outside as I walk through the airport, trying to find my way to the baggage claim as people stride past me, ignoring everyone around them as they trek toward their destinations.

I am definitely not in Texas anymore.

CHAPTER EIGHTEEN

Once I lift my bag from the conveyor belt, I make my way outside to wait for the Uber I ordered. I pull my coat tighter around my body as the chill in the air hits my face.

There are so many noises, so many lights, so many people and cars that I feel like I've been transplanted into a city that feels like another planet.

When my Uber arrives, I hurry into the car, shaking off the snow from my jacket as the driver puts my suitcase in the trunk.

"The Manhattan at Times Square, right?" the driver confirms.

"Yes, please."

"No problem."

My driver pulls out into traffic as I sink into the seat and brace myself for the messages waiting on my phone. But I'm just not ready to face them yet, and impending doom rests heavily on my heart. Instead, I use the ride to scour the cityscape around me and absorb my new surroundings.

On the way to the airport, Evelyn helped me book my hotel and gave me a stern warning that I had to return to Newberry Springs after my two days away when I told her what happened the night before. It was easy to assure her that I would because I'm not sure that I'm cut out for this life, anyway. But I knew that running from my problems wasn't going to solve anything. I just needed to get some distance, some clarity on the matter before I ended up making things worse.

Wyatt said he needed time and space to think, so I decided taking the same for myself wouldn't be the end of the world. However, Wyatt's reaction last night when he found the acceptance letter—a letter that I should have just talked to him about in the first place—was everything I feared would happen.

I know I should have told him, and I still haven't figured out why I didn't. But I never imagined he'd walk away without talking everything out, for his hurt to be so glaring that the entire foundation of our relationship had been shaken.

So I panicked. I needed to escape, if only for a few days. I needed to get my head on straight and figure out my feelings and thoughts instead of swimming in a sea of muddled awareness. And a little suggestion from my best friend was the shove I needed to give in to that pull.

I've never done something like this before, this impulsive decision to take off without letting anyone know. Hell, not even my dad knows that I left. The only person I confided in was Evelyn because she knew —*she knew* how I screwed up, *she knew* why I did what I did, and *she knew* that I needed to take this trip to come to grips with it all.

Plus, I had to see New York for myself. I had to know if everything I imagined was as fabulous in person or if I had built up this idea of studying here in my head.

Buildings stretch up into the gray skies around me, red brake lights flash everywhere the car goes, and I have never seen so many people walking from place to place before in my life. The only street you can walk along easily in Newberry Springs is Main Street, and that's because it's where dozens of shops are located. Getting anywhere else requires a truck or a car.

Once I check into my hotel, I take a nice hot shower to rid

CHAPTER EIGHTEEN

myself of the stench of the plane and help me relax. It was a long night without much sleep, and the anxiety of flying for the first time on a whim had my body riddled with tension.

As I nestle into my bed, I take a deep breath and then turn my phone back on, watching with anticipation as notifications ring out —the most notable ones being missed calls and voicemails from Wyatt. I press the button to listen and hear the panic in his voice when he realized I wasn't home, his concern pulling tears from my eyes.

I don't want to hurt him. That's the last thing I've ever wanted to do. It's why I was so undecided, why I didn't see a way to take this opportunity without some sort of sacrifice.

But he hurt me, too. He sliced through the hope I'd been holding onto. He smashed our future into a scrambled mess with his words. He ran instead of talking to me about it.

As I wipe away the tears, I click on my text messages. There's one from Evelyn asking me to call her as soon as I land, but I'll just send her a text instead.

There's one from Walker asking me to call Wyatt since he's looking for me.

And then one from Wyatt himself.

Wyatt: *I spoke to Evelyn. I know you're in New York. I'm not mad. I'm just so sorry, Kelsea. I love you so fucking much. And I'll be here when you get back. I promise, we can work through this. Just please, don't give up on us. Have a good time. Talk to you soon. And please, let me know that you're safe.*

I type the two words *I'm safe*. And then, for good measure, *I love you, too*, before I hit send.

And then I turn off my phone again.

His words actually ease some of the ache in my heart, but my mind is still swimming with questions and possibilities.

But that was my reason for leaving, wasn't it? To see if this is what I really want?

So that's what I'm going to do. I already have an appointment with the head of the program tomorrow, which wasn't easy to get last minute, especially before the holidays, but I charmed her secretary with my southern drawl and may have lied about an emergency. I have questions, and I hope she has answers, answers that will help me make some decisions of my own very quickly.

～

"Miss Baker. It is such a pleasure to meet you in person." Shaking the hand of Alice Clayton, the head of the Institute's Amateur Photography Program, has me swallowing down the nerves swimming in my gut.

"I can't tell you how grateful I am that you made time to meet with me today. I know the holidays are just around the corner, but I'm sort of conflicted about what to do with my situation."

She furrows her brow as we both take our seats, mine on the opposite side of her desk. "What's the conflict?"

"Well, I know that I accepted the opportunity to attend the program in just a few weeks, but things back home have changed,

CHAPTER EIGHTEEN

and I guess I'm kind of undecided at the moment about whether I can still come."

Her worry lines soften. "I'm sorry to hear that. I will say that this program is very competitive, and our attendees are carefully selected in an arduous process."

My shoulders deflate. "I can only imagine. But—"

"Do you know why we picked you?" she interrupts, surprising me.

"Um. Well, not exactly."

As she rummages through a drawer in her desk, my body shakes involuntarily. "Here we go." She places a navy-blue folder on the desk and opens it, showing me printouts of the photos I submitted with my application. "This was the photo that made the difference for me." She turns it around so I can see it the right way, and the shot has me gasping.

It's a picture of Wyatt at the ranch, resting one foot and his forearms on the steel fence that surrounds the horse pens. He's smiling that casual, effortless smile of his that has always melted my heart as his brothers, Mr. Gibson, and Momma G all stand around. They were mid-conversation about something I have no recollection of, but all I saw was their bond—the family I was a part of, their hearts and souls poured into the world around them. The reverent look Wyatt was giving his family, as if he knew just how unique their connection was—all captured by my eyes first and then captured by my camera.

"This one?"

She nods, her smile building in the span of a few seconds.

"Yes. You see, we get thousands of applications, but rarely do we get photos like these. There's a story here, a message, a moment frozen in time between a family. There's a world in this photo that has me itching for more details. There are laugh lines and wrinkles on those faces that speak of joy and a life well-lived. The beauty in this picture is of a world that very few ever get to live in. We don't see that here in the big city, surprisingly," she jokes as I huff out a laugh and fight my tears from her words. "But *you* took that picture, Kelsea. You have a fresh perspective on something that we don't often see, and that's why we wanted you."

"Wow. Thank you so much. I'm . . . speechless." Choking back the sob that wants to escape, I say, "I had no idea that my photos could make an impact like that."

"They do. And they did, for me and the entire admissions panel."

Tracing over the picture in front of me, I let a confession out. "I guess I was just afraid that maybe my stuff didn't belong here, that I was chasing something so far from where I want to be with my photography."

Alice clasps her hands together on the other side of her desk. "This program can be anything you want it to be. It doesn't mean you have to suddenly decide to shoot models and fashion ads or work for a magazine. It doesn't mean you have to travel the world as a job. This is meant for you to hone your craft, bring your vision and work to life. You just happen to get to do it in the city that never sleeps."

One tear falls as my mouth drops open, a sigh following. "Thank you. I needed this, to hear that."

"I can tell. Now, I know you have a decision to make, so I will reiterate—this program is very competitive. Your seat will be filled if you say the word, but I'd really prefer that you attend so we can push you to be even better."

"I will be here," I declare with overwhelming confidence and affirmation. Come hell or high water, I am determined to grab hold of this opportunity, no matter what the consequences may be.

"Glad to hear it. Then I will see you after the holidays?" She stands and holds her hand out to me once more.

And I gladly intercept it. "Yes, ma'am. Thank you so much again for your time."

"My pleasure, Kelsea. Own your talent. Be proud of it. You're the first person who should be before anyone else."

∼

Evelyn pulls into my driveway at eight o'clock the next night and shifts her car into park. "Home sweet home," she says as I stare up at the porch of the only house I've ever lived in.

"Yeah, it is."

"I was kind of afraid to ask you when you first got in the car, but now I have to know: Was it everything you thought?"

The corner of my mouth lifts up. "Yes. It was amazing. So different from here, Evelyn. An entirely new world with so much to see. I feel like I barely scratched the surface."

"So you're going back in two weeks?"

Inhaling deeply, I turn to face her. "I am."

"Thank God, Kelsea." She rubs my shoulder. "Do it. Don't let anything here hold you back."

I let out the breath I just took in. "I'm going, but it's not that simple, Evelyn. There's still a lot to figure out." I know what my heart wants, but I still have a few strings to tie up.

"Well, whatever you decide, you know I've got your back."

I reach over and squeeze her hand. "I do know that. And I appreciate it."

Just then, headlights bounce behind us as a familiar truck pulls up the driveway. My eyes follow the white orbs as they shut off, and my chest tightens. "Is that . . . ?"

"Wyatt," Evelyn finishes. "I know you didn't want him picking you up from the airport, but I couldn't *not* tell him when you'd be home, Kels. You two need to talk."

"I know." I stare down at my hands in my lap as I gather my courage and open the door. "Thank you again for dropping me off and picking me up, girl."

"Anytime. I hope your night goes well."

Scoffing at the idea that anything we discuss tonight will be easy, I reply, "Me, too."

As I take my suitcase out of her trunk, Wyatt hops down from his truck and stalks toward me. "Hey," he says when he arrives just a few feet from where I'm standing, an uneasiness resting between us. Nervousness radiates from him, replacing the cocky

CHAPTER EIGHTEEN

confidence and reverence I'm used to him possessing when we're together.

"Hi."

"How was your trip?" He shoves his hands in his pockets, almost like he's afraid to touch me. And I don't know if that's a good or bad thing.

"It was . . . incredible," I say on a harsh breath, admitting out loud how I feel. I don't want to lie to him again about how I'm feeling. Look at where that got us in the first place.

"Care to go inside so we can talk?"

I simply nod as he untucks his hands and then reaches for my suitcase, pulling it behind him.

After I unlock the door, I shiver from the cold air in the house. I've been gone for two days so no one has been here to heat the place up since my dad is back on the road. Wyatt stops my suitcase by the door, closes the door behind us, and then moves to the wood-burning stove, starting a fire as quickly as he can. I make my way to the hall, flicking the switch for the heater as well, hoping we'll have this place warm in no time. Though I don't even know if he'll be staying after we talk.

I know he said he loves me, that we'll figure this out, but he also has had two days to think, just like I have. He could have changed his mind, and I'm not sure what I'll do if he did.

"You thirsty?" I make my way back into the living room as I see flames spark to life in the stove.

"No. I'm fine." He stands tall and twists to face me. "Come here, Kelsea." One hand reaches out for me, and I tremble on each step toward him as my heart hammers in my chest. But then he's yanking me into his body, squeezing and holding me so tightly I can hardly breathe.

The truth is, it's been hard to breathe since that night he stormed off, anyway.

"I'm so sorry, Kelsea. God, I'm so fucking sorry." His lips are right next to my ear so I can hear the staccato of his breath, the tremor in his voice, the pain behind his words. His entire body is vibrating from his pulse, and his hands are shaky, but his hold on me is so resolute it instantly brings me peace.

"I'm sorry, too, Wyatt." Burying my head in his neck, I squeeze him back, embracing him as if I'm making up for so many mistakes with my touch. And I feel as if maybe he's doing the same.

"Don't you dare fucking apologize. I reacted all wrong, babe. I didn't run because I was angry. I was just so blindsided and scared that I didn't know what to think. I didn't know why you kept this from me instead of telling me, because we normally tell each other everything. But instead of talking to you, I bolted. I should have fucking stayed. And I promise, I'll never leave like that again."

I lean back now so I can look up into his dark brown eyes, eyes that I hope will still be around when I get back from New York. Regret swirls in the milk chocolate of his irises, and I accept in that moment that everything is going to be okay. "I know, but it's my fault that you were caught off guard. I should have told you. I should have just been honest about what I wanted from the very beginning. I was just so scared of losing you. You're

CHAPTER EIGHTEEN

everything to me, Wyatt. All I've ever known and yearned for. I didn't know how to give that up."

"That's the thing: You don't have to. You don't have to give me up, Kels. But unfortunately, I have to let you go somehow . . ." Suddenly, his face grows serious, and he's increasing the space between us. "And if I'm going to do it, I have to do it right."

"What do you mean?" I ask, panic climbing up my spine.

"Give me a minute. I need to grab something from my truck." Before I can get in another word, he flies through the front door and returns just as quickly, dragging a suitcase behind him.

The gold embellishments on the luggage gleam as the light catches them, highlighting the beautiful tan color of the fabric on the outside.

He bought me a new suitcase?

"I have something for you." He lifts the suitcase onto the couch, unzipping it with lightning speed, and then flips the top open.

When I see its contents, I gasp.

"If my girl is going to New York, she's gonna need a couple of things." He holds up a leather case for my camera. "Every photographer needs a professional case for their equipment." He grabs a book titled *A Tourist's Guide to New York City*. "And a book that will help you capture all the hidden gems while you're there."

My heart hammers as he sets those items to the side and then pulls up the fluffiest, most beautiful navy down coat with a fur-lined hood and holds it up to show me.

"And I can't have my Texas girl freezing up there, so I bought the warmest coat I could find for the days I can't warm you up myself."

My eyes fill with unshed tears. "Wyatt . . ."

He tosses the coat to the couch and then rushes toward me, pulling me into his chest. "I can get you whatever else you need, sweetheart. Just say the word. Letting you go is going to suck, but I support you. Whatever you decide. My heart wants this for you, Kelsea. We can figure out the details together, but if you don't go, you're going to end up regretting it."

"I don't know what to say."

"Well, I have something else I need to tell you."

"Okay . . ."

His face morphs from reverence to seriousness in a flash. "You're fired."

All of the oxygen leaves my lungs. "Wyatt . . . what?"

"You heard me. *You. Are. Fired.*" His body is so tense that I can't even move because I'm afraid to crumble. And I'm afraid he will let me. "That way," he pauses, his lips slowly spreading back up into a smile that has my heart thundering on bated breath, "there is nothing holding you back to enjoy this." He reaches for me again and presses his lips to mine as my mind and heart get knocked off balance.

All of my questions are cut off by his kiss, and instead of searching for clarification, I drown in the swipe of his tongue against mine—a kiss I wasn't sure I'd ever get to experience again just moments ago.

CHAPTER EIGHTEEN

When we part, I stare up at him, fighting for oxygen and clarity. "Wyatt? I'm just . . . I have no idea . . . what the heck is happening?"

Brushing the hair from my face and the tears from my cheeks, he softens his voice and continues. "I know you must have felt guilty, like you would be letting everyone down if you left. But what about *you*, Kels? What about what *you* want? Why did you think that my family wouldn't support and encourage you to chase your dreams when you helped them and *still* help them build theirs? Why did you think that I wouldn't do the same, babe?"

It takes a minute for everything he just said to sink in. "I was . . . scared. To leave, to disappoint people, to sound selfish for going after something I want. Your parents chased their dream, you left to chase yours, and so did Walker and Forrest. But I always wondered when it was going to be my turn."

He chuckles, framing my face with his hands. "It's your turn right now, babe. *It's your turn right now.*"

∼

"Where are we going?" My mind and body may be more at ease now that Wyatt and I have talked, but this little adventure is making me apprehensive again.

Wyatt told me that he wanted to show me something before we settled in for the night, but the road we're driving down is not one I've ventured on too many times before.

Living in a small town, I pretty much know where

everything's at and where everyone lives. And even though I'm familiar with the area, the house Wyatt is pulling up to doesn't exactly bring back many memories for me.

"Where are we?"

"Come with me," he says, avoiding my question and then jumping down from the truck. He runs around the front to help me out of my side. With his hand in mine, we walk up the front porch steps, and then Wyatt leans down to extract a key from a lockbox.

"Um, I don't think we're supposed to be going inside of this house if the key is locked up, Wyatt."

"Then why would I know the combo, Kelsea?" he counters sarcastically, arching a brow at me. With a twist of the key in the lock, we rush inside, out of the wind whipping around in the air. All I can see are shadows and darkness in front of me, but when Wyatt clicks on the light next to us, I gasp.

A giant living room sits to our right with built-in shelves around the wood-burning stove standing on red bricks. To the left is a formal dining room and just beyond that a kitchen that almost rivals his mother's with dark wooden cabinets and light tan marble. A staircase in front of us presumably leads to the bedrooms, but the house has my eyes bouncing all over just from what I can see.

"What do you think?" I spin to find Wyatt leaning up against the arched entryway between the space we're standing in and the dining room.

"This house is beautiful, Wyatt. But why are we here?"

As he pushes himself off the wall and stalks toward me, I

brace myself for what he's about to say. "This is *our* house, Kelsea."

"What?" I shout and then catch myself.

Wyatt laughs as he grabs my hand and leads me into the kitchen. "I bought this place for us. I'm currently in escrow, but if you don't like it or don't want this, I can still back out. Hell, if you decide you want to stay in New York after the program, I'll sell it and follow you wherever you want to go. I could even buy an apartment up there for us to live in while you're in the program, if you want."

I blink, blindsided by how willing he is to give up this home and everything else he has here. "But what about the brewery? The ranch?"

"The ranch is my parents', and I'm sure Walker or Forrest could take over. Or hell, they could sell it. I could sell the brewery, too. Ben is doing a fine job managing, so I'm sure he'd be interested."

"But, Wyatt." I shake my head, now even more confused. "This is your home. That business is your dream."

He presses a finger to my lips, silencing me. "No. *You* are my home. Wherever you are is where I want to be. And I can open up another business. I can buy another house. But there is only one of *you*, Kelsea Anne Baker. There is only one girl who is my best friend in the entire world who *also* has dreams, and I want to help make those come true. I love you. I would do anything for you. So wherever you go, I will follow. Just say the word, and I'm fucking there."

"Oh my God, Wyatt," I exclaim, throwing my hands around his neck. "I can't believe what you're saying right now."

"Believe it, Kelsea. I want you to be happy, but *you* are what makes *me* happy. You are the center of my world; you always have been. So we'll figure it out. Take it day by day. As long as we're together."

Reality slams into me knowing what comes next. "It's going to be so hard to be away from you."

"I know, babe." His grip on me tightens. "It's going to suck so fucking bad. But we've been apart before, so we can get through it again. But I know that you need to do this, and I want you to. I can fly up once a month or more to visit. FaceTime will help in between, and you know damn well I'll want to hear your voice every day. But we can do this."

"Thank you." With no more hesitation, I relinquish to him, allowing us to reconnect in every way I thought I'd lost.

"You don't need to thank me, Kelsea. My only request is that you chase this dream just as hard as you helped me chase mine." As our lips move over one another's, Wyatt backs me up to the kitchen counter and then lifts me onto the surface, digging his hands in my hair before running them all over my body.

"Wyatt, make love to me."

We waste no time discarding our clothes, even though the air in the house is frigid and we can see our breaths.

But I don't feel cold. I feel alive. I gasp like all of the oxygen in the air is mine for the taking as Wyatt lines himself up to my core. "Fuck, I don't have a condom."

CHAPTER EIGHTEEN

For a split second, I hesitate, but then I realize I will face whatever consequence befalls us from this choice. I just need to be with him right now. "I don't care. Fuck me."

"God, I love you, Kelsea," he mumbles against my lips as he thrusts deep inside of me, pulling me up and down his cock, sliding me to the edge of the counter. "I will never stop loving you, needing you, wanting you . . . every fucking part of you." He releases his grip on the back of my head and leans down to suck my nipple into his mouth.

My back arches, pushing my chest toward him. "Oh God, Wyatt. More."

No other words are spoken as we clash, claw, and hold on to each other for dear life, building the intensity and focusing on nothing but reconnecting.

My mind and heart remember how hard we fought to get here together, and that realization alone confirms what I already know in my bones.

We struggle to catch our breath as we come down from our high. But I'm not ready to part just yet, so I stroke Wyatt's back as he rests his forehead on my chest. "I want *this* life with you, Wyatt."

He lifts his head, peering deep into my eyes as he slides out of me. "What life?"

"A life here in Newberry Springs." I flash him a slow grin and then share what I've been thinking about. "I saw the director of the program when I went up there."

His back straightens, but he stays rooted in front of me.

"Okay . . ."

"She got me thinking, and now that I'm unemployed . . ." I joke, which has him smirking. "I want to start my own business when I return."

"What do you mean?"

I lift my hand, running it through his dirty blond locks, and then drag my nails along his unshaven jaw. "Part of what I love about taking pictures is capturing life and love between people, and there's no better place than Newberry Springs to find that. I want to be a photographer in our hometown. I want to capture moments that others may not see, the realness of life and relationships, a moment in time that will never happen again. I could shoot weddings on the ranch, do family sessions, birth sessions, graduation sessions—the possibilities are endless. But I want those possibilities here, with you."

Wyatt lips spread into a smile full of pride. "That idea is amazing. You would be incredible. And I think that's exactly what our hometown needs."

"Yeah?" Hope surges through my chest, and knowing that this is what I want—a life here with him and a career that involves my other passion—takes root in my soul.

"Yes. You've got talent. It's time for others to see it and for you to share it, but only if that's what you truly desire, Kels. I'm serious. I will follow you anywhere."

"New York will just be an adventure I'll get to remember for the rest of my life. But I want to learn everything I can while I'm there."

CHAPTER EIGHTEEN

"It doesn't have to be the last adventure you ever have, babe. I'll take you anywhere you want to go. We can travel whenever we want, explore places you've always wanted to see when you get back. Our life doesn't have to only be *here*, Kelsea, just as long as we live it together. That's all I fucking want." He steps back and then bends down, rifling through our clothes. But when he stands back up, the box he's holding has me fighting for air again.

"Wyatt . . ."

"Marry me, Kelsea?" He pops open the box and reveals a round solitaire diamond that is as beautiful as it is simple. When I flick my eyes up to his, I can see nothing but love, hope, and my future in them. "I want forever with you, if you haven't figured that out yet. I'm not saying we have to get married right away, but I know in my heart you are it for me. You are the syrup to my breakfast, and I can't eat dry French toast, Kelsea."

I blurt out a laugh through my tears.

"So what do you say? Will you marry me?"

"Yes," I whisper, reaching for him to smash my lips to his, faintly aware that we're still naked and this house is still freezing. But none of that matters right now.

What matters is that I get to marry my best friend. And even though that doesn't always work out—my mother and father being prime examples—I know that sometimes it does.

And Wyatt and I will be one of the couples who stands the test of time because I know that some love stories do last, even when they start at just ten years old.

CHAPTER NINETEEN

Kelsea

Six Months Later

"Oh my God, Kelsea. I cannot believe how beautiful you look!" Evelyn covers her mouth with her hand as her eyes well with tears.

"Evelyn, don't you start crying, or you're going to make me cry." I smooth my hands down my dress and face the mirror again, making sure everything is perfect. Each of my curls has been sprayed and pinned in place, and my makeup is flawless. I'm going to start freaking out if we have to redo anything.

"I can't help it. The littlest things set me off lately," she replies, reaching down to stroke the small bump starting to appear beneath her dress.

CHAPTER NINETEEN

I'm one of the only ones who know about the baby—besides Schmitty, Wyatt, and Walker, of course. But Evelyn won't be able to hide her pregnancy much longer.

She called me during the photography program in New York and told me the news, and I didn't know what to say at the time. I knew her and Schmitty weren't in a serious relationship, so I wasn't sure what that meant for them. But she assured me that he was intent on being involved—although lately, I'm not sure that's what he wants, given his behavior.

Today is my wedding day, though, and all I want to think about is me and Wyatt, so I push those thoughts about my best friend's changing world from my mind and focus on my own.

"I know. But if you don't stop, it's going to set off a chain reaction."

Momma G steps into the room at that moment, gasping the second she sees me, and then I notice her eyes welling up, too.

"See?" I gesture toward her with my hand as she and Evelyn both sniffle.

"Oh my goodness gracious. Kelsea Anne Baker, you are just the most beautiful bride on the planet."

"Thank you, Momma." I stare down at my dress again, loving the lace overlay I chose on the mermaid-style gown. "Do you think Wyatt will love it?"

"Girl, that boy is so far gone for you, he'd still marry you even if you walked down the aisle wearing a brown paper bag," Evelyn interjects, making me laugh.

"Wyatt is going to be thrilled when he sees you, Kelsea. My son loves you very much, and so do I."

My bottom lip starts to tremble. "I know. I love you, too."

She walks over to me, gathering me in her arms, the arms of the only true mother I've ever known. She may not be my mom by blood, but she is by heart, and she's the best one I could have ever asked for.

"I know my biscuit recipe is in good hands with you." We part, and then she squeezes both of my hands in hers, winking up at me.

"Wyatt will be happy when he doesn't have to go to the ranch for his biscuits anymore."

"Nonsense. You two better still come around. You were gone for a long time, honey, and we missed you around here."

The photography program ended in April, and I was home the second I could return. I loved every moment of being in New York, and I learned so much about how to take my pictures to the next level. But my heart will always belong in Texas, in Newberry Springs, with Wyatt.

The distance was hard, harder than I thought it would be. Hell, before I left, we saw each other every day. Hearing his voice wasn't enough. Seeing his face helped. But on the weekends he visited, we took every opportunity to be together, most of which was spent in my bed.

The program put us up in rooms at a small hotel just outside Manhattan, so it wasn't fancy or over-the-top. It certainly didn't provide the same comfort as home. But when Wyatt was there, it was the closest thing I could get.

And we had so much sex, it's a miracle I'm not pregnant along with Evelyn right now.

"Well, are you ready?" Momma G pulls me out of my tailspin.

"I've been waiting my whole life for this moment."

Evelyn, Momma, and I walk out the front door of the ranch, where my father is waiting by the horse-drawn carriage that will take us down to the creek and under the tree where Wyatt and I will be getting married.

"My God." My father freezes as he sees me come down the stairs, my hair pulled up on one side of my face with a clip of crystals and baby's breath.

"Hi, Daddy."

"Kelsea, you look gorgeous, baby. I can't believe this is my little girl I'm staring at right now."

"Well, it's me." I look up at him, fighting off more tears as I watch his fall. I'm determined not to ruin my makeup.

"I love you, pancake, and I am so glad that you found the right man for you."

"Me, too. He's my best friend, and I love him, Daddy. And I will always love you, too."

"As I will always love you." He smiles. "I guess it's time to give away my little girl."

He helps me into the carriage before assisting Evelyn and Momma G, and then we're off, headed toward my groom and all of our guests.

While I was away, Wyatt and I decided to get married shortly after I returned. We didn't want to waste any more time not being husband and wife. Time and distance can make a person see very clearly what's important in life, and marrying Wyatt was goal number one when I got home.

Naturally, the only place we wanted to get married was the Gibson Ranch. The reception will take place in the same barn we ran around in as kids, and a dinner of breakfast foods—pancakes and French toast, of course—will be served to everyone a little later.

But the ceremony—well, that had to be where our first one was when we were just ten years old.

The carriage stops at the bottom of the small hill with the creek on the other side. My father helps Evelyn and Momma G down the steps, leaving me sitting here as I see Mr. Gibson, Walker, and Forrest waiting.

"Damn, Kelsea. You look beautiful," Walker says as he stares up at me.

"Thank you." I'm so thankful to him in more ways than one, but I can let him know the extent of that later.

"And you look gorgeous, too, Momma," he says, planting a kiss on her cheek before she walks over to her husband.

"Glad to see my boy has some manners."

"You ready?" Forrest asks Evelyn as he takes one of her arms and threads it through his elbow.

"Yup. Let's get these two lovebirds married."

Walker clears his throat and reluctantly takes Evelyn's other hand. "I agree." He whistles to the guy in charge of the music, and just the sound of the first few notes has my heart pounding even harder.

My father helps me down, and we follow my bridesmaid and future in-laws up the small hill. I watch Momma G get escorted down the aisle by Mr. Gibson, and then Forrest and Walker escort Evelyn down the aisle on the other side of the hill since she's the only bridesmaid I wanted and needed.

But then it's my turn. With a deep breath, I hook my arm in my father's and let him lead me over the hill, absorbing the gasps of endearment when I appear and can see our guests below.

But I'm not even looking at them. My eyes are solely focused on the man standing in front of me, waiting for me as if he needs me there just to breathe, to make sure that this is real.

Wyatt looks so handsome in his dark blue jeans and white button-down shirt, his hair freshly cut, and his brown cowboy boots dusted with the same dirt we used to play in when we were kids.

But his smile is what's holding me captive, along with his eyes that are filled with moisture as he sees me walking toward him —*my best friend, my everything*.

I see my entire future as I walk toward him. I see mistakes and lessons learned and the opportunity to make more with him by my side.

I see my best friend, the man who my heart always knew was the one for me—my head just had to catch up.

And I see every dream, every vision of happiness, and a long life waiting for me in those milk-chocolate eyes.

After my father gives me away, I take Wyatt's waiting hand and then turn to face him as the pastor starts the ceremony.

"God, you look incredible, Kelsea," he whispers.

"Thank you. So do you."

As the preacher leads our guests in a short prayer and discusses the sanctity of marriage, anticipation builds for what comes next.

"Now, it's time for the vows. Wyatt and Kelsea have prepared their own to share with us. Wyatt?" the pastor asks as Wyatt clears his throat and then begins to speak.

"Kelsea, I never thought I would ever get to stand in this spot and make you my wife. It was something I always dreamed of, but I never found the right time to make you mine. Well, if there's anything I've learned over the past year, it's that time only fuels your decisions if you let it. Sometimes, you have to take a moment by the horns and make your life happen because if you wait too long, things pass you by." I reach up to wipe away one of my tears. "You're the syrup to my breakfast, my right-hand man, and my *everything*. You may be the one with the talent for taking pictures, but *you* are the most important subject of every picture I've ever captured in my mind, because you're in every single picture of my future. You are my best friend, and I love you."

I lick my lips, fighting like hell to keep it together for a few more moments, because now, it's my turn.

"Wyatt, I always wondered if I would ever get to stand in this spot and make you my husband. It seemed like just a dream for so long that I figured it would never come true. But then I realized that everyone deserves to dream and have their dreams become reality, and now, we get to live ours. You are the shelter from my storm. You are the shot of whiskey I need to take so I feel brave in my life. And you, too, are the syrup to my breakfast, my left-hand man, *my everything*. Every dream I've ever had has been with you by my side, growing old and still loving being around each other, even when we're wrinkly and gray. I want to have babies with you. And fight with you. And love you until my very last breath. You are my best friend, and I love you more than you'll ever know."

Wyatt swipes away his tears before staring down at me, cupping the side of my face. "Fuck, I love you." We each place our wedding bands on our respective fingers and then itch with the last thing left to do before this is official.

"It is my honor to pronounce you husband and wife. Wyatt, you may now kiss your bride!"

Cheers ring out as Wyatt frames my face with both hands and places his lips on mine in the most important kiss of our lives.

Our first kiss was in this spot, when we practiced getting married to each other at only ten years old.

Our next kiss was here as well, when we were young adults on the road to figuring out who we were.

But this kiss, this kiss defines us together—on the same path, with the same goals, and sharing ourselves with one another for the rest of our lives.

I thought I'd be lucky to marry my best friend one day, but it turns out luck had nothing to do with it. We were fated to be together from the beginning, although a little help from Walker did move things along.

I thought I would lose everything if I gave in to these feelings. But it turns out, I had nothing but the rest of my life to gain by letting my heart lead the way.

THE END

Thank you SO much for reading Wyatt and Kelsea's story! Want to know more about their future? Make sure to download their Bonus Epilogue here.

And keep reading for a sneak peek at Walker's story, *Everything He Couldn't*, which you can pre-order here!

Looking for more smalltown romance? Did you know that Javi and Sydney, the couple from the brewery, have a book? Read their story in *Guilty as Charged*, a sexy, smalltown standalone between the construction worker and the sassy lawyer, full of sexual awakening 😉

Or if series are your thing, start my other smalltown romance series next with *Tangled*, a one-night-stand turned co-worker romance with a surprise twist you won't see coming!

CHAPTER NINETEEN

Walker's Sneak Peek

I reach up and tug on the collar of my shirt. I fucking hate wearing a suit, especially for a reason like this. Not only do I feel like I'm choking because of the shirt, but the palpable tension in the air is suffocating me as well.

The walls of people standing around—all looking solemn and cascading tears as they look on and absorb the preacher's words while my best friend's body lies cold and dead in a casket—are gazing at the scene, occasionally landing on me with a look of remorse I'm not sure I can take much more of.

This is my fault. I couldn't save him.

And there's nothing I hate more than not being able to save someone.

John Schmitt, known to everyone else as Schmitty, is dead. And I'm the one responsible.

I knew we shouldn't have gone into that blaze, but he and I have tackled much worse fires than that one. We had to make sure the building was clear, that there wasn't a family who couldn't get out in time. And even though I saw the hesitation on the chief's face, he trusted us to come out alive.

It's not every day that an apartment complex catches on fire, especially in a town like Newberry Springs.

But it happened, and me, wanting to do what my training prepared me for, insisted that we check out the building and make sure everyone got out okay.

Little did I know that the only person to die that night would be the man who trusted me with his life, the man who followed me into the blaze when we shouldn't have entered in the first place.

And now, as I stand here holding my breath inside because it's easier than the feeling of swallowing knives that scrape my lungs each time I inhale the sadness around me, I let the guilt wash over me.

Because not only did my best friend die, but he's leaving behind a child, a child who will never know her dad.

My eyes find Evelyn, her head hanging low in her black dress that drapes beautifully over the bump carrying her daughter, and I fucking hate myself—for making her cry, for taking away her child's father, and for wishing that it were *my* child she was carrying instead.

Walker and Evelyn's story will release September 2023!

Make sure to sign-up for my newsletter to be kept up to date on future releases!

And don't forget to Pre-Order Walker and Evelyn's book, *Everything He Couldn't*, here.

MORE BOOKS BY HARLOW JAMES

More Books by Harlow James

The Ladies Who Brunch (rom-coms with a ton of spice)

Never Say Never (Charlotte and Damien)

No One Else (Amelia and Ethan)

Now's The Time (Penelope and Maddox)

Not As Planned (Noelle and Grant)

Nice Guys Still Finish (Jeffrey and Ariel)

-

The California Billionaires Series (rom coms with heart and heat)

My Unexpected Serenity (Wes and Shayla)

My Unexpected Vow (Hayes and Waverly)

My Unexpected Family (Silas and Chloe)

-

The Emerson Falls Series (smalltown romance with a found family friend group)

Tangled (Kane & Olivia)

Enticed (Cooper & Clara)

Captivated (Cash and Piper)

Revived (Luke and Rachel)

Devoted (Brooks and Jess)

Lost and Found in Copper Ridge

A holiday romance in which two people book a stay in a cabin for the same amount of time thanks to a serendipitous $5 bill.

Guilty as Charged

An intense opposites attract standalone that will melt your kindle. He's an ex-con construction worker. She's a lawyer looking for passion.

McKenzie's Turn to Fall

A holiday romance where a romance author falls for her neighborhood butcher.

ACKNOWLEDGMENTS

The journey to publish this book has been a wild one. The idea for the Gibson Brothers came to me when I was writing Guilty as Charged. In fact, you meet Wyatt and Kelsea in that book as I was setting up that series, and then I began writing their story in October of 2020. I got stuck, walked away from it, started writing My Unexpected Serenity, and then finished the billionaires series, intent on going back to their book.

And I did. I read what I had written so far, wondered while the hell I stopped, and then finished their book in the summer of 2021. I even dropped my laptop and cracked my screen in the midst of finishing this story. BUT, when I was done, I wasn't happy with the final result. Something wasn't right, and so I decided not to publish it. I never want to put out a book I'm not happy with, and my gut told me it wasn't up to par, so I left it be, thinking I'd never let my readers see it.

Then earlier this year, this story started calling to me again. And with the help of my beta reader, Emily, we found the problems, tweaked the story, brought it up to 2023 Harlow James standards, and now it is in your hands.

This series has been in my mind for SO long, it feels surreal to let it out finally, and I hope you fall in love with these brothers as much as I did. I can't wait to bring you the rest of the series this year. Stay tuned for alerts and news related to my next releases!

To my husband: Thank you for cheering me on and celebrating my success with me as I release each book. Thank you for understanding how much joy this hobby brings me. Thank you for listening to me vent when I'm struggling, and helping me turn this into a business now, including being my "book bitch." 😉 Here's to our adventures this next year doing signings and staying in many hotel rooms with no kids. And thank you for being my real life book husband and giving me my own true love story to brag about.

To Emily: This book would not be out in the world if it weren't for you. Thank you for being my sounding board when I was stuck between two worlds, but my heart was pulling me to this one. And thank you for helping me see that. 😉 I appreciate your friendship and support more than you know, and our friendship means the world to me. Also, I'm sorry for the heart attack I gave you when you read the sneak peek of Walker's book. I promise, his is coming. 😉

To Melissa, my editor: I am SO grateful for our working relationship. I always know that my book is in great hands with you. Thank you for your dedication to my stories and I look forward to working together for a long time.

To Abigail, my cover designer: For three years now, you have brought every vision of mine to life, and this book was no exception. I LOVE working with you. Thank you for putting in so much time and love to my books.

And to my beta readers, ARC readers, and every reader (both old and new): Thank you for taking a chance on a self-published author. Thank you for sharing my books with others. Thank you for allowing me to share my creativity with people who love the romance genre as much as I do.

And thank you for supporting a wife and mom who found a hobby that she loves.

ABOUT THE AUTHOR

Harlow James is a wife and mom who fell in love with romance novels, so she decided to write her own.

Her books are the perfect blend of emotional, addictive, and steamy romance. If you love stories with a guaranteed Happily Ever After, then Harlow is your new best friend.

When she's not writing, she can be found working her day job, reading every romance novel she can find time for, laughing with her husband and kids, watching re-runs of FRIENDS, and spending time cooking for her friends and family while drinking White Claws and Margaritas.

facebook.com/HarlowJamesAuthor
instagram.com/harlowjamesauthor

Printed in Great Britain
by Amazon